nkable

Main

s an excellent example of the struggles all soldiers face—even those far in the future." —*Lightspeed*

"Action-packed, character-rich, and mil spec'd to the max. Empires may rise but this backwater rules!" —Dani Kollin, coauthor of *The Unincorporated Man*

"It's almost a cliche to compare military SF novels to *Starship Troopers,* but this is the real deal. Bauers has created a gritty, complex story Heinlein would have been proud of." —James L. Cambias, author of *A Darkling Sea*

"Tense and fascinating, *Unbreakable* will hold readers captive until the very end." —*RT Book Reviews*

"A little bit *Starship Troopers* and a little bit Esmay Suiza, with a dash of *Firefly* for flavor. W. C. Bauers gives us everything we want in our military science fiction, but never allows the hardware and action to overshadow Paen and everyone else caught in the cross fire." —Dayton Ward, *New York Times* bestselling author of *The Last World War*

Books by W. C. Bauers

Unbreakable
Indomitable

UNBREAKABLE

The Chronicles of Promise Paen,
BOOK ONE

W. C. Bauers

TOR

A TOM DOHERTY ASSOCIATES BOOK
NEW YORK

This is a work of fiction. All of the characters, organizations, and events portrayed in this novel are either products of the author's imagination or are used fictitiously.

UNBREAKABLE

A Tor Book
Published by Tom Doherty Associates, LLC
175 Fifth Avenue
New York, NY 10010

www.tor-forge.com

Tor® is a registered trademark of Tom Doherty Associates, LLC.

The Library of Congress has cataloged the hardcover edition as follows:

Bauers, W. C., author.
    Unbreakable / W. C. Bauers.—1st ed.
        p. cm.
    ISBN 978-0-7653-7542-1 (hardcover)
    ISBN 978-1-4668-4729-3 (e-book)
    1. Space warfare—Fiction.   2. Women marines—Fiction.   3. Space warfare.   4. Women
marines.   5. Science Fiction.   5. Amerikanisches Englisch.   I. Title.
    PS3602.A9358 U53 2015
    813'.6—dc23

                                                                                        2014501975

ISBN 978-0-7653-7543-8 (trade paperback)

Our books may be purchased in bulk for promotional, educational, or business use. Please contact your
local bookseller or the Macmillan Corporate and Premium Sales Department at 1-800-221-7945, extension
5442, or by e-mail at MacmillanSpecialMarkets@macmillan.com.

First Edition: January 2015
First Trade Paperback Edition: July 2016

Printed in the United States of America

0 9 8 7 6 5 4 3 2 1

For my grandfather
CPO William B. Coates, USN, 1926–2005.
He built a nation and a family.

ACKNOWLEDGMENTS

Thanks to Lauren Kaplan and Ronie Kendig for their early reads and encouragement. Thanks to Lt. Col. Gary Foster, USAF (Ret.); Col. Tim Hill, USMC (Ret.); and Maj. Mike Heath, USMC (Ret.). Special thanks to Cmdr. Mark Gabriel, USN (Ret.), for advice and technical assistance. To Bryan DeBates at the Space Foundation Discovery Center. Also, my special appreciation to my mother, Dr. Deborah Bauers, who served as my in-house editor, and my father, Dr. John Bauers, for teaching me that science and faith aren't mutually exclusive (if God made *us*, he most certainly made *them*, too). To my wife, Heather, for her ongoing support. To my agent, Cherry Weiner, for seeing something there. To my editor, Marco Palmieri, and to Tor. To Stephan Martiniere for a fantastic jacket. To Christ, who makes all things new.

NO BASTARD EVER WON A WAR BY DYING FOR HIS COUNTRY.
HE WON IT BY MAKING THE OTHER POOR DUMB BASTARD DIE
FOR HIS COUNTRY.

> —General George S. Patton, Jr., 1885–1945 C.E.,
> Pre-Diaspora

IT'S GOD'S JOB TO FORGIVE THE TERRAN FEDERATION FOR
VIOLATING OUR HOMEWORLD. IT'S OUR JOB TO ARRANGE THE
FACE-TO-FACE MEETING.

> —Kaleb Z. Wolfestein, 2481 C.E., Post-Diaspora,
> the de facto first commandant of the RAW-MC,
> for his role as the senior-most officer of Hold's
> planetary defense forces and militia during the
> war of secession with the Terran Federation

UNBREAKABLE

Prologue

FEBRUARY 2ND, 92 A.E., STANDARD CALENDAR, 1005 HOURS,
REPUBLIC OF ALIGNED WORLDS PLANETARY CAPITAL—HOLD
RNS *KEARSARGE*, PARKING ORBIT WHISKEY-ECHO 3

What is it about *a weapon that leaves residue on your hands?*

First Lieutenant Promise T. Paen rubbed her thumb and trigger finger together beneath her nose, and inhaled the faint, just-fired smell. She then rotated her hand and watched how the particulate glistened in the artificial light of her quarters. She released the question—knowing the answer would come to her more easily if she didn't try so hard to find it—and focused on the charcoal dust on her hands instead: how it shaded her porcelain skin in blacks and grays and filled in the loops and lines for contrast. The answer brushed her consciousness like a whisper in a thunderstorm. *The residue keeps you honest about the people you've killed, and mindful of the people who want to kill you, too. And,* she thought, *a pulse rifle doesn't stain your hands like an old-fashioned bullet fired from a dirty wep.*

A substantial something clanked down the passageway outside her quarters, interrupting her thoughts. Promise fixed her posture, pulled herself into a lotus position, and exhaled. Her antique semiautomatic lay before her in a cloth on her pillow. She'd visited the ship's range with it at 0900 hours. By 0945 hours, she was back in her cabin after shooting exactly one hundred rounds. Perishable skills demanded nothing less, at least once a week. Beside her gun sat an open carton of brass-cased Hawks flanked by a clip. A few rounds had tumbled out of their tray and onto her bedsheets, scattered like childhood memories lost in the folds of time.

Her finger traced the frame of the small semiautomatic. *Black, plastic, and fires every time.* The gun predated the First Diaspora, long before Hiro Mishitoko's jump drive sent humanity beyond Sol in any meaningful numbers. When humans finally took to the stars, the weapons had followed. Her concealment model G-27 had boarded a Colonizer with her great-grandmother. It had graced her mother's hip, and her grandmother's, and her great-grandmother's, going back more than seven generations. *How many generations of women have held this weapon?* Promise didn't know exactly. But she believed her "senior" bound them all together, hip to hand, across the plains of time.

Her eyes shifted from her semiauto to the mirror on the port bulkhead. A polished gold bar rode each of her collar points and stood out boldly against the mat fabric of her tan utilities. She smiled at herself, frowned, acted surprised, and then quickly grew angry. Each face revealed a new landscape. Changing expressions made certain lines disappear completely, particularly the streaks across her brow purchased with blood, sweat, and at times near-paralyzing fear. Other lines were indelible like the crow's-feet and the three-inch shrapnel scar above her left ear. That scar was about a year old, and it still hurt her like it had happened only yesterday. Loss had etched and injured her in the deepest chambers of her heart. She'd camouflaged the most grievous wounds with intense training, and hid others in caves sealed with psychobabble. On more than one occasion, life had quaked and caused cave-ins. But that was fine with her. *Some demons are best left buried where even therapy can't uncover them.*

She looked back at her weapon. It was different from the other small arms in her locker. Older. Dirtier. She'd killed the enemies of the Republic of Aligned Worlds Marine Corps with a variety of modern pulse weapons: conventional rifles that fired hypervelocity penetrators and sniper platforms that threw boosted one-shot-one kills. In six years of service to the RAW-MC, she'd racked up seventy-six confirmed kills. She'd seen the whites of some, and the cold reflective faceplates of others. After each battle, she'd washed the blood away without guilt or regret. But the men and women she'd led and lost in combat were another matter. They haunted her.

Her senior haunted her, too. Humble mechanics, uncomplicated by molycircs and too simple to sync with her mechsuit's targeting computer. It was not a go-gun or a duty wep. It was something else: a relic, a painful memory, a promise. Hell. It was the only weapon she didn't store in her locker with the others, and the only one she'd never killed with.

It was the one thing she owned that had belonged to her mother.

Her eyes narrowed as a soft chime sounded in her cabin, marking the ship's quarter hour—1015 hours, exactly. *About time to bag some sleep,* Promise thought as she stretched her arms wide. Her back arched and her knee brushed the weapon on her pillow. And it struck her, for the umpteenth time, how painfully familiar and oddly out of place her handgun was in her Post-Diaspora universe. Promise shook her head. *My 'verse is way too complicated.* A lot had changed in the nearly eight hundred years since the birth of the GLOCK. Many modern weapons still went boom. But the universe they boomed in required far more space to breathe. In 92 A.E., star nations achieved détente by gobbling up continents across star systems teaming with planets—most of them inhospitable by human standards—and turning them into border zones. Humanity's thirst for more guaranteed that there would never be enough living worlds or buffer systems to go around.

The days of continental rivalries and dirty weps are long gone. Gone and dead. Like my ancestors who once held this.

Promise scooped up the stray bullets from her sheets and rolled them around in her palm. Listened to the *clinks.* Loaded the magazine and fed it to her semiauto. *Click.* Thumbed the slide stop and felt the weapon quake.

"Loaded and lethal," she said aloud.

She drew the weapon in close until the frame fuzzed. Faint traces of solvent and gunpowder tickled her nose. The pungent odor evoked a memory of her mother, Sandra. Promise closed her eyes and found herself on the soil of her birth world, Montana. A trio of moons hung in her memory's sky, barely visible in the morning light. Her mother stood some distance away, in a shooter's stance, arms extended downrange. Promise saw a much younger version of herself standing in her mother's shadow, no older than five or perhaps six years of age. Her mother's breath had turned to vapor in the chilly air. Out, in, and out again. Then Sandra inhaled deeply, exhaled halfway, and fired. *Boom.* Textbook. Recoil. Reacquire. *Boom.* A third shot rang out as her mother's arms rode the recoil upward, rode the groove back to fire again, and again, and again. Until the chamber locked open and spit out the last shell. The casing spun end over end along its axis, clinked, and rolled to a stop against Promise's foot. Then her vision blurred into reality.

She was back aboard RNS *Kearsarge,* in her cabin, pressing her mother's weapon to her own forehead with no memory of how it got there. She breathed in deeply, exhaled halfway, and drew the weapon back to her temple. A faint hint of saffron kissed the air. She canted her head and smirked. *Mom.*

"I wouldn't do that, munchkin. Not if I were you." Promise looked up to find her mother, standing in the middle of the cabin, towering over her.

"You need to lighten up, Mom," Promise said. *And please don't give me that smile. I am not a child.* Before she could help it, she stuck her tongue out at her mother in response, slammed her eyes shut, and dug the cold barrel into her hairline . . . to relieve the itch, of course. "Mmmm." She blindly cleared the chamber and let the magazine drop free. When she opened her eyes, her mom was still standing there. *Still smiling. Well, okay, fine! You really do need to lighten up. Have it your way.* Promise huffed as she laid the weapon back on her pillow, retrieved the loose round and fed it back to the magazine. She made a display of her empty hands and leaned back against the bulkhead. "Weapon is secure, ma'am!" The words came out edgy. "Satisfied?"

"Not quite," Sandra Gration's apparition replied.

Promise stared intently into her mother's bluegrass eyes. "Why are you here?"

"We've mostly established that already, dear." Sandra eyes bounced to the GLOCK. "Wherever she goes, I go. Wandering the ship's been fun, too. Your skipper has a nice derriere."

Promise looked away.

"Well, it was your thought, after all, not mine. I can't say I disagree, though."

"Don't patronize me, Mamma. I asked a simple question."

"Oh, you were referring to why I'm here *this* time?" Sandra turned her hands palms up as if it was patently obvious. "Next time you have an itch, keep your finger off the trigger. Okay?"

Promise snorted. "I wouldn't have. You should know that by now."

"Should I?" Sandra asked. "Munchkin, I don't even know if I'm real. I might just be in there," she said as she stabbed the air between Promise's sights.

"We've been through this countless times. I don't know how I—"

"Yes, yes, munchkin, I know. Why here, why now?" Sandra looked up. "Maybe the Maker will tell us someday. Maybe my soul is stitched to yours, or to the family GLOCK. Maybe you have a trigger spring loose. I don't really know, and I don't really care. What matters is I'm here when you need me."

At the most inconvenient moments.

Sandra tapped the side of her head. "I heard that."

And stop calling me munchkin. I'm a grown woman.

"Habits die hard, dear, particularly when you're dead. But cut your dearly departed mother some slack." Sandra spread her arms out theatrically and did a pirouette. When she came to a full stop, she glanced down at her body, clearly displeased with the uncomplimentary fabric she was in. "This isn't my first choice, you know. Or second for that matter." Sandra cocked her head at her daughter, at the same angle that Promise had cocked hers moments before. "Your off-duty attire leaves a lot to be desired."

Promise frowned. She and her mother were wearing tan utilities, the standard-issue working uniform of the RAW-MC.

"What's the problem?" Promise asked. "One, they're practical. Two, they breath. Three, I don't recall asking you."

"Well, at least you don't have to accessorize it," Sandra said. "Perfect for the range, too, right? Speaking of which, you need to safety that. Now."

"I suppose some things never change." Promise sighed as she gathered her gear in her hands. She kicked her legs out and hit the deck catlike, walked through her mother to the opposite side of her cabin, and pressed her eye to the scanner on the bulkhead, which yawned to reveal two metal shelves. The top one held two spare magazines, a standard-issue e-pistol, a well-worn book, and a sealed carton of ammunition. She fed her senior to the safe and stepped backward, just beyond the proximity sensor's reach. The bulkhead resealed itself.

"Weapon secure, ma'am."

"Now I'm *completely* satisfied." Promise heard the double entendre in her mother's voice. It humored her. And plunged her into a stream of memories, many that had flown high over her head as a child. How her parents had displayed affection in front of her, the kindness of their words, the intensity in their eyes. *I can see, now, how Mom and Dad's relationship was well greased.* Remembering that hurt her terribly.

"Enough wallowing in the past, munchkin."

The sharp hand clap that followed snapped Promise's head around, and then her heels, but she was too late.

Figures!

"Don't forget, munchkin." Her mother's voice echoed about her cabin. "I'm still here . . . and I always will be."

Oh, no need to worry about that, Mother, Promise thought with mixed feelings. *You won't let me forget it.* A moment later she said, "And please don't ever let me, okay?"

One

Six years earlier . . .

Fresh air spilled into her upstairs bedroom through an old wooden window. Promise inhaled the smells of an early autumn shower, which normally calmed her, but not today. She scanned her room in frustration. Anyone walking into it might have thought a vandal had tossed it looking for valuables. She pinched her nose and scrunched her eyebrows, just like her father did, then slowed her breathing and counted to seven, just long enough to temper her words. She rarely let her father see her perturbed and had no intention of doing so today.

"Dad! Where's my comb?" Promise closed her eyes. *I really did try not to yell.* "You know," she said as she forced her shoulders to relax, "the one Mamma gave me for my birthday?"

"Try your nightstand, dear."

"Right." The lamp stood alone, a sea of nicknacks swept to the floor beneath it. Promise imagined her father seated in his hardwood desk chair, sighing in resignation. She didn't even try to keep the edge from creeping back into her voice. "I know it's not approved by the elders, but it's from Mamma, and it's one of the few things I have left."

"Yes, I know," Morlyn Gration answered with a maddening degree of patience, but without ceding the point. "Try not to obsess about it."

"Try some compassion," she muttered under her breath. *Remember, P, he misses her, too—cut him some slack. Just not too much.*

Promise knew her father was hard at work and that she had interrupted him over what he considered to be a trivial matter. She pictured his study vividly: a modest flattop desk, on the right of which sat a pad of paper and a gravity-fed pen because Morlyn Gration refused to use a smartpad or a sensible backup. Rows of calculations foretold the size of the coming harvest and the profits it would net. On a shelf above his head sat a seldom-used book of genealogy. Behind him stood a narrow shelf of books neatly filled with volumes on herbals, horticulture, and husbandry. All very boring in her opinion.

Her family was small and proud. They'd come to the planet Montana many generations ago, on the tail end of the Third Diaspora, which had come to a close with Earth's death. As planetary deaths went, it had been a particularly bad one. Time reset itself, A.E. this time instead of C.E., to keep the homeworld's memory alive, of course. But after one hundred years, no one cared anymore.

The lucky ones had left before "The Event," drawn to Montana by its distance from Holy Terra and their separatist Luddite zeal . . . and just in time, too. Thank God.

After landing, the Grations migrated to Montana's northern hemisphere, to a parcel of land along the foothills of the Fhordholm mountain range, only a day's hike from the tree line. They saw four seasons and winters that dipped deep into the minuses, lived close to the land, and dabbled in tradecraft. In less than a generation, harsh Montana winters took their toll, the deaths mounted—so many children, lost unnecessarily—and time-honored traditions crumbled to dust. The Grations became reluctant technophiles of a sort. And why not? That's what mechs were for, after all. Let them grunt it out for a change. Let the children live.

Big surprise, Promise thought as she kicked a pile of clothes in frustration. Not that using mechs bothered her. It didn't. But it was the principle of the matter, which brought her back to the comb. *He sees the value of machines. I wish I could ask Mom why she fell for him. Dad can be so . . . so . . . stubborn! Can't he see how much this means to me?*

Promise gave up her search. She walked to her closet, reached up high, and grabbed the handgun and holster off the top shelf, making both disappear. She walked down the hall and descended the stairs, which emptied into a plain room. A few solid pieces of furniture hugged the walls, which supported several acrylic landscapes, soft pastorals full of greens and yellows and browns. Her father's rocker sat near a bricked fireplace. Her mother's leather armchair faced to the east. Mount Kinley stood in the distance, a purple dome that had once topped five thousand meters before it blew its top.

"Be back for lunch," yelled her father.

"Don't plan on it," Promise shouted back.

She was already halfway to her ride when she heard the screen door slam shut behind her. Promise swung her leg over the sled and felt her hands mold to the polymer grips. A green light on the steering console came to life and scanned her eyes. Then the sled rose on a platform of countergravity.

Promise glanced behind her and up at her father's office window. She caught movement and knew he was watching her from above, hoping not to be seen. "He looks. Too bad he never really sees me." She pivoted, then urged her sled forward and out of sight.

Two

Promise left the sled by a small creek at the base of the hill. She'd gone there to collect her thoughts and to grieve the loss of her treasure. But there was plenty of time for that and runners didn't waste cool mornings in self-pity. She had only meant to jog a few kilometers. But as her thighs heated, she made the decision to push. Conditioned muscles responded, and three klicks became five, then ten. As she ran, three gray-blue moons floated overhead, a trio of sentinels guarding the hectares of agriculture below them. The air was brisk and wormed its way into her jumpsuit, chilling her slight breasts.

She heard her father's mantra coax her forward as the lactic acid collected in her legs, tempting her to quit. *Rise early, work late, or poverty will knock at your door like an armed man and destroy you.*

How about rest, Dad. Rest is good, too. She'd told him so often enough. *A little sleep, a little slumber, makes a man a kinder soul.* Her father never did know how to take a joke.

Before returning home, she doubled back to the hill to watch the sun crest over the horizon and chase away the night. Her home stood in the distance, about two kilometers away. The path to the hill's top was a series of switchbacks marked by trampled grasses and clay, clear evidence that she had been there many times before. As she neared the summit, Promise heard the roar of engines. She ducked instinctively as a shadow passed overhead. She'd never seen one in real life, just in vids and stills. But she immediately knew what it was. Short-range, blocky, and clearly armed. Two manned sleds dropped from the craft's belly, changed course, and quickly disappeared into the landscape, headed roughly in the direction of her home. Then the larger craft turned that way, too.

A sudden, overwhelming fear washed over her. The nets had reported raids across the planet Garius, barely a week ago, and Garius was only a short jump from Montana.

Oh, God, please turn! But the craft didn't alter its course.

Promise tracked the vessel with growing trepidation. She withdrew a small optic from a band on her arm and used it to glass the land below. The ship came to stop above the ground and a short distance from her rectangular, wood-framed house. Two sleds shot out of the trees and climbed high above them before circling the much larger ship. They reminded Promise of wraiths waiting to collect the dead. The main vessel hovered, impossibly still. Seven figures dropped from its belly and sunk their boots into Montana's orange clay. They drew weapons and spread out. Fear held Promise in place. Time seemed to stretch as one second became ten, and then sixty.

She watched her father exit the front door to face his attackers in The Way—hands raised, palms up, in peace. Like any other day, his dress was plain as his God had intended it to be: a woven hat shielding his eyes; his black vest hanging open and casual (the proper black); the sleeves on his blue shirt (the proper blue) rolled to the correct place on his elbows; his khakis generic, not brand. One of the seven stepped toward him with his weapon raised.

Morlyn Gration's body fell backward in slow motion. Promise waited anxiously for him to rise. *He has to get up. Get up, Dad. Get up!* She screamed in silence. A slight breeze caught his hat and blew it into a mound of flowers, and like that she knew he was gone.

They worked methodically and took everything of value that could be sold or traded: household effects, servomechs, and livestock. They set fire to the rest and then disappeared into the upper atmosphere.

Promise watched it happen from the top of the hill, helpless to do anything about it. She couldn't cry. She couldn't move. She feared going home. What if they returned? She feared moving from the hill and being detected, or possibly taken, or worse. She sat transfixed, rocking herself with her arms around her knees, until the sun approached its zenith.

A brief gust of wind startled her and nearly succeeded in pushing her over. As quickly as the wind picked up, it stopped, and grew strangely still. She reached back to retie her hair and felt her blood pumping in her neck and pounding in her ears. She pressed into the *thrum thrum thrum* of it, as if each pulse was all that mattered. Her father had believed that life and death was in the blood, that it was a cardinal sin to shed it. *Mom would have fought. Why didn't you?* The accusation was aimed at her father but ended up punching her in the gut instead.

"Why?" It was barely a whisper. Then in earnest: *"Why?"* Again, and again, and again. Until her screams turned to gut-wrenching sobs and bruised fists pounding the ground beneath her. She dug her hands into the soil and watched the clumps break apart and scatter.

Exhausted, she began to look for an answer, a direction, a what now?—anything. Lonely childhood memories circled about her, how she'd been raised by a plain, pacifist father who loved God and shop craft as near equals. An avatar of her mother materialized, a fierce fighter who'd charged through life with a 40-caliber sidearm strapped to her thigh.

Her parents had loved each other in spite of their differences. But Promise had been caught between them. Around the time she'd turned seven, she realized she might someday have to choose. It was her mother's sickness that ended up choosing for her. They buried Sandra the following year, on the day the ground thawed enough for digging. After that, her father had grieved in his own way by boxing up her mother's things and refusing to talk about it, or about her.

A memory flashed before her, one she hadn't thought of in years. She was in her mother's room, at about noon. They'd spent the morning in the garden, weeding and tidying up beneath a hot sun. Sandra had pushed her trowel into the earth and stood, arched her back, and brushed the soil from her hands. "Time to come in, munchkin." Promise skipped into her parents' bedroom and sat on the hardwood floor to play with her favorite doll. Her mother appeared sometime later, her hair damp and pulled back, wearing a silk gown with an ornate dragon coiled between the shoulders. Sandra walked to the full-length mirror and stood in silence.

"I feel so old."

"That's silly, Mommy. You're not even close to one hundred."

"I couldn't agree more, munchkin. Thank you."

Promise looked up and smiled. "I love you, Mommy."

"I love you too. Always and forever."

And nevermore. Her eyes shifted, and she was back on her hill, shivering with cold. *Mom was so happy then. That's how I want to remember her.*

Promise pulled herself up off the tear-stained ground, reached behind her head, and let all of her hair fall. She drew her handgun and pulled the slide all the way back, held it for a small eternity. As the round chambered, she found the strength to choose. *Not your way, Dad. Not Mom's either—she wouldn't have wanted that. I choose to live on my own terms. Not for you or for her. For me.*

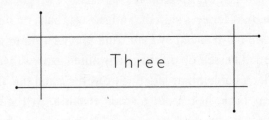

Three

She stood outside the RAW-MC recruiting station in the heart of the Landing, Montana's capital city. A handful of weeks had passed since her father's murder, weeks that might as well have been decades. Nothing felt right. It hadn't for years, really. *Home—I don't even know what that is, what it's supposed to look like. I've lived like an orphan for too long.*

The sign above the doorway read, YOUR TICKET TO THE STARS.

Right. Please scan mine and boost me out of here.

A week before, she'd seen it in the lawyer's office, a brochure about joining up, for the truly "gung ho." An Aunt Janie apparently wanted her. Promise had an idea of what that really meant. Warfighter. Wasn't that the unvarnished truth? Certainly not what her father thought. Paid killers. The brochure had been the only piece of carbonscreen in an otherwise Spartan room. Glass on two sides, sparsely furnished with two withered plants and a virtual painting, a large desk, two side tables, and several abused chairs. The smell of burnt caf. While Mr. Lackett talked her through her father's will, she'd lost herself in a grand what-if. *A Republican Marine? Could I? What would Dad think? And Mom, I don't even have to ask—I know what she would say if she were here now. She'd smile and salute cavalierly and tell me that a Gration woman can do whatever a Gration man says she can't.*

A hollow-point smile consumed Promise's face. From the other side of the desk, Mr. Lackett smiled uneasily. He'd seemed very sorry for her loss and relieved to tell her that she would be taken care of. But it wasn't her inheritance that brought the joy to her face. Realizing she had choices had changed her countenance, and that had settled it.

"Ms. Gration, I'll give you a bit of time to read through your father's last wishes." Mr. Lackett handed her a luminous, razor-thin tablet and a small stylus. "I'll just be in the other room if you need me."

As the door closed, Promise sagged against the back of her chair. She felt her mother's handgun press against her right kidney—she'd forgotten it was there. Her father wouldn't have approved. In his mind, Grations and guns were like blood and oil. Irreconcilable. *So where does that leave me?*

The Last Will and Testament

of

Morlyn P. Gration

I, Morlyn Paul Gration, resident of Bristletown, Montana, being of sound mind and body and at least eighteen (18) years of age, do hereby make . . .

"The mind was very sound, true. But the body—tut, tut, tut—"

Promise jumped in her seat, and her head snapped up reflexively. Between Mr. Lackett's desk and the glass wall stood her dearly departed mother. Sandra Gration's hair glistened. She was dressed in a floor-length robe, cinched at the waist. A tail of some sort snaked over her shoulder and coiled around her heart possessively.

"I'm just joking, munchkin. Your father had a very nice derriere."

"Y-you, you're—"

"Spit it out, munchkin."

"Dead. You're dead. I was there."

"And yet here I am. How positively sublime."

Promise pressed her palms against her eyes and rubbed at them feverishly. When she opened them, she saw that her mother was . . .

"Still here, dear."

Promise stood and began to pace around her chair. "I'm dreaming. No, I'm hallucinating. I have PTS—that's it! That *must* be it." Promise took a step backward, toward the door she'd entered through and away from her mother's apparition. "And you're not my mom. You're just a manifestation of my—"

"Stop psychobabbling, Promise. The fact that you can hear and see me is the important thing." Sandra came around the desk and leaned against its side.

Promise wrapped her arms around herself and stared intently at a woman she knew, *knew,* was long since dead and buried. "You always did cut to the point."

"Yes, well, your father liked to vacillate, and a businessman must be decisive. Someone had to look to our interests, and that someone was me. I made him twice the man he would have been otherwise, and three times as rich."

Promise couldn't decide whether to cry or smile. *I've missed you so much.*

"I know, munchkin. I've missed you, too."

"What?" *You heard that?*

"As if you shouted it for all to hear, like you did when you were born. I remember. God knows you were a stretch—a woman never forgets that kind of pain. You even startled the doctor." Sandra smiled at a distant memory. "And my nether regions were never the same either. The sex got better post you."

Mom.

"Sorry. I'm so glad to see you."

This isn't happening.

"I can't believe this is happening! What a fine young woman you've become. Let me look at you."

Promise took a hesitant step forward.

Sandra cleared her throat and drew a circle in the air.

"Fine." Promise huffed, dutifully turned. "Is it really you?"

"Unless I was body snatched. You tell me." Sandra dropped her chin and smiled warmly at her daughter.

Promise shook her head in disbelief. "This can't be."

"I'd like a hug from my girl." Sandra dabbed at her eyes and opened her arms to receive her daughter.

A tear ran down her face. Promise closed her eyes as she rushed forward and through her mother and into the edge of the desk. "Ouch!" She rubbed at her hip and hobbled around to find her mother standing behind her, smiling sadly, with her arms still open wide.

Sandra shook her head with obvious disappointment. "It appears my body *was* snatched, munchkin—I'm so sorry." A stubborn tear escaped and slid down Sandra's cheek. "Well, at least I'm not one hundred."

Promise choked back her surprise. "I remember that day."

"And I'll never forget it."

"I have so many questions to ask you: Why after all this time? Why are you here? How are you here?" Promise cocked her head and crinkled her face. "I remember the robe. Wasn't it a birthday present?"

"Good questions, most don't have answers—your father would've killed to see me tongue-tied—" Sandra quickly changed the subject. "The robe was one of my favorite things. Silk, from Busan. I remember how it felt. I nearly made your father send it back when I found out what it cost him." She narrowed her eyes, grew serious. "I think you know more about me being here than you think you do."

"Me? I have no idea how any of *this* happened."

Sandra tapped the side of her head and then pointed at her daughter.

"What? So this is just a dream?"

"Maybe I'm just with you. In there, out here—does it matter?" Sandra shrugged her shoulders. "Don't overthink this, munchkin. I'm here and I haven't a care in the world. Except you." Sandra looked over at the door. "You must have been thinking of me; otherwise, I wouldn't be here. Out with it."

"Right." *Deep breath. Exhale halfway. Talk.* But she couldn't pry a word loose.

Sandra cleared her throat. "Dear, it's never wise to irritate the dead."

Promise opened her mouth, closed it. Looked left, opened again, closed again. Her thoughts began to wander in singsong fashion. *I'm talking to my mother . . . my very dead mother . . . this is absolutely crazy.* She licked her lips and . . .

"Munchkin!"

Promise knocked into the chair and nearly fell backward. "Okay. You're right," tumbled out instead. "I was thinking about you . . . and about this." Promise looked down at the crumpled advertisement in her hand. She smoothed out the wrinkles to reveal two lines of words in bold yellow lettering:

SEMPER PARATUS—ALWAYS READY
THROUGH ADVERSITY TO THE STARS

When Promise looked up, she found that her mother was just to the side of her and looking over her shoulder. A hint of saffron hung in the air, and the room seemed a bit warmer than it had been moments before.

"Mom, there's nothing for me here. Dad's gone. So is the house. I barely knew our neighbors, Gene and Tamar Wayvern—you remember them? He's a lot like Dad." They exchanged telling looks. "Three girls. Two are at university. The youngest was a big surprise. They offered me a room until I figure things out. Believe me, they don't get out much either. Mr. Wayvern wants to buy our land, too. Grans is the only family I have let. Her dementia is really bad. She came to the funeral but couldn't remember who I was. There's university. But I've had my head in books for years. I need an out. Out of here. This place. This planet. Out or I'm going to scream."

"Then get out. Go."

Promise inhaled sharply. "You can't mean that."

Sandra nodded at the brochure in Promise's hand.

"You mean enlist?"

"Why not?"

"Dad wouldn't approve. Isn't this *beneath* me?"

"You are Morlyn Gration's daughter. But you are not him."

"I'm still a Gration."

"You are more than that." Sandra looked appalled, and for a moment Promise thought the look was aimed at her. "Your father and I were so very different. We didn't make things easy for you, did we?" Sandra shook her head. "No, we didn't. I'm sorry if we made you feel like you had to choose one of us over the other. In fact, I'm pretty sure we did that, more times than I care to admit." Sandra's breath caught in her throat, and she had to clear it several times to get the next words out. "Promise, please forgive me. Forgive him, too . . . if you can. And please don't carry that burden with you any longer. Make a clean break, here, now. I'll support you, whatever you choose."

"My choice? Huh. That's not something I've asked myself much?"

"Think it over and then decide. No one will rush you, least of all me."

Sandra frowned, and patted her side. "You're clothing is a bit tight at the waist. When you spun for me, I saw Janie imprint. You'll have to be more careful when you conceal-carry.

"Janie?"

"Your GLOCK, dear. That's my Janie on your hip, right?"

Without thinking, Promise cupped the frame of her handgun in the hollow of her back, against her right kidney, and gave her mother a puzzled look. *I've heard that name before. Where have I heard that* name *before?*

Sandra rolled her eyes. "Your father."

Right. You called him the peacemaker and he called you . . .

"Republican-issued Janie. He hated just about everything to do with the government. So I named my sidearm in his honor." Sandra's eyes smirked. "He turned his cheeks, and I slapped them."

Promise heard footsteps in the other room.

"Time for me to leave, munchkin."

Promise looked up from the pamphlet. "Mom? When will I see you again?" But her mother was gone.

"Mom?"

She felt something brush the side of her face, and then a hushed voice whispered into her ear.

"Soon."

As Promise stood outside the recruiting center, she surveyed her birth world for the last time. She watched an odd assortment of vehicles hugging the ferocrete. Butanol-powered cars darted about on antiquated wheels, while their modern counterparts flew high above them, sleek Aerodynes powered by fusion cells and flown by efficient and costly navigational programs. There weren't many of them here. They reminded her of arrogant bees on a planet full of hardworking ants. Montana was a Rim world, part of the "verge," and most Montanans drove on vulcanized No-Flat rubber and preferred it that way. They carried driver's licenses—not "flight" certificates—as a matter of pride, and they holstered guns that chambered metal-cased rounds, some loaded so "hot" they bordered on being unsafe.

One more step and she'd close one chapter, open a second.

Ticket to the stars. Sounds perfect. She stepped through. *Next chapter, please.*

Four

Crystalline glass doors whooshed closed behind her. Directly ahead she found a young Republican Marine staring at her. A white beret with gold filigree graced the woman's head, the Seraph, Globe, and Anchor of the Republican Fleet Forces pinned to the beret's crown. Her face was hawkish and stern with intense eyes, and she had a powerful air about her. The Marine on the poster was good but not safe. She embodied confidence, and Promise found herself longing to be just like her.

A Staff Sergeant Nikandros had taken Promise's call and told her what to expect. She recognized the nasal-thin voice instantly.

"Hold on a sec. Be right with ya."

She heard something slam in the next room and feet scuffing across the floor. The face was unremarkable, average height with balding hair, the sort of man you met and then immediately discounted. His speech was rehearsed. His opening pedestrian, "You made the right choice, Ms. Gration. The RAW-MC is the envy of every star nation, and the backbone of the Republic's Fleet Forces. You don't believe me. Did you stop next door first? Thank God you made it to me before you signed your life away to the bowels of a warship. I bet Petty Officer Bhirn filled your head with fairy tales from the almighty branch Navy. Well, don't let the squids fool you. They may tote us around the 'verse, but we are the fleet's liberty teeth, the Fleet Marine Force. We drop through atmo and put boots on the ground. First to fight, last out, damn the odds."

"Right."

A storm crossed Promise's face. Armored men dropped from the belly of the craft and set flame to tree and porch and screen. She tucked her hands behind her back to keep them from shaking. She pushed aside the image of her father lying dead on the ground. She didn't care what Nikandros promised her, as long as he got her off Montana and gave her the skills to find the bastards responsible.

She held up her hand and cut him off midpitch. "That's all fine and well. But where do I sign?"

"Eager, aren't you." It wasn't a question. "Ms. Gration . . . Promise . . . mind if I call you that? Why don't we sit a bit and discuss the finer points of becoming a Republican Marine."

Promise scowled at him. "This candidate has read the literature, seen the holovid, heard the speech. You have my scores, and you have a quota, don't you, Staff Sergeant?"

At the mention of his rank, perfectly aligned stalagmites beamed at her. *That's right, I did my homework. Now let's get on with it.*

He held out his hand, and Promise squeezed it hard. "All right then. Where do I start?"

Nikandros turned as a mech entered the room. Roughly a meter tall and alabaster white, it hovered on a plain of counter-grav. ELVINA was stenciled on its chest. It withdrew a tablet from its pouch and handed it to the staff sergeant. "Good girl, Elvie. Now off with you." Nikandros turned back to face Promise. "Okay. Wish I had ten like you, Promise. I'll have you sworn in within the hour. Of course, you may still opt out of your enlistment within the next twenty-four hours, should you have a change of heart."

"This candidate will waive it."

"Yes, ma'am!"

Ma'am?

He was only being polite. Gave her the respect a civvie deserved, or an officer of the Marines, after the Corps had chewed her into pieces chased with burnt caf, passed through hellfire, new and improved. Deadly. A leader of Republican Wolves.

No thank you. A stripe and a rifle will do.

The Friday before, she'd met a veteran at Primara Hospital during her military entrance physical. Gunnery Sergeant Seresh Voreche (RAW-MC, ret.) had been a Marine for twenty-two years. Age and doing hard things had diminished his body, forced him into early retirement, and left him with an unkind gait and a cane, but his mind was that of a much younger man. When he retired, he'd taken his pension and gone to Montana, where land was cheap and plentiful. Voreche had told her what to really expect in the Marine Corps. How challenging boot camp and infantry school were. How long deployments could wear you down. How killing a man changed you. Why he almost got out after three tours. How the Corps was more calling than career.

"If you can picture yourself doing anything else," he'd said, "then do that. If not, *then* wear the uniform. It's not for everyone. For me, the Corps became my family. Truth to tell, it still is."

Promise had listened carefully to the retiree. But her eyes had told her more. She'd seen awe and wonder in his gaze, a sparkle that defied easy categorization. Voreche had found himself a place to belong. She'd read about that, too. *Esprit de corps.* She guessed she was after the same.

Nikandros held the tablet up to her eyes. "Voice recognition and your retinal scan come first. Read this line slow and clear."

"See the 'verse in the Republican Marine Corps," Promise said dryly. The words had all the panache of a cheap action holovid, the kind where the acting was piss-poor and the shooting was worse still.

"All right, hold still while the device maps your retina."

A green line drifted across both of her eyes to create her retinal key, the first piece of information in her Republican Personnel Records Jacket. Nikandros handed her the tablet and left her to it. Promise sat down in Montana leather, crossed her legs, and sighed. She felt the unforgiving frame of her GLOCK press against her side.

Names came first.

Great.

"Son-of-a-bi—ah, sorry, ma'am."

Promise looked up from her tablet to stare at Staff Sergeant Nikandros, who was in the process of wiping hot caf off his crotch.

"How old are you, *sir*?" she asked. "And how old do you think I am?"

The staff sergeant sat back. "Ah, old enough to enlist . . . and that's what counts. By the way, don't 'sir' a noncom, ever." Nikandros shook his head and pointed back and forth between himself and Promise. "Remember, we work for a living."

"Then why are you *ma'aming* me?"

Nikandros closed his mouth.

"Never mind." *He's dense like Montana soil.* "Why don't you go back to, ah, that, Staff Sergeant," she said, pointing at his crotch, "and this candidate will get back to this." Promise tapped the tablet with her index finger and held the man's gaze until he looked away.

She scrolled past the basic questionnaire. First name. Last name. At "Next of Kin," she took a deep breath to keep from launching the tablet across the room. "Okay, P, let's take it in reverse." When she reached the last screen, she read the disclaimer. *Yes, I'll release the RAW-MC from all responsibility in the event of my untimely death.* Promise's eyes narrowed. There were all kinds of unpleasant ways to die.

Death due to friendly fire
Death in time of peace and in war
Death from strenuous training
Death due to human error or a mechanical failure
Death caused by environmental toxins
Death due to radiation poisoning

Death occupied nearly an entire screen. And then she came to the final death.

Death due to an act of God

Really? Like God even cares.

Oh, you might be surprised, dear. I know one who's been pissed plenty of times. Do not tempt Him.

Promise nearly bolted to attention.

No, not out there. Inside. Here.

Promise massaged her temples and tried to clear her thoughts, but to no avail.

He barged into a temple—midday, during business hours—and overturned tables, destroying personal property for God's sake. So says the good book anyway.

Get out. I can't think, Promise thought.

Is that any way to talk to your mother?

I'm never going to pass my psych exam. Leave.

Stop obsessing.

You sound like him. Promise banged her head into the wall so hard that it hurt, and then she did it again, even harder. The staff sergeant looked up and stared at her, worry lines creasing his brow.

"*Fine—*" The voice sounded angry, hurt even, and began to fade. "*Before you hurt yourself. Impudent child.*" Then the voice was gone.

She looked down at the tablet. The fields for last, middle, and first names were still blank. She typed her last name slowly, before hitting delete.

Mom said this was my choice. Fine, I'm enlisting and shipping out. That's a pretty big change. "Might as well keep going," she said under her breath.

She saw her reflection in the datapad staring back. But she looked different somehow. It was her face but maybe more at peace. She couldn't say for sure. And then she heard a name call to her. It locked into place, barely seconds old but already fitting like a worn glove. It was the name her mother had brought to her marriage and left behind at the altar. Odd to think of it now. The name said volumes, and it honored the woman who'd carried her for nine months. Most important, it was her choice.

A hard smile consumed Promise's face. The Grations were dead and buried. There was only Paen.

RAW-MC recruit Promise T. Paen.

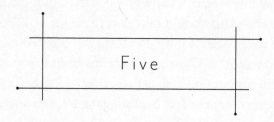

Five

The Android Enemy Soldier stood guard outside the munitions depot, unaware that it was about to die. The RAW-MC was "gung ho," but it wasn't stupid, and it didn't off mechs just because it could. That's what simulations were for. Besides, Aunt Janie's budget couldn't afford it.

Right. Promise took a slow breath and adjusted the rifle's butt against her shoulder to minimize the bruising. *In the Corps, adequate gets the job done,* she thought. *What a crock that is.*

> RANGE: 487.21 meters
> WIND SPEED & DIRECTION: 45° oblique at 1.3 m/s
> ELEVATION: 17.5 meters
> TEMPERATURE: a lot warmer than she liked

She tracked the ANDES through an amber-colored scope and holographic reticule. Bits of environmental data scrolled across her vision until she found what she was looking for. Heat—a variable you felt and respected at long ranges. It was a typical spring day for Eden's equatorial zone, balmy and scorching hot. Promise flexed the muscles in her right eye, and the lens responded in kind, zooming in on the ANDES until it appeared to be standing directly in front of her. *There,* just below the left shoulder. The ANDES's heart. She superimposed a thermal port over the scope's standard daytime presets, and the machine's heart materialized as if on cue, in mottled shades of red. The small fusion reactor was embedded in plating and artificial flesh. She moved her crosshairs three centimeters to the left, to the center of what would soon be a very dead two-leg. But there was such a thing as too much information. Good Strikers took measurements and then shot from the gut. And all that data was making her scope feel cluttered, cramped even.

She slowed her heart rate and breathing, figured one more before mission kill.

Gunnery Sergeant Frederick "Mac" MacGregor's distinct brogue spoke into her mastoid implant. *"All right, Corporal Paen, aim small, steady, squeeze. Kick hell out of the metal-arsed bugger."* A thin smile spread across her face. Not exactly her sentiments, but close enough. The hypervelocity round in the chamber would see to it. In real combat, HV rounds left big holes and little else. Not fancy, zero finesse, but more than adequate. There it was again, adequate getting the job done. *Good enough for government work.*

She turned off her scanners, erasing the telemetry from her field of view, everything but the crosshairs. Released her breath halfway and squeezed the trigger.

Her vision grayed out as the trigger locked up. A soft tone sounded in her mastoid implant, signaling the end of the exercise.

"God bless!" Promise grunted in frustration and slammed her fist into the rocky soil.

"Corporal PAEN."

Promise started, then banged her forehead into the optic on her rifle.

"Corporal Paen." Calmer this time. *"You did not just shut off your scanners. Please, Corporal, tell me after all I've taught you, after all of my hard work, that it wasn't in vain. Please, Corporal, tell me you did not just shut off your optic's scanners."*

"No, Gunny . . . I mean I did, Gu—"

"You are busting my bollocks, Marine. Where is your head? Wait. Do not answer that, Corporal. I will tell you where: up your arse, where the sun don't shine. Because that was bloody paaaiiiiinnnnnn-full. Strikers don't lie doggo for fifteen mikes without running sweeps—all of 'em—all the bloody-merry-live-long-day." Promise heard feet stomping in the background,

timed to the gunny's conniption fit. "*You blew perfect concealment like a frogging greenhorn. I could have done better blindfolded with my scanners on. Keep your eyes on-target and your tech runnin' sweeps. Three o'clock. Please tell me when you find him.*"

Promise checked her flank and saw a stand of trees situated next to a large boulder. No hostile.

"*I am waiting, Corporal.*"

"I don't see him, Gunnery Sergeant." *Not a thing. Nothing. Come on, where are you? Where? Are? You?* Something caught her eye. *You have got to be kidding me.*

The disturbance was barely perceptible, more felt than seen, like a short burst of air through thick tree branches in the dead of winter. But the distortion drew her eyes as a mechsuit slowly materialized between two leaf-bearing trees and waved at her. And it was almost on top of her position.

"I see him, Gunnery Sergeant."

"*Oh, now you see him. Nooowwww you see him.*" The gunny sighed and dropped the volume dangerously low. "*Corporal Paen, if this had been a real op, I'd be officiating over your casket and handing the flag to your next of kin. A fractal scan would have found the hostile that just shot a beam through that expensive head of yours. Even our newfangled Witchfield leaves a small thermal distortion, if you actually bother to look for it.*"

She'd known better and she hadn't.

"*One mistake is one too many. One gets you dead. You are better than this, Corporal. You have let me down, Marine. You have let your toon down. You have let yourself down. Congratulations, Corporal. You're a casualty.*"

"Yes, Gunnery Sergeant."

"*Corporal, use your head for something besides a helmet rack.*"

"Yes, Gunnery Sergeant."

"*And don't make that mistake again, ever! You're a veteran.*" The gunny sounded surprised, and genuinely disappointed in her, which was even worse. "*Remember: act fast; use your gear to look slow. You read me, Marine?*"

"Yes, Gunnery Sergeant."

"*And stop saying, 'Yes, Gunnery Sergeant.*"

"Understood, Gunny!"

"Get out of my sight and grab some chow. Your upgraded mechsuit rolls off the line tonight. You imprint tomorrow. After diagnostics, you head to the canyon for trials. Lights-out at 2200 hours. Understood?"

"Yes, Gunnery Sergeant."

"Piss off."

"Aye, aye, Gunny."

Promise released her trigger hand and pushed herself off the ground. Frustration washed over her face. She forced it aside as she took a knee, rotated her striker rifle, pulled the bolt back, and cleared the chamber, then handed all of it over to her Mule, which had dutifully materialized to hump her gear back to base. Her rifle was old-tech, but Strikers operated at extreme ranges, and bolt-actions were still the most reliable platforms around.

She pulled her helmet off last and placed it on what passed for the Mule's head. The close infantry-support platform was dressed in forest camo and fitted with webbing. It secured her gear, saluted like an ANDES, and dutifully spun around, gliding at high speed toward the barracks.

She watched as the Mule shrank with distance. It would beat her back to base, clean her gear, and return it to her in battle-ready condition. Promise would clean it again because she didn't trust a machine to do a human-rate job. Smart Marines did their own grunt work as a matter of pride and necessity. Life and death often hung on the little details like a thoroughly cleaned wep. Wolves that trusted their tech to Mechs grew sloppy in other areas, and sloppy Marines didn't live long.

Promise arched her back and felt her muscles complain from too much inactivity. She raised her wrist and tapped in a command, which sent a signal to her boots. As she picked up her right foot, she felt the sole remold itself for running. Then the left. When she raised her eyes, she saw the observation post in the distance. The gunny was out there.

She could feel his eyes upon her, somehow sense his disappointment. Gunny Mac could harness the fear of God with a word, melt through peristeel with a look. She imagined him standing at parade rest as he surveyed the field with a dark expression on his face. She'd planned to impress him today, but matters hadn't quite worked to her advantage.

No, P, because you just screwed up by the numbers.

Not that most Marines would've fared better. The Cloak was still on the official secrets list. Promise knew about it because her unit was preparing to muster out with first-generation "Witches." But she hadn't planned to face one. Marine Intelligence believed the Lusitanians and the Terran Federation were still a year or more away from deploying the technology. But that was irrelevant. Now she understood the point of this exercise was to teach her to expect the unexpected. A lesson she wouldn't forget.

The run back to the barracks was uneventful. She jogged most of the first klick, imagining the Republican standard being folded into a triangle and handed to her next of kin, whoever that was. It took her three more klicks to let go of her mistake. She kicked hard through the last thousand meters. The adrenaline brought peace.

As she started up the hill overlooking her barracks, she contemplated the specs of her new mechsuit. The Kydoimos-6 Mechanized Infantry Combat Battlesuit, or mechsuit for short, was the backbone of the RAW-MC. Rugged, ergonomic, and well designed for myriad battlefield conditions in Earthlike atmospheres, in vacuum, and in alien environs. The standard suite of weapons wasn't half bad either:

1. Heavier-hitting, downsized Horde missiles and a denser pod
2. Choice of two tactical rifles: the Marine Corps, 3rd Evolution, Extended-Range Pulse Rifle, or MC^3-ERP (pronounced McEerp), and the FS-7.77 Automatic Carbine
3. A rifle-mounted Flexible Grenade Launcher, choice of over a dozen different rounds
4. Two Heavy Select-Fire Pistols (capable of semi-automatic, full-automatic, and burst fire): E-version or P-version; the P's ammo came in ten mike-mike armor-piercing explosive penetrators; fléchette rounds; hypervelocity darts; and scattershot
5. An EMP-hardened mesh

The mechsuit had compartments for throwing grenades, a medkit, and rations. It also plugged and played an assortment of heavier weapons like the Fuji-P, a particle gun that disrupted atomic bonds, with devastating results.

And it can cloak. Someday the enemy will, too. I'll remember to remember that.

On the other side of the hill, Promise saw her barracks and Corporal

Maxzash-Indar Sindri, who was leaning against the gray-on-gray ferocrete structure, which temporarily housed Victor Company. A just-fired good-luck smoke perched on his lip. The sun at her back cast a long shadow that caught the corporal's attention. He raised his arm and broke into a wide grin, pointed two fingers at his dark brown eyes, and then pointed one at Promise. Promise mimicked him and shook her head in disgust.

Their standing bet was two years old. Whoever did better at the range paid the other fifty chits. Sindri spent like he was on perpetual liberty, so if Promise won, the money went into a retirement account set up in the corporal's name, one he couldn't get to until he aged out of the Corps, retired, or turned sixty-two. Promise didn't drink, and Sindri liked to keep a designated pilot on call. So if he won, he got to spend it any way he liked. And by the look on Sindri's face, he already knew she'd lost, again.

That's Maxi for you. And since I don't partake, I'll have to pay his tab and fly the louse home, too.

Genetics had predestined Sindri to be small, a man nearly passed over by puberty, and his hairless body seemed to argue the point as much as he had tried to argue against it. On most days and particularly during combat exercises, the corporal wore extra socks, claiming that his feet perspired more than most. This was true. You didn't shower or change near the corporal when the socks came off: you bolted when they hit the deck if you knew what was good for you. The members of his toon explained the socks differently—he needed the extra height to see out the visor of his mechsuit. This was also true. Promise knew his height had defined him, from early childhood, and that it was still a sore spot with him.

As she jogged around the barracks to cool down, she passed by and stuck her tongue out at Maxi; then she circled back around and came to rest beside her toonmate. The corporal nodded toward the entrance, and Promise followed. Just inside, her rifle lay on a stand, waiting for her.

"I took the liberty of retrieving it from your Mule. He didn't want to give it to me. But I persuaded him otherwise."

"You didn't hurt Stevie, did you?"

"Nah, but his optics may need recalibrating."

"Stop abusing my Mule."

"He started it."

"Mech bully."

Maxi folded his arms across his chest. "I'll leave you to your cleaning. We can settle up later."

Promise fieldstripped her weapon. She worked methodically, placing each piece with care on a stained sheet until an exploded diagram of the rifle materialized before her. When she was done, every piece shined. A small mound of soiled, square-cut cloth patches sat to the side, and the smell of solvent hung in the air. Her Mule had done a fair job, which was strictly to regulation. But she preferred to leave the solvent in a bit longer than the Regs called for before patching out the barrel. Her first patches were almost clean.

Maxi came back with a sack and cleared away the mess. "Only a Mule, always a human."

It was a running joke between them. He liked to delegate, which is why he was on his fourth Mule. She preferred human hands and bearing her own load.

Promise scolded him and then turned her attention back to her rifle.

The basic elements of sniper rifles hadn't changed much in a thousand years. Bolt-actions and rifle barrels in particular—faithful and eternal friends. But polymers had changed a lot, which meant heavy rifles weren't so heavy anymore. One Marine could disassemble the weapon and carry it alone. Sniper ammo, on the other hand, had bulked up considerably. Modern battle armor required large rounds for one-shot-one-kills, particularly from a distance. Promise preferred the 23 mike-mike long-and-lethals. They were "smart" ammo, armor-piercing explosive rounds that simply did more. A modest electronics suite, longer range than most rounds, deeper penetration, bigger boom. APERs devastated targets.

Promise quickly reassembled the weapon and stowed it in her locker, secured her ammo in a can, then grabbed her minicomp from the shelf above her rack and went looking for the corporal.

Six

"So." Corporal Sindri let the word hang in the air. "The invisible man got you, too."

"I didn't expect cloaked hostiles. Should have at least allowed for it, though."

"Oh, well. Scores are in." Maxi looked pretty unsympathetic.

"So?" Promise broke eye contact with her toonmate and looked around the room. First-world games lined the walls. Some were as old as she was and most were rarely played. To her right stood a worn rectangular table-top, which was split in the middle by a low-hung net. The net had seen better days. Two paddles rested on the playing surface, one cocked just so with a small discolored sphere propping it up. Marine-issue games were typically antiques. Something about the Republic caring more about training and ammo than R & R. Promise didn't disagree there. She preferred tactile games to the digital variety anyway.

She motioned with her head. "Maxi, I'll play you for it. I win, and we call it even."

"I'm afraid it doesn't work that way."

"It never hurts to ask. You can't receive unless you ask."

"Hmmm . . . interesting choice of words, P. Speaking of receiving, I believe you owe me."

The corporal stood and took his chair with him into the next room, which housed their toon's cluster. It was about time for chop, and the barracks were alive with Marines showering, shaving, and packing for the canyon. A hulking Marine walked by wrapped in nothing but tattoos and a towel. Her toon occupied the northwest corner. Five racks sat in a starburst pattern, gear strewn out on top and rumpled sheets below. Two of her five toonmates were busy packing. Lance Corporal Talon Covington nodded toward Promise before he turned back to stuffing his gear into a worn seabag. Private First Class Kathy Prichart smiled like she new something, then returned her attention to stuffing hers with one hand while she ate an energy bar with the other. The fifth rack in the cluster belonged to Staff Sergeant Nhorman Khaine. It was noticeably empty and squared away. Maxi grabbed something from his own rack, then grabbed a chair and pulled up to Promise's. Promise brought up the rear. During Maxi's Striker trials, a cloaked hostile had also M-Killed him. But his scores on the range had surpassed Promise's, a mere tenth of a percentile between them. It was a hairline fracture in their relationship.

"Pay up, Sergeant."

"Sergeant? Not with my range scores. I'll be a two-stripe for the foreseeable future."

Promise leaned over Maxi and grabbed her minicomp. She queued up her bank records and reluctantly thumbed the transfer.

"There, happy?" She flashed him the screen, which displayed a blinking transfer code as the final proof.

"That'll do. Besides, I've already spent it."

Promise feigned exasperation. It was an old argument. "Go on, you might as well show me."

"I know." Sindri raised his hand in mock surrender. "But it was for a good cause—mine. Here, this is for you."

He brought his right hand out from behind his back and handed her a wrapped cube.

"A bow and invisible tape? I'm impressed."

"Mom made sure I touch my feminine side, at least once in a while."

Promise thought of a quick retort, then thought better of it and kept her mouth shut. She looked up at Maxi with delight as she tore off the wrapping and popped the lid. Her eyes narrowed intently, face all business. Sergeant's stripes. Hers? Three inverted gold Vs backed with red flash, nestled in a lined box. For her mess dress. Underneath, Vs on khaki flash peeked out, for her regular dress uniform, utilities, and her beegees on mechsuit underarmor.

Sindri cleared his throat. "They belonged to the staff sergeant. He wanted to give them to you personally, before the skipper made it official. He said to tell you to always remember. That you'd understand what he meant."

Promise looked up, startled to see that the corporal had been joined by her fellow toonmates. PFC Prichart plopped down beside Promise and slapped her back like she was choking.

"Well done, *Sergeant*."

Prichart was a wiry girl. She still had that just-out-of-boot-camp look, with ocean-colored eyes and spiky sea-foam hair. She was also lethal with a tribarrel pulse rifle, and she had a second-degree belt from the RAW-MC's mixed-martial-arts college hanging in her locker. Kathy was as direct in her martial arts as she was with her guns. For a small woman she had a penchant for big guns, and she slapped hard.

"Ouch, careful. Apparently, this *sergeant* isn't made of peristeel." The staff sergeant's empty rack suddenly made sense. Promise made eye contact with each of her toonmates, already sensing a new distance between herself and her new command.

Covington chimed in with his basso voice. His "Ooh-rah" seemed to shake the room. "Maybe not, Sergeant, but I'll grant you polymer, unpowered body armor."

"Thanks, Lance Corporal. Almost unbreakable, huh?"

"And for the times that you aren't, I'll be there," Covington said. The gentle giant smiled as he pressed his gigantic thumbs to his chest, revealing some of the largest teeth Promise had ever seen. His towel shook loose and fell halfway to the deck before he caught it.

"Nice catch."

The lance corporal towered over Corporal Sindri, stood tall compared with everyone else in Victor Company, and the entire battalion for that matter. Covington was a small behemoth, massed 138 kilos. The toon's heavy-weapons expert and one of only a handful of Republican Marines who could heft the MC-390 Mass-Driver, nicknamed the Bi-Polar, in and out of his mechsuit. Bi-Polars typically required two-man crews, one to carry the rail and the other the base. Tucked underneath Covington's arms, both halves looked like errant children. The lance corporal was also a spawn from the planet Ghalt, which boasted the second highest gravity of any settled planet. His great-nanna had been one of the first tube babies genetically altered for HG worlds. Nana's family had arrived in an ark during the first wave of exploration to the harsh environment of Ghalt's equatorial zone. And the bio-enhancements had been passed along in utero ever since.

"And Staff Sergeant Khaine?"

"It's Gunnery Sergeant Khaine now."

Promise nodded, mixed emotions churning inside of her.

"He just bag-dragged," Maxi said. "That's why his cot is squared away and his gear is gone. He meant to say good-bye but didn't have time. He was kicked upstairs to Battalion. Orders came through last night while you were camping at the range. He left at 0600 hours, and he left a message in your queue."

Promise sat silently, looking at her command. "Well, I am happy for him." She reassessed her platoon sergeant's old rack and realized that an unfamiliar boot would soon take possession of it. The room about her felt smaller somehow. Empty. She realized she felt a bit empty inside, too.

Staff Sergeant Nhorman Khaine had taken Promise's training personally and whipped her sorry, scared butt into a competent and confident Republican Marine. Talked her through after her first kill, made her a Wolf. She remembered a particularly unpleasant night, shortly after boot camp. She'd been a member of his toon for barely a month when the dreams had started up again. They began with her father being shot and his body falling toward the earth. This dream had been particularly violent, and she'd cried out in her sleep. When she turned over, she found the staff sergeant at her side with a cup of steaming liquid in one hand and a cold compress in the other.

She'd eyed the cup warily. "Anything in that, Staff Sergeant?"

"Only what you need to sleep, Private. But, before you do, would you like to talk about it?"

"I don't know . . . maybe," she'd answered. But those first few uncertain words had grown into a small stream and swelled into a river of conflict that poured out of her. He had listened, nodded, and held his tongue until Promise lay exhausted on her cot. At the end of her story, the staff sergeant had merely put a hand on her shoulder and told her she was safe, that she had a new home. That he wouldn't let her down.

She never forgot what he said next. "Promise, sounds to me like you haven't buried your dead yet. The tricky part about moving on is figuring out how to own your grief. Right now, it owns you—guilt will do that. But you didn't kill your father. Once you bury that lie, your grief will change and you'll be okay."

"Thanks, Staff Sergeant."

"It's not so easy, though. I know."

"No. It's not."

"Give it time. For now, drink this and bag some sleep. We'll talk again, soon."

"Thank you, Staff Sergeant."

Promise had known her promotion to sergeant was in her not too distant future, and with it would come her own toon. Platoon Sergeant Paen. But she hadn't expected it this soon. Nor had she expected to assume command of Khaine's toon.

Make that my *toon.* Promise shook her head. *Thank you.* Looked up at her Marines.

"Well, we may be down a woman for an indefinite period of time," Promise said. "Platoon sergeants don't pick their people, and the picking is slim these days." This was also true. With new member planets flocking to the Republic of Aligned Worlds, the Corps was strapped for manpower, in the midst of a massive recruiting effort, and struggling to keep their active units at full strength. There simply weren't enough live bodies to fill the mechsuits rolling off the plant.

"Actually, Sergeant, we got lucky, and she's a he. Arriving on a transport later today." Maxi had already jumped into his new role as Promise's number two. "Private First Class Fritz U'baire—he's almost as green as they come, but his jacket seems solid. The staff sarg—I mean, the gunny— pulled some strings before he left. Said he once made a promise to you that he wasn't about to break. Said you understand about that, too. Check your comp."

Promise accessed her minicomp and found U'baire's jacket. Maxi drew up next to her as tiers of holographic data appeared: pictures, weapons proficiencies and range tests, and an early good conduct medal—they were normally handed out every two years, and U'baire had earned his in one, barely a month ago, which said a lot. Promise pursed her lips when she saw the flashing arrow attached to U'baire's "drop" record.

"Thoughts?" Promise arched her neck, found Maxi chewing the inside of his cheek.

"His marks are top ten percent. Expert with small arms, too. A lot of greenhorns tense up in atmo, during drops. He's not blooded yet either. Time will take care of that, and his nerves."

Not unlike a young woman I once knew, Promise thought.

"His mechsuit will need upgrading. Maxi, see to it."

"Aye, aye, Sergeant."

"Good, we'll head to the trials together and I'll shadow him, which will give me a good read on his skills. Let's check with the skipper about a HALO drop sometime this week. We could all use the practice. I want at least three, back-to-back, but I'll settle for one if I have to."

Corporal Sindri smiled. "Roger that. Eden's upper atmosphere should shake the space dust out of his mechboots." He flicked his eyes at Prichart and Covington, who took the hint and walked into the next room. Corporal Sindri waited until they were out of range before he turned back to Promise.

"Promise—ah, Sergeant—I have some reservations about moving out to Widow Maker's Canyon for a live-fire assault exercise with the ANDES."

"Maxi, we're still friends. Let's keep it casual when it's just the two of us. What about the ANDES is bothering you? Afraid of the two-legs?"

"It's not the ANDES that scare me. I worry about the Seabees that programmed them. It's one thing to shoot ANDES on the range. Storming embedded positions held by them, where they shoot back, is another matter entirely. If you don't dial down their strength settings and weapons aptitudes to something we fleshies can handle, we could end up in an untenable position, with injured or worse. And what about Uncle Murphy? What if there's a glitch in the sim? Or an ANDES starts shooting live ammo? I don't want to be on the receiving end of that. Or U'baire. The ANDES are bad karma."

Promise looked at her friend, now subordinate, and tried to sift his worry down to naked truth. Several years back, the Corps had begun using ANDES instead of warm bodies in live-fire trials. Instead of declining, accidental deaths had nearly doubled. The situation was currently "under review."

"You know I don't believe in karma or fate, Maxi, and neither should you. Fatalistic thinking like that will get you killed. We make our own luck, and providence has a hand, too."

"It's not fate but numbers, P—they don't lie. The ANDES are dangerous."

"Maybe, but so are the flesh-and-blood marauders that plague the poorer systems. Too many of them were once Marines like you and me, boots who traded their allegiances for blood money. We've faced a couple of decently funded outfits, but those battles were easy. We had the advantage, better gear, superior intel. But there are more dangerous threats. It's only a matter of time before we face an enemy who can really hurt us." Promise grilled him with her eyes. "Are you prepared for that?"

Sindri turned thoughtful. "Yeah, I'm ready. Besides, this is all I know. The Corps is in my blood. You know, I'm fifth generation on both sides."

"I didn't know that," Promise said sarcastically.

"Mom, Dad, Grams, and Gramps expect big things of me. Nothing like a little generational pressure . . . You're lucky you're first-gen Corps. You get a fresh start and a clean slate."

"Maxzash-Indar Sindri, there's nothing fresh or clean about the RAW-MC." Promise inhaled. "On that note, I believe I need to hit the showers."

Promise let the water and steam knead the tension out of her body. It wasn't every day that a Marine became a casualty, lost a bet, and replaced her platoon sergeant, all within the same hour.

Seven

"Skipper on deck!"

Victor Company went from relaxed to high alert in the span of a second. Most of V Company's Wolves were dressed and quickly mustered by platoon, backs like boards and arms racked to rumps. A few stumbled out of bed wearing nothing but their skivvies and swearing under their breath, breasts and balls swinging freely under loose shirts and shorts.

Captain Paul Remus entered the barracks like God incarnate and came to rest just off Promise's rack.

Wonderful, she thought. *Just wonderful! Why do I have a bad feeling about this?*

Remus was a lanky man with a severe profile and an irritatingly coarse voice. His nose ran straight down the plane of his face and broke left at the last possible moment. The captain could have fixed that, and it said volumes about him that he hadn't. He looked more perturbed than usual.

"Victor Company has had a sudden change of plans. Normally, we'd send you out to the canyon for trials," the captain said, "and give you time to exorcise the ghosts in your new mechsuits before shipping out. But we've got a minor crisis in the Rim. We can all thank another well-financed group of privateers for stirring up this mess. Battalion needs us there pronto to clean it up. And clean it up we will."

Nerves and sweat circulated through the vents. Eyes darted from attention to the faces of friends and fellow Marines, then back to ten-hut! The Rim was the dumping ground of humanity, also called the verge, a place where nonaligned worlds and poorer systems lived from hand to mouth. Rim duty often meant lawless governments and poor supply lines. Myriad questions pressed upon the members of Victor Company as they swore silently, in unison.

"And it seems this little mess may also involve the Lusies. Our spooks believe the Lusitanian Empire is behind several recent attacks upon our Merchant Marines in the Mendelson sector, and the situation is escalating. We've lost six commercial freighters in the past month. The boys over at Marine Intelligence picked up some chatter involving a threat to one of our plebiscites, and because we're just three jumps away from Montana . . ."

Promise's façade cracked, history bleeding across her face. She shook herself mentally and decided that was then; this is now. *Time to get over that, Sergeant. Time to move on.* Promise closed her eyes, *Easier said than done.*

". . . a planet that was only admitted to the RAW fifteen years ago." Remus's eyes briefly met hers. "Montana is still a provisional member of the Republic, but she's well on her way to achieving full voting status in the Senate. More importantly, Montana flanks Lusitanian space, and she's metal-rich. That's why the Lusies want her and why we can't let her go. She's strategically important as the only hab planet in a critical buffer system. And . . . she's our ally. Some of you janes and jacks are old enough to remember her formal annexation. We got into a minor scuffle with the Lusies. Made the nets in the late seventies."

Promise's face heated. What Captain Remus labeled a minor scuffle for the Republic of Aligned Worlds had been a planetary tragedy for Montana. A Lusitanian warship had entered neutral space, encountered a Republican cruiser in system, and fired a shot across the bow, out near Montana's third moon. When the warhead's self-destruct failed, the missile went ballistic and "wandered" into Montana's atmosphere. Like most poor planets, there had been no space-based weapons platform available to engage the threat. Not even a ground-based launcher or a single air-breathing fighter to scramble. Montanans had helplessly watched the missile streak across the sky and done the only thing they could do. Prayed.

A simple kill switch prevented a small holocaust. Otherwise, the Lusies and RAW-MC would surely have gone to war. But the kinetic strike pierced Montana in the heart, killing three hundred colonists, most under the age of ten. Promise had been eight years old. The school drills started the very next week. She had missed them because she was home-schooled. But she'd watched a vid where a principal told the students to get under their desks, where it was safest. Even at eight, she knew that would never work.

Captain Remus crossed his arms as he scanned his troops. Each member of Victor Company was lost in thought, different pasts and different fears surfacing at the prospect of a tough deployment.

"Alright, people, I read you five by five. No one likes Rim duty. But ours not to reason why."

Victor Company barked out the obligatory, "Ours but to do and die!"

"We're going in to fly the flag and reassure the Montanan government that the Republic takes care of its own. Montana has been a problem since the annexation. It's not her fault we're strapped for Marines and fighting a proxy war along multiple fronts. But, and I want this clear as a well-hydrated Wolf's piss, these are citizens of the Republic and we owe them better, so they're gonna get better."

Remus scowled for good measure, a look he normally reserved for a dress down.

"Our mission is part antipiracy and part diplomacy. In case you haven't figured it out, one of Montana's own is among us—our newest platoon sergeant, in point of fact."

All eyes stared straight ahead but might as well have been looking right at her.

Right. Promise's core froze. She stood just a bit straighter and kept her gaze at a regulation three centimeters just off the skipper's right ear, wishing she could crawl into a fighting hole.

"Sergeant Paen. I'm sorry to do this to you. Part of why we're going in is because of you. Battalion believes a native in uniform might help us make inroads with the planetary government and patch things up with the locals. Can do, Sergeant?"

"Can do, Skipper."

Captain Remus nodded his approval and turned back to face his command.

"Marines," he said, addressing the hall, "we're about to be visitors on a planet full of reluctant hosts. They're angry. They're tired of being screwed. I would be, too, if I were in their boots. You're to be on your best behavior. If I so much as hear about one of my Marines giving any Montanan so much as a nasty look, it's half a month's pay and chop duty for an entire month. Have I made myself clear?"

"Yes, sir!" roared Victor Company.

"Good. Drain it, dump it, wolf it down, and pack it up. After that, head over to the morgue. You're being issued standard gear for garrison duty. Those of you designated for Striker rifles and heavy weps will get those, too. Extra MREs are on me." Grins and groans all around. "And don't forget to see your corpsmen and top off your pharmacope. Run down the list, boys and girls; check it twice. We'll be two jumps out from Mendelson SECCOM. That's a lot of light years between us, the Navy, and Battalion HQ. I've been told not to expect reinforcements or resupply either, at least for several months. So get your gear prepped and get ready to mount up."

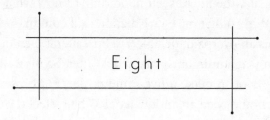

Eight

With Captain Remus's departure came an eerie calm that flooded the barracks as if all the air had breached out. Victor Company exhaled in unison. There were a lot worse places than Montana, which had a respectable gross-system product, the rule of law firmly in place, and little poverty. But the news came as no comfort to Promise. She knew little of realpolitik. She had no desire to return to her birth world either. She was not—*not*—returning home.

Promise found the mission brief already loaded to her minicomp. Pirates, which MARINT suspected were a front operation for the Lusitanian Empire, had set up shop in Montana's system. The Navy's spooks thought the pirates were staging their operations from one of Montana's three moons or from the system's asteroid belt. Exact location was unknown. But the known unknowns weren't the real problem. In the last two months, matters had grown to crisis levels. The loss of the commercial freighters was significant enough to put the entire sector on high alert. Moreover, four separate, unexplained fires on Montana's surface had claimed 113 lives and dozens of businesses and had burned over 250,000 hectares of pristine Montana hardwoods. That had caused a small panic across Montana's thirteen continents. Weather and human error had both been ruled out. And Montanans didn't burn their own land.

In response, a team of Montana lobbyists and senior government officials had flooded the Republican capital planet of Hold and, with temerity and recklessness, had dug into the labyrinthine maze that defined Republican politics. After being bounced between the Senate Frontier Defense Committee and the Homeworlds Alliance Committee, they were dumped into the lap of the Anterior Director of Homeworlds Security. The truth was that the SFDC's left hand didn't know what the right was doing, the H-WAC didn't have jurisdiction and couldn't have cared less, and ADHS was an overpaid, delta-sierra bureaucrat. Fed up, a brash and desperate envoy ignominiously named Walter Scott walked onto the RAW's Senate floor to make a five-minute speech. Midway through his address, Scott brandished an antiquated .357 blue-steel revolver and fired what became known as "Montana's shot heard round the Republic" into the 287-year-old ceiling, shattering glass and the veil of silence. He was summarily tackled by a two-man plainclothes security detail, jacketed, hauled off to the nearest spaceport in an armored Aerodyne, boosted into orbit on the next available shuttle, and sent home without his weapon and with a reminder to Montana's president that his diplomatic immunity would only protect him from so much. But Scott had made his point. Montana would not be ignored.

Shadows filled Promise's thoughts. She'd left her homeworld for a reason. She'd needed to find space, to distance herself from painful memories. She sunk to her rack and put her head between her knees. Her hands started to shake. She reached underneath and withdrew a small box. Opening it, she took out a ball and some needles. Her hands worked in tandem, chaining the wool and her fear together until the shaking became a tremor and the tremor a still, small voice of doubt in a small, manageable place in the back of her mind.

Her mother had taught her to knit when she was five to help her with her fine motor coordination. And the habit held fast, as if Sandra had sewn a piece of herself into the fabric of her daughter's soul. Her hands switched to autopilot as her mind wandered into the past.

During her sixth week in Khaine's toon, she'd led a mock assault on an enemy supply depot. The staff sergeant played the part of her enemy. Her platoon suffered 80 percent casualties, which left her running solo and cornered in a narrow ravine, a no-win situation. The staff sergeant called for her surrender. Her solution had been unorthodox, and it had sent Nhorman Khaine into orbit.

"Private Paen! Stand down. This exercise is over."

Promise heard the staff sergeant in her mastoid implant, on a closed link. Watched as the SNCO broke concealment and stormed toward her with quick, measured strides. Flinched as he grabbed the front of her armor and slammed her up against a boulder. His visor turned translucent, revealing eyes flushed with heat and anger.

"Staff Sergeant—please—I don't understand."

Khaine's words were pitched just above a whisper, scraped across his teeth on the way out. *"Initiating a suicide?"*

"No, Staff Sergeant. Seizing the initiative."

"That's a God-damned way to die, Paen. Do you have a death wish?"

The staff sergeant's words shook her to the core. Her mouth went dry, and she couldn't think. Promise shook her head.

"Not like that. Not ever, understood? This may be a training op, but self-immolation isn't acceptable. Ever. You should have surrendered. What you just did crossed the line."

Promise got hold of her voice and pushed back, full of emotion. "With respect, Staff Sergeant, my mission was to secure the depot and neutralize the enemy." Her visor cleared. "The depot was beyond my resources to take. But I could have taken your toon with me"—she nodded—"Staff Sergeant."

"Maybe, but at what price? Your life is worth more. Better to surrender and live to fight another day than to casually discard your life." Khaine released her and took a step back. When he turned around, his platoon was staring at him. They'd racked their helmets. Faces bleached with shock and uncertainty.

He pulled off his helmet and slicked his hair back. "Sorry, people. Life is valuable. Never forget that." Then he turned back to Promise. "Walk with me."

Promise never forgot that walk, and she never forgot the lesson. "Promise, our jobs are dangerous, and someday we might be called to give our lives for our star nation. But don't court that day. Should it come, die living. You understand?"

Promise felt the breeze soothe her cheek. "Yes, Staff Sergeant, I believe I do."

"Tell me something, Paen. Why do you knit?"

Stopped her in her tracks. "Staff Sergeant?"

Khaine stopped and turned to face her. He raised an eyebrow and waited.

"I guess it helps me relax. It's therapy."

"Yup, I get that. But are you relaxing or trying to forget?"

"I . . ."

"Look, you've had a lot of loss for someone so young. Don't grow numb to it. You've got to embrace your pain, sooner or later, or it will lead you to do something reckless."

"Like what I did today, Staff Sergeant?"

"*Just* like what you did today. Now, enough of that. Have you picked a call sign yet?"

"Ah, no, still thinking about it."

"Well, I have an idea: Slipstitch."

Promise's lips cracked. "Have you been reading up on me, Staff Sergeant?"

"I'll have you know that a slipstitch is sometimes called a 'blind stitch' because it's formed by slipping thread under a fold of fabric, like this." The staff sergeant's hands began talking for him. "It can be used to join two folded edges too, or . . . or . . . ah . . . would you help me out, Private?"

"Why don't I get my needles, Staff Sergeant." Promise managed not to smile and sounded totally sincere. "I can show you."

Khaine crossed his arms and fought the smile until it overwhelmed him. "I think it fits you perfectly, Promise. Your pain is buried so deep you can't see it. Slip beneath it, get a handle on it, turn it into an asset. It's a rare individual that can stare death in the face and make peace with it. You do that and you'll become a truly lethal Marine."

"Okay, Staff Sergeant. Slipstitch. I'll do my best to live up to it."

"All right, then. Get back to your toon. Let's run the op again. But this time, take the depot and my toon without getting KIA. Or offing yourself."

"Roger that."

A shadow moved. Promise looked up to see Maxi standing with his back to her, blocking her view of the rest of the company.

And the rest of the company from seeing me like this.

"Feel tall yet?"

"Not particularly," he said as he turned around.

"Enjoy it because it ain't gonna last."

"Just stretching, Sergeant. Just stretching."

Sindri bent down to adjust his boot-sock, dropping his head lower than Promise's, and looked up to catch her eyes.

"BUMED need to know about this?"

"No, Corporal, BUMED does *not*. I've been evaluated before and cleared for duty." *BUMED doesn't need to know that and a whole lot more*, she thought. Promise immediately regretted the edge to her words. "Sorry, Maxi."

Sindri looked intently into her eyes. Apparently satisfied with what he saw, he nodded. "S'okay. Touchy subject—just looking out for you, you know."

"Yeah, I know. And I appreciate it. Do me a favor and don't stop."

"Aye, aye, Sergeant. Why don't you drop your needles and hit the range for some target practice. That 'senior' of yours has an odd way of calming you. I can handle your gear. That is, if you trust little ole Corporal Maxzash-Indar Sindri not to swindle you out of precious ammo and cells."

"Maxi, you're a good-for-nothing cheat," Promise said, loud enough for everyone in the barracks to hear. "I don't trust you in cards. Why would I with my gear?"

Promise whispered a quick "thank you" and stood. "Time's up," she said.

"Good things never last," Maxi replied, his full height failing to reach hers.

"Actually, some things do." Promise briefly laid a hand on his shoulder and squeezed. Then she turned and walked to her locker, grabbed her shooting bag, and headed outside.

Promise set her weapon down with the chamber open and the barrel pointed downrange. She hung her ear protectors around her neck and threw her goggles on the table. The deck around her was littered with casings, and her fingers were lightly coated with black dust and perspiration. The shells underfoot went flying into the distance. She cleaned her hands on a towel and grabbed her minicomp to hit the recall button. Several seconds later, her circular target appeared directly in front of her.

I think I'll stop while I'm ahead. Promise turned around and nearly jumped out of her boots.

"A little warning next time."

"Not bad, munchkin—pretty tight groupings. The half-dozen fliers are forgivable. What is that? Fifteen meters? I'd say you got her."

"And?"

"And what?"

"There's usually something. Might as well go ahead and tell me what it is." Promise started stuffing her gear into her bag.

"Well, since you asked, you're putting too much finger on the trigger, just a smidge. Don't let your anger crush the gun. Relax. Why don't you give it another go?"

"No thanks. I've had enough for today. You know, this isn't my first time."

Sandra bit her lip. "I remember my first time on the range. I was five, six at most. My mother didn't let me shoot that day, just watch and learn. Shooting came later, after I understood the dangers, and what not to do."

"And here it comes," Promise said.

"I taught you not to shoot angry. It's dangerous."

Promise rolled her eyes. "So is being a Marine. I'll live."

"Stow the know-it-all, bring out my daughter," Sandra said.

"Stop butting in."

Promise tore her muffs off and threw them at her mother. "Of all the places to be deployed, they had to send me back to . . . to . . . back . . ."

"Home."

"Hardly."

"Matters could be worse. This time you won't be alone. You're going home with your company."

Promise closed the bag forcefully, slung it over her shoulder, and started walking. "I don't have a home to go back to. Montana is just a bad memory, a reminder of how unfair life is."

"The Corps isn't asking you to make Montana your home, Promise." Sandra fell in step with her. "Fair has nothing to do with it. Life isn't, ever. You know that. Marines pull a lot of hellish deployments, and this one doesn't begin to—"

"Yes, ma'am. I'll just do my duty. Roger that, Skipper," Promise spun and saluted.

"Don't play military with me, young lady. I raised you better than that."

"You don't have the right." Her voice lowered to a whisper. "You weren't around . . . you left . . . you . . . you left me . . . all alone"

"I left you? I didn't have a choice. I hung on for a year. And do you know why?"

Promise's fingers passed through her mom's hands. "Mom, I'm sorry."

"Shut up and listen for a change. Every day I was sick was hell." Sandra got to within centimeters of her daughter's face, close enough for Promise to feel her breath, if she'd had any to expel. "Every treatment I endured was torture. But I told myself just one more treatment and one more day until tomorrow came. And then I did it again because of your father and because of you, but mainly for you. Your dad was a good man and a good husband. But our life was far from perfect, and his fundamentalism nearly ended our marriage on more than one occasion—you don't need *me* to tell you that. I feared for the two of you, for what would happen to you both after I was gone. I worried you would lose your joy. And then I was gone, and it wasn't my job to worry about you anymore."

"And then my life became hell." Promise crossed her arms and looked away.

Sandra's face softened. "I'm so sorry, munchkin." Sandra reached out for her daughter. "Look at me. Please."

Promise turned back but refused to open her eyes. She shook her head, and the tears came anyway. She longed for the warmth of her mother's touch on her cheek. She imagined the rough texture of her mom's hands cradling her face, the way her mom had pushed her hair back behind her ear and scratched her neck to say I love you.

"I loved you, munchkin, and I still do. You won't have to do this alone."

When Promise opened her eyes, her mother was nowhere to be seen.

Nine

The triplets orbited Montana, visible at all hours and constant like the system's sun. Swallows Helm was by far the smallest planetoid with a diameter of 174 klicks. Pockmarks covered three quarters of the lifeless globe. From the surface of Montana, the moon had the appearance of land masses separated by seas. The moon's weak gravity field had prevented an atmosphere from forming, but it was more than sufficient to catch wanderers and collide with them.

Promise had been assigned to personal quarters aboard RNS *Absalon,* instead of to a rack with her Marines. She felt better about her situation knowing that the rest of the platoon sergeants and the staff noncommissioned officers of V Company had been assigned personal quarters, too. But not much better. To Promise, the cabin didn't feel right, and she found herself longing for the company of her toon.

Absalon was nearing the end of her thirty years of military service. She was scheduled for decommissioning in eleven months, and then she'd be sent to the graveyard in the Valiack System. By modern warship standards, her keel was small and her systems antiquated. Unlike the modern *Vanguard* C-class light cruiser, *Absalon* was an A-class. The *Astro* had been the first class of light cruiser with the dedicated quarters for a company-sized Marine detachment. At the time she was commissioned, platoon sergeants had quartered separately from their Marines, and the ship's quarters had been designed accordingly. Nearly twenty years ago, Staff Sergeant Fitzgerald Cluster had broken half a dozen SOPs by rooming with his Marines instead of separately from them, as the RAW-MC *Book of Lists* at the time had stipulated for an SNCO of his rank and status. Toward the end of his career, Cluster became sergeant major of the RAW-MC, and he institutionalized the practice across the Corps.

Promise gazed through the simulated viewport on the far wall of her cabin, beyond which lay the regolith and craters of Swallows Helm, a deep canyon that plummeted more than a kilometer below the moon's surface and was named for the survey ship that had discovered it. Survey had sent a probe to the canyon's base over three hundred years ago, and scuttlebutt said it was still there, covered by a thin layer of dust. Promise watched a shooting star disappear into the canyon and wondered about the odds of seeing that happen. Of all the places for the meteor to strike, it had died at this particular moment in human history, and she had witnessed the event.

Promise turned toward her quarter's bulkhead door when it intoned a perfect fifth.

That must be Maxi. "Come in."

The door slid out of view to reveal a flag officer wearing dress grays, branch Sector Guard, a single gold star on each collar point, with the crossed swords of Hold gleaming on his breast, white beret tucked underneath his arm. The Republican Medal of Honor was flanked by a mess of glittery over his heart. Her eyes rose in recognition. About one hundred Marines and Sailors from the fleet wore the medal, among the ranks of more than 90 million women and men in the RAW Fleet Forces, the 42-million-plus reservists from the various planetary militias, and the homeworld and system defense forces throughout the Republic. Each holder had earned his or her star nation's highest commendation the hard way. Many of them, posthumously.

She came to attention and gazed at the bulkhead behind the admiral until he chose to address her.

"Stand easy, Sergeant," said Rear Admiral Kristopher Chapayev.

Promise drew her hands to the small of her back and made brief eye contact with her superior. Chapayev wore a groomed goatee flecked with gray. His eyes were light brown with emerald highlights, his face lined and well weathered. His voice was grandfatherly, a voice that might have calmed her nerves, except for the fact that sergeants didn't normally receive private calls, in person no less, from decorated admirals.

What have I gotten myself into, Promise thought. *Stop fretting—it's probably nothing.*

"I hope I'm not bothering you."

Right.

"No bother at all, Admiral." Promise stepped back to let him in.

"You may not feel that way in a moment."

Promise couldn't quite keep her confusion from registering on her face.

"Well, I'm sure you have better things to do than talk with a fossil like me, regardless of my rank. You are wondering why I'm here . . . aren't you?"

Promise pressed her lips together. She allowed them to curve a bit in answer. And she realized by doing so she had followed her late father's advice, one of the bits of wisdom, like it or not, that her Dad had gotten right in his five decades of ascetic living. *Young lady, if you don't know what to say, shut your trap and open your ears.*

Admiral Chapayev stepped into the cabin, which freed the bulkhead door to close behind him. He looked around as if searching for a lost memento, took a deep breath, and turned his attention to Promise.

"You're here because of me," said the admiral.

Her chin rose slightly. The admiral recognized the challenge and raised his hand, palm out, in apology.

"I'm old enough to be your grandfather. I rose through the enlisted ranks, was a sergeant like yourself once, before I jumped ship, about the age you are now when I made ensign."

Promise nodded cautiously to show she was paying attention but without necessarily agreeing with what the admiral had said. The man had read her jacket and spoken with someone who told him what wasn't there.

"I was a commodore when your father was killed."

The non sequitur hit low and hard.

"My father? Sir, I'm sorry. I really don't know what this is about, but—"

"No, I'm the one who's sorry. This must be a difficult subject for you to discuss." The admiral sighed and shook his head. "Will you give me a few minutes? All will become clear, or at least clearer."

"Yes, sir." It came out like a question.

The admiral swore. "I planned to make this quick and to the point, but it doesn't appear to be working out that way. It comes with age and rank you know. Call it an occupational hazard."

"Admiral?"

Chapayev smiled apologetically.

"Sergeant, your father's death, and the many others lost in the raids on your homeworld, made news across the nets. Made waves across the unincorporated worlds, galactic waves, the effects of which we are still dealing with today. Eventually, it was one death too many. Many hundreds died on Montana alone. Entire families slaughtered. Generations lost. The Montanans were up against it when they voted for full incorporation. To our credit, the tax incentives came immediately. We actually poured more into the economy than we took out of it. The private off-world capital investment was even more substantial. Immigration doubled, almost overnight. We still need to build a proper space platform." The admiral cleared his throat. "And the permanent Naval picket and Marine garrison, well, that's where you come in."

The admiral pulled at his collar. "As you know, we're a bit strapped for manpower at the moment." Chapayev shook his head in disgust. "Honestly, we've been strapped since the unincorporated planets banded together, declared themselves neutral, and created the Independent League of Worlds and the 'null zone' between us and the Lusies. Montana led that charge," Chapayev said, finger pointed. "The cold war that followed between the RAW and the LE did more harm than good, to your planet . . . to a lot of planets." Chapayev's hand was shaking. "We took responsibility for the half of the zone that fell to the galactic south, which included your birth world. But because we couldn't annex Montana, we didn't do much for her citizens either. The ILW tried to form a central government. But independence dies hard. Eventually, Montana backed out of the ILW, which mostly fell apart. We were free to pursue formal treaties with Montana and the other willing planets in the zone, on either side, but so were the Lusitanians, which didn't give Montana much of a choice. She had to get in bed with someone just to survive, and we needed the buffer system. Lucky for us, the Montanans didn't want their lands divided up by the Lusies' aristocracy. Her relative proximity to RAW space helped. And the Lusies made it easy for them to choose."

The student in her eased into the lesson, and she managed to *keep* her mouth closed. *After all,* she thought, *Maxi endures mine. And Chapayev's an admiral.*

"While the null zone stood in effect, our duty was clear. We couldn't take planets, but we could police the ILW's systems, protect our Merchant Marines, and develop trade. But when the league crumbled, with it went every kilogram of clarity. The whole sector was suddenly up for grabs. We're talking billions of lives, trillions more in untapped resources. Basing rights. Trade relations. A booming export business that comprised a substantial percentage of our gross systems product. We feared escalation, which might have led to all-out hostilities with the Lusies, which we weren't prepared for and didn't want. So we withdrew the bulk of our assets and took a nonaggressive stance. That was our biggest mistake. We left the door wide open for a horde of miscreants to move in and take advantage of the poorest peoples in the 'verse. Even with piracy running rampant, it still took Montana's planetary government plenty long to get its act together. As you know, Montana's constitution mandates a part-time congress, so getting things done took . . . sorry, I'm digressing again. It's the diplomat in me who likes to hear himself wax eloquent."

"Admiral, with respect," Promise managed to keep almost all of the exasperation out of her voice, "I'm still not clear about how or why this involves me?"

"Which brings me to my real point," Chapayev said, a pained expression crossing his face. "Once Montana formally requested annexation, our government wasted little time absorbing her into the Republic. But we didn't protect her, at least not like we should have. The Montanans have long memories. Frankly, Sergeant, I have a PR problem on my hands, which is where you come in."

"Understood, Admiral. I'm your local connection."

"Yes, you are. I need you to help me patch up our relationship with your people."

My people? Promise looked away as her emotions warred within her.

"Don't quite trust me, do you? Well, this mission isn't purely altruistic. We need breathing space between us and the Lusies. We need it bad like scramjets need air, and Montana fits the bill. Call it an alignment of mutual interests. But that doesn't change the fact that Montana is also a part of the Republic and that her citizens are Republican citizens. As such, they deserve our protection. Whatever our base motives may be, we still owe these people better than they've gotten, and it's time that changed. You're going to help me see to it. That's why I specifically requested a Montana-born Marine to advise me. We've had a small picket—really, a single tin can—in place for years in a nearby system. It jumps in every few weeks to fly the flag, but we've never had boots on Montana soil. Victor Company was up for assignment, and you were born there."

"I see." Promise began to count the rivets in the deck plating beneath her feet, and shook her head to gather her thoughts. "Well, sir, I'll admit it's a bit awkward for me. I'd be lying if I said I was looking forward to returning to this particular planet. But you can count on me to do my duty."

"Yes, I knew that, which is why I chose you. Why I *specifically* asked for you. There were other candidates. I selected you."

"May I ask why, sir?"

"I'm glad you did, Promise."

The admiral measured his words, sifted the need-to-know stuff that she didn't need to know, and told her.

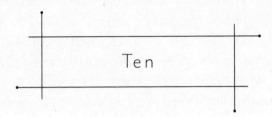

Ten

"**You don't mind me** calling you by your first name, do you?"

"No, sir, that's fine."

The admiral relaxed visibly. "Like me, you came from yeoman stock and enlisted in the Corps. BUPERS almost immediately sniffed you out as officer material, but your jacket says you declined for personal reasons. Most Marines don't say no when the Corps wants to give them a commission. You did, and I wanted to find out why." Promise opened her mouth to speak. "Now hold on a minute, Sergeant. That wasn't a question or a critique, just a statement of fact." Promise clenched her jaw and stomped on her temper. She didn't care for the way the admiral was dissecting her life.

"Your scores are in the top three percent of all officer candidates. Natural command aptitude—that's in your jacket, too, a direct quote. I know you declined a commission last year, citing your preference for the enlisted ranks. But I also know what's not in your jacket, the real reason you said no to becoming an officer." Chapayev paused. "I believe it has something to do with the Montana dirt under your nails. You do the job yourself because you don't believe in leading people where you haven't gone before."

Promise flushed. Chapayev gave her a moment before he continued.

"But it's more than that, isn't it," he said in a voice pitched just above a whisper. "Many planets in the 'verse are quite poor, particularly out in the Rim. The Corps is inundated each year with applicants trying to escape their circumstances—hunger, lawlessness, want, whatever. Frankly, most of them can't meet our entrance requirements. I pity them. The 'verse can be cruel. But Montana is different. She's fairly wealthy by Rim-world standards. Her people are educated, with access to clean water, food, and the blessings of a representative government. You, Sergeant, left for other reasons."

The silence in the room grew pregnant. Promise stared into the admiral's eyes, which seemed to be a tad bit too moist, just like hers were. The realization surprised her.

"Bad memories, sir," Promise whispered. "I wanted to do something about them."

"I know."

Promise believed him.

"You carry your dead with you. Just like all the good ones do. I couldn't know the truth of that for sure until I actually met you. But now I know my gut instinct about you was correct. I see it in your eyes and hear it in your voice. This old man still has it."

Promise couldn't help but grin back at the admiral. She couldn't help herself from liking the man either.

"I carry my dead, too," the admiral said. "My parents came from Telerine." Chapayev withdrew his beret and brushed something invisible from its brim, stared at it a long moment as if deciding something important. Then he looked straight at her. "I was born there. I'm Rim through and through."

Promise's jaw dropped. Telerine was on the Lusitanian side of the 'verse. It hadn't always been, and its annexation stood as a painful reminder of what happened when the Republic got sloppy in Rim-world affairs. Whole cities were razed to the ground, and hundreds of thousands more were displaced, all because the Republic's Marines arrived too late. The Lusies had denied any wrongdoing, blamed the Republic instead for destabilizing the system, and moved in preemptively. And so it had been between the LE and the RAW for decades, both sides inflicting small wounds upon each other, none large enough to warrant all-out hostilities, in a cold war neither side had started or seemed willing to end.

And the unincorporated planets keep paying the price, Promise thought.

Chapayev cleared his throat. "Promise, I'm not here just to rehash our mistakes or to dredge up bad memories. Or to justify this mission either. You're being attached to my personal detail and will liaison between the Marine contingent on Montana and my office. You'll still drill with your company and carry out your responsibilities as a platoon sergeant, but you'll work for me, too. Understood?"

Not much for me to say but, "Yes, sir."

The admiral extended his hand toward her. "Help me build rapport between the Republic and the Montana government." The last sentence came out sounding like a genuine plea from a man Promise suspected was a very genuine man, and a very fine admiral. But it still wasn't enough.

Her temper stood on end as she considered Chapayev's open palm and what grasping it would mean. *What has Montana ever done for me?* "Permission to speak freely, sir?"

Admiral Chapayev sighed and dropped his hand to his side. "Go ahead, Sergeant."

"So, I'm your window dressing," she said tersely, and then she added "sir" to make it proper.

"Safety your temper, Promise." The admiral shook his head. "Try to think this through. And try to think about it from my perspective."

She went to speak again and got out the first syllable before clamping her mouth shut.

"You're walking wounded. I understand that. Montana is the last place you want to be. Lost your father, joined the Corps to get away and to get even, correct?"

Stark truth left her with nothing to say. He took her silence as a yes, and nodded.

"We'll, you're headed back home, and I don't need to remind you of the oath you took to defend the Republic, and that means these people . . . *your* people. Frankly, I need to show you around town, soften up the locals. Be someone they'll be more willing to trust than me. I'm an interloper. You're not. But I also need you to think for yourself and actually get to know these folks."

Promise forced herself to step back from her anger and the long shadow her father's death had cast over her career. She hated to admit it, *really* hated to admit it, but the admiral's request was sound and reasonable.

"Montana calls up bad memories, sir, but they're nothing I can't handle."

"Good. It was never a question in my mind."

"Forgive me, sir. I'll do my best to help you." This time, Promise took his hand and squeezed it firmly.

He let go and stepped back. The bulkhead door slid open for him to leave.

"Remember, Promise, do your duty and be human about it. Half of that will be easy and straightforward. The other half won't be. Your past and your duty might start rubbing each other raw. When you feel like you have to choose between them, just remember that your best command decisions are the ones that you make. Not the Wolf and not the Montanan in you either. You."

Promise nodded.

"Be at Boatbay Three at 0600 hours. I've seen to your mechsuit—it will be on the shuttle down—and I cleared the rest of your schedule this evening, too. Corporal Sindri can handle your toon in the interim. You'll find a full mission brief already waiting in your queue. Spend some time reading up, bag some sleep, and try not to overthink this."

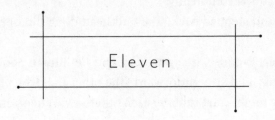

Eleven

The solitary Corvette-class vessel ghosted into orbit on reaction thrusters only, made one last course correction, and then yielded to Montana's gravity well. The diminutive warship had drifted on a ballistic course toward the planet for the better part of five days, past the scattered reconnaissance platforms the RAW had placed along the most likely approach vectors to the Earth-like world, and in spite of the constant scans of one RNS *Absalon*. The bleach-white vessel fell into geosynchronous rotation on the nightside. Passive sensors reached out to sniff *Absalon* as the much larger vessel rounded the opposite side of the planet and floated into day.

Several lightly armored stingships emptied the intruder's gullet. A single scout broke off and fell until it tasted the outer layer of Montana's oxygen-rich atmosphere. Dual scramjets kicked in, pushed the tiny craft into the planet's ionosphere. The two remaining stingers hung back, flanking their mother ship protectively, waiting for the all clear. The stingers were shaped like isosceles triangles and named for their razor-thin wing tips. Officially, they were short-range, single-pilot interceptors. But the merc pilots flying them called them scalpels, surgical instruments of death. And more personal tags, too: *Slit-Throat, Deeper-in-You, Rucking Fugly.* Their pilots tended toward isolation and the macabre, and they cracked shaded jokes about the thin line between mission success and failure, often no wider than the tip of a doctor's lancet.

As the lone predator dropped, her tempered spine and heat shielding absorbed the planet's fury. Then she was through, and blue sky and scattered clouds accompanied her as she overflew her destination. Her skin quickly morphed to shield her from planetary scans. An old-fashioned LIDAR installation adjacent to the spaceport did its best and knifed the air all around her, scoring a number of direct hits, too. But the stingship's skin tingled with life and set about to fool the hands that would kill it. The ground operator never guessed that his skies were compromised. The scalpel pilot ran a second sweep to double-check what she already knew to be true before rejoining her cohorts in outer space.

Montana's fixed batteries weren't in place yet. Another broken RAW promise, which was unfortunate for the people on the ground who were about to die.

The lone stingship rejoined her sisters in orbit. Then they all fell together. A pregnant Assault-class LAC packed with conventional small arms and several dozen raiders rode their wake. Minutes later, Montana's spaceport swam in shuttle fuel and flames.

Captain Sarai Balasubramanian had timed her Razorbacks' arrival perfectly. Her contract had given her no other choice in the matter. Her mission's high probability of failure and its ridiculously small insertion window meant that she'd endured nearly two weeks of restless sleep leading up to the current operation, her constant recalculations, the unyielding second-guessing herself. She'd gone through several dozen pods of caf and carried the ulcer in her gut to prove it. Her crew was annoyed with her because she'd drunk all the Fireberry Dark Roast and most of the Breakfast Blend, too.

This level of coordination smacks Rule #1 in the face. She chewed on a nail while her people sliced through Montana's outer atmosphere. Rule #1: Keep It Simple Stupid. But Rule #2 allowed you to break Rule #1 if the money talked loud enough—and with this op, it had actually screamed—which explained why her merc unit was risking a game of cat and mouse with a much larger and far more powerful Republican warship. RNS *Absalon*. Few merc outfits owned a Corvette-class, jump-capable vessel or the drop units that her Razorbacks did. And Balasubramanian had no desire to squander any of them, or her people, in a no-win situation.

If everything went according to plan, a lot of Montanans—if she got lucky, some Republican Marines, too—were about to die, which would mean a healthy bonus for her and her people. Her employer wanted it that way, which was fine with her. What was another dead 'Publican or a bunch of roasted Rimworlders anyway? Like she'd told her employer to justify three times her normal fee, "*Absalon* will be too close to the *Ex Nihilo* for my comfort level, even *if* she is on the other side of the planet and we're flying through her blind spot. If *Absalon* finds us, and *if* we're implicated in what amounts to mass murder on a RAW planet, my crew and I will never rest easy again. It better be worth our while to go hammerhead to hammerhead with the Republic."

And it had been. *Otherwise, we wouldn't be staring down the launch tubes of a Republican warship,* Balasubramanian told herself.

But the money hadn't stopped Balasubramanian from worrying like a mother spider as her baby mercs spun silky contrails through Montana sky, then broke south until the planetary spaceport floated in their targeting reticules.

Balasubramanian didn't have time to wait for the results either, which was the part of the plan that bothered her the most. *If this is a trap . . .* She cut the thought off with a sip of hot caf and gently nudged her vessel out of orbit using only reaction thrusters. She set a course for Montana's second moon. Once she put herself and her ship safely in the shadow of it, her jumpprint would be next to impossible to detect. She had important cargo aboard, which was due in the Renault system in a little over two weeks. And staying in orbit for too long, or even in the system, was too risky. If everything went according to plan, her people would hit their target and retreat to a prepared base deep in the northern polar zone, hidden underground by a cavern of ice. There they would wait for mamma spider to return and collect them in roughly a month. Only bad luck could compromise their hiding place, unless one of her own did something foolish. And they were too well trained for that.

She'd come back. Rule #3 was as inviolable as #2: Never leave a pirate behind.

Absalon's claxon jarred Promise from her slumber. "*General quarters. General quarters. All hands to your battle stations,*" echoed through the ship's decks and passageways, in the metallic, flat tone of a warship captain steeled for battle. *"All LAC pilots and Marines report to your assigned bays for emergency drop."*

Emergency drop. Promise bolted upright. She'd dressed in her body glove—beegees—before going to bed. The black one-piece wasn't as comfortable as skivvies. But it met ship's regulations, was temperature neutral, and could absorb a limited amount of small-arms fire. It was standard underarmor for mechanized Marines, and it prevented chaffing while operating a mechsuit. The trapdoors made using the head tolerable, barely.

She dropped over the side of her rack and slid into her boots. They quickly molded to her feet. Solid skid-resistant sole to grip the deck plating, stiff at the ankle, with give up the side of her calf.

Promise took a deep breath and rubbed her face down. *Just routine,* she told herself.

Her mastoid implant woke up. *"Sergeant, report to the Admiral, Boatbay Three. Your shuttle is waiting."*

No, that's not fair. My toon needs me.

"Captain, I didn't sign up for this. My toon—"

"Will be fine, Sergeant. The corporal can handle it in your absence. Trust. And follow orders. Remus out."

She silent-screamed, pushed off her rack, and hooked her seabag over her shoulder in one smooth movement. The corridor outside her cabin swam with navies and Marines. She overtook three Marines from Bravo toon who were walk-hopping to the morgue as they tried to pull their beegees on. She'd been caught in a similar situation once before. And she'd promised herself never, ever again.

Just routine . . . in case events aren't just routine. She hadn't planned on suiting up, *but then little inconveniences like emergencies don't give you advance warning, do they?* It was one of her own sayings, a string of words that came to her just before she fell asleep on her last night in boot camp. When she'd realized what all the monotonous training and live-fire drills and yelling and insults and *"Magot, I didn't hear yous!"* were for. To make sure she didn't freeze up in battle, to make sure her body kept going until her mind caught up with it.

Promise tripped through the bulkhead door and slammed into the deck of Boatbay 3. Without her beegees, she would have left a shin on the deck plating. Captain Remus and a few sergeants and corporals had already gathered next to several crates of ammo and cells and heard the deck break her fall. The captain looked up from the holomap in front of him, pointed toward the shuttle to his left, and shook his head. Mouthed *don't even think about it.* Held her gaze until she nodded, then turned back to his men. Promise pulled herself up. Her eyes locked on the steady flow of Wolves pouring into the "morgue" on the starboard side of the bay—skins going in, and mechsuits coming out. The sight of armor—roughly humanoid and covered with interlocking plates, all jeweled with weapons—made her trigger finger itch. The average Marine grew eight inches in mech and weighed over two hundred kilos. Lance Corporal Tal Covington clanked out of the morgue with one gauntlet off and his helmet racked at his side, a "get-some" attitude firmly in place. It took all she had to move in the opposite direction.

So. Not. Fair.

The bay swelled with the battle chatter of Marines grunting, checking gear, trading jokes, racking weapons, and downing rations. Maxi flew past, spun, and gave her two thumbs-up, then ran toward his armor. "Don't worry; we got this." For the first time in her career, Promise thought of deliberately violating her orders and joining them. If her suit had been in the morgue, she just might have. Instead, she told her legs to double-time it to the shuttle. She leapt to the gangplank and entered AS1. The McHaster-class shuttle had the look of polished alabaster and was contoured like a prespace bullet, with undeveloped wings and a diminutive engine. Its primary function was ferrying personnel and staying away from combat. "AS1" was stenciled in black and gold on the nose, where two humble pulse cannons were its only teeth.

To Promise, the shuttle felt like a different kind of morgue, the kind you stuffed KIAs into.

Admiral Chapayev sat alone in webbing, waiting for her. She tossed her gear into an overhead smartrack and secured her restraints opposite the admiral.

"Glad you're finally here, Sergeant," Chapayev snapped.

"Sorry to keep you waiting, sir!"

"That wasn't a reprimand, Sergeant. I'm sorry to keep you from the action," Chapayev replied. "It's gonna get interesting for your unit, hot-dropping into enemy-occupied ground like they're preparing to do. Shouldn't be much trouble for us, though. Most of the hostiles are dirt-side, and our own stingships should tie up the few aerospace assets they do have. I'm sorry you won't make the party, but we're headed straight to the president's office for an emergency meeting."

And directly away from the fight. Promise clenched her jaw and fists. *Can't be helped.*

It came out of nowhere, streaked in on a parabolic arc and fired, peppering the shuttle's thin armor with energy fire. Armament boiled off, exposing the shuttle's belly and counter-grav matrix, which normally bled high-g maneuvers and made them tolerable. Suddenly, Promise felt heavy and began to black out as the shuttle banked hard to avoid a seeker traveling at high v. The missile sped by as the shuttle leveled off.

Move.

The small voice inside her head clamored against the chaos outside, told her to do something she knew she shouldn't. Promise ignored it.

Move.

Louder this time, and the voice was oddly familiar. Female. Promise let it go and hunkered down in her webbing, prayed for a quick descent and the assurance of terra firma.

A Marine didn't leave her harness during planetfall. Certainly not in the bowels of a shuttle flying evasive maneuvers because it was being shot at. *But my mechsuit is tethered in the rear, just behind the crew compartment. If we take a direct hit, I'll . . .*

MOVE!

Promise jumped in her webbing. This time the voice was unmistakable. Montana drawl laced with parental discipline. Promise did as she was told.

Admiral Chapayev screamed at her as she clawed her way to the rear of the vessel, rung by rung. *As he should be,* Promise told herself as she grasped another bar. *One ill-timed maneuver will turn me into red paste. P, you are out of your mind.*

BRACE YOURSELF!

Promise sensed the sudden movement, too, almost anticipated it. Threw her arms through two rungs and back around and managed to lock them together as the shuttle spun along its axis. Pain blossomed in her shoulders, down her arms. She found herself inverted and staring at a still-screaming Admiral Chapayev. His jugular bulging with every incoherent word. Her shoulders whined, and metal smashed against soft tissue. Then the vessel righted itself. Promise pushed off and around a small corner to her mechsuit's webbing. She spun around and stepped into her battle armor at the precise moment the shuttle dove. The sudden change in v slammed her up and against her suit's shoulder pads, gashing the back of her head. She grunted as the suit sealed itself and made the appropriate hookups to her front and back doors.

Suddenly, she was back in infantry school, during her first walkthrough. *How do you piss in a mechsuit? Just. Like. This.*

Canned O_2 flooded her helmet. Promise flexed her jaw to equalize the pressure in her ears and addressed her AI. "Identify Sergeant Promise T. Paen, Alpha-Zulu-Niner-Gamma-Two-Two-Three-Gamma-Zero-Five-Six."

The shuttle dipped sharply and pulled up hard. One of her mechsuit's tie-downs broke loose, causing her armor to rattle around the shuttle's cramped bay.

A flat metallic voice responded. *"Voice identification confirmed. Initializing retinal scan."*

A green light mapped both of her eyes. A moment later, her heads-up display and AI booted. Her semiautonomous-reasoning grunt spoke with a gentleman's brogue. SARG's vowels said more than his consonants. *"Hello, Sergeant. Biometrics and telemetry are online. Your fusion plant is cycling up. All weapons systems nominal."*

During her off-hours in basic, when she'd needed to detox from all the crap her drill instructor had heaped on her and her fellow recruits, Promise had devoured the nets, particularly old action movies filmed on Earth. She'd stumbled on an archive of pre-Diaspora films featuring the many faces of an attractive secret agent, one double-aught-seven. *Odd name for a call sign,* Promise had thought at the time. He'd been a debonair, philandering male spook with a penchant for survival that stretched plausibility to the breaking point. One in particular had had a voice like a demigod. To her it was *ear candy*. She'd uploaded his speech patterns into her AI and gendered her suit male. A very masculine sophisticate who made her weapons sound sexy and required nothing in return.

"Mr. Bond, run a systemwide scan and give me a verbal on my weapons mix."

The AI read her weapons manifest like poetry:

Shoulder Mounted Hordes—ready.
Triple-7 CAR—ready.
Heavy Pistols—ready.
Striker Rifle is webbed and ready.
Ammo feeds are green and fuel cells are fully charged.

There was a momentary pause before it finished. *"All systems nominal, Serg . . ."*

A missile strike ripped open the starboard side of the shuttle. The atmosphere bled out of the shredded artery, along with cabin detritus and one silent, screaming Admiral Chapayev. As the shuttle corkscrewed, Promise forgot which way was down.

"Hull breech, Sergeant. I suggest you exit this craft."

"That's an understate—" The shuttle lurched again. Promise felt her stomach slam into her brain, then turn inside out and try to crawl out her mouth.

Her suit's gyroscope kicked against the ship's inertia and stabilized her inner ear so she could determine which way was up.

Promise risked a glance—she couldn't help herself, really—and stared at the ship's wound. A rough circle ringed in jagged teeth, bronzed by fire, taunted her. Through it her point of view blurred between sky and land. The wall between the cargo hold and the forward compartment was gone, too. And so was Chapayev.

I should have died with him, she thought. *No, P, should haves do NOT count. We either make it . . . or something breaks us. You need to get out, now.*

Blood and copper filled her mouth. She swallowed and tapped into the shuttle's comm net to speak with the pilot.

"Sergeant, I've already tried to access the shuttle's computer. It's down. I'm afraid the pilot is dead. Guidance systems are offline as well."

"Can you trip the manual override to the bay door?"

"Negative, Sergeant. The servos were severed in the blast."

Promise gripped the frame around her, then stretched to free her mechsuit from its restraints. She rotated her torso toward the shuttle bay door and raised her carbine, loaded with explosive rounds. Squeezed the trigger as the shuttle blew apart.

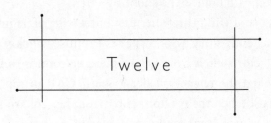

Twelve

She was plummeting in a controlled fall, with the north quadrant of the spaceport rushing up from below. Her chronometer told her she'd blacked out for more than thirty seconds.

"Bond, you little bugger! You're a lousy nav." She was two klicks up, falling fast, and bearing down on uneven terrain and buildings. While she slept, her AI had deployed her grav-chute and activated her mechsuit's stealth suite. Her HUD had already identified heavy weapons fire from multiple enemy signatures, numbers unknown. "Well, you're a half bugger. At least I haven't been shot down."

"My apologies, Sergeant." Her SARG sounded like a pleasant and unrepentant waiter.

"Shut up! And get me a link to the skipper."

"Negative, Sergeant. We're being jammed."

"Keep at it. Calculate time-to-deck. Identify optimal LZs with maximum cover."

"Scanning," replied the AI.

Her HUD refreshed with a schematic of the ground below. Promise found what she was looking for, a twelve-story building with a reasonably flat roof.

"High-ground, there." Promise ringed the target. "Give me a thermal scan of the first three floors, and a body count."

"One moment, Sergeant . . . Thermals make it sixteen. Ten are stationary. Six are standing or moving. I am detecting some nominal heat sources, too. I may be able to tell you more as the distance closes."

"Keep flying," Promise ordered reluctantly as she dropped below half-a-klick elevation. "I'll handle the shooting."

A sudden gust of wind threw her first burst wide of its intended target and through a tenth-story windowpane. Promise quickly recalculated, tripped the selector switch from armor-piercing rounds to hypervelocity darts, and stroked the trigger on her Triple-7 CAR in rapid succession. Multiple bursts stitched the rooftop sentry from her collarbone to the opposite side of her torso. The woman crumpled to the floor.

"One," Promise counted to herself.

"Would you like me to count, Sergeant?"

"No. Fly. Zone . . . Tango 3—magnify!"

A pirate on the opposite side of the rooftop sat nestled in an autoturret. The antiaircraft battery whirled around to range on Promise's suit. Even the best jammers couldn't mask the origin of energy fire, and the turret was equipped with a basic AI suite, which quickly backtracked her locus and started scoring hits.

Promise launched a salvo of Hordes in return. The small, hypervelocity missiles honed in on their target as their onboard sensors received real-time updates from her targeting computer. Six missiles streaked in, and three found joy. The turret returned fire before erupting in flame. Seven meters of building materials vanished with it, leaving a substantial wound in the structure's side.

Two, Promise said, this time in her head.

"Direct hit on your starboard shank. Armor down to forty-five percent."

"Acknowledged. Deploy smartmetal to reinforce it."

"Aye, aye, Sergeant, but you'll deplete your reserves if you do."

"Belay that, save it, and monitor that leg."

"Gladly, Sergeant."

Gladly? Bond's words sounded sultry and suggestive. He was leaching personality. Promise set a mental reminder to tweak his speech patterns later.

"Ten seconds 'til breaking thrusters," her AI said.

She lased the corner of the roof. "Drop me there, near that ventilation shaft. Looks like two hostiles are on the next level. We'll take them next."

"Too late, Sergeant. Here they come."

———————

Promise burned in, found herself wading waist-high in ferocrete and covered in gray rubble and dust.

"I seem to have miscalculated," her AI commented.

"You think?" Promise pulled herself up and into a crouched position, seeking hostiles. She didn't have the time or energy to give her suite a tongue lashing.

"A third pirate appeared unexpectedly and blew a hole in your grav-chute right before landing, which threw my descent calculations off by—"

"Shut up," Promise snapped, "and find him."

"Three o'clock, behind those crates." A ring appeared on her HUD and dropped behind a wall of unmarked containers encircling a thermal blur that was holding a long stick.

Promise aimed her carbine at the slatted wood, toggled back to armor-piercing explosive rounds—two-meter penetration, about head level—and squeezed the trigger once. She advanced and checked her flank, skirted the crate, and found a headless mess of blood and brains sprayed across the rooftop and an intact set of false teeth smiling back at her.

"Three," she said. "Deploy whiskers. I want a good look at the next level before dropping down."

A small panel opened on the side of her helmet. Three remote probes flew off and darted between louvered vents. They briefly hovered just inside the mouth of the ventilation shaft before diving down into it.

"Visuals coming up now."

Promise's HUD momentarily flickered, and then split into two halves: the top compressed her normal field of view while the bottom half divided into three equal panels, one for each whisker. Her suit's targeting computer automatically designated them, Alpha, Bravo, and Charlie.

"Charlie has a hostile on the south side of the building. He appears to be laying down suppressive fire for his cohorts on the ground. Alpha has a second hostile who's guarding seven hostages. He's raised his weapon and . . ."

Her AI paused.

"I've detected a low-powered energy discharge near the hostages' vicinity."

"How powerful is the whisker's suicide charge? Enough to kill him?"

"Checking . . . It's really not designed for that. More to keep the technology from being captured and reverse engineered, but perhaps . . ."

"Never mind the weapons specs. Fly the whisker near the man's head. Jam it in his ear if possible, and blow it."

"Aye, aye, Sergeant. Almost in position." Promise watched Alpha's screen as the whisker zeroed in on the hostile. The pirate was a tallish man with rakish hair and a foul mouth. Every other word was four letters and an "ing," then four more for the noun. Then two "ings" trumped by hell.

"He has a limited vocabulary."

His words sounded stretched and distorted through the whisker's mike. A hostage lay motionless on the ground with a head wound. The woman next to him was sobbing hysterically. The swearing pirate raised his rifle, butt first to silence her as the whisker made its terminal move, buzzed into the man's mouth, struck the uvula, and blew.

"Blown, Sergeant."

Four.

Promise crouched on the rooftop, watching her remaining two whiskers through a split screen. The sniper hadn't moved from his position, though he was clearly on edge, switching from his sniper scope to a naked-eye view, all the while screaming into his comm.

"Fisher, you there? Fisher. Fish! This ain't funny. You get that Marine? Haas, you read me, Haas? Where you guys be?"

"He's not one for proper grammar, is he?"

It was rhetorical, but Promise couldn't help herself. "You and your proper Terran Standard."

Promise opened the rooftop door and made a noisy entrance. Mech-boots on stairs. She broke through several because of her suit's weight. Hit the landing and crossed the deck, advanced through a cordoned hallway and into a pod of workstations, which had been smashed and tossed aside. A group of frightened, wide-eyed Montanans was huddled in the corner. The screen on the wall behind them was cycling through stills of interplanetary spacecraft.

She raised an armored palm to the hostages as she approached the far end of the room and peered into the next. The hysterical woman was now screaming uncontrollably and covered by pirate blood and brains. Promise saw her target pressed against a ring of sandbags, already reorienting himself to face her. Leading with her carbine, she stepped all the way into the room. Mr. Bond's voice boomed over her suit's external speakers. Something about men responding to men.

"This is Sergeant Paen of the Republic of Aligned Worlds Marine Corps. You've violated Republican space, damaged Republican property, and killed Republican citizens. Toss your weapon and get facedown with your hands on the back of your head. You have until five, four, three—"

The pirate hesitated at the sight of her, looked to his right and his left for an exit strategy, down at his weapon, and back at Promise. His smartly pressed fatigues suggested two very different possibilities: either the man was fastidious or his clothes had just come off the rack. Judging from his panicked face, Promise guessed he'd recently landed his first job as a gun for hire.

He chose poorly. The last thing he saw was a faceless suit smile before his head exploded.

"Five," Promise said over her suit's speakers. She spared a second to wonder why.

The dead man didn't answer, and she didn't have time to dwell on it. There was at least one more hostile in the building.

Promise regrouped with the hostages in the opposite room. Focused on the hysterical woman. She selected a hypo from her medkit and closed the distance. The woman went limp in her arms. Promise handed her off to a remarkably composed gentleman wearing a mustard fedora and asked, "Are you former military?"

The man with the yellow hat nodded. "Aye. I was Navy Corps of Engineers in another lifetime, Ti Jezrel, ma'am," he said as he laid the woman on the floor, stood with effort, and saluted. Promise returned the gesture and frowned. His bulging waistline suggested he'd been out of circulation for a bit. Sweat dripped from his nose. Promise winced as she handed Jezrel a Heavy Pistol and a three-second explanation. "Both hands, Mister Jezrel, or you'll sprain your arm." Heavy Pistols were made for armored Marines, not the relatively weak human hand. "Point and fire." She prayed the man didn't shoot himself or a friendly. She found the stairwell and moved toward the last hostile, who quickly dissolved from reds into greens and blues before fading into black.

Thermal masking? she wondered. *Pretty sophisticated tech for pirates.*

As she left the stairs, she tripped a sensor mounted on a micronetic charge the size of a pebble. The blast tossed Promise back into the stairwell and slammed her headfirst into the far wall. Her faceplate failed and split along the side, and heat poured into the crack and blistered her cheek. As her primary power plant went offline, her suit's systems started flatlining.

Her auxiliaries cycled up five seconds later. Five seconds she would never remember.

Promise's AI initiated a systemwide diagnostic. It isolated a skull fracture and a clean break in Promise's right femur. Forty-five percent hadn't held after all. The AI deployed a wave of nanites to the bone. The tiny robotic medics created an atom-thin shell around the break as strong as peristeel. A second wave set to work to seal the wound and repair the femoral artery. Painkillers blocked the neural impulses between Promise's leg and brain, effectively blinding her to the pain. Were it not for the head wound, she could have walked out and continued to function at full combat capacity.

The femur was easy. The head wasn't. As her brain swelled, armies of neuroinhibitors and cortical suppressants bathed her neurons, arresting almost all electrical activity to keep her cool. A cocktail of steroids fought off the swelling, while the suit's pharmacope activated the Brain-box attached to her cerebellum. With Promise unconscious, her "NCO Brain" merged with her AI's combat matrix and started giving orders. Her eyes opened and she stood up. Less than a minute passed between her injury and her next kill. She fought another thirty mikes at a "reduced level of combat effectiveness."

Seven more kills later, Lance Corporal Roxi Zahn, the company medic, entered the override sequence to shut down Promise's mechsuit and her Brain-box. The lance corporal cracked the mech's chest, put Promise in a stasis collar, and medevaced her to RNS *Absalon* for emergency surgery.

Thirteen

"She's suffered massive brain trauma," said the distant, muffled voice of a woman.

A second woman spoke. This voice was more familiar. "I already know that. Tell me her prognosis."

An older male responded. "True, but we've addressed the edema. The H-CAT detected no permanent damage. She should make a full recovery. My greatest concern is memory loss."

"Mine, too, doctor. Only time will tell," replied the first woman. "Ah, looks like our gal is coming around."

"Easy, munchkin."

"Hold still, Sergeant." Promise felt a large, firm hand push down on her shoulder.

"Aooowww. My head . . . is . . . throbbing."

"Well, young lady, you're lucky to be alive—thanks to your mechsuit's triage capabilities. Without them, your brain would be mush and you'd be a stiff in a launch tube."

Promise recognized the doctor's attempt at humor and rewarded him with a thin smile. "Is that supposed to cheer me up, sir?"

"Well, now, nice to see you can still appreciate humor. Something in your noggin must be functioning right. How about those peepers? Try opening them. Slowly."

Promise did and winced.

"Sergeant, I thought I said slowly. Surely you take orders better than that?"

"Not this one," replied Promise's mother, who was leaning against the back wall.

"You're gonna be sensitive for a while," said the doc. Here . . . let's try these on."

Promise opened her eyes to the dark outline of a well-groomed face barely a breath away from her, smelling minty fresh. "Better. Thanks." She squinted up at a shock of jet-black hair and a square jaw that appeared to be in two places at once. Glanced left and saw her mother over the doc's shoulder, leaning against the bulkhead, arms crossed and blinking hard to contain her worry.

As the doc looked down to consult her chart, Promise mouthed, "I'm okay, really."

Sandra shook her head.

I will be, all right.

Sandra went to speak, changed her mind, and walked out of the room.

"So . . . what's my prognosis, doc?" Promise looked for his rank. "You're a civilian."

"Correct, good. I came up with you. I'm the chief neurosurgeon from Primara Hospital. Got the call for help from your ship's doctor, Commander Tamm. She's in surgery now."

"What's my prognosis?"

"Well," the doc said dramatically, "you've looked better."

Promise scowled at him.

The doctor kept a straight face. He waved his hand in front of her and cleared his voice. "First things first. I'm Doctor Mitchell. That's Doctor Pharrington; she rode up with me." A petite woman with red hair waved and then excused herself from the room. "Who the 'verse are you?" The doc held up a finger and then pointed it at her.

"Right, Sergeant Promise Paen, sir. Service Number MM-I 163 524 436."

"Uh-huh. I'll take your word for it." The doc motioned to the side of her bed. "You mind?"

"No, sir. Please take a load off." As he got closer, his features got finer. *Real easy on the eyes. But about a quarter century late.*

"Secondly, where the 'verse are you?"

I think that's two fingers. Maybe four, which would give him ten on a hand. That's not right. "In a hospital bed, wearing a lot less than I'd prefer, sir."

The doc smiled. "True, on both counts. When was your birthday?"

Three fingers. Definitely three. "Same day as last year, doc."

"Humph." The doctor clicked his tongue. "The burns on your face weren't too bad; skin's already recovered. Your leg's responding well to quick-heal. The break was clean, all the way through. No muscle damage to speak of, and your PT at the Health and Wellness Center will be short and sweet."

Then he shrugged into the bad news.

"Your sponge is another matter. Initial scans suggest some amount of memory loss. Maybe permanent, maybe not. Thankfully, I didn't have to go in. Brain injuries are tricky. Your mind can compensate for damage, reroute neural pathways, adapt, and even completely heal itself. Time and more diagnostics will tell us a lot."

He squeezed Promise's shoulder. "But your sense of humor is still there, you've oriented times three, and, from all indications, I have every hope that you'll walk out of the infirmary and forget all about me and my good looks."

"Sorry, doc, but you're not my type," she heard her lips say while her brain thought *but your younger self might have been.* Promise shook her head, immediately regretted it, and yelped in pain. She closed her eyes to stop the room from spinning. "Doc, what can you tell me about the blast that put me in here? And the hostages—did they make it out all right? I remember exiting a stairwell, and that's about it."

"Don't really know about the blast. That's above my pay grade." He smiled back. "But I do know the hostages came out just fine. Nice work, Sergeant." The doctor hesitated a moment.

"I'm afraid I have some bad news. Your captain took a serious beating. Lieutenant Ffyn Spears should pull through fine, though his body will need regen therapies to replace a leg and possibly his right hand. Captain Remus is another matter. He's worse than critical. The captain sustained massive trauma to his brain stem and spine. Commander Tamm is working on him now. Better keep him in your thoughts and prayers."

Promise and the doc shared a moment of silence for a good Marine and an even better skipper.

"And the admiral?" Promise already knew the answer, but it was one of those questions that still had to be asked.

The doc shook his head, forced a smile, and changed the subject. "In the meantime, *rest*. That's an order. Drink lots, pee pale—a good liter or so—and I'll pull that tube from your most holy of holies and get you up and out of here, and over to the HAWC."

Promise's laughter discovered her cracked rib. She doubled over as her cheeks heated to a fine crimson glow, too. "S-sounds like a plan, doc."

"Sorry. Those ribs will hurt awhile." The doc stood to leave and said, "Oh, you may want to button up your backside. Tomorrow, I'm transferring you dirtside for the rest of your convalescence. I hear Montana's president wants an audience with you ASAP. I'm not happy about that, at least not this soon, but the powers that be have spoken, and I'm just a lowly healer."

Promise winced as she flexed the still-healing muscle one last time to complete her set. Her leg quivered as it lifted the virtual equivalent of nine kilos, less than half the weight she pressed in her normal routine. And neither "routine" nor "normal" came remotely close to describing her convalescence. Here she was in *Absalon*'s HAWC, straining under grav-weights so she could sojourn to a world painted in hostile colors, the planet she'd been orphaned on. Tomorrow would come far too soon. *I've had enough of Montana for two lifetimes. And here I am, returning for a third go at it.*

Promise locked down on her pain as she pressed her leg up and squeezed at the top, then resisted gravity all the way down. She was in the process of standing when she heard, "Excuse me, Sergeant. You aren't done yet, are you?"

Navy Nurse Lieutenant Commander Skyller Towns got up from her duty station and gently nudged her charge back into position, adding one kilogram. "There, Sergeant. Happy?" she said with just a hint of satisfaction.

Promise scowled at her matronly warden. They'd bonded immediately. Skyller liked to do hard things, too.

"All right, Commander—have it your way." Promise heaved the weight up and threw her nurse a defiant look. "Happy, ma'am?"

"Not until you walk without a limp."

"Yes, ma'am! Then I guess I'd better do a few more reps."

"Why, Sergeant, that sounds like an excellent idea. We need to push that leg through a good kind of pain, just not too hard. Now, mind Nurse Towns, you hear?" And with that, the lieutenant commander waved Promise back to work.

"Aye, aye, ma'am."

Over the last few days, Promise had felt like a toddler with a bad gait. Doctor Mitchell told her it would be at least two days before she shed her limp and another four days after that before he approved her for a brisk jog on the treadmill. But only after she'd undergone several more rounds of quick-heal to address the soft-tissue damage. The brain was coming along fine, and her memory was clearing up like fog at dawn, though she was struggling to recall new acquaintances—a very mild case of short-term memory loss and a lingering headache were the likely culprits. But nothing a few pills couldn't ease. On the whole, she was no worse for wear.

Montana's spaceport was another matter, a total write-off, in fact. She'd crash-landed into the enemy and caused a modicum of damage. But Victor Company had chosen a circuitous route to the hot zone with a longer approach—two klicks out from the port's epicenter. The approach had been costly, building by building, and blood for terrain. The toll grieved her. Three lost souls plus the skipper. In exchange, Victor Company had killed several dozen hostiles and hospitalized two more, who were hanging on thanks to their stasis collars. Once the enemy wounded healed, if they healed, they'd be facing a swift trial and a firing squad. Republican justice had a one-strike rule when it came to pirates. Get caught in the act and your shuttle got grounded, permanently.

Say hello to the deck, say good-bye to the deck. Her leg hurt in both directions. She distracted herself by rehashing the battle damage.

The terminal, all three landing pads, the docking and refueling stations, and a fleet of civilian crafts sat in ruins. The vids had been depressing. Two runways that intersected looked more like cratered regolith than takeoff and landing strips. Cluster bombs had flattened the control tower and ground up the emergency-response crews. A few fingers and a man's appendage were the only recognizable parts found. In sum, 762 civilians either died from the explosions or burned in the terminal itself. It was the second-worst atrocity in Montana's history. And she'd been around for the first one, too.

Lucky me.

"Last one didn't count," came from her right. She'd almost forgotten her nurse was standing over her, keeping track.

"Says who, ma'am?" Promise looked up into her nurse's shadow.

"Says Nurse Towns. You want out of here today? You better give me two more."

"Fine. Two more."

Lieutenant Commander Towns cleared her throat and this time removed a kilo.

"Really, ma'am?"

"Really. You're getting fatigued. A tendon in that leg might *really* give if you don't let me do my job."

Promise chuckled. Skyller did, too.

"All right, Sergeant, think you can manage the shower by yourself?"

"Yes, ma'am. I and my modesty will be just fine, such as it is."

"Honey, you've got nothing to be modest about. Now, get yourself a shower and back to bed. I want you off that leg and rested. I hear you have a very important meeting tomorrow morning."

"Don't remind me."

"A word of advice, Sergeant?"

It wasn't a question. Skyller didn't ask questions. "Of course, ma'am."

"Just do what she tells you."

Fourteen

Montana's presidential limousine settled onto the shuttle pad at Primara Central. Landing's premier hospital housed the only level-5 trauma center on the planet, complete with a quad of stasis chambers and a top-notch nanorobotic surgical team. It had been one of President Annie Buckmeister's signature achievements in her first term in office. As the limo's engine hummed on standby, a two-person security detail got out. Both wore two-tone boots, dark slacks, and sports coats that bulged slightly at the hip, the primary strapped to the thigh in a tactical holster, clearly visible. The taller of the two subvocalized with the air car circling the perimeter and confirmed the all clear. The shield opened the limousine's back door, and a tall, lithe woman got out.

Two men fanned out on either side of the president. Her presence was palpable like moisture in the air on a sultry summer afternoon. She looked at the LAC resting at the far corner of the shuttle pad and frowned. She'd meant to beat Sergeant Paen here and welcome her back home.

Well, no use crying over spilt milk, Annie told herself. She strode through the hospital's side entrance with a measured gait, flanked by her sentinels, one in front and the other behind her.

The president had a problem. Her citizens were threatening a government shutdown by withholding their taxes. They objected to their hard-earned chits paying for the medical care for two wounded pirates who'd tried to kill Montana citizens. She couldn't really blame them for feeling that way. As she rounded the corner to Sergeant Paen's room, she overheard someone say, "If hell is their last stop anyway, why don't we yank them out of stasis and get 'em on their merry way?"

It got better.

"Shame on the Republic," read *The Beast*'s cover story by Kyle Vooster, a pretentious reporter with a knack for finding the planetary nerve and pinching it. He'd dubbed his piece THE RAPE OF SPACEPORT ANNIE. His op-ed went on to opine an impressive list of pithy diatribes attacking the Republic, things like "Promised us peace and broke it instead" and "Knocked on our planet's door; delivered a knockout blow to our economy."

As much as the president hated to admit it, she really couldn't blame Mr. Vooster or his inflammatory journalism either. She was just as angry as a startled mother hexapuma with a pack of cubs on the tit.

But this mother, she reminded herself, *wears presidential panties. Watch your mouth, Annie.* One of these days she'd decide to follow her own advice. *Well, probably not.* She smiled and shrugged her shoulders while her guards weren't looking.

Montana's spaceport bore her name because she'd managed to attract the off-world funding to build a first-class port of call on a third-rate world struggling to pull itself from the verge and to achieve full incorporated status. *A population of one hundred-fifty million souls earns me a vote in the Republican Senate, too. What's another fifty million, give or take one or two?* Thus far, the spaceport was the crowning achievement of her second term in office, and she wasn't finished yet. The destruction of spaceport Annie was a personal wound to its namesake, one that would bother the flesh-and-blood Annie for the rest of her life. She'd built the place on prayers and five-year, zero-rate tax incentives, using thousands of volunteers to keep the labor costs low.

Her Montanans were a proud people, pride best exemplified in a simple maxim: Love your neighbors and the land. They helped each other out and didn't take kindly to people who broke faith with them. Or star nations, like the Republic of Aligned Worlds, which had been too late, again.

In perhaps the biggest twist of providence, Sergeant Promise T. Paen's dramatic rescue of the hostages in the spaceport's business complex turned the young NCO into a planetary hero, almost overnight. Made page 2. MONTANA MARINE GIVES PIRATES SOME OF THEIR OWN, the caption read. The article almost made you forget Paen was also a 'Publican. Almost.

Another sign of the public's disgust and distrust, she thought.

Annie found the room she was after and stopped at the door to square her shoulders. A nurse was just inside helping the sergeant get settled. Annie waited as she considered the actions of her Marine, from a discreet distance. One of the hostages the sergeant had saved was her niece once removed, a fine girl with a square head on her shoulders. The day of the attack, her niece had toured the spaceport's grounds with a group of her peers from the Montana Aviation and Propulsion Academy. An hour earlier and they would have died when the terminal went up in flame.

Annie shook her head. *Right place. Nearly the wrong time. Sounds like my niece. But not like my Marine.* She smiled because she knew something the young sergeant didn't.

The nurse left the room and President Annie Buckmeister walked in.

Promise was fighting with the back door of her hospital robe when her visitor arrived. She flushed as she took stock of Montana's head of state. The woman was, in a word, regal. Subtle makeup enhanced high cheekbones and jade-colored eyes. Her chocolate hair fell straight and beveled, accentuating an already-long neck. But her rugged clothing made her a walking study in contrast: tight-fitting jeans and a frayed leather vest. Stiletto boots? An occupied tactical holster wrapped around her thigh. Promise immediately recognized the woman from her mission brief.

The president's sidearm looked like an ancient revolver with a custom turquoise grip and a blued finish, but the vents along the barrel gave it away for the modern energy weapon it truly was. *And either Annie is in mint condition for a lady who has to be in her late forties, early fifties, or she's had a lot of bodywork. I'm guessing the former.*

"Sergeant Paen," the president said, extending her hand.

"Madam President." Promise stood to her feet. Her hospital gown chose to malfunction at that moment and nearly slipped off her shoulder. Thoroughly flustered, Promise caught the gown before it exposed her while managing to shake the president's hand, all in one fluid stream of motion.

"Madam President, I'm sorry, I'm . . ."

"Bare-assed and busted up," the president finished for her with a firm shake and a winning grin. "I should be the one apologizing for barging in on you like this, and for what I'm about to do."

I don't like the sound of that, Promise thought.

"No need to apologize, Madam President."

"Annie."

"Yes, ma'am."

The president's expression went hard as she absorbed Promise's appearance. Promise had no difficulty visualizing what she saw: the gash above her ear was now just a faint line highlighted by a lock of missing hair. Annie waved her hand, and Promise turned to give her a better look. The president "uh-humed" and "oh-my'd." The mottled black and blue colorations on her neck and collarbone had faded but not wholly disappeared. The leg brace told another story; the knee joint was proving stubborn even for the miracles of modern science.

"Well . . . s'ppose it could be worse."

When the president had seen enough, she drew in a breath and met Promise's gaze directly. "You obviously know who I am—Annie Buckmeister, planetary president," she said dismissively. "Please call me Annie. I keep things on a first-name basis in my administration. I'm sure you know about my niece. Pam's a good girl and smart, too. A real knack for shuttle engines, too. I'm sure glad you were there to pull her out. Thank you."

The president snorted and cleared her throat. Her eyes watered up, lashes fluttered, and then the dam broke. Annie stared, fanning with both hands. "Hang it all, my liner's gonna run. I told myself I wouldn't cry. This didn't happen, we clear?"

Promise shook her head no and handed Annie a tissue. "I seem to have extras."

Annie took a second to regain her composure, gingerly dabbed at her eyes, blew several puffs of air to dry them out. "You . . . ," Annie said, heart in her throat, "you, young lady, you're a Montanan first. You remember that. A *Montanan* first. And then a Marine."

Promise inhaled sharply.

"A very fine Marine sergeant at that. I meant no disrespect. It's just that I've got a conundrum on my hands. Honey, hand me another tissue. Make it two. Thank you kindly. Like I was sayin', my government's threatening secession from the Republic over her failure to protect us. How am I supposed to argue with the truth? Some of my constituents took out their anger against what was to be your barracks, and burned *it* to the ground. Others are refusing to pay their taxes. Our constitution actually gives them that right. It's called free speech." Annie look disgusted. "When you get out of here, remind me to show you the mound of hate mail in my office. The doll with the noose around her neck was uncalled for. I had that man arrested." Annie sighed like the weight of a planet rested on her shoulders. "I have a revenue problem that may shut down my administration, and the economic policies I ran on, which all hinged on growth through planetary exports, just went up in a blaze of shuttle fuel. It's a bad day to be president."

"Yes, ma'am?" was all Promise could think to say. It came out like a question.

"You think? Sergeant, I've got a bigger mess than I know what to do with." Annie's eyes flared. "But I also have you."

Promise sensed a smartmine and tried to sidestep it. "Ma'am, I was just doing my job and . . ."

"Sergeant, keep your trap shut. And listen. Good."

Promise shut it but not before a half-cocked smile broke free.

The president tilted her head, raised a questioning eyebrow. "What?"

"Sorry, ma'am, you just reminded me a bit of someone."

Annie's face softened, and she motioned to the foot of the bed. "You mind?"

This is becoming routine, Promise thought. "Please, have a seat such as it is, ma'am."

"It's Annie in private. Now, I may be old enough to be your mother, but I'm not old . . . and I am not a *ma'am*. Let's get that clear from the start."

"Yes, ma'am, ah—Annie."

"Relax, Marine. I don't bite, at least not often." Annie took Promise's hand in both of hers, and looked intently into Promise's eyes. "Promise, what I need right now is a hero, someone the good people of Montana can celebrate. I need you to be that for me. Yes? Good. I'm so glad to hear it."

"Ma'am . . . Annie, like I said, I was just doing . . ."

"Like *I* said, keep your trap shut and let me talk."

Promise nodded.

"Better. Are you like this with your superiors?" Annie frowned. "Never mind, my point is there are a lot of angry and bitter people out there." Annie looked toward the window. "I need to help them focus all of the hurt and pain they're feelin' and turn it into something productive. They need to see past this tragedy and catch a glimpse of hope. Montana's seen too many broken promises, and it's time that trend stopped." Annie turned back to face Promise. "Hello, Ms. Hope. You just beat the living daylights out of those pirates. The whole planet knows it. And we're gonna celebrate you Montana style." Annie patted Promise's good leg. "I'm awarding you the Planetary Medal of Freedom for service above and beyond the call of duty, both to Montana and to the Republic." Annie looked down the bridge of her nose. "Don't let it go to your head."

Promise went to speak but thought better of it when Annie glared at her.

"Our Medal of Freedom is a new award, one I just created in your honor, in fact. And, frankly, my actions aren't wholly altruistic. This planet needs the Republic, even if her citizens can't see the truth of it at this moment. I need to help them see it and help them clear their vision before their blindsidedness drives us right off a galactic cliff."

Annie let that sink in and gave Promise time to think it through. Then she told her how it was going to be.

"So, you will accept this award and help me do that, okay? Yes. Wonderful." Annie looked pleased.

"I don't believe I have a choice."

"Smart girl." Annie stood and racked her hands on her curvy hips.

It was Promise's turn to snort.

"I hear you're being discharged later this week. Sorry to do this to you beforehand, but the ceremony is tomorrow morning at, ah, zero nine hundred. I say that right? Good news is, I'm breaking you out early. Wear your leg brace with pride. I want everyone to see you roughed up but unbroken when I pin your medal on you. That's an order."

"Yes ma'am. I mean Annie."

"All right then." Annie slapped her hands together and bared her teeth. "This is gonna be fun."

Fifteen

When is this going to end?

Promise saw eyes, everywhere, looking straight at her: adults and children, strangers, Montanans, and Marines. An immense avatar of her floated above, surveying the crowd like a specter out of *Immortals in Love*. Her mechsuit was scored by weapons fire, her helmet racked to her hip, her hair matted with sweat and grime, and her eyes ablaze with what the president later called Montana moxie. As Promise stared up at herself, a stout little girl named Myla took her hand and pulled her up the steps, gently nudging her until she was standing in front of her chair. The girl smiled, rocked her feet, and waited. When Promise didn't sit, her attendant turned and motioned "What now?" toward a handful of government officials. Promise saw Landing's police and fire marshal, the mayor of Landing, Annie's vice president, a pack of state governors, and the president herself.

Worry creased her brow. *Where are the others going to sit?*

"Oh, don't worry about us," Annie said as she crossed the stage. "And don't say I didn't warn you, either. Please, have a seat, Sergeant Paen, or you're going to make young Myla here believe she didn't do her part." President Buckmeister nodded toward the chair. "Now sit."

Promise's buttocks hit the cushion on the downbeat of the Landing Diamondhead's signature fight song. She nearly bolted back up to attention at the *bum, bum bum bum—bum, bum bum bum,* all in syncopated time, sounded to a rapid-fire 3D montage of the Battle of Landing. Live-actions of her and her fellow Marines floated above the stage. Shots of V Company as they killed the enemy, shots of her taking fire, shots of her firing back, shots of her being medevaced to *Absalon.* A solitary LAC rose into the sky, and the screen went dark. Promise covered her mouth to hide her dismay. *They're mostly shots of me!* Promise wanted to bury her head in her hands. She fought the urge to fidget, and barely restrained the impulse to walk off the stage and run the rest of the way back to RNS *Absalon.* She locked onto the air above the back row of spectators. *Don't make eye contact and you'll be fine.* Then the president's speech began, and matters grew even more embarrassing.

"...with a singular resolve, Sergeant Promise T. Paen faced the enemy, vastly outnumbered, yet with little regard for her own life. Saving our people was her only concern."

Promise tried to block out the speech and the piercing reverberations. She didn't dare look at her company. *I'm going to pay for this later.*

For most of the last millennium, star nations had honored their finest with the five points. But the president was a true-blooded Montanan, and Montanan's were known for bucking tradition. Promise stared down at the body of the medal. Everything fogged. She couldn't recall being pinned, and it had only just happened. She almost laughed. It was shaped like a bull's head. Annie's prize stud had modeled for it. It had black onyx horns. Its chest displayed Montana's planetary crest. Its head held deep-set eyes that glowed ruby red, all of which hung on a ribbon of Montana green and gold. In the wrong hands, it would have been a garish caricature from a "neobarb" planet, but the craftsman managed to make the bull appear just this side of elegant and as fierce as a Marine raider.

To Promise's shock, the medal came with a hefty reward, or about half a year's pay for a Marine of her rank. The Corps didn't let active-duty personnel accept bonuses for doing their jobs, from anyone for any reason, unless it was awarded by the RAW-MC as prize money, an enlistment or MOS bonus, or "imminent danger pay."

After the ceremony, Promise quoted Annie regulation 247.20.2B, which didn't sit well with the president. Annie fired back with one of her own from the Republic's Articles of Federation. Article 15 prescribed the proper use and mobilization of the planetary militia.

"But I'm regular Fleet Forces. Ma'am, with respect, what you're proposing is, well, illegal."

Annie didn't care. "According to Article Fifteen, the president commands the planetary militia and may assign combat bonuses at her discretion, from federal funds block-granted to its member planets."

"But I'm not militia," Promise repeated, as politely as she dared.

"But you *are* active duty, which automatically makes you a reservist on my planet, should your services ever be required." Annie's eyes flicked upward in thought. "And I require them." It sounded like Annie added the last bit on the fly.

"Ma'am, when did I become a reservist?"

"About noon yesterday, when I exercised an obscure clause on the books and activated your reserve status. You'll start drawing a small stipend at the end of the month."

"*Madam President,* the military cannot operate under the jurisdiction of a local planetary government. It's prohibited by federal law." Promise almost pleaded. Her voice sounded weak, which irritated her immensely.

"No, it isn't. At least, not exactly. You need to understand a thing or three about politics. Best I start your education.

"As a Republican world, Montana falls under Republican law. We keep our own laws, as long as they don't contradict the Republic's bylaws. According to the Defense of the Homeworlds Acts, and I quote, 'Members of the Republican Fleet Forces, and other uniformed military as may arise, may lawfully operate in tandem with and as an integrated member of a Republican-sanctioned, local planetary militia or system defense force, providing said operations don't interfere with the primary duties of the officer or enlisted personnel in question, and to the extent that no legal distinction may be drawn between the two in either case.'"

"Come again, ma'am?"

"Congress passed the DOHA and slipped in this proviso. It's a loophole in an otherwise airtight prohibition against federal uniformed soldiers interfering in purely local planetary matters."

"You might be stretching the limits of DOHA. Operating in tandem is one thing; operating under the direct order of the planetary president is another."

"Maybe—well, probably—but we'll let the high court decide afterward. In the meantime, you're a Montana reservist. And I've just activated you. Bam!" Annie slapped her hands together for effect.

"So you're just treating me like one of your own."

"You *are* one of my own, Promise. I'll ask for forgiveness later. By the way, everyone in Victor Company is getting a combat bonus, too."

"You've got to be kidding me."

Sixteen

"You have got to be kidding me, sir. I'm *what*?"

"*The new CO of Victor Company, effective immediately*," said Lieutenant Spears. "*Congratulations, Lieutenant.*"

Promise grabbed her caf, took a sip of the hot liquid, and barricaded herself behind the mug. First Lieutenant Ffyn Spears stared out at her from the monitor on the desk, gray eyes dimmer than usual but just as focused. He was slumped in his medchair. An amber-colored liquid dripped in the periphery. Though the lieutenant was in orbit aboard *Absalon*, the feed was essentially instantaneous. Promise wished she'd accepted audio only.

"*I'm awarding you a battlefield commission to second lieutenant. You can't dodge the bars, Promise, not this time. If I have anything to say about it, BUPERS will let you keep them, too.*"

"Sir, there are SNCOs in our company with substantially more leadership experience than me." Promise shook her head in protest. "What about the gunny?"

"*You're right, Gunnery Sergeant Ramuel has a career's worth of experience. But Tomas endorsed your promotion without hesitation. You have his full confidence, and I have his word that he will assume command of Victor Company should something happen to you.*" Spears paused to make his next point. "*Lieutenant, don't let that happen. Understood?*"

"Roger that, sir."

His laughter took her by surprise. *"And, by the way, Promise, second lieutenant would be a significant step down for a lifer like Tomas. I wouldn't dare offer him a field commission. But that didn't stop me from making him your official XO."* Promise's spine stiffened. *"Don't worry about it—I won't tell him you said so."*

The lieutenant took pains to sit forward until his face nearly filled the monitor. His voice turned professorial, the voice Promise guessed he'd used as a history teacher in his former life.

"Listen closely: command isn't just about the years or seniority. Look at me. I'm old for my rank. I joined up late. Most of my immediate superiors are younger than me. My handicap for running the five k is the same as most captains and a good number of majors, too."

Spears's pained smile filled the frame. It was obvious he was enjoying making Promise squirm.

"Being in the right place, ready to step into command when an op goes south or a unit takes casualties, is how a lot of Marines make rank. There are only three paths to promotion: expansion, retirement, and death. Just happens to be the latter in this case. I wish the skipper had pulled through. He was one of the best. It'll be tough filling his boots."

"Yes, sir. It certainly will."

"But I don't just need a Marine with the bars on her collar to play lieu-tenant in my absence. Unlike me, you're still relatively young for the rank. Well . . . so what. I need someone with aptitude and ability—both have a lot to do with my decision. You've demonstrated each in turn and"—Spears said, stabbing his side of the screen—*"my Marines respect you."*

"And I'm Montanan," Promise added.

"And you're Montanan. But don't sell yourself short. You happen to be from Montana. That's a plus in my book, but not a necessity. Other aspects of your jacket are equally attractive: successful completion of the NCO Leadership Academy with top marks; the degree you earned in Pre-Diaspora Military Conflict from the University of Salerno, during your off time, I might add; your weapons proficiencies." The lieutenant quirked an eyebrow. *"And I know you go easy on your Mule. Stevie, I believe."* He waited for Promise to nod and then added, *"I like a Marine who cleans her own gear."*

The lieutenant crossed his arms and flashed Promise a skewed smile. When Promise didn't lighten up, he quickly grew angry.

"*Lieutenant Paen, you've just been promoted. How 'bout a thank you, sir!*"

Promise's face heated. "I'm sorry, sir. Thank you, sir. I just don't know what to say, sir."

"*Stop 'siring' me. One will suffice, Promise. Look, life happens and calls upon us to respond. Some sergeants become staff sergeants and gunnys. Some become officers. Like you.*"

Promise searched for something to say. "I . . . Thank you, sir."

"*See, it's not so hard. You can like it or lump it. But my decision stands, and you have your orders. I know you'll rise to this occasion.*"

Promise sat up straighter and nodded. "I won't let you down, sir."

"*I never doubted it, Lieutenant.*"

Lieutenant Spears leaned back and winced. "*'Verse this infernal disk. I'm off to SanStar Medical for treatment. Booked passage on a commercial freighter. I'll be away from Montana for at least a few months. Maybe take care of another problem, too. After five kids, the Alpha Unit would be grateful.*" He wagged his finger and smiled. "*You're not the only one being promoted either. BUPERS made me a captain. And I plan to come back and resume command of Victor Company unless the powers that be say otherwise. I expect to find my command in tip-top shape. Have I made myself clear?*"

"Crystal, sir. Congratulations, Skipper."

"*Skipper—I like the sound of that, especially coming from you, Lieutenant. Did you get the package from me?*"

"Yes, sir, right here with your orders to leave it unopened until after speaking with you."

"*Well, we've talked, haven't we?*"

Promise tore the bag open and dumped a small box into her hand. She cracked the top, revealing two polished onyx second lieutenant's bars.

"*Sorry I can't be there in person.*"

"I'm honored, sir."

"*You're my choice, Promise. Officer material. Rise to the occasion like you've done before and you'll be fine.*"

Her company. Her Marines. It was going to take a while to get used to that.

"Lieutenant?"

It took Promise a moment to realize Maxi's question was directed at her. "Mmhmm?" Promise turned her head to the side and frowned at her reflection in the mirror. She was sitting in the CO's office, in her office, and she was struggling with her new authority . . . and the weight of new responsibilities. She felt off-kilter. The bars on her collar looked strange. They certainly felt strange. She kept glancing at her reflection and what she saw wasn't matching what her mind said should be there. "Yes, Maxi," she replied, lost in thought. "Sorry." She inhaled deeply and made herself smile, then turned toward him.

"Company's moved in more or less. Your president's a shrewd woman."

"*My* president, is it?" Promise said as she pushed back from her desk and crossed her legs. "Do you disown her and the chits she just transferred to your personal account?"

"Quite the opposite, ma'am. I'm rather taken with your president . . . and I've already spent her money."

Figures. Promise gave Maxi her most disapproving glare. The "ma'am" wasn't lost on her either. *I suppose that comes with the bars.*

"Anyway, ma'am, she's shrewd and calculating. Our barracks rate four stars, which is three better than usual. But we won't have much privacy. She loaned us Summit Elementary. Summit merged with another school and no longer needs the building. It's ours until our new barracks gets built. We're situated in the middle of a planned community in South Landing. We won't be able to so much as take a piss, let alone run an op or training mission, without the locals knowing about it."

"Shrewd and calculating, Corporal. Maybe the president wants us highly visible for the benefit of our new neighbors. There isn't a better way to build rapport with the locals than to let them see us flying overhead *and* pounding neighborhood ferocrete. The more hands we shake, the better."

Maxi grew thoughtful, then nodded.

Promise changed the subject by looking about her. "I like my new office. I've never had one before." And then she turned back to look at Corporal Sindri with a newfound excitement that surprised her. "Please tell me about our new home, ah, Summit Elementary."

Maxi grinned. "Well, ma'am, we've got a lot of space to take up." Maxi started ticking off fingers. "Trees cover the grounds, the green grass rolls on, there're grav-bars and lots of parking. PTA meeting is tomorrow evening."

Promise snorted. Maxi tapped a command into his minicomp and brought up a schematic of the school. A holographic layout appeared between them. Maxi pushed his index finger and thumb into the projection, spread them apart, and magnified the lower right quadrant.

"The auxiliary gym is here, which is now the morgue. All mechsuits are prepped and ready to deploy. The playground and soccer field on the north side should do fine for morning PT. We could even invite the locals to join us if they like. Barracks is in this wing. Here. Our command center and your office are in the music and band rooms. We even have our own mess hall."

"Won't that make the cook happy. Where's our LZ for the LACs and stingship? They're heavy. Civilian-grade ferocrete will cave. We'll have to pour."

"No need. Turns out the south parking lot was paved with military-grade materials. It doubles as a helipad for flight-for-life. X marks the spot. We're sharing it with Primara Hospital. I tell you one thing, these people think outside of the box. This school sits dead center of Southfork, the largest suburb in Landing, which is about seven klicks as an HV missile flies from the only level-five trauma unit on the planet. Summit Elementary is the perfect place for an evac."

"Hmmm. What do they fly?"

"Nothing fancy, ma'am. Mainly antiquated rotary copters that burn fossil fuels, all subsonic. Grav-assisted VTOLs are too expensive for Rimworlders. Their helos may be slow by our standards, but they run clean, and I'm told they're pretty responsive—up to two hundred KPH. With your permission, I'd like to get checked out on one. While skimming the planetary nets, I found the same LZ footprint across Montana, all using school parking lots."

"And there you go," Promise quipped. "The more I see, the more I like them."

Maxi looked at her funny.

"You have to remember, I didn't get out much as a child. I never darkened the doors of a public school. I learned at a distance, up here"—Promise touched her head and then her heart—"but not here. My dad forbid it. When he died, I enlisted. I probably know more about the RAW-MC than I do about my homeworld."

"That's too bad. These are good people."

Promise nodded. These people were growing on her, and her Marines. That was a good sign, a very good sign indeed.

My Marines. It may take a lot of time to get used to that, too.

Without warning, the weight of command started rubbing her shoulders wrong. She squared herself up and felt the burden settle across her back and neck, still uncomfortable but bearable. She rolled her shoulders until the fit settled, wrinkled her nose, and nodded sharply.

"All right, Corporal, the chrono's ticking. Assemble the company and meet me"—she checked the schematic and found what she was looking for—"in the Jeannie Miller Amphitheater at seventeen hundred hours."

Seventeen

"**. . . So that about covers** the situation. We've got one understrength company of Mechanized Marines—us—to police and secure a planet of ninety-eight million people and keep the Lusies at bay and a few banged-up VTOL platforms we scrounged from the locals, plus our three LACs and an aging stingship, to do it with. *Absalon* has one additional LAC, which will stay aboard her as a reserve. Up top, there's a small orbital platform, the Lucky Lady, to handle customs and shuttle goods to the surface. She's unarmed and won't be of help in a stand-up fight. The good news is we get to keep *Absalon* in orbit to fly the flag. *Absalon* will make any pirate think twice."

Promise rocked back on her heels, hands lying thoughtfully against the small of her back. "Questions."

"Ma'am, this is bullshit. One company . . . for an entire planet?"

"Private, watch your language around the lieutenant. She doesn't care for it." The gunny caught the private's eyes, held them 'til the young Marine nodded.

"Sorry, Gunny," and then, "ma'am."

Promise dipped her head toward the gunny. "Private Koval, correct?" Mild amusement drew her brow upward. "I asked for questions. Would you care to rephrase?"

Private Oliver Koval turned white as a warship's hull. *They're all still getting used to you.* Koval had been a last-minute replacement before Victor Company shipped out to Montana. His youth and inexperience were showing him up. *We all learn sometime,* Promise thought. *It's time I start his education.*

"Isn't this, uh, well, isn't this total BS, ma'am?"

His question won her over.

"Yes, Private, it is a crap load and more." Promise wrinkled her nose. "And it stinks to high heaven." Promise drew her hands to her hips. "But your observation doesn't change our predicament, does it?" Promise chuckled inside. Now she was the one asking rhetorical questions. Koval sat up straighter and looked astern of her. Promise wasn't out to embarrass him. But she needed him to calm down and make peace with the inequities of their deployment. Koval, blond as the sky was blue and just the other side of eighteen, was nearly fresh out of Book Camp and his inexperience was showing. After Boot, he'd been rushed through the RAW-MC's School of Infantry, in less than sixty percent of the time the SOI should have taken to complete. The Corps had been trying to garrison too many planets in the verge for years, and protect the Republic's core worlds too, and maintain parity with the Lusies in a cold war that was well above freezing, all of which meant too many green boots were deploying before they should have. Private Koval was so wet-behind-the-ears he hadn't even made private first class before BUPERs sent him to the fleet.

Careful, P. Privates break easy.

"Private"—she said, sweeping the room—"we are down five Marines, and the skipper, and Lieutenant Spears—make that *Captain* Spears—was severely injured." At the mention of the skipper, a surge of anger washed over the company, an invisible wave felt more than seen. Promise matched eyes with a number of Marines, nodded in understanding. "We won't see replacements for months, if we're lucky. Montana doesn't even have a proper space station, probably won't for several more years. The Corps is too strapped to shake loose the garrison that would normally come with it. Look, this may be the Rim, but Montana is still a Republican world. Which means I need you to clone yourself and help me be three places in one Marine minute."

Every jane and jack in the room smiled, even Koval.

She let her words sink in and hoped the humor tempered them a bit and made them more palatable. *Like a cold MRE, if I'm lucky. Well, maybe not . . .* While the silence lingered, she thought of something else her father used to say. *Always preach truth, but use as few words as possible. Gives people time to do their own thinking.*

Promise watched Koval chew on what she'd said. Slowly, his shoulders dropped and he relaxed into his seat. *Good.*

"But here's what we can do and what we will do. We will fly the flag and wave it high and proud. I'm detaching Private First Class Fitzholm, Lance Corporal MacDevit, and Corporal Na'go with one of our LACs to the Lady as Montana's first official Marine Customs Support Team. You're our first line of defense should some of Private Koval's BS hit the fan space side."

The three Marines sat together, already briefed, and nodded back at their new commanding officer.

"That leaves us two LACs and a lot of sky to cover," Promise said to the rest of her company. She'd stewed about how best to break the next bit of news to her people. If there was a better way, it had yet to reveal itself to her.

"It appears we have an insurgency to deal with, too. The pirates that hit the spaceport were reconnoitering the base and the local establishments for at least a few weeks. Landing's chief of police, Hess Krause, has the instincts of a gunny. He took snapshots of the pirates still in one piece, the ones in stasis collars, and posted their faces across the planetary net. Several business owners in Landing recognized them and had actually done business with them, with the receipts to prove it. I'm willing to bet there are more. We've got an infestation. Who wants to play exterminator?"

Every dominant hand shot skyward.

Private Koval blurted out, in carefully edited speech, "God *bless*! Lieutenant, what are we mucking waiting for?"

Fast learner, Promise thought. "My sentiments exactly."

Promise's eyes swept over her people, her Marines, her janes and jacks, chests swelling with pride, shoulders proudly burdened by a long, storied tradition.

In its nearly three hundred years, the RAW-MC had lived, breathed, bled, and died in mechanized companies of forty, eight platoons per company,

five Marines, or "points," per toon. Since the war of seccession with the
Terran Federation.

In the year 2481 C.E., the TF had swamped Hold's meager system-
defense forces and militia. Hold couldn't win. Others had already fallen.
It was only a matter of time before Hold did, too. Hold was a chartered
Terran colony after, all. What did the colonists expect? Its taxes were appropriate to its position in the Federation, slowly phased in like all the
others. Independence from Holy Terra was off the table, a nonnegotiable.
After just days of fighting, the TF's victory seemed all but guaranteed. In
the scope of the war, the battle of Lake Tilyar was insignificant. A poorly
equipped band of forty citizen-soldiers were cut off, pinned down in a
swamp near the southern shore of Tilyar. They held out for three days,
used mud to mask their thermal prints, pissed in neck-deep water rife with
parasites, ate raw snake flesh and vegetation, and buddy-bagged at night
to stave off hypothermia. On the eve of the fourth day, they'd had enough
and decided to end things one way or another. Their raid behind TF lines
caught an inbound dropship gutted up with TF gear and much-needed
ordnance, taking it down in flames. Few of the forty made it back to the
swamp. It was a small victory that rallied a planet and birthed the Republic of Aligned Worlds and the RAW-MC.

Earth- and space-based Marine Corps had organized by platoons twice
as large, if not a dozen or more men, for as long as anyone could remember. History had scoffed at the Holdians for defying tradition. A "toon" of
five Marines was inadequate, a company of forty understrength. What
did one planet in a fledgling system know about prosecuting wars anyway? The first commandant of the RAW-MC hadn't cared. He'd fought
for and won his independence with understrength militias on an understrength planet in an unwinnable war against an unbeatable foe. Then
he'd helped other planets band together to do the same.

The corps' central ethos hung in Wolfestein Hall, enshrined above the
archway in the central quarter of the RAW-MC's School of Mechanized
Infantry, just off the "drop-off" and not far from the symbolic line of
mechboots cemented in ferocrete that every class had stepped into before
starting training. Promise still remembered stepping into those boots and
thinking about the price paid to put them there. The words ghosted over
Promise's lips.

Sisters and brothers, warriors true, Forty and Company.
Into the jaws of death. Uah! Rushing the mouth of hell.
Besieged by beam, shot and shell
Through smoke and fog 'cross stream and line
All forty charge—now twenty-nine.
Oh, glorious victory! Yet death's sting. The cost too great to bear.
Paid by the faithful, valiant few. Lives spent by them—for you.
Now charging back, bruised flesh and bone
'Cross bloody fields, none left alone.
No better friend, no fiercer foe
Janes and jacks, dead and gone, but Forever Company.

—"Forever Company," by First Commandant Kaleb Z. Wolfestein,
after the battle of Lake Tilyar, fought between Hold's System Militia
and the Terran Federation, during the Holdian war of secession.
Read at the dedication of Hold's National Cemetery.

Promise noted the empty chairs in the back row, compartmentalized the loss for another time. She was down a toon, but she'd make do. She'd have to.

Every toon had an NCO (usually a corporal or sergeant), a heavy-weapons expert, Striker-rated Marine, corpsman, and demolitions expert. All were riflemen. Every point had a secondary MOS, too: shuttle or LAC pilot, GravCraft coxswain, dropmaster, linguist, TacWitch, armorer, MechTech. The possibilities grew every year. Regular companies were led by one or two officers (typically a captain and a first or second lieutenant) and a gunnery sergeant to grease the troops. And toons were trained to operate independently, for long periods of time if necessary.

I will need them to operate solo, for extended periods of time. They have no idea what I'm about to ask of them.

Promise looked down at her minicomp, hit transmit, and sent her orders to every member of Victor Company. She watched as her people acknowledged her instructions in their own way: pursed lips, raised eyebrows, jock checks, and grunts. "We'll run three eight-hour watches per day, two toons per watch, giving us a small reserve that will be off duty . . . theoretically." Everyone smiled—Marines didn't get time off, in theory or in practice.

"Gunnery Sergeant Ramuel, Staff Sergeant Hhatan, and Sergeant Felix will command first, second, and third watch respectively. The gunny is working up a crew rotation and will make sure everyone receives liberty."

Promise knew rule 1 for green lieutenants. Make nice with the gunny. After all, he's one step from God and knows it. But she wasn't *that* green, and she definitely wasn't some "ninety-day wonder" who'd earned her commission after a ridiculously short training period. She and Gunnery Sergeant Tomas Ramuel had enlisted days to fall back on.

The gunny stood in the corner. He was a small giant used to being singled out for his height as much as his rank. Gray lines streaked his hair. A faint scar bisected his jaw, and the tip of his right ear was noticeably absent. With fourteen years in the Corps, Gunnery Sergeant Ramuel showed no sign of slowing down. He was her effective XO, too, standing where at least a second lieutenant would normally.

Promise looked at him as she finished her brief that he'd helped her rehearse earlier that afternoon. "Gunny, I'll expect you to handle any personnel conflicts that arise. Unless it's major, I don't want to hear about it." Said for a reason. "Keep me apprised of anything interesting." The gunny nodded and turned toward Sergeant Richelle Felix and Staff Sergeant Moya Hhatan.

Promise continued. "I'll also need you three to set up flybys and sensor sweeps of the most logical places where pirates might be hiding. It's a tall order, I know. But we're tapped into the planet's sats. Put your minds to it this afternoon and get me a preliminary report by 0830 hours."

The three veterans nodded. Promise moved on.

"During each watch, one toon will run flybys and sweeps, wave the flag, hunt for pirates, and visit the locals. This is police and PR, folks. On your best behavior. Let's get out there and help the Montanans get to know us and build a reserve of trust." *Maker knows we may need it.*

"The second toon of each watch will remain here in Landing, on standby. For the time being, the second toon of the watch will also provide security at Annie while the Montanans rebuild her, at least until the locals can take over their own OPSEC. We need those launchpads up and running ASAP. Our neighbors need to know that the Republic is covering their sixes while they work. You'll police the site in mechsuits, augmented by VTOL platforms for rapid transport to potential hot spots. We'll keep the stingship here at the school. Corporals Sanchez and Porter, and Lance Corporal Hendricks are flight certified for the ship. Sorry, gals, until we get a few more of you checked out on her, you'll be perpetually on standby. I want each of you to find a replacement, train her or him. Pronto. Until then, it can't be helped."

Each woman groaned outwardly. Some days it didn't pay to have special skills in the RAW-MC.

"I'll be politicking with the president's office and will from time to time tap one or more of you for social and political functions."

"Poor bastards," came from midway back.

"I heard that, Mic," Promise said. "There's a special place in my heart for insubordinate PFCs. I'm tapping you as my personal chauffeur. Your cap and coat are on order." Private First Class Mickie Hong stood up and gave his fellow Marines a deep, perfunctory bow.

As her people laughed freely, the task suddenly seemed more manageable, and perhaps not quite impossible. She was asking each woman and man in her command to shoulder the weight of a planet and to stretch social muscles most had never exercised. Some simply didn't possess them and probably never would. The Corps turned out disciplined, well-trained riflemen, not PR officers. Schmoozing wasn't covered in RAW-MC's combat bible. You were either good with civilians or you weren't. And a small percentage trained for it. She hoped her troops could spit and polish their behavior, act nice, and befriend the locals.

"Lastly, we need to loop in the planetary militia." Genuine surprise registered across her Marines' faces.

"This particular revelation caught me off guard, too, something *my* Montanans are growing quite adept at doing. Their population is on the small side and scattered across the planet. I expected local city militias, at least for the largest population centers, not something larger, certainly not coordination on a global scale across multiple continents. But they are forward thinking. These are resourceful people, and there's a lot of talent to tap in Landing alone. I'm creating a training regimen to get a small contingent of locals up to speed on modern weapons and basic tactics.

With a few months of training"—*and a small miracle*—"we'll be able to bolster our numbers with some homegrown bootstraps."

Promise looked out at Victor Company. Many were young and inexperienced, just like she was, truth be told. But they were the best-looking lot she'd ever seen.

Her eyes caught the gunny's. The veteran looked at his new CO and gave her two thumbs-up.

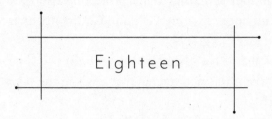

Eighteen

"Time to next waypoint?" asked Staff Sergeant Moya Hhatan. She sat in the pilot's chair, flying A-LAC3, which was stenciled across the vessel's conical nose. The RAW-MC encouraged cross-training, and Hhatan had opted for flight school. Fourth Platoon was strapped tightly into the aft compartment of the craft, most of which was unoccupied, built for a much larger complement of Marines. They hit a pocket of turbulence at nine hundred klicks per hour, a slow crawl up where mountains looked like molehills and all but the grossest features blurred below into a sea of arctic white.

"Ninety seconds, Staff Sergeant," replied Corporal Brad Forester, a leathery-looking man with channels carved across his face. "There's another pocket ahead. Suggest you climb to niner thousand meters." Corporal Forester was seated a meter behind and to the right of the staff sergeant, riding the copilot's chair and NAVCOM. A holographic array of blues, greens, and yellows wrapped around him. He ran fingers over virtual boards, inputting coordinates and updating the LAC's heads-up display.

"Roger, that. Climbing to niner thousand meters." Hhatan's light touch nosed the craft upward. "Course change in . . . one mike." As the last second ticked down, Staff Sergeant Hhatan executed a shallow bank to port and lined up on their next destination in the sky, which appeared on the HUD as a small red diamond projected into the distance.

Corporal Forester suddenly jerked in his seat. "SAM launch at one o'clock! Elevation eight hundred meters!" barked Forester. He opened a screen to the staff sergeant's right, projecting real-time tracking info on an incoming bogey moving fast, almost directly ahead. "Deploying countermeasures."

Two birds fell astern of the craft, then split in two along different vectors; suddenly there was not one but five LACs in the sky, squawking the same signature.

"Brace yourselves!" Staff Sergeant Hhatan nosed the shuttle hard toward the planet's surface to create a miss and throttled her engines to full.

A drop ring opened in the aft compartment, Hhatan's voice blaring over the shuttle's comm. "Bail, bail, bail." But she knew there wasn't time. "Corporal, punch—"

A burst transmission relayed via satellite and downloaded to Promise's terminal. A long minute later, Promise sat in her ready room reviewing Fourth Platoon's final moments. Moya and Brad had done a fine job. Promise wished she could have told them so. Instead, she listened to the last words Staff Sergeant Moya Hhatan spoke before she died.

"*Bail, bail, bail. Corporal, punch—*"

Out, Promise added. They'd had no warning. *And no chance to bail out.*

The transmission ended abruptly. Promise pulled up the visual recording. She didn't want to, but part of doing her duty meant being with her Wolves . . . until they'd met their end. *I owe them that much.* She watched Staff Sergeant Moya Hhatan fight the controls in a staid panic, trying to generate a miss. Heard her bark desperate orders. And then . . . Private Kami Sneider, Private Ryonda Petersburgs, and Lance Corporal Bane Ri had sat aft of visual, and each had died from the missile's impact. The blast had worked forward, taking Hhatan with it. She clenched her jaw as Corporal Forester took the controls, unable to punch out. Brad didn't stop fighting, didn't stop trying to stabilize the LAC, and didn't lose command of himself, even in the midst of chaos.

Tears began to run down her face.

Promise switched to the pilot's vantage point and played the vid a second time. Her screen momentarily froze. Suddenly the terrain visible through the LAC's armorplaste started to spin about the ship, as if the ship were the one calm and the world outside had gone amuck. The proximity claxon sounded in the background. Armorplaste shattered and the ship lost pressure. Everything aft that wasn't bolted or tied down was suddenly sucked forward. Hhatan slumped into the camera's view. *Merciful God, at least it was fast,* Promise thought. She switched to Forester's vantage point. Fighting the helm, before he blacked out. His vitals kept reporting loud and clear until impact. Then he flatlined, and the recording defaulted to "End Transmission."

Promise pushed the screen away and only then wiped away her tears. They were her first casualties as an officer. She'd sent them to die and at the time hadn't known how much she would ask of them.

"So this is how it feels."

The knock at the door pulled her into the present. The gunnery sergeant and Corporal Sindri walked in, both looking somber. Promise didn't try to hide the pain in her eyes. Both men sat opposite her and waited for her to speak. She leaned forward and spun the screen on her desk to face them, and hit PLAY. When the transmission ended, all color had drained from their faces. Maxi was visibly angry. The gunny's eyes radiated strength and understanding, and told Promise that what she was feeling was okay, normal, and part of commanding Marines. The weight of command bound them together in a moment of sacred understanding.

Promise thought about Staff Sergeant Hhatan, a solid Marine and an even finer woman. When Promise had met her nearly five years ago, she'd been old for her rank. And the powers that be had given her a glowing FITREP but passed her over for gunny, twice. A single sentence had sealed her in grade.

POSSESSES THAT SPARK OF LEADERSHIP, AND AN
INNATE ABILITY TO LEAD AND MAXIMIZE
PLATOON-LEVEL COMMANDS.

The promotions board had officially denied her the rank of gunnery sergeant because she was invaluable in her current role, which was a kind way of telling her that she'd hit ceiling, stalled out.

Promise remembered the day she'd met the small, unassuming woman. Her plain features and petite frame had starkly contrasted with the uniform. Two blue-on-green ribbons for service and three theater ribbons with red Vs for valor earned the hard way. God only knew how much glittery the woman wasn't wearing. Promise had stood in awe of the staff sergeant.

Hhatan had welcomed Promise to Victory Company personally—even met her at the spaceport, which had surprised Promise. That's what privates were for. But there were a lot of things that surprised Promise about the staff sergeant. Every Marine got "the speech," which ended with a dose of cold reality. "Every Marine has her limitations," said the staff sergeant on the ride from the port to the barracks. "Learn to recognize yours. I recognized mine several years ago, after I didn't make gunny the first time. Then I didn't make gunny the second time. The powers that be saw my limits long before I did. Good thing, too. I might have gotten a lot of good Marines killed. Took me a bit to swallow my pride and get over myself. But eventually I did."

The staff sergeant's eyes had drifted out of focus, lost in old memories. Promise remembered her silence. A smart private kept her trap shut when a SNCO spoke. But it was more than mere military courtesy or the healthy fear of a superior that kept her from talking. She'd recognized the sacredness of the moment, knew Hhatan was peeling back a part of her soul and that she didn't have to do that.

"I'm a platoon leader, Promise, a real good one, too," the staff sergeant tacked on after a small eternity. "I know how to think small and maximize my toon. I can handle one or two platoons of Marines better than most can. My unit becomes another part of me, like an arm or a leg. I know exactly what to do with it. It's like a puzzle in my mind, and all the pieces fit together just right. But give me command of too many souls and I start losing track of a piece here and a piece there, and suddenly I can't tell what the picture is supposed to be anymore. I used to hate admitting that. Saw it as weakness. But not anymore. I'm stronger because of it, because I've made peace with it and learned to maximize what I do best. No, I'm where I'm supposed to be. Staff Sergeant Moya Hhatan. I was born for this, and I'll retire here, too—if the Corps will keep me that long."

Promise learned more from the staff sergeant in a day than she'd learned in all her leadership courses combined. Know your strengths, recognize and make peace with your weaknesses, and then Marine up.

Promise said a quick good-bye, knowing a time would come when she would grieve for the dead. She stood and walked over to the small sink mounted to the wall of her office, let the water run cold, and rinsed away the pain. She toweled off and looked at her complexion. *It's okay, P, if they see you hurting a bit. Just not much. There's time for grieving later; now is not that time.*

"All right, Marines. You want those responsible. So. Do. I. And we're going to get them. But let's be smart about it. Right here, right now, stuff your payback in your seabag. We do this like the professionals we are." And then she bore her teeth. "We're going to kill these bastards by the numbers."

As she looked at her people, she saw a cyclone of feelings. Several Marines appeared to be on the far side of rational, jumpy, and unfocused, which could get too many of them killed. It was her job to take the blunt, pained object in front of her and hone it to a fine point, and then plunge it into the eye socket of the pirate who'd keyed the launch.

"First, we know where the launch site is. Or was. Fixed or mobile? That's one thing we don't know. Are there more launchers? That's another. The staff sergeant's sensors got a decent look at the SAM before it took her down. Its guidance system was frontline, military-grade hardware, and expensive for your run-of-the-'verse backwater pirate. Given that, we should assume its owners own nastier tech and that they know how to use it."

Her company seemed to settle a bit as it prepared for battle, sifted through the data for useful intel. *A bit less jumpy, a bit more alert. Good.*

"Secondly, the missile that took our people out may have had range to spare. We don't want to fly into another kill zone. Which gives us two options: we skim the surface and land well outside of the potential KZ, and hump it in, or we drop from orbit under stealth. I prefer the former, which is less risky, and it gives us time to scout the land. So I'm ordering four platoons to this location, a glacier just outside of the Arctic Circle. I'll be commanding."

Will you follow me into hell? She wondered.

Promise looked over at the gunny. He simply nodded and waited, stone-faced, totally unreadable. Promise realized she only had herself to look to. *My op, my company, my orders.*

"Suit up, configure your mechsuits for heavy assault, and toss in a mag of sleepies." That earned her a roomful of scowls and complaints. "Remember, Wolves, I want prisoners." *Maker help us,* she thought, *and the pirates, too.*

The bowed head in the corner of the room caught her attention. *Not a bad idea.*

"If you're the praying sort, get your account settled." Promised bowed her head. One by one, her Wolves followed her lead. She heard soft, steady breathing and a boot tapping nervously. *Words, words—I'm not the praying sort. What do I say?* She opened her eyes, realized she didn't have to say a thing. Each Wolf was finding her or his own way. She remembered her father's voice blessing the land as he'd done each day, both his morning glory and his evening grace. *Sir, if you're up above, I could sure use some help down here. Watch over my Marines. Please take my best and make it better. Amen.*

She heard someone approach. Looked up to see the gunny close the distance between them and square up beside her.

The gunny cleared his throat. Said, "For the Republic, for the RAW-MC, and for Staff Sergeant Hhatan and the Marines of Fourth Platoon!" Victor Company jumped to its feet and collectively roared.

The gunny's bark cut through the noise. "Where do we go?"

Lieutenant Paen's Wolves pumped their fists in unison. "To hell and back. Ua! Ua! Ua!"

Nineteen

The temperature outside was minus thirty-three degrees Celsius and visibility was down to twelve meters. *Both are dropping fast,* thought Corporal Raauel Baker-Preston. *We need to get in and out, and quickly.* The cold front heading their way promised colder weather still, a thick blanket of snow and ice, and high winds. Montana's newly formed Joint Combat Intelligence Command, run by Montana's militia and the lieutenant, was estimating 65–95 kph bursts and near zero visibility. According to the J-CIC, their veritable winter wonderland was about to become a hostile wasteland. The corporal intended to be long gone before that happened.

The comm crackled to life, the lieutenant's voice on the other end. *"Three-Charlie, this is One-Alpha. Give me a SITREP, over."*

Corporal Baker-Preston, a man with two last names and two right feet, scouting ahead of his toon, was out several klicks, near the southern flank of the storm, when he stubbed his mechboot on a rock and heard metal strike metal and say hello.

"Stand by, One-Alpha, I may have something, over."

"Roger that, standing by."

BP knelt down and scraped clear a hexagon-shaped access point, just large enough for a suited Marine to fit through. Sniffed it for traps. *Smells like roses,* he thought.

BP reported back using proper voice procedures. "One-Alpha, this is Three-Charlie, over."

"*Three-Charlie, this is One-Alpha, Go ahead, over.*"

"Probable entrance located. Scans are negative. Could be rigged, over."

The lieutenant's voice bounced back. "*Three-Charlie, proceed with caution, over.*"

"Wilco. Going in. Stand by."

The hatch popped easily enough. He sent two whiskers down and out, found no hostiles, sniffers, or mechanical demons nearby, and dropped himself inside for a closer look. His mechboots struck rough ice that had been grated for walking. After advancing a half dozen meters, he encountered an orphaned thermos sitting in a pool of frozen brown liquid. Two smokes lay discarded nearby, both resting on discolored snow.

The corporal licked his lips. He never wasted a smoke, not even a shorty.

From around the first bend came an off-key tune in three-quarter time. The first whisker found the cup's owner dressed in arctic camo, shouldering a pulse rifle wrapped in white skin.

Probably looking for her drink and a fix, the corporal guessed. He took a knee and raised his Heavy Pistol, wrapped his off hand around it, and aligned his sites. The faint smell of smoke and nicotine started singing its own tune. *God help me,* he thought. BP hadn't had a smoke since earlier that morning. Ops made him jittery, which is why he smoked before, during (when he could), and after combat maneuvers. But he chose to restrain himself. He loved nicotine but hated germs even more.

He envisioned his target's heart squarely in his sights. A cold weather suit rounded the corner, blue eyes peering through narrow slits, weapon pointed up and useless. The woman's eyes went wide as three sleepy rounds punched through her parka and into her left breast. Her hand went for her rifle as her legs noodled and took her down on a cushion of ice. Her head hit with a dull thud. BP walked up and nudged her side with his mechboot, to be sure she was out. You might have even called it a small kick, because he could. Satisfied that his prisoner wouldn't be getting up anytime soon, he grabbed her by the nape of her parka and started dragging her back toward the hatch.

"One-Alpha, this is Three-Charlie. Echo-Victor-One. Falling back to your position, over."

"Negative, Three-Charlie, hold position. Bravo-Zulu. Will come to you, over."

"Wakey, wakey," Promise said. The Echo-Victor, "Eve" for short, was bound and propped up against an embankment, hands trapped behind her waist and clasped by a zip tie. Old-fashioned, double-knotted bootlaces made great makeshift restraints. Promise smiled thinly behind her suit's visor as her captive opened her eyes, looked up, and realized she was surrounded by a ring of faceless, armor-clad Marines staring back down at her.

"Oh, shit."

"The can's over there." Promise pointed to her left and Ramuel dumped his suit's catch pocket as if on cue. The thin stream of yellow liquid froze before it hit the ground. The gunny picked up his stream, snapped it in two, and tossed it over his shoulder.

"Gunnery Sergeant, looks like you need to drink a bit more."

"Just excess vitamins, Lieutenant."

Promise turned back to her ward. "You may use the can, but as you just witnessed, you do so at your own peril. Given the weather we're having, I'm afraid your tushie won't like it much—ice up your down-there hair, if you know what I mean. We're low on paper, too. But I might be able to find you a few squares . . . *if* you tell me what I want to hear."

"I'm not telling you a thing, 'Publican." The last word groaned out of her as she hunched forward, clutching her side.

"Corporal, did you do that?"

"Ma'am?" Corporal Baker-Preston's tone gave him away.

"Right." Promise addressed the prisoner. "Well, now, I was hoping for a different answer. Tell you what. You and your cohorts downed my shuttle and killed five of my Marines. Right now, the only thing keeping you alive is my good graces. See the Marines behind me? I told them they could use enhanced interrogation techniques if you didn't sing. Nothing permanent, mind you. An ice bath should do. The Terran Conventions don't apply to you. No uniform, see? Well, little lark, guess who just made their day?"

Promise turned and walked away. The gunny and PFC Prichart stepped forward, one on each side of the woman, and forced her to her feet.

"Interrogations make me hungry," said the PFC. "Gunny, what'd you bring? All I've got are e-rats."

Gunnery Sergeant Ramuel snorted at his subordinate. He pulled out a fixed combat blade. "Private First Class, you're a bottomless pit. Speaking of pits, over there should work nicely. Let's dump her clothes in the crevasse and count the seconds until they strike bottom." The gunny's externals made his already-deep voice sound even more ominous.

Promise started counting to herself, wondering if the woman would call her bluff. She got to four when she heard a panicked, "Wait!"

"I'm listening?"

"I'm not taking the blame for this. I talk, I want immunity or, or something. Agreed?"

Promise kept her back to the woman. "How about I agree not to put you in front of a Montanan firing squad? She turned around, drew her sidearm, and pointed it at the woman to bring her point home. "The locals might hang you, though. They are partial to a good hangin'." Promise's metal shoulders shrugged. "That's as good as it gets. You have three seconds to accept the offer or I'll rescind it."

The prisoner sputtered as Promise holstered her gun and started counting "Three, two . . ."

"Wait! All right, okay. I'll take it!"

The gunny grunted, clenched his gauntlets, and spat out, "I was hoping you'd say no." He shoved the prisoner and walked to a nearby mound of rock and ice, punched a quarter meter into it.

Once the prisoner got started, she sang like a Montana hummer. She divulged the basic layout of the base—which had locations named after popular movies, cameras, sniffers—as well as how many colleagues she had and their weapons mix. She also produced a small minicomp from a thigh pocket.

Corporal BP stepped up and stripped his hands down to his smartgloves. He rubbed them greedily and then held them open to Promise like a kid waiting for Christmas.

Promise grinned up at him. At 235 centimeters, the corporal was the tallest man in her unit and had a long face and geeky topography. "Want to play, Corporal?"

"Yes, ma'am!"

Promise tossed the toy into his waiting hands. At twenty-one, he had close to four standard years in the Corps and a hacker's reputation that rivaled many Wolves with twice the number of stripes.

Several white tendrils snaked from BP's right glove and into the mini-comp as a small screen opened in his HUD.

"Jacked and ready, ma'am."

"Go ahead, Corporal." Promise started counting from ten and got to three.

"I'm in, Lieutenant."

"Impressive, Corporal. Now, shut it down."

Another minute later, the Corporal hit a wall. "Not gonna happen, ma'am. Getting in was easy, but the local defenses are protected by an outer ring of lockouts and a randomizing cipher matrix fit for a warship. But," he said, pushing bad news away with good, "I've found our guest's ID responder. I can copy and upload it to my suit. One pie-rat coming up. That will get me through the exterior ring and to an access point, where I can jack directly in and disable their net. Easy, ma'am."

"Good enough for me," Promise said. "Okay, Corporal, off you go."

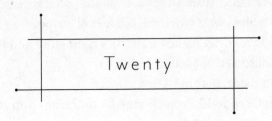

Twenty

Private First Class Kathy Prichart came to a halt at a fork in the ice and raised her fist, signaling to the First and Fifth Platoons behind her to stop the advance. She commed the gunny, who was leading the Third and Sixth through a similar ice tunnel roughly a half klick away. Kathy reverted to call signs, still proper voice procedure but more casual. "Rabbi, this is Carbs, give me a SITREP, over."

"Carbs, this is Rabbi. All's quiet on the western front, over."

"Copy that, Rabbi. But it won't stay quiet much longer, over."

The gunny's silence spoke volumes.

"We are not youth any longer," Kathy quoted somberly. "We don't want to take the world by storm. We are fleeing. We fly from ourselves, From our life. We were eighteen and had begun to love life and the world; and we had to shoot it to pieces."

"Very good—I see you read Remarque's masterpiece—it's a sobering book," replied the gunny.

"Roger that, Rabbi. It was downright depressing, over."

"You've sighted in the point, Carbs. War is never glorious. God help us if we ever forget it."

"Roger that. Moving up. Stand by."

When the sergeant had stepped into the mechboots of a field-promoted second lieutenant, Kathy had "moved up" to become her guardian, and the gunny had begun her education. Told her to think less like an individual Marine and more like a commander of Marines. Because the lieutenant was a student of history, she would need to become one, too. Her queue was now full of must-reads like *We, Few, Bastards All,* followed by *On Killing, The Unforgiving Minute,* and *Starship Armageddon.* Officers were expensive to replace, which meant guardians went in first, first and always. It simply wouldn't do to have the CO fall in battle because no one was watching her six while she watched everyone else's. If there was a beam or bullet out there carrying the lieutenant's expiration date, it was Prichart's job to kill the shooter first or take the hit.

While First and Fifth Platoons held fast behind her, Prichart crouch-walked ahead to take a look-see and found herself facing yet another fork with a left and a right leading God only knew where. *'Kay, this was definitely not on the schematic.* She tasked two whiskers to take point for her. *Left or right. Um—both.* The tiny probes sped forward and banked away from each other before disappearing completely. Prichart's HUD split into three panels to accommodate, Alpha on the left, Bravo on the right, and her own POV below. Alpha encountered a dead end. Bravo came to a relative stop and reported, MAIN CHAMBER LEFT, TWENTY-SEVEN METERS. Her HUD lit up with multiple heat signatures.

Left it is. She looked back and waved her hand over her shoulder, brought her hand forward and pointed to port. Saw the lieutenant give her a thumbs-up in return before turning around herself and echoing the order. Prichart smiled in anticipation and turned round. *Suits in motion. Let's make some commotion.*

Prichart reached the opening and took a knee behind a few crates marked FRUIT SALAD. A large cavern yawned into a vast, dimly lit expanse punctuated by an uneven ceiling made of metamorphic rock and crystallized minerals. She heard the lieutenant come up on her six and settle on her three for a look-see behind a crate marked TRAIL MIX.

Prichart touched Promise's suit to establish a hard link. "Hungry, Lieutenant?"

"Kathy, you buy that and I'll sell you my mansion in Rolling Pines Estates on Hold," Promise answered.

"Sounds nice, ma'am? Jacuzzi?"

"Ooh-rah."

"Ocean view?"

"A nonnegotiable."

A squat man in arctic camo caught their attention. He hurried over to a nearby wall of crates, which were marked FREEZE-DRIED POTATOES, and struggled to pop the top off one with a crowbar. The man was greasy, disheveled. Wild hair pointed in all directions, and ashy rings circled his eyes.

"Sweaty palms, that one," Promise filled in.

"Mashed or baked, ma'am?" Kathy asked.

Promise sighed. *"Fried."*

"Mmmm, my kind of side."

The two women watched as Greasy lifted a shoulder-mounted hyper-velocity launcher from its cradle, instead of a sack of starch, and then dropped it. Both women held their breath, then audibly exhaled when nothing happened. Greasy recovered the launcher, slung it awkwardly over his shoulder, and grabbed a clamshell of ordnance. He reached a side table, hastily spread his gear, and began to load the weapon.

"Civvies," Prichart chimed in. Prichart tapped her visor, which went clear for a few telling seconds, and grimaced at her superior. She pointed two fingers at her eyes, then swept her field of view before looking back at Promise with a look of disgust. Then she made an L shape with her finger and thumb, held it against her visor, and mock-offed her brains out.

Half-packed crates and trash filled the expansive bay. Energy weapons, gear, dead power cells, and MREs littered the deck. Floodlights hung at odd angles from spikes driven into the overhead, casting intermittent lowlight across the deck. Several were cracked and dark. Warm bodies ran about, packing and loading gear into an Assault-class LAC pregnant with weapons pods, its engines hot. Racks of close-quarter weapons stood to one side of the ship, waiting to be loaded. Many had fallen over and were pointed in precarious directions.

"Would you look at this place," Promise remarked.

"Messy pirate techs. Let's ring necks."

"Roger that."

"Orders?" Prichart said, sounding impatient.

Promise drew her right hand to her side. In response, a Heavy Pistol disengaged from her suit. It was loaded with a magazine of sleepies. The first shot was hers.

Promise opened a company-wide channel and said, "Flash-Flash-Flash—all toons, nonlethals, engage!" She fired a trio of sleepy darts into Greasy's rear and watched in satisfaction as he spun round to look at the fire in his ass. His face sagged and his legs buckled in one fluid motion. She ticked him off before he even hit the ground.

One.

Then the rest of V Company opened up and dropped a half dozen more.

Kathy swore over the comm as a stocky woman ran to a rock face and tripped an alarm, took a burst of sleepies in the buttocks and thighs, and canted sideways into a rack of weapons. *Uh, oh.* She brought her tribarrel to bear. A raucous claxon filled the chamber. She saw them first, a trio of miniguns dropping from the overhead, pivoting toward her. Gatling-style barrels started whining. Kathy kicked backward and into Promise, knocking the lieutenant out of the way. Hellfire chewed up the ice underfoot, pinged off her suit. She went lethal without orders, raised the barrel of her tri-b and uffed the cannons quiet.

"*No damage, Lance Corporal.*" Kathy's AI accessed the carnage. "*Looks like they forgot the heavies. I read light penetrators only, nonexplosive.*"

"You copy that, ma'am?" Kathy asked.

"*Roger that. All toons, be advised . . . ,*" the lieutenant said.

Clearly whoever these people were, they hadn't expected to face Marines in powered battle armor. Kathy scanned for hostiles as the lieutenant barked orders over the company-wide comm. And then she heard music to her ears. "*All toons, dump the sleepies. Load and lethal.*"

"'Bout time," Kathy snarled. She continued firing while the rest of Victor Company ejected the sleepies and chambered bullets and poured into the chamber. Rounds flew, energy hummed, and pirates died.

A grenade whistled past Promise and ricocheted into a stack of pylons meant to shore up ice tunnels. The explosion threw them like javelins, impaling the overhead and tunnel walls, littering the deck. PFC Mickie Hong staggered into view, hands gripping the pylon in his chest, trying to pull it out. His icon blinked from green to crimson red on Promise's HUD. She watched him career backward, crumple to the ground. Heard him collapse over her suit's externals. It unfolded like a well-acted vid, every detail painfully correct. Surreal. Promise responded with a quarter cell of rage. A chunky pirate hiding behind several barrels stenciled with "H_2O" on the side devolved into a watery pile of flesh and goo. Blood and real water flowed and promptly froze.

Promise bared her teeth. *Two.* "Carbs, I've got your six, move it."

Prichart led First Platoon deep into the main cavern, Promise, Lance Corporal Talon Covington, Corporal Maxzash-Indar Sindri, and Private First Class Fritz U'baire covering both flanks in a V formation.

Promise pointed up. "I need eyes in the sky."

"Aye, aye, ma'am." U'baire dropped out of formation, shuffled right, and disappeared.

Up ahead, a quad of pirates in arctic camo darted behind their ride out. Steam poured from the LAC's engines, parking lights sprang to life forward to aft. Blast doors on the far side of the bay began to part. From the outside, natural light and freezing air rushed into the craggy ante-chamber.

Promise jinked toward the LAC with Prichart hugging her starboard side and two-handing a tri-barrel pulse rifle. The weapon belched fire. *Stroke*—a young woman attempting to bring a hypervelocity launcher to bear simply disappeared. *Stroke*—energy bore through the cockpit of a Lancet-class stingship and tore the head off its pilot. *Stroke*—the trio of beams consumed another body but left the legs.

For a brief moment, both women found themselves out in the open and completely exposed. Prichart rotated her torso to the left and fired her tri-barrel at a pirate in unpowered body armor, just as a hostile stepped around a crate and prepared to fire into her exposed right side. Promise felt the threat more than she saw it, released the stock of her pulse rifle and shifted the full weight of the weapon to her other arm, barked at her guardian to get . . .

"Down!"

Prichart fell and rolled underneath the blast. Promise brought her weapon forward and kept moving. She didn't need to see the target fall to confirm the kill.

Three.

Promise spotted a small command center rimmed with hardware and holographic screens in a recess on the far side of the bay and designated it a high-value target. A red ring appeared on her HUD, dropped around the HVT, and uploaded to the company's battlenet.

"Two-Alpha, I want that tech secured. Will lay covering fire, over."

"*Two-Alpha affirms. Target in sight,*" Corporal Sindri replied, then pinged Lance Corporal Covington to follow him.

Promise and Prichart took up new positions to cover their advance. From high above, an explosive round howled in and struck the ground between them. It cooked off before they could react and tossed them to the deck. Then a small circular disk attached itself to Prichart's armor and began pulsing.

"*Null Ring!*" Kathy barked out in warning. "*I'm . . .*" She abruptly dropped out of the net.

Promise rolled for cover behind a crate marked MOLYCIRCS. Spun on the ground and fired a tow rope at Prichart, who lay facedown on the deck. Anchored her foot and started reeling Kathy in. Promise raised her right hand and tried to make a fist; her fingers refused to comply.

"That was close. Carbs, do you read me? Kathy? Private First Class Prichart, report!"

Prichart was still swearing when her systems rebooted and her voice appeared in Promise's head.

"Status?" Promise barked.

"*Net just spun up. When I get my weps back . . .*"

"Too late," Promise replied, already hunting.

Kathy's attacker was of medium height, kneeling on a catwalk ten meters above them, downrange from their position. Promise tapped the power setting of her pulse rifle to maximum yield, continuous beam. Popped up and sliced through the woman's torso, just above the naval. Her mechsuit's fusion engine spiked with heat as it poured additional power to the pulse rifle, instantly recharging the weapon.

Four. Promise wrinkled her nose and scanned for a fresh target. A wall of crates to her left suddenly fell over, revealing a toothy pillbox. The first blast knocked her to the deck, again.

"Bond!"

"*Already on it, ma'am,*" replied her AI.

Promise watched in horror as the turret acquired a solid target lock on her mechsuit. Her HUD screamed as the follow-up blast struck true, and then everything went dark. A moment later her visuals rebooted. Promise opened her eyes and found herself encased in a ball of cerulean energy. She watched in sick fascination as blast after blast spent itself on the shield. Then the field faded, flickered on and off.

"*Failure imminent,*" her AI said. "*Diverting all power to the forward screen.*"

"Slipstitch to ALCON, taking heavy fire from a pillbox. Carbs is down. Enemy bird is about to fly. The shuttle's priority one. Who has the shot?"

Private First Class Fritz U'baire's deep voice rang over the battlenet. "*Four-Alpha has the shot.*"

PFC U'Baire had hauled his metal carcass and light bipolar rifle onto the catwalk at the other end of the chamber. Elevation and a big Marine with a scaled-down rail gun did the rest.

Sight, steady, squeeze.

U'Baire switched targets to the LAC. Double tapped. Then triple squeezed. *K-thwack, K-thwack, K-thwack.* Punched two holes into the LAC's starboard side, through the craft's armor and skin, and into critical components. Two at the cockpit, one to weaken the armorplaste, the other to punch through. Shifted his aim to the stern of the craft. The last shot severed the power relays to the starboard engine, which began to spark and spin down. Flame shot out the side of the engine and licked a crate of frag grenades. Several cooked off and tossed what was left of the miniturret into the air. It crashed wrong side up.

"*Slipstitch, this is Four-Alpha, Tangos down. Down, down.*"

Promise grunted in satisfaction. "Well, done, Guns. Stay put while we tidy up the deck, over."

"*Wilco, ma'am. Four-Alpha out.*"

"Two-Alpha, I need a SITREP on that HVT? Where's my tech? Over."

A long moment later, she heard Maxi respond. "*Almost there. Stand by.*"

Corporal Maxzash Indar-Sindri typed furiously on his virtual keyboard, inputting commands that traveled through his link into a small mainframe. He wasn't getting anywhere. And Lance Corporal Talon Covington was getting jumpy.

"This isn't working? We need to bug out," Covington said.

"Hang tight, I'm transmitting the tunneling worm now—almost there, almost there."

Covington ducked, came back up, and returned fire. "Screw this. Rip the console off its anchors before our visit turns permanent."

"Sounds good to me." Maxi tore the console off its moorings, secured it in webbing, and slung it over his shoulder. "Two-Alpha to Slipstitch, correction, I have the package. Request covering fire, over."

"Wilco, Two-Alpha, on my mark."

Maxi placed the crosshairs of his pulse rifle over a crate marked MIXED VEGETABLES, dialed the power of his McEerp to maximum, and fired. The vegetables erupted in a series of explosions, transferring fire to a few surrounding crates. Flame engulfed the two pirates hiding behind them. The blast licked a crate of "dried fruit" and one of "toilet paper," both of which blew up. The blast tossed Covington right on top of Sindri.

"Definitely not veggies," Talon said. He cleared his visor so Maxi could see the stunned expression on his face. Talon smiled as he hefted Maxi to his feet. "Time to bug out now?"

Maxi broadcast his warning to the entire company. "Two-Alpha to Slipstitch," Maxi said as he ran. "Cargo is secure, cache of ordnance about to cook off, all toons evacuate. Repeat, all toons evacuate."

"Roger, that, Two-Alpha. Slipstitch to ALCON—bug out. I repeat, bug—"

The next explosion knocked Maxi and Talon to the deck, too, showered them with loose rubble. The air above ignited. Then the LAC's fuel cell ignited, tossing what was left of the vessel into the cavern's side. Its remains rained down upon a dozen unfortunate souls, and a trio of pilotless stingships.

They found the prisoner laying facedown in the snow with a gaping hole in her head. Frozen blood and tissue were splattered about.

"Never trust a pirate," the gunny said.

Promise took a knee and scooped the brain hole with a metal finger. "Brain pill?"

"Looks that way, ma'am. Someone else knows we're here."

Promise scanned the blood and told her AI to run a diagnostic. She turned to face the gunny and said, "I don't like what that implies, Tomas."

"Me either, ma'am. Me either."

The gunnery sergeant turned his attention to his lieutenant's mech-suit, which was bronzed and burnished from helmet to boot treads.

"Ma'am, back in the cavern, what was that?"

"You mean the Banning Shield."

"The BS?"

Promise's lips curled upward. "An engineer at BUWEPS named Trantor Banning invented the thing. It's called a Banning Shield after him. Kidding aside, it's new, a one-off, still in phase-1 rollout. Lieutenant Spears—ah, the Captain - gave me his before he shipped out to SanStar Medical. They're expensive and classified. Congress appropriated just enough funds to outfit every officer at the company level. In time, I'm told we'll all be issued one. But you know the Corps."

"Adequate gets the job done."

"Adequate and cheap."

"It's impressive."

"It better be. It's a defensive measure of last resort that all but slags your fusion engine. Because we don't have a proper mechbay, Mr. Bond tells me I'll need a complete pull and replace . . ."

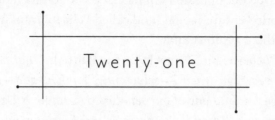

Twenty-one

Promise whistled softly.

Corporals Sindri and BP had labored for the better part of the day and night on the captured data core, coaxing out its secrets. When the core refused to divulge more, Promise commed the president.

"Madam President, we've discovered over a dozen account numbers spread across Montana's banking sector, with combined deposits of more than thirty-three million chits. Each account traces back to a start-up tourism company doing business under the name Contiki Journeys. Where the money originated remains a mystery. We've hit a wall there. We know that frontier start-ups raise seed capital. But thirty-three Ms is an awful lot of liquidity for a new business, and when you consider that last year's gross receipts didn't reach two Ms . . . And there's an interesting transfer trail, too, with receipts for unusually large purchases of nonperishable foodstuffs. The crates of 'potatoes' and 'TP' we found are beginning to make more sense."

"What else?" Annie asked. The president's hand drew close to adjust the screen. Promise's field of view widened to take in all of Annie's upper half, the large window behind her, and the darkness outside. Annie sat back and rubbed her face, trying to wake up.

"Quite a bit, I'm afraid," Promise said. "Each account was opened by an employee of Contiki Journeys. The company sells extreme sports packages out of a small office in the suburbs of Landing. Ten million chits were moved out of more than half of the accounts in question, and into an off-world venture capital fund called Pelican Trans-World Investments. From there we don't know."

"*Pelican? I believe I do,*" Annie looked disgusted. "*That name surfaced more than a year ago when I—reluctantly, I might add—authorized a closed investigation into one of our senators. His name is Uzi Kofferteine. He's a two-term populist and a homegrown muck—unfortunately, we have a few. He's grown quite wealthy off of some highly speculative investments, including Pelican. We know Pelican is just a front. My Secretary of Homeworld Security has some connections on Hold. Turns out Pelican is on a watch list. Kofferteine may have been suborned.*"

"By the Lusitanians," Promise said.

"*By someone. But, yes, the Lusies are suspected. But Justice doesn't have enough to make a case against the senator stand up in court, not yet.*" Annie rocked forward in her chair. "*We need to make a house call to Contiki Journeys.*"

"Agreed."

"*I'll send Landing Enforcement to Contiki to close her doors, seize her assets, and arrest her personnel on charges of sedition against the Montanan government and the Republic.*" Annie looked upward. "*And, I'm awarding your company ten percent of the take as prize money.*"

Promise sat back, a bit startled. "Ma'am, that's . . . unnecessary. My chain of command won't approve. We earn prize monies for thwarting pirates in space, by capturing vessels engaged in illicit activities. This is a local police matter."

"*Lieutenant, I thought we covered this? We're looking at a well-funded operation backed by off-world capital, the full purposes of which we have yet to discern, a specious chit transfer to Pelican, which may implicate a sitting member of Montana's Congress, and a well-funded merc outfit that razed our spaceport to the ground and killed your Marines. This isn't just a Montana matter anymore. It's a Republican matter. Where the battle took place is immaterial as far as I'm concerned. But your intervention did matter, and your unit should rightly benefit from its work.*" Annie shook her head. "*Lieutenant, as Montana's president, I am duly authorized to award combat bonuses to the planetary militia as I see fit, of which Victor Company is part. Have I made myself clear?"*

The search and seizure of Contiki Journeys went smoothly. The manager of the company claimed to know nothing, the employees asked for their lawyers, and Promise's Marines stood by in mechsuits with weapons ready, itching to pull triggers.

No direct links were found to the Lusitanian Empire. *Figures,* Promise thought. Too many cutouts and third-party shells obscured the truth. What records they did find implicated Contiki and employees in seven counts of securities fraud and tax evasion, sedition against the Republic, aiding and abetting terrorists, murder and attempted murder, and twenty-two other counts.

Promise leaned wearily against the prison bus, just outside Contiki's main office and surveyed the circus about her. Yellow tape ringed the block and passersby ringed the yellow tape. Her Marines ran traffic control along with the local police, as the large and growing crowd of Montanans witnessed the spectacle. Two news crews hovered at a respectable distance and captured it all for posterity . . . and for the evening vids.

A little redhead who couldn't have been more than five caught Promise's eye. Promise walked over to the girl, who promptly shrank back at the sight of her towering mechsuit. The mom reached around her daughter and looked up at Promise through cold eyes.

Smooth, P. Way to frighten the locals.

She popped her helmet and racked it on her hip, then got down to eye level with the frightened girl.

"I'm Promise. What's your name?" she said as she pulled off her gauntlets and ruffled her sweat-soaked hair.

The girl remained silent. After an awkward moment, the girl's mom rolled her eyes and answered, "It's Emily."

Promise pulled a wipe from her rations pack, cleaned off her paws, and grabbed a bar of sweet chocolate. She gestured to the mom, who thawed a bit more and gave her a quizzical smile.

"You mind splitting this with me? I don't think I can eat it all."

"Ah, sure," Emily said with huge eyes. She looked up. "Mom, can I?"

"Go ahead, Em," her mother said with just a slight trace of reluctance.

Promise let Emily take the first bite before she indulged in chocolate decadence. Promise and Emily chewed, smacked their lips, smiled at each other, and then started laughing at nothing in particular.

"Could I wear one of those someday?"

"A mechsuit?" Promise asked. Emily bobbed her head cautiously. "Sure, you can do whatever you set your mind to. Don't let anyone ever tell you differently."

Promise stood and spoke with the mom for several minutes and told her what a cute little girl she had and what a polite young lady Emily was. Mom beamed.

It was a good day. No one died. New friendships formed. She was slowly building that reserve of trust.

As she walked back to her troops, she heard little Emily say, "Mom, when I get big, can I be just like her?"

Twenty-two

Promise bent forward over a cup of steaming caf, a small mountain of crisp bacon, and two fried eggs, not the freeze-dried reconstitute the RAW-MC usually served its boots at chop. At the moment, the hall was vacant. She inhaled deeply, added cream and sugar. At the bottom of her mug she saw a distorted image materialize and nearly spilled the hot liquid all over herself.

"How are you holding up, dear?" Sandra said as her image sloshed about the mug.

I'll be better once I drink my caffeine . . . while it's hot, if you don't mind.

"Very funny, munchkin. Oh, very well. It's a bit weak for my taste anyway."

Promise eyed her mug suspiciously, saw only herself this time, and took a sip. "Mmmm." Looked up and found her mother sitting opposite her, arms crossed on the table, head cocked and worried.

Well, so much for some quiet time to think.

"Well, would you like to talk?"

Promise took another sip. Sighed. "You were always direct. I'll give you that." Set her mug down and took a bite of bacon. Chewed and savored the fat in her mouth and sipped more caf. A tear slipped out against her instructions. Promise kicked the table leg and squeezed her fork like a knife.

Sandra looked at the fork. "Okay, I get that you don't want to discuss your feelings. But I wouldn't run to bacon to drown your sorrows."

Promise half smiled as she stuffed more bacon in her mouth and downed it with the rest of her caf. "Twenty-nine Marines, Mother," Promise said as she crammed egg into her mouth, and another piece of bacon. "I have twenty-nine Marines left to protect this planet with." Promise grabbed the salt and doused her food with snow. Rolled a piece of bacon and tossed it in. "And six families who lost Marines. What am I going to say to them?" More eggs. "They are parents and husbands and wives . . . and children." She nearly choked on her last word.

Sandra shook her head. "Chew first, dear."

Promise swallowed, cleared her throat hard, and scowled at the bottom of her mug. "I don't know what to say."

"Tell them the truth," Sandra said softly.

"The truth? I sent their loved ones to die. And it was my job to protect them."

"Yes, it was your job, and because of that you'll never forget them. You will carry them with you as long as you live. Just like you carry me. How did your father tell you?"

Promise sat stunned by the question and the memory it dragged up. She'd been six. Her father had woken her early in the morning and carried her downstairs and into their living room in her nightclothes. He'd knelt down beside her and taken her hands in his. She remembered the penetrating heat from the woodstove in their home. "Momma's gone to be with the Maker," he'd said. They'd cried together. It was the only time she could remember her father doing that.

"You tell them the truth," Sandra said again. "Your Marines died serving their star nation. They spent their lives defending people who couldn't defend themselves. Your job was to give them their orders. Their job was to follow those orders and to honor the oath they made when they enlisted."

"Just like that, huh?"

"No, not *just* like that. You tell them as Lieutenant Paen—you owe them that much, but you can offer them more." Sandra spoke softly. "Tell them as a daughter who's lost loved ones, too."

Promise inhaled deeply. She reached for the carafe and refilled her mug.

"I wish things were—"

Her wrist comm chimed. Comm-forwarding was both a blessing and a curse.

"Later, munchkin. And go easy on the pig."

Promise swished her mouth clean with more caf and reluctantly welcomed the day's first test. She gazed at the crystalline screen and saw the presidential crest staring back at her. Tapped accept, and a holo of Annie Buckmeister's face appeared.

"*Good morning?*" It came out more like a question. Annie frowned, "*Promise, are you okay?*"

"Yes ma'am. Though I am a bit tired."

"*Then my timing couldn't be better. The locals want to thank you and your Marines for their service. In fact, a little girl who's a friend of yours*"—the president looked off screen for a moment—"*Emily Braunmeir, a youngster from Landing Elementary, suggested as much to her schoolteacher. Your unit's been adopted. Emily's school plans to grill in your honor, and after that, a carnival. Apparently, Emily is partial to them. Looks like standard Montana fare: a clay-pigeon contest, a strongest civilian competition, pie throwing, calf roping, and a dunk tank. I'm taking a turn myself. You mind getting into your suit and spelling me?*"

"I don't know what to say, ma'am. Whatever happened to the orbital wheel and Tilt-a-Whirl?"

"*Now, Lieutenant, do I really have to answer that? This is Montana. We always put our own stamp on things.*"

Promise snorted. "I guess that was a stupid question."

"*No, not a stupid question, just a tired Marine,*" Annie replied. "*Your people need to have some fun for a change. And you need to let your hair down. Well, maybe get some extensions first.*" Annie grinned. "*Laugh more, too, Lieutenant. So show up. That's an order.*"

"Aye, aye, ma'am. We'd be honored."

"*Good. Dress casual for the dinner and wear boots fit for dancin'.*"

"Dancing?" She didn't dance and she definitely didn't have the social graces for it, or the wardrobe. She could face down a pulse rifle, but she felt like a recruit in zero-g out on the dance floor.

"*Just a bit of two-stepping. Nothing a can-do Marine of your ability can't handle.*" Annie's lip curled upward. "*Promise, command sometimes requires you to fly the flag with the locals. In this case, that includes dancin'.*"

"You're using my own sense of duty against me."

"Get used to it," Annie said. *"You might end up enjoying yourself. Just remember not to follow with both feet."*

It took a healthy bit of nudging, but Promise enjoyed herself and the company.

Maxi nudged her to kit up for the evening. After Annie's call, she'd started fretting like a teen without anything to wear to her sixteenth gala. Tactical gear and beegees filled her locker. She couldn't remember the last time she'd dressed for a nonmilitary social function. After a quick bit of recon, Maxi found a local boutique called Wranglers and offered to take Promise and a few of the boots of V Company shopping. Maxi had a fetish for tailored clothing and the rolling credit to prove it. Two hours later, Promise stood in her officer's quarters scrutinizing a stranger in local couture. From bottom to top, she looked the part of a "hand" out of an Earth vid, circa mid-twentieth century: her knee-high kickers shined; the denim hugged and lengthened her legs and rear; the blue gingham shirt flirted without showing the ranch, with a little help from underneath, too.

The dancing nudged her out of her comfort zone, into a world where she couldn't lead. Being denied line of sight disconcerted her the most—Marines just didn't walk (or dance) backward unless a second Marine had their six. But she made herself do it anyway and paid for the effort the next morning with blistered heels. And it turned out Maxi was quite a dancer, too. He took her out and two-stepped her around the floor until the locals started cutting in.

"Boss, you mind if I take over?" drawled a tall man with blue-gray eyes and a groomed upper lip.

Maxi bowed out gracefully, much to Promise's consternation. She drilled him with her eyes—*Don't you dare!*

As Maxi backed away, he raised both of his palms upward as if to say, *What do you want me to do?*

Rescue me!

How? Maxi shrugged and shooed her toward her new partner.

Nudge.

"Name's Jean-Wesley Partaine. I run the planetary militia and a ranch up north," was all he said as he held out his hand. Promise kept staring at Maxi until Partaine cleared his throat, hand still in midair. Empty.

Oh, fine. Just one dance. Promise looked up and swallowed, placed her hand in his.

"I was surprised to learn Montana had a militia," Promise said, as their eyes met. *Nothing to this, P, a nice friendly dance with a colleague. Strictly professional. Gorgeous brown eyes.*

Her expression froze in place when Partaine pressed his hand firmly on the small of her back and led her to the middle of the floor.

Nudge.

"It's not much yet, but I hear you have plans to get us into shape. I'd like to officially offer you my help." Partaine spun her out and around and righted her as she lost her balance. As he pulled her back in, Promise tripped over her feet and fell into him.

"Well, Mr. Partaine, I'd be happy to whip you into shape." Promise immediately regretted having said it. "Ah, I meant your militiamen, of course. Whipping them, no, not that, I mean . . ." She looked frantically for the exit, the ladies' room—anything to be free of the man's firm grasp.

"Whips are a bit harsh, ma'am. I'd suggest a live-fire demonstration and some training exercises for starters." Partaine raised his brows and smiled.

"Right. I suppose that sounds reasonable . . . and less painful, too," Promise answered. She cleared her throat and smiled weakly. "Thank you."

"Humph, it's not every day you get to help a lovely lady pull her foot from her own mouth."

Nervous laughter spilled out of Promise's mouth. *Stop it, P. You are not going down this road. Not. Not. Not!*

Partaine changed the subject as the musicians changed keys. "Annie and I go back aways. We dated in college for a good spell. But she broke my heart, kicked me to the curb for my good-for-nothing roommate," he said with a straight face. "I guess we didn't stay enemies for long, though. Her husband and I patched things up years ago. And the two of us drew up some contingency plans when it became clear that the mighty R-A-W wasn't coming and we'd have to look after ourselves. Typical 'Publican horseshit, if you ask me. No offense."

Suddenly Promise didn't feel so attracted to Mr. Partaine. More like pissed off at him. *But I can't blame him for feeling that way.* "I suppose that's fair criticism, Mr. Partaine." Promise thought about that a moment and decided there wasn't much else to say. "But that was then. This is now. I'd be happy to work with you to prepare Montana's militia."

"Fair 'nough. My friends call me Jean-Wesley. Annie swears by you, which is good enough for me."

"All right, Jean-Wesley, you have a deal," Promise said.

Partaine dipped her back to ink the contract and whispered in her ear. "You know, for a Marine type, you dress up real nice. Ma'am."

They weren't quite nose to nose. A shiver raced down her spine, sped up as it hit the curve of her back, then made a U-ee on her hip and parked on her front. Promise inhaled sharply.

Jean-Wesley pulled his head back and held her in limbo for a solid three count, grinning ear to ear. He let her hang in the awkwardness of the moment, obviously pleased with the impression he'd made.

Promise's cheeks grew hot. She turned her head sideways and saw Maxi and half of her command grinning back. Annie gave her a nod and raised her drink. Promise looked back at Jean-Wesley, gave him the meanest scowl she could muster, and said, "Time to put me on my feet, mister."

"Yes, ma'am." The music ended and Partaine motioned for Maxi. He looked at Promise and removed his hat in genteel fashion, revealing a shock of jet-black hair with thin gray wiring. "Thanks for the spin. I'll call on you to discuss things. Enjoy your evening, ma'am." He tipped his hat, turned on his heels, and ambled off the dance floor.

Promise was doctoring another cup of caf when Annie pulled her into the dance hall's kitchen. Annie smiled at the staff, held up a finger, and pointed toward the door. The room cleared in under a minute.

"I wish my Marines listened that well."

"I wish the Senate did, too. Here. I have something for you—we only just found it." Annie smiled conspiratorially at Promise and handed her a small leather satchel. Inside was a soft linen cloth wrapped around something hard and circular. Her heart started racing as she tore off the wrapping. Nestled inside was a small holographic disk monogrammed with her mother's initials.

"H-how? It was lost in the shuttle explosion."

"The shuttle's black box turned up about an hour ago, with most of the shuttle's wreckage, at the bottom of a lake. That's an amazingly resilient piece of tech. I know how important it is to you. We had to activate it to find its owner."

Promise tapped the disk with her trigger finger. A 3-D montage of her mother came to life, fading from scene to scene. Sandra Paen at university, wearing her cap and gown. Sandra Paen signing her marriage certificate, her face aglow. Sandra Paen on the podium at a shooting event, her "senior" in one hand and a first-place ribbon in the other. And Sandra Paen, now Sandra Gration, with her arm around a little girl who couldn't have been more than three or four years old.

"Cute little girl."

Promise looked up and found that the president's eyes were slightly moist.

"I found that vid of Mom and me on the nets. She had posted it on a class-reunion board."

"She must have been some woman. And she had good taste in firearms, too." Annie sniffed and slapped her hands together. "Your GLOCK's a good gun. You can dunk it in water, roll it in sand, and it will still fire, every time. Outside of the histories, yours is the first one I've actually seen. I'm jealous."

"I don't know what to say."

"You don't have to.

"Well . . ." Promise's voice caught in her throat.

Annie reached for a stack of cloth napkins and handed one to Promise. Then she grabbed another and carefully dabbed at her eyes. "This is becoming a habit with you."

"How can I thank you?"

"No need, Promise. Here, you'll need this, too."

Annie withdrew a hand-tooled black leather thigh holster from a cinched bag. It was embossed with PP on the side and came with adjustable straps and a magnetic thumb break. She gave Promise a quick hug. "Welcome to the family."

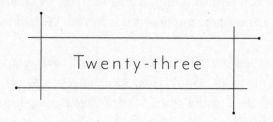

Twenty-three

Sir Geoffrey Theodore Samuelson, commodore of Cruiser Squadron 13 of
the Imperial Lusitanian Navy, surveyed Montana from his perch aboard
the HMS *Intrepid,* in geosynchronous orbit around the planet. Shrouded
oceans and continents filled his command screen. Montana's axial tilt of
24.7 degrees was very near to that of humanity's cradle. Three lifeless
planetoids circled the oxygen-rich planet, which was suffering a particularly violent electrical storm near the equator.

The six warships of Samuelson's CRURON had parked in high orbit
like stray clouds in a pitch-black sky. About as black as his Navy utilities,
red piping running down the lengths of both sleeves. The Crossed Anchors
and Charger rode each shoulder tab. A large gold star flanked either side
of his collar, the Navy anchor embossed into the pentagon in the middle.

CRURON 13 had jumped into Montana's system six hours before and
made for the planet at a modest burn without delay or challenge. Montana had no system-defense force, no mobile or static minefields, and
only a scattered satellite net armed with small anti-asteroid batteries.

The commodore had expected as much.

Not so the Republican vessel at the lower corner of his screen, in a
geosync orbit. He cursed the sight of the light cruiser, which was situated
directly above the planet's capital. Its message could not have been clearer.

The commodore's orders were officially oblique. A monthlong deployment to the verge to shakedown his new command. He had broad discretion

regarding which systems and ports he called on. But the Minister of War had been abundantly clear on three matters: fly the flag, build unit cohesion, and, most important, make friends with the neobarbs. After all, yesterday's neobarbs were tomorrow's taxpaying patriots. That meant three things: be nice, be nice, and, unless he wished to piss off the queen, be nice.

The Republican warship was a clear and dangerous problem.

"Hell," Samuelson said under his breath.

Several heads swiveled around to find the source of the outburst. Officially, he was prepared and responsible for rendering assistance to "any Rim world, which might seek outside intervention to quell an urgent domestic problem" (page 22, paragraph 3A of *Captaincy and Command*). Unofficially, he should have intercepted a distress call from Montana's planetary government more than three days ago. When the call never came, he'd activated contingency plans for Operation Sea Change and jumped his command into its current predicament to investigate.

The challenge from RNS *Absalon* had been both brief and pointed. Officially, his Navy and that of the Republic of Aligned Worlds were interstellar neighbors, nothing more. But even a wet-nosed junior lieutenant wasn't that naive. *It's coming. Only a matter of time. We both need the space and the resources, and neither one of us wants to share.*

Absalon's captain—a man named Dimitri Tsveokiev—had been polite but to the point. *"What an unexpected surprise, Commodore. I do hope you enjoy the Montana system on your way through."*

"Yes, I expect I will, *Captain*."

"Feel free to top off at the Lucky Lady, Commodore. We like to take care of our neighbors. I'd be remiss if your ships left our system without full tanks."

"CRURON Thirteen is most grateful, *Captain*." Samuelson said. And then he'd wrapped up the niceties, killed the channel, and nearly ripped the arms off his command chair.

The screen filled once more with cloud-covered landmasses and blue oceans, which brought him to the present moment and that single indulgent, off-color word that had raised the eyebrows of the bridge crew. Because it was so unlike him, at least while on duty. Not like the fools at the Circle and the Ministry of Naval Intelligence. Lax discipline showed up in all sorts of ways. And all of them had a penchant for screwing the pooch, repeatedly. Sir Anthony Wigglesworth was perhaps the worst, a self-indulgent prick at the head of the Ministry of Naval Intelligence with the stomach to match his inflated ego; only being distantly related to the queen had kept him in the best possible position for causing the greatest amount of damage to Her Majesty's Navy, and it usually meant a lot of good and decent Naval officers and Sailors got spaced in the process.

Absalon complicates things immensely. Now, how to go about dealing with her? Hmmm . . .

Wigglesworth and MONI had promised Samuelson a problem and cut his orders to solve said problem.

The problem is, there's no howling problem, at least not anymore. Wonderful, I've taken a light CRURON into Republican space—at least by loose interstellar definitions that recognize ownership as nine tenths of the law—and I have no crisis or convenient excuse for staying. Now what? What are you doing here, Geoff? Almost anything you say will sound suspect. The Montanans won't even have to guess why. Simple math and the order of battle at your back will add it up for them.

"Sir, we're being hailed by the Lucky Lady," said Samuelson's communications officer of the first watch, First Lieutenant Gerald Zimmerman.

"Patch it through to my command chair, Lieutenant."

A balding man appeared on-screen. He looked competent and tense. Samuelson watched the man's mouth move in real time.

"This is controller Orin of Montana's orbital platform, Lucky Lady."

Orin paused and several seconds passed in awkward silence. Samuelson only realized why a few moments later. Orin hadn't lased Samuelson's flagship. The poor man probably didn't even have the array at his disposal to do so, which meant his platform was revolving blindly without I-Dent. Montana wasn't on the best of diplomatic terms with the Lusitanian Empire either, which was putting it mildly. The LE's history with Montana didn't help—firing upon a planet tended to turn its populace against you, accident or not. And Samuelson blamed the Congress for its ill-fated tax policies on Rim protectorates and plebiscites, too. The path to full planetary status in the Lusitanian Empire was almost predatory. Rocks like Montana were ravaged for several years by repressive tax policies, often with only the bruises to show for it and in worse monetary shape than before joining. After a trial period, a planet could become a plebiscite and would then be able to borrow money at low interest, which was usually made available by the empire's Ministry of Finance just before a planet's economy entered fiscal collapse. End to end, Imperial planets were like dysfunctional children, always dependent on their beneficent parent. Rarely, they were allowed to mature into teens, but never into adults.

Samuelson cursed his star empire, too, this time in his head, where no one could overhear him. He hated unwelcome welcomes and had no intention of getting off on the wrong foot with this particular Montanan. No doubt, he was being recorded, and his words would be parsed by Captain Tsveokiev, too.

Wonderful.

"Controller Orin, I am Commodore Geoffrey Samuelson of the Lusitanian Navy, commander of Cruiser Squadron Thirteen." Behind Orin, the Republican colors burned brightly on the screen like an O-class star.

Samuelson narrowed his eyes as he thought about what that particular icon meant.

"Commodore, may I offer your ships assistance?" Orin said. Clearly, the man didn't know what to say. *"Our tanks are full,"* he continued with just the smallest pause, a clear indication that he was internally editing his words. *"We just received a shipment of reactor mass last week. We can top you off if you like; Lusie credit is as good as gold out here."*

Orin smiled tightly. "Lusie" wasn't exactly a complimentary word. Samuelson thought he heard a nervous tick over the channel, perhaps the soft tapping of fingers on a communications console.

Hmmm. Samuelson smiled warmly, hoping to disarm the man and disabuse him of his nerves. He'd learned long ago that nervous types like Orin didn't do well with silence and tended to fill the void with needless chatter. And anxious people were potentially valuable sources of information because they seldom thought before they spoke.

"Our little platform's not a proper port of call with local entertainment for your troops. I'd offer you liberty, but things are a bit of a mess dirtside."

"Really," the commodore said as he leaned forward in his chair, managing to sound genuinely alarmed. "Mr. Orin, is there anything Her Majesty's Navy may do to help?"

"If we'd had this conversation a month ago, our president might have

taken you up on the offer. As it happened, the Republic sent RNS Absalon *and a full company of Marines out our way and just in the nick of time, too. Pirates hit us hard. Killed hundreds of good and decent Montanans. We're patching things back together best we can, but we won't have even a provisional spaceport open for at least a week."*

"I'm sorry for your planet's loss," Samuelson replied, and he genuinely meant it, too. In his experience, conflict generated unintended consequences, and innocent people usually paid the price. Samuelson believed in the rules of warfare; the proper rules of engagement meshed with a personal code of ethics. Civilian casualties were to be avoided at all costs.

The two men exchanged pleasantries for another minute, and then the commodore signed off. He sat back in his chair and rubbed his aching neck, which was working up to a full-fledged cramp.

His second in command stepped into view and waited for his CO to speak.

"Commander, I assume you heard that?" Samuelson said without making eye contact with his XO. A pained expression crossed his face as he kneaded the knot in his shoulder.

"Yes, sir," Commander Niall Mouser said, pitching his voice just loud enough for his CO to hear.

"This is not the mess I expected, Niall. Not one bit. This mission went straight into the crapper before our first sensor sweep hit the Rim."

Commander Mouser paused a moment and pursed his lips before saying, "Pirates, sir?"

"Pirates. How typical."

"The spooks at MONI seem to be partial to them."

And now the Navy has to go in and mop it up, Samuelson thought.

"Niall, what didn't you hear?"

"The question any platform controller worth his august pay would have asked—why we're here. A light task force in Rim space is a rare sight. We brought more tonnage with us than most Rim systems see over the course of several years, and some in a lifetime. He knows something."

"And if you think *they* think our being here is just some cosmic coincidence ..."

"Then with all sincerity, Skipper, I don't deserve to wear the uniform."

"You or the spooks at MONI? Commander, don't answer that."

"Yes, sir." It was Niall's turn to smile. Samuelson looked up at him and shook his head in apology.

A mere five months had passed since Niall had become the Commodore's XO, and an easy rapport had already developed between them. Commander Mouser was his second, still new to the four small gold stars on his collar points that were arranged in a diamond formation, as well as to his current post on HMS *Intrepid*, but he was already sliding easily into the role of Samuelson's alter ego. Samuelson liked everything he saw in Niall, even what he didn't like. Niall was one of those rare officers who could come to terms with his own shortcomings and then fix them. In another navy, Niall would have filled the billet of his flag captain. But, unlike other navies, commodores of the Lusitanian Imperial Navy were not flag officers. They directly commanded their own vessel as well as smaller formations like CRURON 13, which meant that Samuelson was simultaneously the skipper of *Intrepid* and commodore of the CRURON. If Samuelson was killed or incapacitated during combat maneuvers, Commander Mouser would assume command of *Intrepid* and pass command of the CRURON to the next most senior captain in the squadron.

Which reminds me. I need to speak with Kharl on the captain's board about short-listing Niall for his first command. He's ready, Samuelson thought.

Samuelson filed the thought for another time and returned his attention to the matters at hand. He stood, giving his last order before retiring from the watch. "Lieutenant Hans, dock us with the platform and top off our tanks, and inform the rest of the task force to do the same."

"Aye, aye, sir."

The commodore motioned for Niall to sit, and command passed without a word. Niall returned his attention to the forward screen, the planet Montana, and the sleek outline of the 'Publican cruiser in orbit around her. Samuelson heard bulkhead doors whoosh closed behind him. Only then did he let the anger he was feeling envelop his face.

Twenty-four

"Captain Tsveokiev's on the comm, ma'am. He asked to speak with you immediately. He said to tell you we have visitors."

"Thank you, Corporal. I'll take it in my office."

Promise killed the screen on her wrist comm, pushed her plate aside, nodded toward the Marines at her table, and left the mess hall at a determined stride. The Wolves around her did likewise and headed in the opposite direction, toward the morgue, presumably to check their mech-suits, in case they found themselves suiting up to receive uninvited guests.

Promise closed the door behind her and seated herself before her monitor. She touched it, and Captain Dimitri Tsveokiev's image appeared.

"Good afternoon, Lieutenant. I'm sorry to disturb your meal."

"No apologies needed, sir." Promise cocked her head. "I take it our *visitors* are of the potentially unfriendly sort."

"You could say that, Lieutenant. I just got off the comm with a Commodore Samuelson of the Lusitanian Navy, a rather smug man with a decided weight in tonnage at the moment." Captain Tsveokiev paused for effect. *"He brought a light CRURON with him on what he said was a routine deployment."*

Promise sat up straight in her chair as claxons went off in both hemispheres of her brain. "Did he say how long he would be in system?"

"Actually, he did. For at least a week—maybe more—as he works out

some of the 'kinks' in his command staff, I believe is how he put it. He's of-ficially petitioned Montana's government to run mock search-and-rescue operations along the edge of the belt and offered to police the system from pirates while he's at it. Considering what recently happened here, that's go-ing to be a tough offer for the president or the Congress to pass up."

"SAR, sir?"

"Sounds about wrong to me, Lieutenant. I suggest you accelerate your plans for Montana's militia. I'm transferring the rest of the weapons you requested immediately."

"Thank you, sir."

"Then I'll leave you to it. Good luck, Promise." She went to kill the screen when the captain cleared his throat. *"I know you didn't expect the com-mand pressures or expectations you now find yourself forced to cope with. But Captain Remus thought quite a lot of you."* Tsveokiev paused. *"I know he pushed you toward OCS. I doubt he told you just how impressed he was with a certain young sergeant that 'shined brighter than most.' Saying so just wasn't his way."*

"Thank you for telling me. And sir," Promise added before Tsveokiev signed off, "take care."

"Thank you, Promise. You do the same."

Twenty-five

Staff Sergeant Billy "Bear" Aryson, a balding, dry-behind-the-ears veteran in the Lusitanian Imperial Marine Corps, brought up a virtual schematic of the Lucky Lady. He selected the quadrant he was looking for and spread his fingers to explode it. A scaled-down holograph of the secondary fusion plant appeared with entrance and egress points illuminated in green. A simple two-stroke command overlaid a schematic of the power grid and security lockouts on top of it, the former in orange and the latter in blue. Satisfied that he had his bearings, he sent a heavily encrypted message to his handler on the bridge of HMS *Intrepid*. He chased the message with a scrubber to erase the data trail and wipe the ship's central memory core, too. A neurotic tech who went looking long enough might theoretically find the residual ghost, but not without running a full-system core scan, and deployed vessels simply didn't run them. Espionage in space dock was a constant threat, and yard dogs were neurotic about security and ran myriad scans, in triplicate, before releasing one of their charges to her captain and the vacuum of space. But after a ship deployed, space provided a level of security that mere mortal efforts could not—with one perilous exception.

The enemy within. Aryson smiled.

A message appeared on Junior Lieutenant Chalatie Borek's display, which she read promptly before deleting it. Borek tucked a lock of hair behind her right ear and quickly stole a glance at her commander, who was seated behind her, one level up on the bridge. Her part of the ruse was simple. Thirty minutes after *Intrepid* docked with the Lucky Lady to take on reactor mass, the warship would suffer a boatbay accident, and an unfortunate loss of pressure in Boatbay 3. Hopefully, no hands would be lost, but some valuable gear would vent into space, including the suited, powered-down body of Staff Sergeant Aryson. Her job was to run interference on the bridge and make sure his suit didn't register on her sensors while he swam in vacuum toward his target. Under her watchful eye, he'd be nothing but a ghost in the machine. Aryson would do the actual haunting.

Borek keyed the prearranged response and returned her attention to her regularly scheduled duties, simple routine sweeps of the planet's continental landmasses, looking for Republican Marine Corps boot prints. Her mouth twisted in satisfaction as she queued up the next quadrant, input a set of coordinates, and began to scan.

Staff Sergeant Aryson reclined inside a storage locker on the starboard side of Boatbay 3, breathing canned air, wishing he could scratch his crotch. He'd volunteered for the third watch to help maintenance tear apart the fuselage of a LAC the evening before. He'd stayed late, long after the rest of the watch had retired for some rack time. Aryson had blamed a glitch in one of the servo panels that was going to keep him up all night if he didn't get to the bottom of it. Boatbay 3 was primarily an auxiliary bay and not staffed round-the-clock, which meant the next watch wasn't due for several hours. The bay's cameras recorded Aryson as he methodically stripped the panel down, part by part, double-checked that each was operating to spec, and then reinstalled them. Forty-seven minutes later, he stood and arched his back and slapped his hands together, apparently satisfied with himself. As he stepped through the bulkhead door, the bay's internal cameras began looping to footage of the previous night, when Boatbay 3 had been empty. As the bulkhead door closed, Aryson reentered the bay, suited up, and sealed himself in a vacant storage locker. For all intents and purposes, Boatbay 3 was empty. When he felt the locker he was in shift abruptly, he knew the bay was now open to space.

Aryson waited several mikes for the debris field to clear. He visualized the plan for the fourth time, perhaps it was the fifth. *Best get it right the first time,* he thought. The habit had held fast after multiple schools and years of training. His SERE instructor had yelled the loudest, and his words still echoed in Aryson's thick skull: "Marines think ahead; they draw up primary, secondary, and tertiary options. The Marine that commits himself to a single set of options often succumbs to his own ingenuity and overlooks his blind side. This Marine gets himself killed in the process. You want to be KIA? I didn't think so."

Aryson likened his present assignment to the game of chess, which had recently surged in popularity, particularly on the nets. Outthink, outmaneuver, and then put your enemy into checkmate.

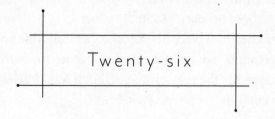

Twenty-six

MARCH 26TH, 91 A.E., STANDARD CALENDAR, 1130 HOURS,
VICTORY COMPANY TEMPORARY BARRACKS (SUMMIT ELEMENTARY),
PLANET MONTANA

After her morning run, Promise showered and shaved her legs, too, which she did about twice a week, and she was grateful today was one of those days. The school's air-conditioning wasn't working, and her "shorty" one-piece was less than forgiving.

She had just settled into her chair with a fresh cup of steaming caf. Dozens of surveillance reports waited patiently in her queue. As the first sip went down, Jean-Wesley knocked on her door, which was sitting wide open on its hinges.

"Howdy."

When you said you'd call me, I expected you to comm me. Isn't that what normal people do?

Mr. Partaine wore a tailored suede sport coat with fringe, straight-legged denim, and an onyx necktie—something the locals called a bolo.

Promise used the cup to mask her smile, which spread across her face and got away from her anyway. Partaine made a point of noticing. "Business or pleasure?" she whispered under her breath. Then she set her mug down and gave Jean-Wesley a curt nod as she stood and offered her hand.

"Pardon?" Jean-Wesley said as he grabbed it and held it just a tad longer than protocol dictated.

"Ah . . ." Promise ignored the question. *Business, definitely,* she thought.

"Good morning, Jean-Wesley." She squeezed his palm firmly and motioned to the chair facing her desk.

Partaine removed his hat. "Ma'am."

Promise watched him place his duster on a small table and settle himself without breaking eye contact. It wasn't quite the same smile with which he'd dipped her the previous night, but it was close enough.

Well, I can enjoy my work, too, right?

"That was some mighty fine dancin' last night."

And a little pleasure never hurt anyone, Promise told herself. Promise pushed back from her desk and crossed her legs. She'd strapped her gift from Annie to her right thigh. Her senior came up as her heel came down.

Jean-Wesley's eyes dropped like stars, and immediately shot skyward to meet hers. His lip went very stiff. She wasn't sure if he'd noticed the piece on her thigh, or just her thigh.

"It sure was," Promise added as she rolled back up to her desk. "And it's Promise in private."

Partaine nodded and visibly relaxed.

"You're a great lead, Jean-Wesley. I had fun—thank you."

Partaine cocked his head to the side. "But not too much fun. I noticed your beverage looked mighty clear. Either you like hard stuff or you're an abstainer. I believe I know the answer to that, but I'm curious all the same. You mind?"

"Ah, *that*"—Promise waved her hands dismissively—"that's simple enough." *Liar.* "Um, my father didn't permit alcohol in the house." *Mostly true, except for Mom's stash in her closet, which he never let on about.* "He believed spirits and guns were instruments of the devil." *That's completely true.* "My mother had a glass occasionally, in private. But she respected his wishes in his presence." *Why am I going there?* "Besides, alcohol and I don't mix. I tried to hold my liquor once, and it wasn't pretty. So I took to caffeine instead," she said as she held up her mug. "It's my poison." Promise cocked her head. "Care for a cup?"

"No, can't stand the stuff. I'm fine, thank you."

Mighty fine. Eyes on target, P. No, no, no—Jean-Wesley is not my target. He's just, he's just . . . a colleague. Right. Maybe a friend. Maybe a collegial friend. Oh, dear God, help me.

Promise looked into Partaine's eyes as if her life depended on it.

"Why do you ask?"

"Just curious. That advice about guns being from the *devil* apparently didn't take—that's a nice piece, ma'am."

"Ha! You have a point there." Promise suddenly felt disappointed. "Guns and I have a bit of a history." *Now that, P, is a vast understatement.* From under the table, Promise patted her semi-auto. And for the first time in her life, the textured polymer brought her nothing but comfort. *Hmmm . . . maybe I'm making peace with my history.* Her mind began to wander.

Promise's mother had read a lot during her lifetime, particularly the history of war. Her mom had often said, "If you don't read about the past, you'll just stumble through your future." When she passed away, Promise went looking for friends, and the only ones around were on the page. As she grew older, she took an interest in mysteries. Inspector Vanders remained her favorite literary hero, a character out of pre-Diaspora crime literature. Vanders was an "extractor" who solved crimes through postmortem analysis of gray matter by jacking into the memories of victims of violent crimes to find out what had happened to them. The books were gruesome, and Promise had loved every line.

In her midteens, she stumbled upon her mother's trunk in the attic, where her father had hidden it behind an old mirror. She'd gone up there to look for a box of winter clothes and banged her head against a rafter. Her light dropped from her hand and rolled out of sight. She discovered the trunk while on all fours and quietly pulled it across the wooden floorboards and out into view. It was covered in dust. Promise traced the wood grain as one might follow the line of a map to a specific destination. Her finger came to rest over a crack in the wood, put there years earlier—she remembered—by a little girl who had tripped with a candlestick in her hand.

Promise founder her mom's semi-auto at the bottom, on top of a badly worn book that was dog-eared and marked. A single phrase was bookended in quotes and recopied onto the title page: "Know thyself, know thy enemy." Next to it was Sandra's own, brief commentary, "Sometimes they're the same person."

Jean-Wesley cleared his throat. "I'm sorry, Promise, if my question stirred up a mess of bad memories."

"That obvious?" Promise shook her head and told him not to be sorry. Then she pushed her mug aside and stood. "Caf just hit me. Give me a sec."

"I'll be here."

"Well, we'd better dig into the question at hand," Promise said as she took her seat.

"Promise, I . . ."

She held up a hand. "Really, I'm fine."

"All right, then." Jean-Wesley uncrossed his legs and leaned forward. If her words had hurt him, it didn't show on his face. "I believe I know where we should start. With your permission?" he said, reaching into his coat for a fold of papers.

"By all means."

What might have been regret flashed in his eyes but didn't stay there long. Partaine spread several sheets across her desk. "What I have here is a list of the names of our active Rotary members in Landing. Rotary is our civic club for gun enthusiasts. This is just a sample of the total membership that lives in the precincts of Landing. We have Rotary chapters across Montana. All the major cities have them, and most of the smaller towns have at least one, too. Rotary is also our citizens' watch group. We don't have much of a law-enforcement profession on this planet. We police ourselves through the Rotary, Rotary members organize volunteer watches, and our judicial system is mainly staffed by volunteers, all Rotary. But you already know most of this, being a local yourself."

Promised smiled and shook her head. "True, I am from here, but that doesn't necessarily translate into cultural fluency. Why don't you assume I know next to nothing about your Rotary and start from scratch." Promise spread her arms wide. "Please, enlighten me."

"All right, ma'am. Back to the Rotary, then. On the legal side of things, nearly all of our judges are Rotary members. Local chapters handle local matters. More serious matters are settled at the township, city, and state levels. Anything major gets referred to one of three planetary district courts. We also maintain a small Federal Bureau of Investigation that's funded by the taxpayers to investigate crimes across state lines. The Supreme Court here in Landing has the final say."

"Okay. I assume this all relates to the militia, correct?"

Partaine quirked an eyebrow. "It gives you the backstory, yes. Rotary was the brainchild of our mutual friend Annie Buckmeister. She asked me to lead it; I wrote its bylaws and had them vetted by the Supreme Court for constitutionality. Then, the bylines were ratified by the states and voted into law by the Congress. In essence, any woman or man who joins the Rotary is a reservist in the planetary militia and the president has limited emergency powers to activate them. Which means, within three days, we can mobilize almost thirty thousand members, and all of 'em own weapons. That number can go up substantially if need be because the vast majority is married and most of the spouses are Rotary, too. But someone has to mind the store and the ankle biters."

Promise whistled. These people might belong to a backwater planet, but their forward thinking was nothing short of impressive.

"Forgive me for asking this, Jean-Wesley, but how many of those re-servists really know how to handle a firearm?" Promise asked. "There are a lot of Imperial Marines in orbit and they may not stay there. What if I have to send your people out there to face them? I have no desire to throw lives away in a meaningless show of strength."

Partaine quirked the other eyebrow, like he didn't understand the question. "Why, all of them, ma'am. *All* of 'em can handle weapons. And just to set the record straight, Montana is their home. They won't sit idly by if their planet is invaded. If you don't command them, a lot of them will probably die unnecessarily."

"Jean-Wesley, you may rest assured that I will command them. I *need* them. But I also need a feel for their competencies. It's one thing to handle a firearm periodically. It's quite another matter to hit a living, breathing target that's trying to kill you while you try to kill it."

"Understood. But *you* need to understand how competent my people are. Montanans, by and large, learn the care and use of firearms from a relatively early age. Remember, we have few professional law enforcement officers—most are Rotary volunteers. Part of being a citizen of Montana is providing for your own and your neighbor's safety. So, to answer your question specifically, all of our Rotary members can handle small- and large-caliber rifles and handguns. More than ten percent of them are small-arms instructors themselves. Their weapons are low-tech com-pared to Republican standards, but the basics are there to build on, and a substantial number of them are crack shots, too. Even as good as some of your Marine snipers."

"And how are the individual chapters organized?" Promise wondered aloud as her mind raced through the possibilities and hurdles ahead.

"Pretty loosely, but you might think of one of our larger chapters as the equivalent of one of your companies. They range in size from five or more members in the rural areas to upwards of fifty to a hundred or more in the larger cities. Each chapter has a president, typically an older, more seasoned type—an expert among experts—who takes responsibility for training and such. Larger chapters have more organization, more officers in various positions: warden for the local prison, secretary, finance officer—you get the picture. Each chapter has a small weapons locker with extra handguns and rifles, ammo, and some provisions, just in case."

"How many chapters are there in Landing?" Promise asked.

"Chapters?" Partaine scratched his chin. "Around sixty, with a combined membership north of four thousand."

"I certainly don't have the manpower to train all of your people. But I think we can tackle a portion of the Landing chapters for starters."

"More or less what I was thinkin', ma'am."

"Good, can you set up a meeting with your senior chapter officers? You, me, your officers, and my own command staff to start."

"Should be easy. That'll be around one hundred and fifty bodies or so. Give me a few days."

"In the meantime"—Promise changed direction—"I'd like to introduce you to my people and show you some of the toys I'll be handing out to your people in case the Lusies come looking for a fight."

"Ma'am, now you're talkin' my language."

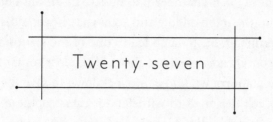

Twenty-seven

Staff Sergeant Aryson touched the skin of the Lucky Lady, grabbed a rung to kill his momentum, and turned to gaze at the surrounding darkness. The platform hung on the nightside of Montana. Aryson drank in the emptiness of space, drawing strength from it. The Lady was an old facility. It lacked the heat sensors and security measures common to modern military platforms. Effectively, the Lady was blind to his presence, which suited Aryson's purposes perfectly.

Aryson thumbed his suit's thrusters and pushed off toward his entry point, about fifteen meters away. The hexagon was an old-tech access hatch hardwired to a twelve-button interface with two lights, which at the moment was glowing an angry red. Light from the panel reflected off his faceplate and illuminated a small bit of the station's outerhull. Slowly, Aryson typed in the code he'd been given by his handler in the Ministry of Naval Intelligence.

If the commodore knew what I was doing, he'd toss my ass in the brig and have me court-martialed, Aryson thought as he hit ENTER. *But he's not in the need-to-know, now is he?*

The staff sergeant smiled when the status light turned green. With his free hand, he muscled a cantilever ninety degrees and then pulled it down and toward him. Aryson swam through fifteen meters of access tubing until he reached a stark white bulkhead hatch marked LL-15. He checked his schematic to confirm his location. On the other side were the station's aft fusion plant and cells, which provided half the platform's power. The cells sat in a hexagonal chamber like bullets in an antique six-shooter, with the mag bottle in the middle and access hatches equidistantly placed around the perimeter. Each hatch led to one of the station's extremities. The Lady had bulkheads, plenty of them. If she lost containment, whole sections of the platform would go into lockdown to save the rest. But her bulkheads weren't designed to withstand a catastrophic blast. And hot fusion cells, while stable, didn't take well to explosive compounds. If something ignited the cells, the resulting torrent would annihilate nearly half the platform with it, which is exactly what Aryson had in mind.

Aryson opened the chamber's exterior hatch and swam inside and toward the number 4 cell. He reached behind it, a gray stick about one finger's width in diameter in his suited palm, and fixed the remote detonator on the interior curve, where it was least likely to be discovered. (Scuttlebutt said maintenance wasn't due for three more weeks, which was more than enough time for his purposes.) Then he retraced his flight in vacuum, back through both hatches and toward the emptiness of outerspace.

Micronetic charges left atomic calling cards that were traceable to the manufacturer. Aryson's orders were to leave no trails. The blown fusion cell would take care of that for him by flooding every compartment within fifty meters of the central node with thermal plasma. Aryson swam up the final meters of the tube, closed the outside hatch, and pushed off toward his ship.

Clean, Aryson thought proudly. He'd come and gone without leaving as much as a speck of cosmic dust. He skirted the hull with short bursts until *Intrepid* came back into sight. As he expected, the boatbay was still open to space.

Twenty-eight

Promise and Jean-Wesley made their rounds among the various groups of Rotary assembled in the Saint August ballroom. Jaxon, Aero, and Fern were midway through their second set. "More Like You, More Like Me" had already been requested twice and the evening was far from over. The young, old, poor, and well-to-do comingled and clinked their drinks. "To the Rotary," said a man. "To the Marines of Victor Company," said another. "To the queen," said a young woman. The men and women around her grew deathly silent and shot daggers at her—an older gentleman even spat on the floor—until the young woman cracked a smile and gave the queen her middle finger. "God save the queen!" Then they all toasted the queen's good health.

The evening dress was casual: a short-waist, military-style jacket adorned with pockets over both breasts and braided piping along the shoulders, along with a holstered weapon, mostly semi-automatics. A handful of old-timers sported revolvers. The red and blue harplike crest of the Montana Rotary stood out boldly against the black of their jackets.

Jean-Wesley nursed a stein of Blue Monk while Promise sipped a mug of caf. They had joined in a lively discussion about the merits of trading with Imperial corporations, even though Republican law strictly forbade it. Sometimes Rim planets had to make do with what they had, even if that meant bending the rules a bit, right? Everyone agreed it would be nice if it were possible. Montana needed the trade and the job growth it would bring. Half the group advocated for it outright. Rim planets could get away with more, after all. But it simply was not possible, right? Could not be possible, said the remaining half of the group. Wasn't even right. The antitrade faction cited strong moral grounds against establishing open trade. Chief among them was Marsali Grounds, a thirtysomething chapter officer with brown hair and hazel eyes. Trading with the Lusies— even a private-sector Imperial consortium—was "unpatriotic" and "un-Montanan." "But, but, but," chimed in Tonnie White, a seasoned Rotarian sporting honest blue hair. "We aren't at war with the Lusies *now,* and we hope to never *be,*" she exclaimed precisely. "We might as well benefit from their cheap exports and, while we're at it, sell them some of ours, too." And so went the discussion, until someone caught Partaine's attention.

"Excuse me for just a moment." Jean-Wesley tipped his hat and stepped away. As if on cue, Annie walked up to take his place.

"He's a troublemaker, that one," Annie whispered as she pointed to the dark-haired man Partaine was talking with. "His name is Brederick Tarnes. He's known for his mouthful of fighting words." Annie wrinkled her nose in obvious distaste.

Hmmm . . . I wonder if those fighting words were meant for me, Promise thought.

Tarnes pointed in Promise's direction. Then his hands flew wildly in the air. Partaine appeared to threaten Tarnes, and Tarnes immediately stepped back from him with his palms in the air.

Uh, oh. Promise made a mental note to ask Jean-Wesley about it later. At the end of their encounter, Tarnes was laughing uneasily over a shared joke.

Promise tried to pick up the thread of the trade conversation, but she found her eyes lingering on Partaine. He possessed an enviable way about him, natural with people, easygoing, but hard as peristeel when he had to be. *Hard in other places too,* she thought, remembering his firm hold on her and sinewy frame. *And that's enough of that.*

"Give me a sec, Promise," Annie said. Promise found herself surrounded by a sea of people and feeling utterly alone. When she turned back to find Partaine, he'd disappeared into the crowd.

Over the last seventy-two hours, Jean-Wesley had acted the role of her civilian guide with practiced ease, steering her around Landing and the pricklier members of the Rotary with the finesse of an expert Navy shuttle pilot in a field of smartmines. By her count, this was her sixth Independence gala in the span of three days. Most of the Rotary members were hospitable and treated Promise with respect and a genuine willingness to judge her on her merits, not on the marred reputation of the Republic's failed promises. But a few were snide. Several members had barely restrained their hostility in her presence, rancor that Promise felt was blind and misguided.

There he is. Promise relaxed a bit as Jean-Wesley disappeared into the men's bathroom. *I wish he'd hurry up and get back over here. Now hold on, P. Don't go making attachments with a man you hardly know. Besides, you probably won't see him again after this deployment ends.*

"Young lady. I'd like a word wis' ya about those overgrown rhino-saursss you call Mar-eenss."

Great.

The voice arched upward every other word and howled like the wind through a too-narrow cavern. Promise pictured a grumpy old man missing his front teeth. She shook her head and sighed, put on her best win-me-over smile, and turned around. *I was right, and he looks really mad. Uh-oh.* The man's breath nearly bowled her over, smelled of hard spirits.

"Let's get one thang straight. I ain't got no love for your kind. We don't need yer help and we don't want yer help neither."

"My kind? Sir, my kind is here to serve the likes of . . ."

"Shut your howling hole, Kauffee Saks!" Jean-Wesley Partaine's voice boomed from halfway across the hall. He appeared from nowhere, cursing as he parted the Rotary sea. "Son of a hexapuma split-tale. Kauffee, I told you to leave the lieutenant alone."

"Nothin' I'm saying ain't what half the planet's thinkin', JW," Kauffee spat back.

"Might be true, but she's here to help us," Jean-Wesley said. "Why don't you get yourself sobered up and useful."

Kauffee scowled, locked his jaw, and dropped his head like he was preparing to charge. After a moment of posturing, he apparently decided

Jean-Wesley was right, or that it didn't matter because JW had him by over a head and was big enough to throw him out on his butt if he misbehaved, so dear Kauffee conceded the point and staggered away.

"Sorry about that," Jean-Wesley said to Promise in a voice loud enough for everyone within earshot to hear. "Kauffee's a good soul. He loves this planet and considers the Rotary his family, and for all of Kauffee's faults, we consider him family too. He's just seen a lot, I reckon. A lot of bad, second-rate equipment shipped in by the Republic, and a lot of broken promises. His sense of justice tends to run roughshod over any social graces his mamma taught him."

Scattershot laughter ricocheted across the room.

"He seemed really sweet," Promise said, rolling her eyes for effect. "And harmless, I suppose. I can't say that I blame him, though. I may be from here, but I've been off planet for a long time and I've grown accustomed to the best that the Republic has to offer. I can understand being fed up with the dregs."

"That's about the sum of it. How about another drink?"

"I could use a warm-up."

"Good, follow me . . ."

As they made their way to the open bar, new Rotary members stepped up to introduce themselves. Conversations started. She never did get that warm-up. Promise found herself discussing Montana politics one moment, the history of the break-open, double-barrel shotgun the next. Vids of families and kids appeared at random, and if it wasn't one Montanan it was five that handed her a glass of the *best* microbrew in Landing. She said thank you, clinked glasses, and found the nearest tray to set it down on or a willing soul to drink it for her. Partaine downed two.

After running the gauntlet, Promise retreated to the ladies' room. *This isn't like me.* She preferred direct actions, like starting the training regimen now to get the Rotary up to speed on modern tech. Sooner versus later. But Jean-Wesley had counseled patience and a handful of social gatherings.

"Get to know them first before you toss them into the deep end of the 'verse by demonstrating just how antiquated their weapons really are."

At first it was just one. Then two. Tonight's gala made half-a-dozen meet and greets, and Partaine wasn't done.

"Another gala? You've got to be kidding."

"Promise, these folks don't take kindly to change or to directions from outsiders," he'd explained, "especially from Republicans. You need to make the rounds."

"So I've noticed," Promise snorted and saluted. "Message received, loud and clear, sir."

After doing her duty, Promise washed up and doctored her lips. She found Jean-Wesley sitting patiently nearby and wondered if this was how the married half of the population lived. When he spotted her, he stood up and removed his hat. Promise grinned up at him as she looped her arm in his.

"Where to, boss?"

"Back through the crowd. There are a few more people you need to meet on the other side. Here, I got you that warm-up."

Promise took the mug of caf from him and breathed deeply. "Mmm, what's that I smell? Did you spike this?"

"It's called Jasper juice, and it's completely nonalcoholic. I assure you. Just try it."

Promise took a sip. It reminded her of earth and rain and fresh mint swirled into one deliciously hot concoction. "That's amazing! What's in it?"

"I'll let the roaster tell you himself."

"Then by all means, lead on."

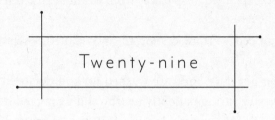

Twenty-nine

Promise walked the line. Ranks of eager Montanans stood with their backs to her and their eyes fixed downrange, firing antiquated low-V rounds into red and white concentric circles tacked to target stands. Promise needed to see what the Rotary could do with their own weapons before arming them with hers. On this point, Jean-Wesley had backed her one hundred percent.

As Rotarians reloaded, fired, cleared jams, and called shots, Promise stepped into training mode. She adjusted the stance of a pretty young blonde, maybe eighteen or nineteen years old, and worked with her on her follow-through. "Hold the trigger for a one count, then release." She spoke words of encouragement to a middle-aged man. "Not bad. Tighten your grip a bit." And said, "A little less finger on the trigger" to a steely octogenarian. She praised a group of older teens on their marksmanship. "Tight patterns, sirs. Well done." She booted a youngster from the line who wasn't yet sixteen—the age you could join the Rotary—and mollified his pride with an offer. "How about a private shooting lesson with me, later this week?" And then she came to Juri Kade, who must have been just shy of eighty and had no business carrying a "hog leg." His toothy six-shooter nearly rocked him off his arthritic feet with each shot. Promise stood to his left with a light hand at his back to absorb some of the recoil.

Age over youth, she thought. *Juri it is.*

"Juri, how would you like to try your hand with a RAW-MC fléchette gun?" Promise took the man's revolver and swapped it for a smaller profile weapon that took a clip. Juri's eyes danced with delight. As Promise showed him how to load the weapon, a small crowd gathered around them to watch one of the "newfangled" Republican weapons in action.

"Fléchette rounds are in many ways like buckshot," Promise explained to the crowd surrounding her and Juri. "Only instead of small metal spheres, fléchettes hold dozens of razor-thin darts made of a high-density metal-reinforced polymer. They are ideal for starship search-and-seizure operations because the darts won't penetrate bulkheads. But they will penetrate lightly armored personnel, and they function as scaled-down spread weapons, too. A fléch round at a distance of twenty-five meters will spread its payload over a sphere roughly half a meter in diameter. The barrel has a screw-in choke, too, with five standard presents. The *round* exits the barrel at a very high velocity, about three times the speed of the ammo in that takedown of yours, Juri. Against human targets—well, let's just say this load doesn't take prisoners."

Promise heard murmurs and low whistles of appreciation. Juri looked like a kid on Christmas morning. He took a textbook isosceles stance and emptied nine rounds into his target. When he was finished, there wasn't anything left to see.

Twenty-five minutes later . . .

"Roger that, Maxi. I'll be done here in another hour or two. I'll see you this evening, Paen out."

Promise removed her muffs, killed the link, and walked back to the firing line.

They might have the basics like Jean-Wesley said. But what am I going to do with them? Not one is an actual combat veteran. They've never seen real action, and some of them can't even vote yet.

Promise took a deep breath. *I can't change their past. But, God help me, I'll do my best to see they have a future.*

She wasn't the praying sort, but she found herself mouthing words she'd heard her father say on many occasions. "Sir, please cover me."

"He prayed that a lot," Sandra said, "particularly when he felt he wasn't measuring up."

Promise looked to her left and saw her mother walking beside her, staring into the distance.

"Measuring up to what? Dad never admitted his faults," she replied.

"I can see why you'd think that," Sandra said. "But he was a man of many faults . . . and believe it or not, he knew it, too. They haunted him, Promise. He rarely discussed his feelings, but he went to bed most nights believing he hadn't done enough with his days. And he constantly worried about failing you. He asked God to 'cover him' a lot. It was his way of asking for forgiveness."

Promise found herself struggling to accept her mother's words. "I wished I'd known that about him when he was alive. Instead of asking God, he should have just asked me. I never understood what he meant by it anyway."

"Supposedly, an ancient king named David offered up that prayer before each of his battles."

"The slayer of tens of thousands? *That* King David?"

"Ironic coming from your father, isn't it? No. To your father, David was the man after God's own heart. David was constantly at war through most of his life, but he longed most for peace. In some ways, I think your father related to that."

"At least David was willing to pick up the sword and fight."

"You're right. Your father chose not to fight back when those men came, and he paid for it with his life. But had he fought, he would have betrayed who he was, and it would have destroyed him."

"And I've been paying for it ever since."

Sandra stopped walking and turned to face her daughter. "I'm sure he thought he could reason with those men. He was wrong about that. But he was right to pursue peace. You saw the odds—if he had fought back, they would have shot him anyway." Sandra pointed to the row of Rotary members. "If your commodore invades this planet, will they survive? You may have to decide the price they will pay, and many of them have daughters and sons the same age you were when your father was killed. All I'm saying is to weigh the costs carefully. Seek peace first. And then go out and slay your giants."

"I hate it when you're right, Mother."

"And I'm almost always right, dear."

Promise laughed. "Love you."

"You too. Now get."

Promise walked to her rover, grabbed a bullhorn, and ordered a cease-fire. Then she walked out far enough so everyone could see her. Jean-Wesley kept with her, to her left and back a few paces. He was there to make a point, and that point was that she was clearly in charge.

"All right, people. Thank you for showing up today. The last week has been a lot of fun. I've spoken with and met many of you over drinks and been offered some of the finest microbrews in the 'verse. In the short time I've been back on Montana, I've grown to see your home world—*my* home world—in a new light. You're a good sort, my kind of people. You love your neighbors as yourself and love your guns even more."

The crowd responded with scattered laughter and obscenities. Several members yelled out a string of expletives followed by the word "Lusie" to bring the point home, which started a chain reaction of hoots and hollers and even more raucous laughter. Partaine indulged the crowd before hushing them with two fingers and a shrill whistle that left Promise's ears ringing.

"I know many of you are worried about your homes and families," Promise stated without pretense. "Frankly, I'm more worried about the Lusies. If they land on our soil, Victor Company and the Rotary are going to make their lives a living hell."

The crowd broke into uproarious cheers, punctuated with pumping fists and handgun and rifle fire that rang out for an unforgiving minute. Promise instinctively hit the deck. When she looked up, she was the only one on the ground. Everyone else was smiling down at her. Partaine offered her his hand. She stood and then took a moment to brush herself off. Turning to her left, she ordered Stevie to join her. Her Mule hovered over and handed her a pulse rifle.

"Before I give you one of *these*, there will be no more of *that*. Understood?" Many in the crowd looked startled. Some cocked their heads as they decided if she was joking or not. Finally, she arched an eyebrow and both sides of her mouth rose to meet it.

The crowd grew quiet as Promise hoisted the rifle into the air. They all knew what she held in her hands from the pictures on the nets, but they'd never laid their eyes on one before. And behind her lay several crates of sleek, modern, military-grade pulse rifles that were waiting for willing hands to ply them in the art of warfare.

"This is the standard-issue RAW-MC pulse rifle. About a third of you will leave here with one of these. You may be asked to use it. So pay close attention and forgive me if I bore you with the basics. I'd prefer to start small and then build on those basics, to ensure we are on the same screen. Understood?"

Promise scanned her volunteer troops. A number of folks gave her nods of encouragement. Some were obviously uneasy with her leadership. Crossed arms and stern expressions were pretty easy tells. *But they're here, P,* she told herself. *So what if they don't trust me. They seem to be sitting on their feelings and paying attention. I want more from them, but I can work with that for now.*

"All right, then. The pulse rifle is a modern, all-around energy weapon and one of two RAW-MC standard-issue duty weps. In standard atmospheric conditions—what we call the SAC—our best snipers can drop targets up to three klicks out with a modified version of one of these. It's an accurate, robust weapon. I expect most of you to do quite well at two to three hundred meters to begin with, and then out from there. What you have to keep in mind is this rifle's ammo travels at the speed of light. It is not affected by wind or gravity the way conventional bullets are. So you don't need to compensate for normal drag, drop, or drift. You can also submerge it in water, bury it in sand, throw it in a campfire, and leave it outside to freeze overnight, and it will still fire for you in the morning, every time."

A few of the Rotary got funny expressions on their faces, causing Promise to hop back a system. "But I wouldn't go out and try any of that if I were you. There's always the rare exception when the weapon fails. You wouldn't want that to happen to yours, now would you?"

She let the question hang in the air a moment until she was satisfied that the more curious sorts in the crowd weren't about to go out and test the waters. Literally. To make sure, she said, "And one of these babies costs seventy-two thousand chits." Economics did the rest of the talking for her.

Promise held the weapon vertically with the business end pointed up, giving everyone a side profile of the assault rifle. "This is the trigger . . ."

"Ah, hell, you've got to be kidding me" came from someone in the crowd.

"Like I said, let's start small and build upon the basics."

She counted to ten and started again.

"In case you missed it, this is the trigger." Colorful metaphors flew from multiple directions.

Promise glared at her students, daring someone—anyone—to pop off. Angry Kauffee from the other evening decided not to disappoint her.

"Ma'am, you know the difference 'tween a rifle and a gun?" Snickers everywhere. The women near Kauffee flushed; others scowled and shook their heads in disapproval. The men around Kauffee, all old and wrinkled like he was, elbowed him in the back and ribs and egged him on.

"Kauffee, by the looks of you, I'd say you don't have much use for the latter anymore. As for firing a rifle, I'll be the judge of that." Promise might as well have tossed a grenade, because the crowd exploded. Kauffee turned crimson red and stomped off toward the rear of the crowd.

Promise looked over at Jean-Wesley, fearing she'd gone too far. Instead, she found him doubled over laughing so hard he could barely catch his breath. A stream of tears started running down his face. As he struggled to pull himself together, he spun his hand in a circle and told her to get on with it.

"Let's try this again. For those of you struggling to keep up, this is the trigger."

Silence. No one said a word. She could have heard a leaf skip across Montana bluegrass. "The trigger is designed to prevent accidental fire. Pull it from the center—if you trip it up top, down below, or from the side, it won't release. That's a nice safety feature."

Promise turned the weapon over and held it tightly to her chest. "Your power cell loads here." She pulled a small cylinder from the cell well and held it up. "A standard charge gives you thirty shots."

She had their undivided attention now. Her show. Her militia. No sign of Kauffee. *Wait, there's the little schmuck.* She saw him near the back, still mad but keeping his trap shut while he peered between the shoulders of two taller men.

"In combat, adrenaline floods your nervous system, which makes it harder for you to think. Your basic fight-or-flight instincts can easily take over. That's where your training comes in. Practice now until basic skills become good habits. When you're in a firefight, you won't have time to think about what you should do . . ."

Energy was/is ammo. Promise thought a moment more about how best to explain this part of the demonstration, and she realized her first instinct was still the correct one. She'd decided to keep with the vernacular the locals knew best—ammo, shots, and rounds. "And you'll end up holding the trigger and wasting ammo."

Promise paused to let her cautionary words soak into the crowd.

"Back to the trigger. Under stress, you'll default to holding the trigger back, and blow through your ammo doing it, too, which brings us to the selector switch, here. It's ambidextrous, situated just above the thumb rest. Flipped up, your rifle's a semi-automatic. Flipped forward, it's 'full-bite.' Pulse weapons don't kick like conventional rifles do. What's good about that is they won't fatigue your shoulder or affect your aim, which makes you more accurate at distance. But zero kick encourages bad habits, like spraying rounds, which is why the RAW-MC limits full-bite to three-round bursts. I prefer semi-auto and suggest you do the same. One shot per trigger pull. Full-bite is more aggressive . . . and a lot of fun. But you'll blow through your ammo, fast. The governor is set to three-round bursts. Be mindful.

"Keep a light touch. The 'surprise break' still applies. Pulse weps don't 'boom' when they fire, but they still fire, and you still have to pull the trigger. Don't try to time or anticipate your shots. You'll jerk the wep and throw your shot. Squeeze, squeeze, squeeze as you pull the trigger. Practice gets you smoother. Smoother gets you speed. Too much finger on the trigger will still affect your aim, just like one of your long guns.

"Use your cells wisely. Each pulse rifle comes with five extra cells. A single shot will burn through three centimeters of military-grade ferocrete or punch a bullet-sized hole through the center of a man's chest cavity and keep going."

Worry crossed a few faces. *Good, they need to respect this. A little fear will keep them careful and alive.*

"The pulse rifle has a power governor with five settings: one is minimum power; five is max." Promise showed the crowd a side profile. She pointed to a small readout just above and forward of the trigger that included a yellow power bar and a touch pad. "Don't worry about this feature for now. The rifle defaults to power-level three, the standard setting for combat. Remember, level three gives you thirty shots. But if you have time and want to play with the settings, feel free—just watch where you point the thing. And use a berm behind your targets. If you miss, you could take something out unintentionally, at distance."

No one laughed. Most of the Rotary members stood silently, rocking on their feet and anxious for their turn to fire one of her rifles.

"Finally, your cells are rechargeable. I'd like to introduce you to the mobile recharging station, or the MRS—we call her the Missus."

During the meeting, a small crate about a meter tall marked with block type, MRS MODEL C, had sat to the side of the field. Promise tapped a short series command into her minicomp and the front of the crate fell away. Out came what looked like a standard-issue Mule, but the torso was oddly out of proportion with the rest of the mech's body.

"Looks like a slotted spoon to me, ma'am," said a substantial Montanan in the front row.

"You're not too far off the mark. May I have your name, sir?"

"Tullivan Sands, ma'am. I run a local eatery. Come by and I'll serve you the finest burger and fries in all of Montana. I like a good burger myself, as you can see." Sands slapped his belly and ho-ho-hoed to himself.

From his sparkling green eyes and rosy cheeks down to his fleshy ankles, Sands epitomized a jolly old man. He wore hikers and knee-high socks (which takes bravado any way you look at it), shorts, and a checkered red and black short-sleeved shirt that appeared close to bursting.

"And Tully never met a burger he didn't like . . . or eat," Partaine added.

Tully feigned modesty. "You should know that Jean-Wesley supplies all of my beef and his is the *finest* beef in all of Montana. We scratch each other's backs, if you know what I mean."

"Well, how about that," Promise said. "I know the restaurateur, cook, and rancher—a complete supply chain. Tully, plan on seeing me there."

"I'll have a half-pounder waiting, ma'am."

"Fried sweet potatoes?"

"Surely."

"Good man."

Promise turned back to the Mule. "As Tully already pointed out, the Missus' torso is slotted. Each slot is a cell receiver. When your rifle's cell runs dry, just pull it from your weapon and feed it into your Missus until you feel it click. She's powered by a small fusion plant that will supply her energy needs and charge twenty-five cells simultaneously in under a minute. She's designed to service a platoon of regular Marines in unpowered body armor. Mechanized toons always deploy with at least one as a backup. I'm providing the rotary with five Missus. But be careful with them. Each Missus is programmed to defend herself if attacked. You push your cell at her too forcefully, and she may misunderstand your intentions and lay you out flat."

"Sounds like my Missus," Tully said.

The crowd started laughing and nodding in agreement.

Promise fought hard for her composure. "All right, then. Any questions?"

"Uh, ma'am," said a blond-headed beanstalk to her right. "What happens when the cells run down?" His buddies jabbed him in the ribs and showered him with collegial insults.

"Good question, Mr. . . . ?"

"Roderick Krieton, ma'am."

"Good question, Roderick. I'm glad to see someone is thinking about that possibility. If you run down your cells, you run out of ammo. That's bad. You need at least a three percent charge to fire at all. Below that, the trigger will lock into place in the forward position and refuse to retract— that's your physical cue to swap cells. But if you bleed all of your cells dry, you're not completely out of options. Every rifle has an emergency cell, which is housed just forward of the trigger assembly, right here. If this was a pump-action shotgun, I'd be holding the slide. But pulse rifles don't have slides. The emergency cell is good for thirty shots. When your main cells run dry, you have to manually activate the backup. Grab the frame of the rifle here, depress both pads to disengage the pins, and twist 180 degrees. It's a safety feature. Your last thirty are defensive shots only. If you're living on your last three-zero and you don't have a backup wep, then you're of no use to anyone; find the fastest route off the battlefield and get your butt out of harm's way, sit tight and call for your Missus, or find more ammo."

Promise turned her back on the militia. She tucked the rifle's butt against her right shoulder and fired several single-shot bursts downrange. She pointed the business end down and turned around to wait and see who the quickest study was.

Five seconds passed. Then ten. At twenty, most were still wondering what she was doing just standing there. One lightbulb went off at the half-minute mark.

"Ma'am, did you just fire? I didn't hear anything."

"What's your name, son?"

The youngster flushed. "Jonas Morg, ma'am."

"Well, Jonas, you're observant, which will keep you alive when it counts. Unlike conventional weapons, energy weapons make very little noise. I'm about five meters from you. At that distance, you probably won't hear the weapon's capacitor discharge. Holding it, you'll hear a soft buzz and feel a rush of heat as the weapon vents energy through the thermal ports along the length of the barrel."

Jonas scrunched his brows.

Keep going, kid, what else didn't you hear? "Jonas, you've got more on your mind. Why don't you share it with us?"

Jonas shuffled from one foot to the next to vent his own nervous energy. "Well, ma'am," he said and his voice cracked. More jabs.

Promise smiled and encouraged him to go on.

"Seems to me that knowing someone is firing near you is pretty important, your enemy or your friend. If you can't hear an enemy weapon firing at you or your buddy firing next to you, well, how do you handle that?"

"Another good question, Jonas. Who is this boy's mamma?" A proud hand went up in the middle of pack. "You've done a good job with him, ma'am," Promise said. Jonas's mother beamed, and Promise made herself another friend for life.

The young man turned sunset pink and took several more jabs in the ribs, only these were of the congratulatory sort.

Promise took off her sunglasses and held them high in the air. "This is the BMR—the Battlefield Mapping Reticule. A pair of these serves two purposes: it protects your eyes from the sun, enhancing your vision, and it projects a compressed three-dimensional display of energy signatures into your field of vision, out to five hundred meters from your position. As most combat typically occurs within two hundred and fifty meters or less, that's the standard default. A friendly signature comes up green; a hostile signature comes up red. The BMR also detects energy discharges from pulse weapons, both friendly and foe. When a friendly combatant fires, his green dot pulses, too, emitting a ripple like a rock dropped in water. Works the same way for hostiles, only in red instead of green."

She'd have to repeat herself later. The "getting-started" guides Maxi made the night before would be useful, but they wouldn't replace a live body explaining it.

"If you think about it, you only know a rifle has fired a conventional round after the fact, and far too late to dodge the bullet. The same holds true for pulse weapons. You can't dodge energy, and you really can't dodge bullets either. What the BMR does is give you spatial reference. What you lack in sound you make up for with visual reminders. Your eyes will take over for your ears. With time and practice, you'll begin to compensate just fine."

She didn't say what she was thinking, that they might not have enough time to make the adjustment before some of them started dying.

She toyed with telling them about the rifle's self-destruct feature but thought better of that, too. If Murphy stepped in, some pimple-faced miscreant or someone's grandfather like Juri would trip the thing by accident and blow himself and everyone nearby into the next 'verse. She'd chosen to deactivate the feature before dispensing the weapons. Better to rest easy at night.

"I'll be happy to go over the finer points of the pulse rifle later today. For now, let's turn our attention to the basics of the FGL—the Flexible Grenade Launcher." That weapon took more time to explain than the pulse rifle because of the different kinds of ordnance it fired, and Montanans loved to talk about ordnance.

The next hour passed quickly. Only later that evening did it dawn on Promise how easily the role of instructor had come to her. And that she'd had fun, too.

Thirty

Montana's primary asteroid mining operation floated in the extreme outer system. The debris field, flat like a two-dimensional disk, encompassed the seventh planet, Ramshacke. The field circled the planet more than twenty-five thousand kilometers rock to rock. Asteroids ranged in mass from large bits of debris to small behemoths, including an asteroid that spanned seventy-seven klicks and spun on its axis every eighteen minutes. AC-2673 generated a modest amount of gravity, and 129 miners called it their home away from home. They lovingly referred to it as the Rock.

At 1200 hours, Tramper pilot Rhaymond Garcias was headed home to the Rock after a double run. He sat at the helm of his light tug, the *Mary Jane,* towing 127 tons of newly harvested "roids" and ore, all of it destined for AC-2673's smelters. He sang an upbeat, rhythmic song about striking it rich, which in fact he had done. An unusually large find of thorium sat near the center of his catch, a mere three hundred meters astern of his diminutive vessel, in the clutches of a grav-net. Garcias anticipated a healthy bonus, and for good reason. Thorium was a profitable, albeit radioactive, material. And unlike its neighbor, uranium, which lived two homes over on the periodic table of elements, thorium was far more abundant, powerful, and safe. Montana's colder continents and antique-yet-reliable fission reactors would rejoice over the radioactive fuel for the next five years.

Garcias's mind began to wander to the girl he was dating, a ravishing cocktail waitress from Blue Sands, who was the latest in a long line of casual affairs of the heart. He hadn't seen her in five weeks, and he still had three more to go before his rotation home for the upcoming holiday. He'd buy her something nice and make sure she remembered their time together and . . .

The proximity alarm howled. He jerked the flight stick left and forward as he tried to generate a miss, found a pocket of open space underneath a twenty-two-ton spheroid that rolled across his screen at a deceptively fast speed. He pulled the stick back and angled his little tug up the other side of the asteroid and through a small field of rocks that bounced harmlessly off his tug's deflectors.

Convinced he was now out of harm's way, Garcias replotted his course to the Rock and began to sing again. A small, very faint blip appeared on his scanner, one moment a hard contact and the next, an indeterminate ghost. Garcias wrote it off as a sensor glitch. He was tired and nearing the end of his double shift. When the red dot appeared much closer to his vessel, his fatigue gave way to suspicion.

Probably that fool Metaxas out for an unscheduled joyride, he thought dismissively.

Garcias pinged the vessel and received deafening static. He tore off his band and howled. The mystery contact wasn't squawking, which lent credence to his "ghost" theory. It started matching his ship's speed and course changes, and Garcias tried to hail what he now knew to be an unknown vessel. *When I get back, I'm going to kill him.* Garcias sent a short-burst transmission to the Rock, which was never received. The bogey disappeared once more and then materialized on his scanners on a convergent course and traveling at multiple g's. His proximity alarm screamed. Garcias punched the aft thrusters to maximum burn and dropped the tug's nose, after which he tried to open another comm channel with the mining station. His mayday never traveled beyond the cramped walls of his command couch because it was being jammed. His heads-up display died, and his cabin suddenly went dark. He sat alone, dead-sticking his vessel without even reaction thrusters to adjust course. His insides froze as he watched a light attack craft with foreign markings come into view and belch out a half-dozen armored figures.

Three minutes later, space enveloped Garcias's body as it spun away from his tramper. His face was contorted and iced over, preserving his last breathing moment of abject terror.

Thirty-one

Promise was in the shower, getting ready for her night out with the gunny. She figured the evening would run her around two hundred chits.

She'd lost fair and square, two rounds to his three. Her half of Victor Company, suitably named the Bars, had almost beaten the other half of V Company in mock combat. But the Stripes, led by Gunnery Sergeant Tomas Ramuel, had triumphed in the end, thanks to one good toss. The grenade had bounced and rolled to a stop. A dud. When she turned her back on it, it had decided to pop up on its spindly little legs and sprint to her position. She saw it at *boom*. As the commander of the Bars, she owed the gunny a round of his choosing, and his choosing was expensive. Geneva Ale. Ramuel drank to make it count. *And he always holds his liquor,* Promise thought with admiration.

The gunny's Marines knew that liberty meant less "liberty" and more "monitored R & R." They took their gunny's caveat literally. "Drink 'til you're sober and not a drop more." Every boot under his command had heard the speech at least once. Ramuel made sure of it. He was master, commander, and moral compass, and his command loved him for it. But if he thought little of a drunken boot, he thought even less of a Marine that drank cheap alcohol. Or a boot that threw it back up. *Which is why tonight is going to be a drain on my account.*

Promise was lathering up as Maxi ran into the woman's locker room, stopping short of the water and tile while he kept his eyes carefully averted. "Lieutenant, we just received an SOS from up top. It's the Rock."

Promise instantly turned her back to Maxi, dropped her bar of soap, and started rinsing rapidly. "Go ahead, Corporal."

"An emergency beacon blazed into Montana space about five mikes ago. Started squawking on all frequencies. There's been an explosion and casualties—at least three dead and an unspecified number of injured. The station's O_2 plant is down, and there's wreckage blocking the entrance to the station's only shuttle bay."

"Wreckage? That's no ordinary explosion." Cutting the water and reaching for her towel, Promise found that Maxi was already holding it out to her while still keeping his gaze elsewhere.

"No, ma'am," he answered. "The station was fired upon, and the Lusie CRURON just broke orbit for the Renault system."

"Try that for coincidence. So the miners are trapped," Promise said as she toweled off. "How long have they got?"

"Not long, ma'am."

"All right, Maxi. All clear."

Maxi turned around and locked eyes with her. "Sorry, ma'am."

Promise smirked. Maxi's face was a tad bit flushed, and he was doing his best to act as if nothing was out of the ordinary. *Me in skin, in the shower with a man. Mom would be thrilled.*

"The situation is stable . . . for now, ma'am. The miners have the fire under control, too. But their scrubbers are off-line. They have roughly three days of canned air before hypoxia sets in."

"All right. Get a message off to Captain Tsveokiev on *Absalon*. Give him a SITREP and request immediate transport to the field. He may expect us at 1830 hours. Mobilize first and second toons, and tell the gunny I'll make it up to him. He'll have to hold down the chicken coop while mother hen is away."

"Mother hen? Is that how you're styling yourself these days, ma'am?"

"Just a phrase I heard the president use the other day. She makes an impression."

"She's one tough mother fu—Ah . . . sorry, ma'am. I meant a tough mother hen."

"Aye, that she is, Maxi. That she is."

"I'll leave you to dress, ma'am."

"I'll do that." Promise's lip curled upward. "And Corporal, we bring the heavy weps this time. Just in case."

"I was hoping you'd say that, ma'am."

Promise walked to her locker and opened it, revealing her skivvies, her beegees, and a three-quarter-length mirror. Her GLOCK sat on the top shelf with the grip facing toward her. She brushed it as she reached for a bottle of lotion.

"You're a natural trainer."

The voice startled Promise, and her towel came loose. She made several attempts to grab it and cover up and ended up banging her head into the locker next door. "A little warning next time."

"You don't usually startle, dear."

Promise saw her mother in the mirror and immediately looked away. "Well, I'm not dressed, and I'm in a hurry."

Sandra's expression changed like a light going off. "I've embarrassed you," she said softly. "I'm sorry."

Promise turned around but didn't meet her mother's eyes. "I feel, um—never mind."

"All right, if you'd rather not talk about it. Perhaps when you get back."

"Mom, look at me," Promise said as she stared at the deck. "I'm more muscle and angles than curves. And you're, well, you're"—Promise outlined with her hands—"you."

"Last time I checked, anyway." Sandra turned away.

Promise grabbed her skivvies and quickly pulled them on. She ended up with two legs in one hole before she finally got them up. "I'm no good with men. I don't know how to be around them, and I don't feel pretty."

"Well, Mr. Partaine sure thinks you are."

"Yeah, and that scares me."

"If I was Partaine, dear, I'd go for you."

"That's disturbing."

"That's better," her mother said. "Better finish getting dressed. You've got miners to save."

"Thanks."

"S'what I'm here for. Be careful, munchkin. You know they're probably waiting for you, right?"

Promise finished toweling off what little hair she had, holstered her GLOCK, and shut the locker door. Then she commed the gunny.

"*I just got off the comm with the corporal, ma'am,*" Ramuel said.

"I'm taking two toons with me and *Absalon* to assist with search and rescue. You'll be in charge while I'm away. Sorry to leave you this way."

"*We'll manage, ma'am. But you may not if you encounter a task force of Lusie warships and Marines.*"

"Frankly, Tomas, what's left of Victor Company isn't enough. But it has to be, doesn't it? I can't leave the planet completely defenseless, which is why I'm leaving you here, and Montana doesn't have a search-and-rescue unit that can operate in a vacuum. It's up to us to get those miners out."

"*You might be doing exactly what the Lusitanians want you to do.*"

"Agreed." Promise hesitated, and it must have showed.

"*Lieutenant, if I were in your shoes, I'd be doing the very same thing,*" the gunny offered. "*You can only deal with the here and now, and right now those miners need your help. Absalon's CO is sharp as they come, and he'll be looking for a trap. You can trust him. You should also trust your instincts.*"

"Thank you, Tomas."

Promise heard the hesitation in Ramuel's voice. "*It might be a good time to call the president and put the Rotary on standby.*"

"Good idea. And you'd benefit from a little personal time with President Buckmeister, too. When we're done, give me a few mikes to comm her myself and give her a SITREP, then you do the same."

Ramuel pushed his misgivings aside. "*Aye, aye, ma'am. Take care of yourself and good hunting. I expect to see you back here, soon, to relieve me of command. Besides, the Rotary are pretty rough around the edges, and they respond to you better than anyone else.*"

"Thanks, Gunny. Watch your six."

Thirty-two

Ensign X'atti Quartz sat at his station on RNS *Absalon*'s bridge, on the secondary command level, which was situated directly in front of and below the captain's chair. He'd just completed his third scan of the watch, looking for anomalous readings within the asteroid field encircling the planet Ramshacke. The results were next to impossible to decipher due to the field's wealth of heavy metals, which interfered with sensors. On his fourth scan Ensign Quartz—XM to his closest friends—picked up a ghost, which he attributed to a pocket of radiation from a rather dense thorium vein in a cluster of asteroids. *Probably throwing off a false positive,* he figured. But XM decided to use the ghost for practice and ordered *Absalon*'s forward array to isolate the anomaly.

As several mikes passed, XM was no closer to an answer. Just when he thought he had a firm fix on whatever it probably wasn't, and just as he thought he was close to being able to cut through the radioactive interference to actually prove nothing was really there, his readings rescrambled themselves.

Impossible. Noise doesn't flow like this, he thought. *It's random and this—something tells me this isn't as random as it's trying to appear. Unless, there really is something out there. Hmmm.*

Quartz's mind ticked off the possibilities. First, the proverbial ghost was in his machine, possibly a glitch in the calibrators. Second, the relay cones were damaged. An unlucky strike from a small chunk of rock could have caused such damage. The deflectors occasionally missed something. Third, maybe the static was coming from a derelict mining beacon. Fourth, an as-yet-unidentified alien craft bearing an as-yet-undiscovered race of being was mucking with his sensors, which was about as likely as a black hole materializing within Montana's gravity well to gobble up the planet whole. And then he smiled at how ridiculous it all was. The fantasy of aliens and the fact that he was an ensign sitting at a post he was grossly underqualified for. *Yet here I am nonetheless.* He allowed himself a brief moment of private revelry at his very good fortune.

XM was young for his post, with a pubescent face and the wiry, developing frame to match it. A first lieutenant normally filled the billet he now sat in, and on occasion a second lieutenant stepped into a manpower shortage, not a lowly ensign with one bar on his collar. But top marks at the Naval Academy on Hold and perfect scores in both astrophysics and geospatial calculations, plus the behind-the-scenes meddling of an academy patron, had created the perfect confluence. Much to his surprise, he was short-listed for his first staff position and assigned to his current role as *Absalon's* senior Electronics Warfare Officer, first watch.

He sat at his station and counted his blessings. Here he was, eight weeks into his snotty cruise and already a bridge officer. In reality, XM held a slightly higher opinion of himself than he should have, but confidence, according to his silent benefactor, who unbeknownst to him was good friends with XM 's own captain, was something to be fostered in young officers, even manipulated into being if necessary. Particularly officers as young and as naturally gifted as one X'atti Quartz.

A soft tone told the ensign that his latest sweep hadn't swept up a thing. *Mucking asteroids!*

Sensor sweeps were rather boring endeavors, but they played an important part in the life of a ship's EWO. Space was rather boring, too. It was filled with very little other than, well, space. But a rescue mission was anything but boring. Navigating along the perimeter of an asteroid field was anything but boring, and his ghost in the machine was certainly not boring. All of which told XM's gut that his nothing might just crystallize into a something and that he better do something about it. Sooner rather than later. He nodded his head and squared his shoulders, and then he cleared his throat and spun around to make his report.

"Captain," Quartz said with all the confidence he could muster. "I believe I have something on my scanners."

"Go ahead, Ensign," Captain Tsveokiev replied. Tsveokiev's deep green eyes sparkled with an energy utterly lacking in his pale complexion. His thick brows knitted in concentration while he waited for the ensign to make his report.

"I detected it roughly seven minutes ago, sir. At the time, it was acting more like a sensor ghost than a true bounceback—one moment there, the next gone. I didn't think much of it at first—perhaps an anonymous reading caused by a cluster of radioactive isotopes. But I tried to isolate the source for practice, and the thing is, sir, it's not just ghosting in and out. I can't prove it, sir, but I believe my sensor sweeps are being jammed."

Tsveokiev sat upright, almost spilling the cup of steaming liquid in his left hand. "Jammed?" He asked tersely. "Elaborate, Mr. Quartz." The captain rose from his chair and walked down the side ramp to Quartz's position.

"Well, sir," XM began in a neutral voice as he swung back to his readouts and punched in a new set of commands. He'd only served under Captain Tsveokiev for two months, but he already knew the skipper to be a methodical and exacting officer who appreciated specificity and preached against jumping to conclusions. "The closer we get to the source, the better my sensor resolution should become." As Quartz stated his thesis, his voice cracked. The youngster turned three shades of red and ducked under the moment, only to be yanked up by his CO.

"And?"

"And, sir," XM said, grateful for his captain's single-mindedness, "at our approximate distance from the anomaly, I ought to be able to peer through the noise, if what we're seeing really is a ghost. Or, I should be able to localize the source, within a small margin of error, if something is there. I can't do either."

Captain Tsveokiev narrowed his eyes and nodded. "Ensign, what do you recommend?"

"It might be nothing sir," he said with more confidence, about an octave lower. "Could be, like I said, just an unusually heavy concentration of radioactive rock. But I'd feel better if I launched a drone for a closer look."

"Under the circumstances, I'm inclined to agree. Proceed. And why don't you bring it in under stealth. Let's get some practice with the Shadowdriver drone BUWEPS was kind enough to provide us, passives only. As close as you can get."

The captain gave his young charge a wicked smile, which Quartz couldn't help but return. Shadowdriver was still on the official secrets list. Quartz turned back to his holoscreen and licked his lips in anticipation.

Seventeen minutes later . . .

Commander William Kim leaned over Quartz's terminal and shook his head in disbelief. "Mr. Quartz, you just found what looks to be a pair of stray Lusitanian cruisers."

Kim felt adrenaline hit his bloodstream. Time seemed to slow down, and the routine noises of the warship grew louder until he could no longer screen them out. His pulse became a beating drum. Muscles twitched, yearning for release. If he'd been in his day cabin, he'd have changed into his dobok and centered himself, then progressed steadily through his forms, until he calmed down. *But not on the bridge,* he reminded himself. *Because commanders lead by example. Decisively. They make snap decisions based on limited data, and they don't act like nervous pups.* He settled into a gentle sway, back and forth on his boot heels, as he sorted the data on Ensign Quartz's screens. Sweat started slicking his face, and a drop slid off the end of his nose and fell to the deck.

Kim had long ago learned how to handle the stress of being a ship's officer. He'd seen more than his share of small wars and anti-piracy operations, and it had taken a toll on him. He had the blood on his hands to prove it. An eidetic memory that wouldn't let him forget it, either. He'd compensated by isolating his feelings from the facts, and he'd spent dozens of hours of therapy building the necessary walls to keep the two apart. Together, they would have emotionally incapacitated him. But apart they were far less lethal, even manageable. He'd faced his demons and survived. The one thing he'd not been able to change was how his body vented stress. When combat came knocking, his glands always gave him away. *Once again,* he thought, *I have the pit stains to prove it.*

"Nice job, X'atti. That is obviously not a sensor ghost."

"Thank you, sir. No sir, it's definitely not."

Two cruisers blipped on the scanners where none had been moments before, both with the mass and beam length of the Lusitanian Ares-class warship. The unidentified vessels were powered down and running passive scanners only.

"Nice work, XM." The commander took one more look before he squeezed the ensign's shoulder, and then he walked back toward the skipper. Kim cleared his throat. "Captain, CRURON Thirteen broke orbit just ahead of us and headed out of the Montana system. None of those warships were Ares-class. It's Lusie SOP for them to operate in tandem, typically as a system picket, so finding two together makes sense. We assumed the Lusies jumped out. But we don't have the hardware in system to prove it. Regardless, this pair is new. But I believe it's likely they arrived with CRURON Thirteen."

"You think they were detached before the Lusies made Montana orbit, don't you?" Captain Tsveokiev said. "If that's true, Commodore Samuelson's arrival was a setup from the very start."

"Sir, I wish I could disagree." Kim return to his chair and turned to face the captain. "I realize I'm jumping to conclusions, but the timing for this confluence works out rather well. And I don't believe in coincidences, not when it comes to the Lusies."

"Neither do I, Wil. Given what little we know at the moment, I'm inclined to agree with you." The captain folded his hands beneath his chin. "I don't like what their presence implies either," Tsveokiev said.

"My thoughts exactly, sir. We've been suckered, and we left Montana uncovered." Kim flared his nostrils—his other tell, which had nothing to do with stress.

"I know that look, Commander."

"Sir, Occam's razor comes to mind. The simplest explanation is often the correct one. We are responding to an SOS from the Rock. We've got two possible hostiles running dark at the edge of the asteroid field, pretending to be innocent chunks of rock. Our unidentified warships are sitting parallel to our least-time intercept between Montana and the mining station. Given CRURON Thirteen's recent presence in this system, they are almost certainly Lusitanian Cruisers. And they're in perfect ambush position. They are ignoring an all-channels SOS, too, which is against our laws and theirs. These ships are not here by accident."

Silence filled the room. Tensions between the RAW and the LE had been ratcheting up for years. Neither side was anxious for open conflict with the other. When two powers of near parity went to war, they usually succeeded in just smashing each other into debris. History had illustrated this truth many times, and in horrific detail: the Anglo-Spanish War in the late 1500s C. E.; the four India-Pakistani wars of the last half of the twentieth century; and the NATO-Russo/Crimean War of the late twenty-third had each left no winners, and millions dead.

Kim watched Captain Tsveokiev tap the bridge of his nose and imagined what he must be thinking. *Perhaps something's changed on their end, made them willing to force a confrontation with us. Maybe the Lusies think they can take us here and no one will be the wiser. Whatever this is, it's pushing too far.*

"Captain," Kim said, "their actions could be construed as an act of war."

"Possibly. Assuming those actually *are* Lusitanian warships out there."

"Not much else they could be, sir."

"I think you're right, Commander. But I'm not going to be the captain who goes down in history for starting the RAW-LE war, only to find out that he destroyed two civilian ships by mistake."

Tsveokiev turned toward Quartz. "Ensign, how close can you get? Enough to give me a hard scan on their drives?"

"Would a hull number suffice, Skipper?"

The captain looked surprised. "I believe it would, XM. Be a good EWO and go get it for me."

Five minutes later . . .

Quartz turned around to face his captain. "Sir, I can't get a positive read on the second vessel. There's a large asteroid between them, which is throwing off my scans, and getting around it might give away the probe. Even Shadowdriver isn't that good. However"—and Quartz inhaled sharply—"CIC positively ID'd the first vessel. She visited the Tagon sector more than a year ago and one of our Merchant Marines got a good look up her skirt. She's the HMS *Tolerable,* Ares-class light cruiser, commissioned eighty-nine A.E., out of the Lusie's BlueStar Naval Yard. She masses forty-five thousand tons with a complement of roughly 550. At the moment, she's running silent."

Tsveokiev laced his hands together beneath his chin. "Those vessels are watching us close the distance, and there's only one plausible explanation why."

"They're suckering us in," Kim said, "so they can take us out."

"Exactly. And they've refused to answer the Rock's SOS. That's the most damnable part."

Every member of the bridge crew turned toward Tsveokiev. He met their gazes directly as the shipwide claxon sounded three times. Then he opened a shipwide comm and sounded general quarters.

"Lieutenant Riccio, it's time for a live-fire exercise. Please select a few asteroids for target practice—gunner's prerogative. Tag and map them with active sensors, and then make them disappear."

Tactical Officer Second Lieutenant Sean Riccio stared at her captain like a Marine with ruined night vision. "Sir?"

"You can't always trust what you see, Lieutenant. I'm going to show the Lusies one thing and do another."

"And set a trap of your own, sir?"

"Precisely."

Commander Kim walked to Riccio's chair and leaned over her console. "Here, this one looks promising. Don't worry, Sean. I'll walk you through it."

One minute later . . .

"Fire!"

"Aye, aye, sir. Firing tubes three, five, and nine—missiles away."

Lieutenant Sean Riccio kicked six warheads into the drink. A dozen seconds later they unleashed their thermonuclear energies like compliant WMDs. Reduced several quarter-klick-length asteroids to fine cosmic dust. The blasts momentarily blinded every active and passive sensor in range. Just before Riccio's birds found their marks, two shifted to secondary targets, and made small terminal maneuvers that took them outside the blast radius, then powered down at the precise moment their sister warheads detonated. They disappeared from Riccio's scanners, as *Absa-*

lon's bridge collectively held its breath. A half mike later, the warheads began to blip in and out thanks to the ship's FTL Burst Relay.

"Skipper, I have them. And they have eyes on target. T minus two mikes."

"Thank you, Lieutenant." Tsveokiev turned to his XO. "Wil, I'd say things are about to get interesting."

Commander Kim exhaled. "Yes, sir. Best seal up, Captain."

Tsveokiev nodded and reached for his helmet as the countdown dropped below ninety seconds. He was newly dressed in a standard-issue vacsuit, helmet racked to his command chair. He reached for it but didn't put it on. *Plenty of time for that later.* Tsveokiev racked his helmet to his belt instead and smiled at his XO, who'd just done the same thing. The Regs called for suiting up, and both men knew it. But the reality of leading women and men into combat dictated otherwise. There was enough stress on the bridge without adding canned air to it any sooner than necessary.

A compressed, three-dimensional map blazed at the heart of the bridge. It danced with lights, tracking movement, both friendly and hostile, at a compressed rate, and in real time. A thin rail about waist high circled the holotank, and both the captain and commander leaned on it as they contemplated the start of an internecine war. A small pinprick of green indicated *Absalon*'s precise location relative to the two red enemy dots on the far side of the tank. Twin streaks of blue coasted along a dotted ballistic course toward their target. A tone sounded across the bridge as the warheads entered the enemy's countermissile envelope without challenge.

Captain and XO exchanged glances. At T minus ten seconds, Tsveokiev donned his helmet and closed his eyes.

Captain Gerald "Light Foot" Tamanend sat on the bridge of the HMS *Tolerable* nursing a cup of tea with heavy cream and honey. He'd watched the distance fall between his ships and the unsuspecting Republican cruiser for the majority of an hour, and he'd refused to fidget his way through it. Waiting for battle was an art form, one he believed even the best commanders were pressed into. *And combat is one of the best teachers I know.* As he waited for *Absalon* to close the range, he had little to do but contemplate his orders, fret about how they'd been executed, and worry about what he'd missed. *Perhaps I've misinterpreted a critical bit of data or overlooked something completely.* He hated his self-doubt. He was certain *Absalon*'s missile launch was nothing but a drill. Still, it had surprised him.

A flashing icon caught Tamanend's attention. He gazed into *Tolerable*'s holotank and frowned . . . again. Starships in proximity concerned him, particularly when his vessel was one of them. HMS *Tolerable* and *Century* were both powered down, which meant the actual threat of collision was minimal. But Tamanend had plenty of reason to worry. A starship not under her own power was as responsive as an ancient galleon with her sails down. Unexpected storms tended to crop up at the most unlikely, inconvenient times, and strong swells could capsize even the most robust of vessels.

Why was Tamanend frowning? Because his sister ship, HMS *Century*, hung in space off his starboard side, essentially rubbing shoulders with his own vessel, with a mere seventeen klicks of separation between them. Roughly one quarter of the correct distance the Regs called for. He'd essentially "stacked" the vessels under his command, one on top of the other with an oblong planetoid in the middle to help hide them both. If *Century* and *Tolerable* were somehow detected, Captain Tamanend probably wouldn't live to find out the who's and how's. And the proximity of the large asteroid between them all but eliminated evasive maneuvers, if they became necessary. But if all went according to his plan, the Republican warship would vanish with all of her hands aboard.

He was about to break an interstellar treaty and cause the first of many, many deaths. Assuming *Absalon* lived through today and reported the breach of compact. *Which of course she won't,* he assured himself. He didn't mind killing her and her crew. He was a Naval officer who'd ordered men to kill members of their own species. But striking from the shadows like he was about to do upset his black-and-white reading of the rules of war.

Tamanend grimaced as *Absalon* crept closer, raised his cup for another sip.

The launch clock on *Absalon* ticked down to T minus zero as the first missile "knocked" on *Tolerable*'s hull within one kilometer of a direct hull strike and blew. Radiant energy smashed through seventy-five meters of peristeel, weapons, ship compartments, and bulkheads, as well as the humans they were designed to protect from the ravages of space. *Tolerable*'s forward missile tubes vanished, along with Engineering-2. As atoms split apart, 15 percent of the ship's beam length became a crematorium and 123 Lusitanian Sailors lost their lives. A secondary explosion sent a plume of heat and neutrinos through the rest of the ship's hull, burning Sailors, vaporizing precious armor, and tearing deep into the ship's internal organs. *Tolerable*'s GravMatrix died, and hundreds found themselves at the mercy of zero g. Food, personal effects, and less pleasant things blobbed through *Tolerable*'s passageways and interpenetrated with her crew. The veterans swore as they swam to reach their assigned battle stations. The less seasoned Sailors spewed stomach acid and undigested food into the flat, recycled air.

A steady voice boomed throughout *Tolerable*'s compartments. "Partial gravity coming online. All hands to action stations."

Moments later, Engineering restored gravity as suddenly as it had died, and everything flopped to the deck. A handful of unlucky Sailors died from blunt-force trauma. As *Tolerable* came about to meet its attacker, the second missile bore down upon her and contacted with her hull midship. *Tolerable* literally broke apart. Forty-five thousand tons of weapons and peristeel and her full complement vanished at the center of an explosion as hot as an M-class sun.

RNS *Absalon*'s bridge witnessed the complete destruction of HMS *Tolerable* in utter silence.

Captain Tsveokiev turned to *Absalon*'s communications officer. "Let's hope they received our message in the spirit in which it was meant. Lieutenant?"

"Aye, sir," said First Lieutenant Reshe Bua. Gray streaks punctuated Bua's short mop of spiraled hair and ebony skin. She was a mustang and quite old for the three gold bars of a Naval first lieutenant, which were pinned to the collar points of her dark green utilities. A Marine staff sergeant in her former life, she'd gotten fed up with the pimple-faced, green-as-get-you-killed Naval officers who thought they knew something about hauling "ground-pounders" around the 'verse. She gotten so fed up she'd decided to do something about it. After a branch transfer, she graduated top of her OCS class, proving the old maxim true: sometimes the only way to do it right is to "do it like a Marine."

"Recording, sir," Bua replied.

"This is Captain Dimitri Tsveokiev of the Republican Naval ship *Absalon*. We have fired preemptively upon your sister vessel. We deeply regret her loss with all hands." Tsveokiev paused for a three-count. "However, your vessel is powered down and running silently along our intercept to the Rock. Masking your presence in such a fashion, in a classic ambush position, in Republican space—*that* action may be construed as an act of *war*. Said action contravenes the treaty between our two star nations, which requires a full disclosure of potential training maneuvers in foreign territory and the permission of the host nation for said maneuvers to proceed. To my knowledge, as the duly appointed commander of this star system, your government made no such request of the Republic of Aligned Worlds. Furthermore, *Absalon* is answering a mayday broadcast on all bands from Montana's single mining station in the field, and your vessels noticeably aren't. This means your vessels' actions may be construed to be obstructing this vessel's nonmilitary, purely humanitarian effort, which places you and your star nation in specific violation of the Ngolobe Accords. I expect you are intimately familiar with Ngolobe and understand that firing upon or refusing to offer aid to a civilian installation in distress is considered a dereliction of your duty and a flagrant violation of accepted interstellar law. You are hereby ordered to stand down your vessel and prepare to be boarded. Any attempt to flee this system or resist our boarding parties will be further construed as an escalation of hostilities between our two nations and will be met with lethal force. This is your one and only warning. I will not repeat myself. Captain Tsveokiev, out."

"Got that, Lieutenant Bua?"

"Clean recording, sir. Ready for transmission."

"Transmit. Let's see what their CO is made of."

Thirty-three

"Captain Vrayson, we're being hailed." Second Lieutenant Shana Foreigner, the communications officer aboard HMS *Century,* turned in her chair to face her commander.

"Put it through on an open channel, Lieutenant."

An impassioned, steely voice filled *Century*'s bridge. Her crew listened in genuine shock to the Republican captain and the severity of his terms. Less than a minute had slipped by since their sister ship, HMS *Tolerable,* had vanished with all hands. Not a single pod had spilled from her ruptured bowels, and not enough time had passed since her destruction to process the overwhelming loss, let alone compartmentalize it in light of the massive intelligence failure staring them in the face.

Not one pod, Vrayson thought. *Gerald's people never had a chance.* Vrayson stared into an empty plot, looking for a sea of missing red pinpricks, each a soul now banished for all eternity. The enemy captain's ultimatum continued and ended as abruptly as it began. Words Vrayson heard but didn't fully comprehend. Not yet. He sat in silence, waiting for someone to make a decision, and then he realized that someone was him.

Lieutenant Foreigner cleared her throat. Her unvoiced question pulled Vrayson back to his senses.

"Lieutenant, play that back again . . . please."

Vrayson listened for the word "surrender." He keyed upon this word. He knew surrender wasn't an option, because the Navy he served in had little experience with losing, and he knew his career would not survive if he capitulated to this enemy, a mere single ship from an inferior Naval tradition. He imagined his time in captivity as a prisoner of war and his repatriation, followed by a swift court-martial and the sound of the gavel crashing down upon his career in the Lusitanian Navy. He stroked the arms of his command chair, knowing either way that *Century* might be his last command. Complete intelligence failures happened. He'd known a few men, men once proud and resolute in their own competence, men now diminished by failure and haunted at night by the screams of their dead. Decent and honorable men disabused of the moral rectitude of their actions by the best of teachers—defeat in combat. The sheer weight of destruction and death bore down on Vrayson like a too-heavy seabag shouldered across grueling terrain. It was almost more than he could bear.

Yet, ultimatum or not, he would not stand down his ship. His orders were clear: leave no witnesses. Capture the survivors and bring them back with him. Violating either directive meant not only breaking his empire's treaty with the 'Publicans but also broadcasting that fact to the entire 'verse and saddling his star nation with the blood guilt.

Not today, not this ship, not Century.

"No."

Vrayson spoke the word, barely audible, a word he needed to hear, even if no one else on the bridge could. One single, solitary word, an oath of fidelity to his people, his ship, and his duty. "No." That single word was all it took to get him moving.

He ordered his command to action stations. HMS *Century* slipped from the shadow of a nameless planetoid to engage her enemy.

A missile duel between equals was a slow, grinding sort of exchange, once described by a wet-Navy tactician as "death by a hundred different flesh wounds that together cause the victim to bleed out of every bulkhead, bulwark, and beam." Energy duels were entirely different. The longest recorded was seventeen seconds, and few souls had lived to talk about it.

RNS *Absalon* belched atmosphere first. Captain Tsveokiev gritted his teeth behind his visor as his ship shuddered beneath him. His countermeasures were stopping fewer missiles, and *Absalon*'s armor and her internal organs were absorbing the slack. He white-knuckled his command chair and willed his ship to shrug off each blow. He ignored the groans of the dying vessel around him and urged *Absalon* onward. Commander Kim sat slumped in his chair, dead, a serrated shard of molycirc protruding from his chest.

Tsveokiev embraced the inevitable. His ship was dying. A direct hit had blown through Boatbay 1 and continued down the radius of his ship and through *Absalon*'s secondary fusion plant. Thirty-seven meters of *Absalon*'s starboard side sat open to space. *Maker only knows how many were vented.* Tsveokiev became one with his ship. Her wounds were his. His mission was hers. The cruiser started to corkscrew along her axis as her propulsion systems died. She labored for breath, not yet a derelict but no longer under her own power.

Damage reports flowed across Tsveokiev's screen. He ignored the casualty list, focusing instead on *Absalon*'s schematic. Over sixty percent of his ship glowed orange with serious damage. Another ten percent blinked red with critical and irreparable wounds.

Tsveokiev clasped his hands together and pressed them hard against his chin in concentration.

Engineering-2 and Fusion-2: destroyed
Engineering-1: open to space
Fusion-1: offline . . .
Missiles numbers 2–11 and 14: destroyed
Forward armor: down to 15 percent . . .

"Deploy all smartmetal to the forward sections," Tsveokiev barked. "Transfer auxiliary power to the weapons. Concentrate on their forward missile tubes!"

"Aye, aye, sir." Lieutenant Sean Riccio's left hand danced across her holoscreen, redirecting the few weapons she had left to return fire, while her right hand prioritized which holes in the hull to patch first. Blisters covered both of her forearms, and her face was drenched in sweat. She finished her firing sequence and executed it. More birds launched, and a half minute later they tore chunks out of *Century*'s ravaged hull.

"Lieutenant Bua—it's time to go. Give me a shipwide channel, please."

"You're live, sir."

Bua's calm voice made the captain proud.

"All hands, this is your captain speaking. We've done what we can, people. Abandon ship. I repeat, abandon ship. Get to the pods. Boatbay Three is still operational. The lifts are down, so use the emergency tubes. It's your best bet."

Tsveokiev paused and searched for the right words.

"Good luck and . . . Maker be with you." He turned to Bua, his de facto second in command.

"Lieutenant, get down to Bay Three and coordinate the evacuation. You're no longer needed here."

"Sir, I . . ."

"You're the XO now. I need you down there, coordinating the evac to make sure as many as possible of our people get out."

"Sir, I cannot let you—"

"Lieutenant, that's an order!"

Bua abandoned her post, slowly.

"God's speed, Reshe. I'm . . . I'm sorry."

She stood and came to attention. "No need, sir. It's been an honor."

Absalon convulsed along the length of her keel. The bridge's overhead lights died, and several consoles spat embers, briefly silhouetting the lifeless bodies across the bridge. After a brief moment of darkness, the emergency floodlights cycled on, and Tsveokiev's heart sank. The crushed body of Reshe Bua lay on deck, half-covered in debris, visor shattered and covered on the inside with blood. In a flat voice, he ordered Lieutenant Sean Riccio to handle the evacuation. When Riccio didn't respond, Tsveokiev turned to her and saw that she was still strapped into her chair and that her chin was resting on her chest.

Captain Tsveokiev acknowledged their deaths without feeling it and queried the ship's computer for the senior-most surviving officer on board. His eyes tensed before spreading widely in disbelief. None. Engineering, Medical, Weapons, Supply—he read down the list of departments as his ship labored about him, searching for an ensign or warrant officer to pass command to. *My God, how can they all be dead?* His screen momentarily froze, flickered out, before spooling up to a darkened version of its former self. And then he thought of his Marine detachment. *There.* The list was surprisingly intact. Two Marines missing, the rest assembled in Boatbay 3, including Lieutenant Paen. *Thank God she's still alive.* The only surviving officer other than himself, in either branch, aboard his vessel. A small "(S)" appeared next to her name, which confirmed the lieutenant was already sealed in her mechsuit.

He opened a channel with her mechsuit. "Lieutenant Paen, this is Captain Tsveokiev."

"Aye, Skipper. How may I—"

"There's little time, Lieutenant. I'm placing you in command. This ship is dying. Get my people out. Head for the Rock. I'll do my best to draw their fire."

"Sir, I—"

"Good hunting, Lieutenant. Make sure their story gets told."

"Aye, aye, Captain," Promise replied. *"I will si—"*

The feed died. Captain Tsveokiev tried to reestablish it but heard only static. He slumped back in his chair and stared into the plot as the Lusitanian warship closed the distanced with his command, still spitting missiles, still trying to kill him. He scanned his bridge, which was bathed in red emergency light. It was a tangled mass of electronics and bodies.

He sat alone.

Tsveokiev queried his weapons manifest. One laser mount and three solitary green dots glowed in response, his only operational tubes, waiting for further instructions. He transferred tactical command to his chair. A virtual console materialized around him. Tsveokiev typed frantically, aiming his remaining offensive assets at *Century*'s jump drive. He ordered missiles 1, 12, and 15 to full auto, until the tubes ran dry, and he prayed. He prayed for his people to live. He prayed for the enemy to die. In his last minute, he prayed for his wife and daughter to live on without him.

His last request was for himself. *Grant me a good death.*

Absalon's command deck sagged under the weight of fire from *Century*'s forward-mounted heavy laser. *Absalon*'s bridge opened to space, sucking the bridge clean of every scrap of matter not strapped in or bolted down, including the lifeless body of Captain Dimitri Tsveokiev.

Acting Captain Shana Foreigner couldn't stop them all.

HMS *Century* crossed into knife range, firing her particle-beam weapons into *Absalon*'s battered hull. Her computers recorded a direct hit on *Absalon*'s bridge, noting several larger ship fragments that spun away from the vessel, one with three trapped Sailors inside. Three of *Absalon*'s missile tubes continued to return fire. Too many missiles were closing in on Foreigner's seconds-old command. And she couldn't possibly stop them all.

The ship killers closed as her countermissiles raced out to greet them. They picked off four. Her point defenses fired. Five more disappeared. Three warheads punched through everything she had and granted a Republican captain his dying wish.

Thirty-four

Promise heard Captain Tsveokiev in her mastoid implant, and she heard the ship's claxon sound over the channel and echo throughout Boatbay 3. She noted the strain and control in his voice. And then she heard him tell her to abandon *Absalon* without him.

"Sir, I—"

"Good hunting, Lieutenant. Make sure their story gets told."

"Aye, aye, sir," Promise replied. "I will sir. Sir? Captain? Bond, I just lost my link with the bridge—I need that link now."

"The bridge is not responding. Absalon's primary command-and-control net is off-line. I'm attempting to access the secondaries through Engineering-One. One moment, please."

Promise's stomach knotted. She looked for an open container as a wave of nausea rolled over her and contemplated ripping off her helmet but refused to do so. *Swallow it, P. Swallow it!* Space battles were the stuff of Marines' nightmares. Becoming stranded in the boatbay of a dead warship was every Marine's worst fear.

RNS *Absalon* death-rattled once and went dark. Three seconds later, red light flooded the bay from rectangular panels spaced equidistantly around the perimeter, from deck to overhead.

Two of hers were still out there, cut off by a blocked bulkhead door. But she couldn't wait for them any longer.

I'm so sorry.

She boarded the LAC last, walked through two rows of Marines and Navies strapped into webbing on either side of her, and forward to the LAC's cockpit. Corporal Sammi Porter sat at the helm. Her mechsuit's helmet was engraved with a trio of stars, one for each shuttle school she'd graduated from, all with top honors. Promise ducked her head into the cockpit, spoke over her externals. "Take us out."

"Ma'am, I'm patched into Absalon's *sensor logs and have something you'll want to see,"* her AI reported as the shuttle dusted off.

"On my HUD."

Her screen shifted to open space, and the hull of a Lusitanian warship breaking apart.

"Belay that order, Corporal. Set us back down. But keep the engines hot, just in case."

"Aye, aye, ma'am—hot and holding," replied Corporal Porter.

As the senior surviving office on board, it's my job to carry out Captain Tsveokiev's last order and to evacuate Absalon. *But as the Marine commander of Victor Company and the de facto captain of this vessel, it's also my job to exercise my own command authority. I will not leave anyone behind if I can help it.* Her wounded deserved a fighting chance, the wounded in *Absalon's* medbay, the wounded trapped in corridors filled with debris and crushed bodies. Her wounded. The irony of the situation hit her. She was now in command of Marines and Navies alike. They were all *hers.*

Sergeant Richelle Felix, Corporal Maxzash-Indar Sindri, and Private First Class Kathy Prichart unstrapped their webbing as Promise clanked past them and down the gangplank. The PFC and two non-comms fell in lockstep behind their lieutenant. The rest of V Company and a few seamen disgorged from their webbing and followed suit. They all assembled on the deck of the now derelict *Absalon.* A collective *what now?* washed over them.

Is this what a ghost ship feels like? Promise's gut knotted again as she stood in the center of the bay and thought about the carnage that lay beyond it. She looked about her and saw a relatively orderly boatbay, Marines and Sailors suited should a hull breach occur. She knew that the rest of *Absalon* looked little like its former self, and a part of her wanted to do the easy thing—leave and live—and realizing that shamed her. The ship's crew, her Marines, and her planet needed her to do the opposite. They needed her to stay and breathe new life into a warship perched on the abyss. And the people behind her were waiting for their orders.

My orders. What would Dad say? Oh, yes. "The Maker won't give you a rock too big to plow under." Well, all I've got is a trench shovel to move this mountain. I better get to it.

"Bond, I need a SITREP on the hull's integrity."

"Stand by . . ."

"Private First Class Prichart, I need a triage center," Promise said over her externals, pointing to the right. The first order was the hardest. After that, it was like rolling rocks down the hill. "There's wounded out there . . . somewhere. Fire up the M-bot and prepare to receive casualties."

"Aye, aye, ma'am." Prichart peeled off and headed back up the LAC's ramp for supplies. A tall spheroid-shaped mech with four surgical arms came to life and hovered down the ramp, passing the PFC on her way.

"Sergeant Felix, I need SAR teams. We've still got people out there," Promise said, "Find them."

"Aye, aye, ma'am," replied Felix. She pivoted on the balls of her mechsuit and pointed both hands at her Marines, quickly dividing them into search-and-rescue teams. A holomap blossomed in their midst. Felix pointed quickly. "Teams Alpha, Beta, Charlie, Delta—go, go, go, go. Then she pivoted again and stared at Promise, smiling behind her suit's visor.

"I need you to fix this ship, Richelle."

"I wish we hadn't lost all of propulsion," Felix said. "My familiarity with the mechsuit's fusion plant might come in handy. But it's not my primary MOS. Might is the operable word, though. I've never tried to patch a warship's fusion plant back together."

"See what you can do to seal the hull breach at Fusion-Two for now, and then worry about assessing the damage as best you can. There's a ship's manual in the data core. If all else fails, read the instructions." The two women exchanged wry smiles. Promise added, "I need propulsion, if at all possible. I need it to be possible, and I need it now."

"You don't ask for much, do you, ma'am?" She scanned the bay and set off for a small hatch on the forward side of the boatbay.

Promise turned her focus inward. "Well?"

"Major hull breaches have been sealed off," Bond said. *"Primary bulkheads are holding. A number of compartments are open to space, and there*

are dozens of microbreaches on the outer hull. The inner hull is at forty-nine percent. This bay is vaccum-tight. I suggest recalibrating the deflectors to shore up overall hull integrity."

"Do it. I need you to access *Absalon's* medical net. If Sailors are still alive, their I-Dents will tell us. Also, stand down *Absalon's* noncritical systems. We need to conserve power. Tell me what still works on this ship, and prioritize what needs repairing."

Her AI finished his report several mikes later, and lines of names and numbers started scrolling across Promise's HUD.

First, the living.

She was the senior officer aboard, from either service branch. She'd known that, but she'd felt compelled to confirm that command had indeed rightly passed to her. Promise quickly scanned the officers' list. Each was flagged in red, KIA. She checked the engineering and medical rosters next and found it to be the same, which is as much as she'd expected, except for Engineering Apprentice Fingers and a Commander Tamm, the ship's doctor. Both were listed as MIA, which meant they'd probably been vented in the carnage. Farther down the ship's roster, she found several names highlighted in orange, which indicated they were still alive but critically injured. Amazingly, all her Marines were still alive.

Next, the dead.

Over 91 percent of the ship's company was dead, less than 1 percent were injured, and the rest were missing. Compartments throughout the ship were open to the stars. Thankfully, the environmental plant was still making air and scrubbing CO_2. *Absalon's* gravity was nominal but more than sufficient to keep her mechboots on the deck plating. Auxiliary power was feeding on reserves. For the immediate future, they wouldn't freeze to death. The jump drive was down. *That's bad, but things could be worse. I have air, heat, and food. No engines. Three out of four—it could be a lot worse.* Unfortunately, the hull breach in Engineering-1 was a problem. Both plants were down. Fusion-2 was destroyed, and Fusion-1 sat open to space. *Getting to the feeds to repair the plant and restore power—if that's even possible—probably means spacewalking and a level of expertise my people simply don't possess. I need a space dock and yard dogs.* What she had was a lot of space between her command and home and a bunch of angry Marines itching for a target. A hard smile crossed her face. *Remember, P, you're immortal until you die. Feel like dying? Me neither.*

Promise removed her helmet, racked it to her side, and took a deep breath. *I can do this.*

And that's when a Sailor dressed in a green Navy vacsuit fell into the boatbay, and into Sergeant Felix's arms. A whining motor caught Promise's attention. Promise turned toward the source of the noise, a hexagonal access hatch, which proceeded to slide half-open, before it seized up and whined to a halt. One of the tallest men she'd ever seen turned sideways and snaked through, almost dropping to the ground at Sergeant Richelle Felix's feet before the NCO caught him midair. An armored Marine scraped through next and forced the doors to open fully, followed by a much smaller Sailor wearing the bleach-white vacsuit of a ship's doctor. Both suits showed signs of damage and had been hastily patched. Promise's other missing Marine brought up the rear.

Felix led the pair of Navy lost-and-founds toward Promise. "Slim" pulled off his helmet and presented first, snapping a slightly off-kilter salute to his new CO. "Engineering Apprentice Fingers, reporting—"

"Excuse me, Seaman Fingers." Promise held up a finger and turned to address the senior-most officer standing in the boatbay. She wore commander's insignia—two globes flanking the caduceus, the centuries-old symbol of the healing arts. Her vacsuit's arms and torso were freshly painted red. She struggled to remove her helmet, which fell to the deck as she lost her balance. Promise caught her under the arm. "Forgive my abruptness, Commander . . . Tamm," Promise said as she read the woman's name off her vacsuit, "but we need to attend to your wounds."

"Blood isn't mine, Lieutenant." The commander's voice quivered. "I, ah, I believe I'm okay. Give me a moment," she said as she pulled at her collar. "Okay, you can let go."

"Roger that, ma'am." Promise held tight. "Are you sure you're okay?"

"I was in the medbay, trying to stabilize a young man with a crushed pelvis, when . . . when we got hit. I was thrown clear, and Lieutenant Commander Towns took the brunt of . . ." The doc broke off, clearly struggling for words.

Promise laid a hand on the woman's shoulder and squeezed gently.

"We've all lost good people today, Commander. I swear to you that we will honor them."

The doctor looked into Promise's eyes and slowly nodded.

"Ma'am, the captain passed command to me when he couldn't confirm your condition or whereabouts. Now that you're here, command is rightfully yours. I stand relieved."

Tamm actually smiled, which warmed her otherwise pale face. "If I have my branch trivia right, every Marine, regardless of specialty, is still a rifleman. A warfighter. But in the Navy, medical personnel stand outside the chain of command. I may be a commander by rank, but I'm really just a doctor. I know how to mend broken bodies, not lead in combat. No, Lieutenant, the fighting is rightly left to you."

Promise nodded. "All right. I need you to prepare for wounded. What do you need?"

Tamm appraised the boatbay and nodded. "An assistant and space to work."

"Done. Private First Class Prichart is already on that." Promise waved her guardian over. "PFC Prichart, you're with the doctor."

Promise turned back to the young Sailor dressed in a scorched vac-suit. Standing before her was indeed a small miracle. *A Gaawd-blessed engineer!* "Now, Sailor, you we're saying . . ."

"Right, ah, Engineering Apprentice Fingers, reporting for duty, ma'am."

"My AI said you were MIA. Glad my own two eyes just proved it wrong."

"You and me both, ma'am."

"And I'm glad to have an engineer at my disposal. I need engines, Seaman Fingers."

"Well, engineering apprentice, ma'am. But I'll certainly do what I can."

"At this very moment, Seaman, you are the entire engineering department. My condolences."

Fingers blanched and looked away.

"Sergeant Felix, you have a new friend," Promise said. "Why don't all three of us head toward Engineering-One and have a look-see."

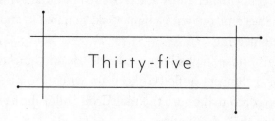

Thirty-five

Promise, Sergeant Felix, and Fingers climbed into the narrow passageway lit by the angry glow of red emergency lights. Upon reaching an L, they began climbing vertically. Several meters up, they encountered a blackened access hatch with unreadable markings. A pale foam coated it and the nearby bulkheads. Promise used her augmented strength to punch through it.

"Seaman Fingers, what do you know about repairing engines? Can you do it?" Promise asked as she exited first, turned, and helped the engineer through.

"Hopefully enough, ma'am." Fingers did a three-sixty, checked his minicomp for directions, found his bearings, and headed right and down a dark corridor. The two Marines activated their lights, and both saw the metal rafter that angled from the overhead to the deck.

"I'll certainly try, ma'am," Fingers replied as he misjudged the beam and rapped his head on it. "Son of a sea donkey!" Sergeant Felix caught him as he fell backward.

"That makes two, Sailor. Shall we go for three?"

"No, uh, no, Sergeant!"

"Easy, Seaman Fingers," Promise said. "I need that head of yours intact if we're to get out of this mess."

"Yes, ma'am," Fingers said as he rubbed his temple. "I'm partial to it myself."

Promise stepped around Fingers and over a pile of debris. She noticed a nearby emergency panel and walked over to it, punched the plexi, and fished inside. She came out with a light stick, snapped it, and handed it to her head of engineering.

"Try this." Promise stepped over more debris and quickened her pace toward Fusion-1. Fingers huffed to keep up while Promise led and the sergeant followed, to make sure the maladroit Sailor didn't lose his head before getting to their destination.

"We can't work in there without vacsuits, ma'am," Fingers said when they reached the bulkhead, which accessed Engineering-1 and the primary plant. "And we can't open the bulkhead without venting a good part of this section of the ship with it. But . . . if we move back two bulkheads"—Fingers clicked his tongue as he weighed his options—"um, yes, we can turn the middle compartment into an air lock between the section with atmosphere and the one exposed to space. I won't know more until I get through the air lock and assess the damage."

Promise peered through armorplaste and saw stars, as well as the edge of the asteroid field peeking around a sensor console on the left and only remaining bulkhead of the main compartment. She imagined the young Sailor that must have stood at her station to the end, now entombed in space. She cleared her throat and turned around to face the young engineer apprentice before her.

"All right, Seaman Fingers, off you go."

Eight hours later, Fingers came through, with the help and steadying hand of Sergeant Felix, several spacewalks, and a LAC full of plug-and-play components. Together, Navy and Marine nursed Fusion-1 to fifteen percent.

In the interim, Promise returned to the boatbay and downloaded the ship's manual. She scanned the section on navigating a warship without a bridge and discovered a small storage compartment that housed a modular bridge assembly. After several pots of caf and two tantrums—they took turns—she and Maxi managed to assemble an underwhelming command center with navigation and passive sensors.

"Well, Maxi, two out of three isn't bad," Promise said. "Though I would feel better with weapons."

"You always feel better with weapons, ma'am."

"True." Promise rubbed her hands together. "Let's flip the switch. Fingers crossed."

One by one, the boards turned green. When the last status light turned solid, they both sighed.

"Corporal, I'm promoting you to helmsman. Tell me, how long before we reach the Rock?"

Maxi sat on a crate of rations, typing coordinates into a small keyboard, the ship's manual spread across his lap.

"Hmmm . . . according to this, seven hours, give or take."

"Give or take what?"

"If the plant gives, it will take a lot longer."

The *Absalon* took another nine hours to reach the Rock. While in transit, Promise turned over command to Sergeant Felix and climbed into her rack, leaving orders that she be woken only in an emergency. She slept a little over six hours and woke to a soft chime.

"Lieutenant Paen." Promise rolled to one side and ran a hand through her finger-length hair.

"Ma'am, you asked me to wake you when we were ninety mikes out. No other hostiles on scanners."

"Give me ten," Promise said and killed the line.

Thirty-six

"Ma'am, I have a little surprise for you." The Rock's station chief, Mark Swanson, directed Promise to an old-fashioned, two-dimensional digital map of his station and stabbed a dotted square with his finger.

Chief Swanson was a thickset man with a crate-sized chest and cannons for arms. He'd been a collegiate power-lifter before joining the Terrestrial Miner's Union on Montana and then working in the asteroid field as a conveyor operator.

"This here is the station's hangar, where we keep our little fleet: tugs, UAVs, and a few support craft." The chief raised both eyebrows and grinned port to starboard. "And we keep a little something special in there, too. Ma'am, it will make more sense if I just show her to you. If you'll follow me," the chief said, offering her his arm.

The gesture struck Promise as old-fashioned and provincial, but the involuntary smile that swallowed her face made her realize she didn't mind the sentiment in the slightest.

The chief led Promise down a rough-hewn corridor near the outer wall of the asteroid. The incline was steep, and Promise found herself having to duck in several places as she fought against the sensation that she was falling. Several minutes flew by as Swanson entertained her with a monologue on the station's history. Then they came to two large blast doors that were large enough to fit an armored personnel carrier through.

Beyond the doors lay a vast cavern many times larger than the bays on most capital battleships. Floodlights illuminated the ferocrete deck and a small fleet of mining vehicles, tugs, haulers, and UAVs. Several shuttles rested at the far side of the bay near a much larger bullet-shaped vessel. Promise was surprised to see her, and she began to pick at the oddities of the vessel, particularly the odd bulge along her belly.

"Chief Swanson, just what are you doing with a Bengal-class assault LAC?"

The Republican Navy of thirty years ago had relied heavily on the Bengal as its chosen assault boat for the Navy's Monitor-class of battlecruisers. As the Monitors decommissioned, so too had the Bengal LACs. Surplus vessels were sold off to the aligned systems, to the RAW's allies, and to several private security firms. And many of the ships were then resold to nonaligned planets, corporations, and multisystem consortiums.

The chief shrugged. "We take care of ourselves, ma'am. Montana may have joined the Republic years ago, but we haven't seen any of her promises come our way or come true."

Promise acknowledged the criticism, fair as it was, and nodded for the chief to go on.

"And this mining platform is a long way from home. We're a sitting duck out here in the field. We don't even have static defenses. A bunch of us miners put a resolution up before the union a couple of years back, suggesting we get proactive in defending ourselves, and the *Maven*'s the result. Bought her on the junk market two systems over near Clear Harbor. The union's been banking dues for decades and saving them for a bad solar flare. We all figured it was time to spend some of our hard-saved chits on an insurance policy."

"I assume she's space-worthy."

"Yes, ma'am, with her original weapons suite, too. Her guns won't stand up to your *Absalon,* but they'll sting like the over-sided, three-inch deviljacks back home. Four small particle cannons and two Sparrow missile tubes," Swanson said, beaming with pride.

"I'm glad you didn't try to fight her," Promise offered. "We managed to ambush one of the Lusie cruisers that boxed you in; the other nearly knocked us out."

"Truth is, we would've tried if those bastards hadn't blocked the bay doors," the chief replied. "The Lusies must have detected her drive lighting off."

The chief pointed to the bulge in her midsection, just behind her forward section and the cockpit. "Ma'am, why don't you take a closer look along her belly?"

"I noticed—she's thick in the keel, Chief. Just what am I looking at?" Promise tried to puzzle out the oddly shaped vessel. It looked, for lack of a better word, pregnant, like the vessel's skin had been stretched from the inside. Swanson's laughter told her she was overlooking the obvious. It was clear that the *Maven* had been customized and that the addition, whatever it was, required more cubic meters than the vessel's hull normally permitted. Only the chief's remark about being far from home tipped her off.

Her head snapped around. "No."

Swanson nodded vigorously.

"I don't believe it." Promise said.

"Seeing ain't all there is to believing. But it surely beats blind faith!"

"A jump drive?"

"A God's-honest *jump* drive, ma'am." The chief flexed his suspenders. "It's short-range, twenty light-years max, with a full charge. We had to gut her crew compartment to make space for it. She'll only hold a complement of six. We retrofitted her ourselves with salvaged parts from a mothballed frigate. The *Maven*'s probably the only Bengal in the 'verse that's jump-capable." Swanson snapped his suspenders again. "I know a schemer when I see one. I'm bettin' there's a nasty little plan formulating in that pretty little head of yours. Um, no disrespect meant, Lieutenant."

"None taken, Chief. Thank you." Promise turned back to the ship as she thought aloud. "Chief, I think your investment is about to pay a fat dividend. I need a huge favor."

"If it's doable, it's yours."

"I made a promise to my captain that I intend to keep. Would you be so kind as to prep her for launch? I need you to make a house call for me."

"My pleasure, ma'am. Anything to pay back those bastards for what they did to my station."

"Good man. You're headed to Mendelson sector HQ, with this." Promise raised her minicomp and hit TRANSMIT. Swanson looked down at the comp attached to his work belt, which chirped to attention. "It's a code Omega, Chief. It means 'Invasion Imminent.'"

Swanson's expression paled. "Ma'am, it'll take me nearly five days and multiple jumps just to get there. The recharge and transit times in system will slow me down. I'm sorry she's not faster, but . . ."

Promise held up her hand. "Chief, you can only do your best with what you have. You didn't make this mess, and I don't expect you to clean it up, either. Make haste, don't stop to relieve yourself, and bring a lot of firepower back with you." Promise gave the chief a winning smile.

"Well, that I can do, ma'am," the chief said as he puffed out his chest. "I'll bring back the entire Republican Fleet Forces if I have to."

Promise slapped him on the shoulder. "Good man. You bring them back for me, and I swear the Lusies will pay."

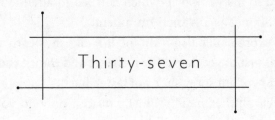

Thirty-seven

"So, Seaman Fingers, you're suggesting we shut down all of *Absalon*'s systems, correct?"

"Yes, ma'am."

"*All* of them, including life support? And you want me to direct every bit of power to the jump drive?"

"Yes, ma'am."

A crowd of Marines, Sailors, and miners stood behind Promise and Seaman Fingers, listening as *Absalon*'s new skipper and de facto head of engineering talked through a potentially deadly gambit for getting them all home. It was a gamble of the first order.

"You believe she's got another jump in her?" Promise asked. "I thought the damage to the drive was so extensive that we needed yard dogs to fix it."

"So did I, at least at first," said Fingers. "Power isn't the problem. We've got enough power, ma'am. *Absalon*'s banks are fully charged, too. And I've checked her relays and capacitors. I believe they'll hold."

"If they don't?"

The young engineering tech looked even younger at that moment. He broke eye contact and looked down at the deck plating. Promise cleared her throat.

"If they don't hold, ma'am, the excess power will have to bleed somewhere, which could create a cascading effect and blow the whole assembly."

"And most of the ship with it. That's a rather unpleasant prospect, wouldn't you say?"

To his credit, the Sailor met her gaze directly. "It's about time, ma'am. And we're about out of it."

He has a point. And if I ignore his recommendation and we keep to our present course? Promise turned around to face her people. Hard eyes and determination stared back at her.

"Folks, we need to get home quickly. *Absalon* is falling apart. If she doesn't kill us, our enemy just might. Our best option is a microjump to Montana. But if we make the jump, we might not make it back at all. And if we don't, our odds aren't much better. So we're taking the shortcut, and hopefully we'll materialize in Montana space in one piece."

"What if we don't like that choice?" said a voice near the back.

Promise scanned the crowd for its source.

"You're free to stay on the station and enjoy what little air is left. Frankly, your odds of surviving may be better if you do."

"And if we get home, then what?" The question came from the same man, a tall miner who began pushing his way forward.

"When we get home, we prepare for a ground war. I can't fight with *Absalon*. She's in no shape to defend the space around Montana." *And I'm no starship captain either.* Promise kept that revelation to herself. "So we're going to lose the high ground. But I have no intention of losing Montana."

"Other questions?"

The same miner piped up, louder this time and more obnoxious. "I'm no soldier, ma'am, but I ain't stupid neither. Without a ship, you ain't got a pot to piss in. How you gonna save our planet?"

"What's your name, sir?"

"Ray Tokavid, laser cutter on Team Four."

"Well, Mr. Tokavid, you're right. You aren't stupid and you just pinpointed my dilemma. The Lusitanians have us outgunned in space. I can't do anything to change the weight of metal we're facing. But they still have to put boots on the ground to take the planet. If they do, I'll fight them, and they will pay for it. And by the way, I'm a Marine—I don't need a pot to piss in."

It was the right thing to say at the right moment. Long memories of broken pledges gave way to open smiles. Many were missing teeth; several others had left their dentures behind. Tokavid roared with laughter and slapped the back of the man next to him.

"Any *more* questions?"

Tokavid had moved close enough for Promise to see him lean over and whisper to the man next to him. "Real spitfire, that one. I like 'er."

"All right, people. Get your gear stowed on board the LAC. Any loose items in the bay need to be secured first before you strap yourself in. If you are the praying kind, now is a very good time to get your account squared away."

Promise scanned her people and nodded.

"All right then. That's the plan. May the Maker bless it." She heard amens all around.

Promise jerked her head back toward the ship and hefted a nearby crate of medical supplies up the gangway.

At about the same time, aboard the Lucky Lady, Montana orbit . . .

The Lucky Lady circled Montana, falling closer to the planet with each revolution. Her insides were gutted and marred with plasma burns and blood. Dozens of corpses floated through her corridors with pained expressions frozen into place. From the planet's surface, she looked like a half moon because sixty-three percent of her orbital ring was missing. A handful of work crews swam through her remains, rushing from one emergency to the next, putting out fires, rescuing the wounded, sealing hull breaches, and fighting to stabilize the Lady's vitals. One by one they flatlined: gravity, life support, propulsion, and finally auxiliary power. The station went dark, and the men and women of the Lady made the hard choice to retreat to the safety of space. The final decision was kicked downstairs to the president's office. Two hours later, precision charges tore the station apart.

A minute of silence was observed across the planet in every time zone and city, township and homestead. Farmers and ranchers looked upward, removed their straws and felts. Schoolchildren squirmed in their chairs with their eyes glued to the in-room screens, not really comprehending the magnitude of the loss yet knowing their planet had grown somehow smaller. Later that same night, Montana's youth marveled at the unusually high number of shootings stars that lit their sky, beauty born out of the ashes of the Lucky Lady. The collective prayers of the old fell from the heavens, seemingly forgotten and unanswered.

At dawn, *Absalon* blinked into existence between Montana and her second moon. Fingers maneuvered *Absalon* into a stable orbit before abandoning his station.

"I won't forget her," Fingers said.

Promise cleared her throat. "If I have my way, the Navy won't either"

"Thank you, ma'am. She's earned her keep."

"That she has, Seaman Fingers. That she has indeed." Promise held the young man's gaze. "Now, we need to continue to earn ours." Promise looked across the overcrowded compartment of personnel: Sailors, Marines, and miners. They had fought, bled, and died together. To fit everyone in, they'd ripped out the LAC's webbing, racks, and emergency equipment. It was standing room only except for the wounded, and half weren't even suited, which violated at least a dozen regulations.

Promise crossed her arms and looked out the cockpit's armorplaste as the LAC departed RNS *Absalon*'s darkened bay. She focused upon the space where the Lucky Lady should had been and flinched. *No platform, no* Absalon. *We're on our own.*

The "we're" wasn't lost on her either. She'd thought it intentionally. Despite the difficulties ahead, Promise was glad to see Montana's lands and seas, the checkered patterns of farmland, and the telltale signs of urban sprawl, and she realized she was exactly where she wanted to be, with the people she cared about most.

Welcome home, Lieutenant.

Thirty-eight

Annie Buckmeister and Jean-Wesley Partaine stood at an appropriate distance from each other. She was the president of her planet, and he, the head of its all-volunteer military. Though they were friends, and while most people close to either of them knew theirs was a friendship both deep and clear like a still lake lit by morning sun, it was important for them to draw certain lines in public, namely that the government and the militia weren't too cozy and that the latter wasn't in the pocket of the former. Montana's constitution and her citizens had a problem with standing armies, which is why Montana had a Rotary-style militia but no regular military units. In a world of guns and butter, butter ruled the day. But that was about to change, which explained their distance from each other as they waited at the provisional spaceport for Montana's most recognizable and in many ways most reluctant citizen to arrive home.

The LAC approached from the east, touched down, and taxied to a stop. The landing was old-fashioned and as gentle as the pilot could manage for the passengers stuffed inside. Promise disembarked in her mechsuit with her pad on the trigger, not knowing what to expect and believing it best to be "hot" in case her welcome party turned out to be a coup d'état. A quick visual confirmed her scans: the provisional spaceport and Montana's government were still intact and in the service of the planet's citizens. Promise frowned at the number of Rotary members assembled across the landing strip, many of whom carried Marine-issue pulse rifles with belly-mounted FGLs and MOLLE gear stuffed with ordnance.

"Looking for a fight," Promise said as she approached Jean-Wesley and Annie. She racked her helmet to her mechsuit and ran her fingers through a mess of matted, greasy hair. She met Jean-Wesley's eyes fully and found a reason to worry about him.

"Only if the Lusies want one," he said. Jean-Wesley held her gaze a bit longer than protocol dictated. He said a lot in that look. Then he glanced behind Promise as several stretchers came down the ramp behind them. Medical personnel swarmed around the wounded. Those in regulation gray body bags were met with silence. Partaine's eyes closed, and his fists balled up.

"We lost a lot of good people on the Lady and the Rock," Jean-Wesley said. "They deserved better." His eyes opened and stared into the distance. "About a dozen made if off the platform alive, including your people, and we still don't fully know what happened." Partaine looked back at Promise. "But we do know that platforms don't normally blow themselves up. Before you arrived, we were leaning toward a massive systems failure. Probably a tragic accident. But now . . ." He dropped his head. "Now, my people just want revenge. And I want those bastards to pay for their sins."

Vengeance is mine. They were words she'd read in a dusty book once, words her father had lived and died for. A few times in her life, in the most difficult of times, she'd sensed her father looking down upon her and felt his reproving eye and simple faith prodding her along unpaved roads. She remembered his voice—its deep timbre and somber cadence—and how often he'd scolded her for being overemotional. *Sometimes, Promise, we ask the Maker for justice and he gives us the opportunity to be just. When the time comes, we must reject vengeance and wait for His justice to catch up to our timetable.* This time, Promise couldn't have disagreed more.

"Jean-Wesley, if the Lusies come looking for a fight—I pray to God they don't—but if they do we don't have enough to stop them. Your friends and family will pay the price. Do you really want that?"

"I won't just sit by and let those Imperial bastards kick up a storm across our planet. This is our home. Those folks up top were our sons and daughters. They deserve justice, and the men responsible should be punished," Partaine said. His voice shook at he spoke.

"Justice? I want that, too," Promise replied evenly. "But I won't send you or your people out just to die in a show of force to satisfy some code of honor. The Rotary isn't equipped to repel Lusitanian Marines in shock-gear and modern weapons. If they attack the planet, the fight will come to your cities and homes, and many will die. Too many. Neither one of us wants that."

Promise let the wind carry her words around the landing pad, to the minds that needed to think upon such things. Partaine fought off unshed tears and shook his head in response. "No, Promise, I don't want that. No more needless dying."

"That doesn't mean we won't fight, Jean-Wesley. It just means we'll use different tactics."

Partaine looked at her, clearly confused, but it was Annie who spoke first. "What do you mean?"

"I intend to make a show of force, and your Rotary will help me do that. Mainly, though, I plan to appeal to the Lusie's humanity, and if that fails, exploit their desire to live to fight another day. We have a saying in the Corps: 'Wars are fought by flesh, paid for with blood.'"

Annie's brow furrowed. Then it dawned on her what Promise meant.

"Exactly," Promise said. "Their commodore . . . what's his name?" Fatigue was setting in and her short-term memory hadn't been the same since the head injury.

"Samuelson," Annie offered.

"Right, Samuelson, he's certainly aware of that, too. He can take the planet, but he'll have to face a rifle behind every tree, and a lot of his Marines and Sailors will die in the taking. His empire will have a massacre on its hands and high casualties, and a PR nightmare that will take on a life of its own. I'm betting he doesn't want to be the officer who gets blamed for either outcome. War may come someday, but not today," Promise said.

"What if you're wrong?" Jean-Wesley asked.

"Then God help us all."

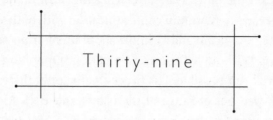

Thirty-nine

APRIL 8TH, 91 A.E., STANDARD CALENDAR, 0615 HOURS,
HMS *INTREPID*, OUTER MONTANA SYSTEM

Commodore Samuelson sat at the head of the antique mahogany table in his ready room, scrutinizing his captains and commanders as they nervously settled in around it. A few matched eyes with him; the rest stared straight ahead. His steward leaned against the wall with a hot pot of caf in one hand and several mugs in the other. Samuelson motioned him forward, grateful for the warm stimulant at the dawn of what promised to be a very challenging day aboard ship. Then he motioned to the rest of the table, too. This was going to be a long meeting, and they would need all the focus they could get. The ship's clock behind him marked the twenty-five hours of the capital world of Lucitane. The royal family crest was mounted above it and everything else in the room. Just like the queen, first above all, first by blood right, first in everything, the chain of succession unbroken for almost four centuries. The color red for the will to power. Black for the absence of fear.

Samuelson swept his hand across the smooth table, leaned forward, and saw his reflection looking back at him, looking appropriately grave for the occasion. The table had been a gift from Her Majesty, delivered through appropriate channels, of course. Samuelson wasn't important enough for an audience. *Not yet,* he thought. The wood was beautifully grained, from timber felled in Her Majesty's redwood. *And a none-too-subtle reminder that she's watching me.* The clock struck 0615 hours. Very early indeed for a command staff meeting.

Two weeks had passed since the commodore dispatched *Tolerable* and *Century* to picket the outer system. During the burn in, he'd positioned several hyper-relays to maintain communication with both vessels. As far as he knew, the "Publicans didn't know about them or possess comparable technology. Without FTL communication, Operation Sea Change would not have been possible. His orders had kept both vessels, as a reserve of force, well out of range of the planet and RNS *Absalon* in case matters took a turn for the worse. And then he'd sent his picket to the Rock to intercept *Absalon*.

And matters definitely turned for the worse. Samuelson felt like slamming the table with both fists. He imagined how it would feel. His flesh smarting from the impact. His officers would rear back, utterly stunned by his violent outburst. He saw himself lifting the table up on end—even though he knew he didn't have the strength to actually do it—and shoving it and all those mugs of hot caf into the bulkhead. And then he came to his senses. Tolerable *and* Century *had a decisive numerical advantage, the initiative, and the element of surprise, too. What the hell had gone wrong?*

Samuelson knew the rules of warfare. The first one was inviolable as the rest: one side always loses. He knew that commanders expected losses to happen. He knew real losses often exceeded the best casualty estimates. He knew his lot as a Lusitanian commodore was to cope with fewer ships, fewer men, and to rise to the occasion in the service of queen and country.

And rise to it I shall, he thought.

Samuelson continued to sit quietly as the room filled to capacity. When the last seat found an occupant, he rocked forward in his chair and stood to address his people.

"You all know why you are here. Two warships from this task force are no longer with us. Now we know why."

Every back in the room sat up a bit straighter. Most gaped at him as they struggled to grasp the enormity of his words. A few risked glances to fellow officers, all of whom looked confused.

"*Tolerable* was lost with all hands." The silence in the room was palpable. "We managed to find a small number of the lifepods from *Century*; they were picked up by the *Mako*." Samuelson nodded briefly to the *Mako*'s senior officer, Captain Trumage.

Shock and indignation made its way around the table, and a low mur-

mur slowly swelled until it filled the room. Samuelson raised his hands and spoke over the cacophony until only his voice was heard. "We found a debris field of sufficient size, plus the survivors to corroborate both ships' destruction. How *Absalon* managed to take our vessels in a battle that was heavily weighted in our favor, and what our response should be, are matters I wish to discuss with you." Then Samuelson sat down.

The way Samuelson said "you" made it clear to every officer present that his response was already decided. This meeting was merely a formality to ensure everyone was on the same screen. It was the Lusitanian way. The CO was expected to come to the table with his mind made up. It was the job of his subordinates to change it.

Captain Lindsey Trumage, a short woman with spiky brown hair and a thick waist, raised a finger. "Sir, I've been studying what little sensor data we have of the wreckage. I've also interviewed all of *Century*'s survivors on my ship, and their stories corroborate what we already know. *Tolerable* and *Century* were powered down, and they were hiding in the shadow of a large asteroid. They should have been invisible to *Absalon*'s sensors. Obviously, *Absalon* found them or both ships would be here, with us. I believe the most pressing question we need answered is how *Absalon* detected our ships in the first place."

"That, Captain, is a most disturbing question," Samuelson conceded.

Commander Bertrand Hawkwood from the *Black Prince* cleared his throat to speak. At 115 kilos, he was by far the weightiest officer present, with a wide chest and a matching voice.

"Go ahead, Commander."

"Sir, we could be looking at a simple systems malfunction, maybe radiation bleed from a fusion plant due to faulty shielding. Or a stray asteroid that generated a hit and gave away our ships' locus."

Samuelson shook his head. "No, I've thought of similar possibilities, Commander. While I agree with you in theory, my gut tells me we're looking at something else entirely. Those crews were full of veterans. Oh, I know, hiding in an asteroid belt is tricky work, but this one isn't particularly dense, and our ships were positioned along its edge. Stray asteroids are easy work for an alert crew with grav-nets—it's simple catch and release—and even several sizable asteroid strikes may not have given either ship away. As for radiation bleed, *Century* and *Tolerable* are relatively new vessels, and both saw dock time less than three standard months ago. Faulty shielding so soon after yard dogs? It's possible, yes—but probable? I think not."

Hawkwood shrugged his massive shoulders and sat back, lost in thought.

Captain Regina Vines of the *Merryweather* brought her hands together and leaned forward. Neatly trimmed eyebrows flanked a severe nose. The light in the room caught the amber flecks in her eyes, which made them appear to dance with fire. Scuttlebutt said she was headed for her own TF and a commodore's star, soon.

"Commodore, if I may?"

Samuelson nodded. He'd hoped, even expected, Regina to weigh in. She'd recently wrapped up a stint at the Ministry of Weapons, where she'd contributed substantially to Her Majesty's missile doctrine. Her white paper on marrying stealth technology to a recon drone platform was trickling down to the assembly plant. Barring the unforeseen, the first prototype would pass out of clinicals in less than a month and the first warships would deploy with the new birds another eighteen months after that. None of Samuelson's officers were privy to this at the moment, nor did they know of the classified reports from neutral merchant vessels, which documented odd sightings of the same Republican warships, system after system, which seemed to be following the same merchant ships while staying out of sensor range. As the reports mounted, the Ministry of Naval Intelligence had come to its own conclusions about just what was going on and how the Republic was probably doing it. The Republic had stealth-capable drones.

Commodore Samuelson knew the scuttlebutt was actually true.

Vines continued. "Sir, during my stint at the Ministry of Weapons, I . . . ran across some information, which may suggest the Republic has equipped and deployed a new generation of recon drone with a miniaturized version of their Invictus-class stealth suite. Up to this point, we've primarily deployed drones in theater on a ballistic course to prevent detection, which severely limits their usefulness. Obviously, without a powered flight pattern, once a drone is launched, it must stay on that course or risk detection. But a drone under power is maneuverable and infinitely more valuable, and a drone possessing stealth technology . . . well that's nearly priceless." She scanned the room for effect. "We can all imagine the ramifications for any future engagements between our forces and the Republican Navy if this information turns out to be true."

Samuelson nodded for her to continue. Commander Hawkwood whistled and cut in. "But Captain, Commodore, the mass-to-power ratios make what you're suggesting almost impossible. The energy requirements alone are prohibitive. Marrying a stealth suite to a recon drone would require an enormous, continuous power supply, perhaps as much as a shuttle or light LAC, and in a platform as small as a drone?" Hawkwood crossed his arms. "I don't believe it's possible. We can't do it, and Republican technology is roughly comparable to our own."

"True, Commander," Captain Vines said, "but, with any technology, time and experimentation leads to breakthrough, which translates to two things: evolution or miniaturization. And both typically evolve in tandem. What if the Republic *has* found a way to do it?"

"Then *Absalon* could have dropped a drone right on top of our ships," Commander Hawkwood added.

"Precisely," Vines confirmed. "If, *if*, the 'Publican cruiser launched a drone under stealth, that could possibly account for her having found our ships. I'm sure Captain Tamanend and the *Tolerable* tried to sucker her well within energy range to destroy her with beam weapons. But he ended upon getting suckered instead and was fired upon before he could get his vessel's active defenses up."

Vines took her time scanning the room. "What we're looking at, ladies and gentlemen, is a preemptive strike," she said with finality as she barred her teeth.

"But how would *Absalon* know to launch the drone in the first place? We still haven't answered Captain Trumage's initial question," Hawkwood interjected as he pressed the matter.

"No. We haven't," Vines said. "But improved recon drones go hand in hand with the improved sensors and the telemetry required to track them. Maybe *Absalon* saw through *Tolerable*'s stealth, or *Century*'s? Or maybe *Absalon* saw just enough to make her suspicious.

The room fell silent. Then one by one each officer present turned to look at their Commodore.

"For what it's worth, I believe Regina's theory is probably correct. I will say as much in my official report."

Commodore Samuelson let that sink in. It was rare to hear a senior Lusitanian commander cede any advantage to his enemy, no matter how likely it was that he indeed possessed it.

"But right now, how *Absalon* pulled it off is largely beside the point. We know *Absalon* is back; she microjumped into the Montanan system, just 135,000 kilometers from Montana, which is a remarkable piece of celestial navigation, I might add. The ship made orbit, and then all hands abandoned her. The sensor net we left behind has reported back since, and no further traffic has entered Montana's space since. The planet is vulnerable."

"Sir," Commander Victoria Perez of the *Mastodon* raised a hand at the far side of the room. Perez was from Saigon. Petite, with a slender face and almond-colored skin. Her eyes were more brown than black, and her hair was auburn. An altogether striking combination that never failed to turn heads.

"Why come back to Montana? Why not run for help?" Perez said.

"A very good question, Commander, and one I've been puzzling over. I'm afraid the answer may not be to your liking, or to mine for that matter."

"Another ship jumped out for help," *Black Prince*'s captain stated flatly. Captain Jeremy Taragon was among the tallest assembled. He was thin, with a spidery appearance that made him look both frail and alien. But anyone who'd seen him spar in the ring knew better. He was both spindly and lethal.

"Possibly, Captain, though I doubt it. *Absalon*'s been operating alone for months. The single-ship picket fits with the Republic's SOPs for plebiscite systems, particularly for planets as far out in the verge as Montana is. To our knowledge, no jump-capable vessel has left Montana in the last standard day. There aren't many in system anyway. Montana's government declared a state of emergency and commandeered them, so for the moment they aren't going anywhere. But there's always the possibility of an outlier, I'm afraid," Samuelson replied. "Either that, or *Absalon*'s crew felt she couldn't handle an out-of-system jump and decided the best she could do was get home. I believe it was probably the latter."

"We may have another problem, sir," Second Lieutenant Viany Kiriloff said. Half the room turned around to peer at the young officer, who stood behind his commodore and wore two small stars on each collar point.

"Go ahead, Lieutenant," Samuelson said with genuine interest. It was a rare lieutenant who dared to offer his commodore advice in preaction briefings, particularly with so many captains and commanders present. It was a trait Samuelson openly fostered in all of his officers, regardless of rank.

Kiriloff's even voice did the young officer proud. "We left a lot of miners stranded, sir."

"Yes, we did, *Lieutenant*. We may be making a bid for this system, but we are not mass murderers."

"Commodore, I didn't mean to . . ."

Samuelson raised his hand and cut him off. "I know that's not what you meant, Viany. You just happened to be in the way of this old spacer's wrath. My apologies. Please, continue."

"No need, sir. Well, ah, like I said, we fired on a civilian installation and left those miners for later. Some will say we left them to die. Thankfully, Captain Tamanend got his report off before the *Tolerable* . . ." Kiriloff's voice trailed off and he cleared his throat. "Captain Tamanend's report could not have been clearer. We know he intended to rescue the miners, at least before we learned about his ship's destruction. We know he fired preemptively to prevent them from launching their LAC, which would have been suicide. But . . ."

"But the Montanan's and the Publicans don't." The hard edge in the commodore's voice was unmistakable. "No, they won't see it that way. They won't believe that by firing on the station we saved lives, either. Those fools were powering up an oversized LAC and meant to take her out to meet us. It would have been a massacre . . . for them."

Kiriloff nodded stiffly and retreated back to the wall.

Prior to the briefing, before the first of his officers had arrived, Commodore Samuelson had swayed in his chair, reconstructing the events in the asteroid field. The *Absalon* had likely settled into a parking orbit about the mining station, made emergency repairs, and evacuated the miners. If they did get word out, the Empire could be staring at a war-crimes accusation. Firing on civilians violated at least a dozen interstellar laws, not to mention what it meant for the treaty in place between the Lusitanian Empire and the Republic of Aligned Worlds. It wouldn't matter how he'd try to spin it or what his real intent was. He was the TF commander, which meant he might be disavowed by his government in order to allow Her Majesty to hide behind plausible deniability.

"Lieutenant Kiriloff has made a chilling point. I believe our problem is twofold." Samuelson summarized. "First, we have a PR nightmare waiting to happen. We need to get ahead of it and get our own story out before this thing bites us in the heel."

Samuelson turned to face his most senior captain. "Regina, you're the best person for the job. I'm sorry." *And I'm doing you a favor, my dear. If this op goes south, you'll be out of the way and your career will survive.*

The captain sighed and nodded.

"I know you're not keen on running from a fight, but I won't need you to lob missiles for me. *Absalon*'s out of commission so the system is ours, and your seniority and expertise in drone technology will be vital to explaining what happened here. Please transfer your Marine contingent to the other ships and make haste to Saint Helen's Naval Base in the Antwerp system. We need to get word to the sector commander and request immediate relief. I'll transmit my official report within the hour, which will include an after-action summary and the detail of our side of this wretched story. We were, after all, fired upon first. Godspeed, Captain."

"Sir, Captains, Commanders," she said as she stood and left the room.

To the remaining officers, Samuelson said, "When we make Montana orbit, we'll deal with the second problem piece by piece. Why they didn't scuttle *Absalon* is a mystery to me. While I'm sure they wiped her data core, I'm equally sure that they secured her sensor data, which will eventually surface unless we get to it first. There might be a hard copy somewhere, but our main priority will be infiltrating Montana's planetary net. We accomplish that, and we'll find our sensor data and track it to its source.

"If we can get out ahead of this thing with our version—and Regina will see to that—and secure matters on Montana, we might just win the media war and push Montana into our corner of the 'verse."

Samuelson turned toward Kiriloff. The young lieutenant nodded and trotted off to his quarters. He had very little time to craft a compelling and slightly biased report of the past several days.

"The remaining units of CRURON Thirteen will microjump back to Montana," Samuelson continued. "Once there, I will file an official complaint with the office of the president and demand to know why our units were fired upon. Since we will be down two ships, we will have presumably taken on the survivors of the others, and our ships will be packed like squids, our environmental plants tasked beyond specifications. Which will give me the justification I need to request liberty."

Several officers were clearly unhappy about the situation, which Samuelson duly noted and addressed head-on.

"Captains and Commanders, I don't like it either. But at this point, we have little choice. Let's be honest with ourselves. Our presence here *is* an act of war. This system barely has a pot to piss in, but its astronomical location might well make it as critical as a core world. We secure this system, and we effectively pull in another seventeen light-years of territory with it, creating a strategically important buffer between the RAW and us. Failure here isn't an option."

"And once we're there, sir?" Commander Hawkwood asked cautiously.

"I'll request temporary quarters for our people until a transport can reach our location. This will give us an excuse to shuttle most of our Marines to the surface, get friendly with the locals, wave the flag, and defend the honor of the queen."

Samuelson took a sip of his caf before continuing.

"Then, we'll wage our own media war. The locals need to know that their dear Republic fired upon our vessels without warning or provocation. The 'Publicans won't expect us to make the accusation in the first place, and it will have the benefit of being essentially true. Let's not forget that they did fire without warning. The initiative will throw them off-kilter. Until I can get to the bottom of things as the official representative of Her Majesty's interests on Montana, I'll have no choice but to stay in orbit until matters are resolved to the queen's satisfaction."

"What about the miners, sir?" asked Commander Perez. "We have to assume they made it home."

"Yes, we do. It will come down to our word against theirs. But Montana is a big planet. Accusations will fly. Emotions will grow out of hand. Many will be frustrated and confused, all of which will work to our advantage. We will be the side of reason. We'll state matters plainly, without emotion or rancor, and let their miners and the Republican Marines get hot and do something foolish. We'll push their buttons until someone gives us the excuse we need to seize the planet for the safety of her own people."

Forty

"He said what!" Promise rocked forward in her chair and onto her feet. Her chair smashed into the wall behind her. President Buckmeister stood in the doorway of her office, arms crossed, angrier than Promise had ever seen her.

"Samuelson is claiming your warship attacked his vessels without provocation." Annie's voice shook. "According to his story, *Absalon* fired on his ships without warning, which resulted in their destruction. And he's claiming his remaining vessels are overcrowded with the survivors and his environmental plants are straining to keep up. He's requested liberty for his Marines and Sailors, a secure location on the surface for temporary housing, and he's offered to pay for all of the expenses until additional vessels arrive to ferry his folks home."

"And he just demanded to speak with you?"

"Not in so many words. My assistant, Saxena, took the call. Samuelson was cordial but to the point. He said that he, and I quote, 'wished to avoid a potential misunderstanding that could lead to more hostilities.' Saxena took him to heart—smart girl, that one—woke me up with my best blazer in one hand, my independence boots tucked under her arm, and a cup of steaming caf and a tube of lipstick in the other. I've never been a kept woman. God only knows how I'd do my job without her." Annie nodded toward the other chair in the room. "You mind?"

"I'm sorry, Madam President. Please sit down."

Annie smirked. "Don't go formal on me. And don't go digging a ditch only to bury yourself in it, young lady." The president leaned back, crossed her legs, and sipped her caf. Steam rose, and the pungent smell of freshly roasted beans punctuated with cinnamon filled the room.

A young woman, singing an unfamiliar melody, came walking down the hall and into the room. She placed a file on Annie's lap and gave Promise a second cup of hot caf.

"Cream and sugar, Lieutenant Paen, just the way you like it."

"Thank you, Ms. . . . ?"

"Ankit," she said as she headed for the door. "But please call me Saxena or Saxy."

Her head was the last thing to disappear.

Promise followed her voice down the corridor as it faded away.

Annie opened the folder and briefly scanned the contents. She handed Promise a copy of the transcript of Samuelson's call. Several terse words stood out against the text: "preemptive," "without cause," "misunderstanding," and "war."

"We did fire on his ship preemptively," Promise said as she looked up at Annie. "But *with* cause. Did he mention that his ships were hiding in ambush? Did he mention that we gave the second ship, HMS *Century,* due warning before engaging her? Or that *Century* nearly took us out? Annie, his story is a lie, and you and I know it. How did he explain firing upon the mining station? Did the miners attack him, too?"

"Actually, his response is rather convincing. He said he dispatched two vessels." Annie looked down at her file and then back at Promise. "The HMS *Tolerable* and *Century*—he dispatched both ships to the asteroid field to play what he called one-on-one." Annie raised an eyebrow. "A mock battle, correct?"

Promise nodded.

Annie clicked her tongue. "He says his ships contacted the Rock and made their presence and their intentions known. Then, shortly thereafter, one of his ships suffered a temporary power failure, and the second ship was assisting with the repairs, which, according to the Commodore, is the reason both vessels were 'keeping station' when you detected them. At that point, Samuelson said the lamed vessel—ah, *Century*—contacted the mining station again and explained the situation. This time, words were exchanged, which devolved into threats, and the captain of the *Century* said he detected at least one LAC drive powering up, which is when *Century* dispatched a wing of LACs to the station. Samuelson's arguing he fired on the station's bay doors to prevent the miners from launching what he referred to as a 'suicidal act of lunacy.' He's claiming his actions saved lives."

"He's lying . . . through his teeth," Promise said. "He fired first, on the mining station, and then he left the miners to die in space. We responded to their SOS."

"And that's when he says *Absalon* fired upon his vessels."

"So we not only fired without provocation, but we fired on a wounded vessel not under her own power," Promise summarized tartly. "What about *his* wounded?"

"The most seriously injured are headed to Saint Helen's Naval Base with Samuelson's report," Montana's president said.

"Perfect," Promise said. "Just perfect."

"Can't say I disagree with you. I'm afraid this is what we rancher types call a mess of night clouds. It only takes one to touch down and wreck your holdings. But we've got a sky full of 'em to deal with. I've got the word of my miners and your Marines against a Lusitanian commodore with three starships in orbit around my planet. We are as defenseless as a penned mare in breeding season. And the Rock's data core crashed shortly after the incident. Mighty convenient, if you ask me. There's no recorded proof to dispute Samuelson's version of what happened."

"I've got *Absalon*'s sensor data to dispute it!" Promise snapped back.

"Yes, you do, but that doesn't cover the altercation between his warships and the mining station. Samuelson says he has his own sensor data taken from his search-and-rescue operation, plus the survivors, to corroborate his story."

"Let me guess. He won't let us interview his people."

"Nope. He considers us or at least you the aggressors. He's keeping his survivors and the rest of his wounded in orbit and will ferry down other personnel to Montana's surface to free up space aboard his vessels."

"But this story will never stand up under scrutiny, and . . ."

Annie held up both hands, palms forward. "Yes, it will. We've got a case of 'she said, he said' and three boatloads of firepower pointing at us, which more than tips the scales. Montana is a big planet and there's a mess of people across her continents who hate—literally hate—the 'Publicans and the Lusies. You take my point? Until we can get the truth out—the real truth—you're fighting a political battle and spin, and the vids are going to eat you alive. Remember, a lot of the locals have come to respect and even like you and your Marines, some personally, but all of that goodwill has pretty much stayed here in Landing. Most of my planet—most of *your* birth world—still distrusts the Republic."

Annie went on. "You know the saying that people will believe whatever sounds right until they hear something else? That works in reverse here. Folks have come to expect little of the Republic, and they're used to thinkin' of you as a negligent bunch of snooty, inner-sphere elitists. Sorry, but it's true. For Montanans, it's tough to believe anything but that. The commodore's spinning a clever tale that feeds into our misconceptions. It has the ring of truth, right down to his request to evacuate some of his men to the surface due to overcrowding on his ships. You did fire first, and you're still here to talk about it. Tell me how I refuse his requests and save face with my constituents? I might as well resign from office. And if my own people don't show me the door, I'm sure the good commodore will be happy to oblige."

Promise raised her cup to her lips and nearly burned her tongue, thinking hard about what Annie said. She gingerly took a few sips that sent welcome comfort down her throat. It mixed with the anger and stomach acid churning at her core. As she cupped the mug, she felt her hands heat up. *Too hot and you can't drink it. Too cold and no one wants it.*

"I guess we give him what he wants, Annie. And a whole lot more," Promise said, nostrils flaring.

"I've seen that face before, young lady, and it spells trouble. Spill it."

"I was thinking a dance, or maybe a carnival, was in order. A good Montana welcome. Grant them liberty. In fact, as the senior Republican officer on the planet and the effective head of your military and militia, I officially recommend that you invite Commodore Samuelson's command for a little socializing. Let the local brewers show off. Let's give his Marines and Sailors a chance to reveal their true nature and give the locals an opportunity to get to know the real Lusies."

"And?" Annie asked.

"And we convince Samuelson that he should think twice about invading our planet."

Forty-one

Annie, Saxena, and Promise sat conferring in the president's day room. Montana's sun had dropped below the horizon hours ago. A small table held a tray for finger foods and two highball glasses filled with generously sweetened tea. But for a few crumbs, the platter was bare. The tea was gone, exposing mostly melted ice in a bed of sugar crystals.

Promise nearly choked on the last of her iced tea before setting it down. "I'm sorry. You want to bring their Sailors and Marines down to the surface and help them out of their skivvies?"

"That's right, Lieutenant," Saxena replied. She cocked her head, tapping several commands into her datapad before looking up. "Yes, that's exactly right. If I may, ma'am, I'm not tackling the problem as a Marine Corps officer. I'm approaching it as a young co-ed. Sure, their Imperial Marines are soldiers and trained killers, but first and foremost they're men. All men have certain needs."

It was all coming down to skivvies, breasts, and libidos, and Promise didn't like it one bit.

Unlike the RAW, the LE had a relatively small number of women in its uniformed services, and the male-to-female ratio was close to twenty-five to one in the Lusitanian Navy, and almost 150 to 1 in the LE's Marine Corps. A quarter century ago, Lusitanian women had finally won the right to enlist. A few had become officers. But the Empire still strongly discouraged women from serving in the Marines, and those who did filled staff positions well away from the front lines. The LE's female Marines weren't lookers, either. Lusitanian women with prospects married, raised a family, or entered professions like medicine, education, or one of the sciences. In the Lusitanian Navy, the men made war, alongside a small number of women with similar talents.

Promise sat back in her chair, clearly worried. "I don't know, Saxena. Showers? Really?"

Saxena nodded and crossed her arms. "Yes, ma'am. *Real* showers."

"Showers," Promise restated. "You can't be serious."

"Do Republican warships have showers?" The way Saxena asked made it clear that she already knew the answer.

"Yes, but they are a luxury. We mostly use sonic scrubbers to conserve water."

"That was my understanding, too," Saxena said. "A good, hot shower will take a lot of the fight out of a man and soften him up for the likes of me."

"Wait a minute. I thought we were keeping the likes of you"—Promise said, tracing the air generously—"far, far away from these jarheads and their man-brains."

"Once the beer starts flowing and dark comes out, my friends and I will be long gone," Saxena said.

"Right." This was about the most ridiculous thing she'd ever heard. All she envisioned was it backfiring on them all . . . and several young women getting raped in the process.

"Lieutenant, consider what I'm saying, beyond just the obvious. We'll welcome the men proper-like, hand out guest bags: a softened towel, a bar of soap and tasteful pinups, and fresh fruit. We'll quick-wash their uniforms while they shower and then send them to the arboretum for a pint. Then, we'll disappear; you'll have happy spacers who got a good look instead of hundreds of pent-up, space-sick men."

Promise still didn't like it. "There's way too much room for something to go wrong. One of your girls could find herself in a bad situation."

"I can see to it that there's no chance of *that* happening," Annie said. "I'll have Jean-Wesley coordinate with Landing's police chief. Several dozen uniformed Rotary and some plainclothes, too, to patrol the grounds. We can circle the showers with barbed wire, subtle and friendly-like."

Annie slapped her hands. "And we'll post signs where they can't be missed. 'Rape is a capital crime on Montana, punishable by *castration* and life in a work camp.' This will be fun."

Promise's eyes nearly popped out of their sockets. That kind of frontier justice shocked her inner-sphere, adjusted, egalitarian view of life.

Annie and Saxena nodded in unison. "So" Saxena said, " the way I see it, we give them some jollies, bathe and feed them, and send them off stuffed and happy. If they get out of line, that's what prison is for. Or the brig, right?"

"We do *that,* and we'll just be giving Samuelson a reason to pull the trigger," Promise countered.

"Maybe." Annie bit her lip. "We already know the commodore is looking for that reason, Promise. But he can't argue with us locking up drunken Sailors, or Marines who can't keep their hands to themselves. If he does, we might as well provoke him with a stein and a jail cell, on our terms, and try to steer this situation to the outcome that we want. The more of them behind bars, the less we have to shoot."

To Promise, the room suddenly felt a lot colder. "Madam President, I'd hate to be the commander that squared off against you."

"All right, then." Annie stood up, ending the meeting. "I'm due to talk with Chief Krause and Jean-Wesley in a few minutes. Saxena, I'll let you get back to coordinating the welcoming committee. Promise, you're with me."

Annie, Promise, Chief Krause, and Jean-Wesley worked through most of the night, selecting the best locations to deploy the Landing PD, the Rotary, and Promise's Marines as inconspicuously as possible. Promise lit up when the chief offered her ten unmarked armored vans from a local security firm for her and her Marines to travel in. The gunny made the assignments. Two Marines in mechsuits per vehicle, with a reserve of another half dozen Rotary members riding shotgun and armed with modern weapons. She was shocked by the number of Rotarians already deployed throughout the city.

"Fifteen hundred? We weren't able to train that many."

"No, we weren't," Jean-Wesley replied. "But those that were trained gave the rest a crash course. It's the best we could do."

Promise nodded. They were all doing the best they could do, which still left a lot not done, as well as a lot of vulnerable areas around the city. But they had been able to secure the most critical spots, including the congressional buildings, the president's office, key power relays and communications nodes, and the spaceport.

They were as ready as they were going to be. Promise prayed it was enough.

Forty-two

Promise looked skyward as six cobalt-black, light attack craft plummeted through Montana's atmosphere. They overflew the city in a flying V formation before circling back to land the old-fashioned way, one by one, using the full length of the runway outside the college grounds. In a world of VTOLs, the old-fashioned touch and taxis made a bold statement.

He's coming in smarter, Promise thought. *If the LZ looks wrong, he can just punch it and go. Well done, Commodore. You don't trust me, and I don't blame you.*

The LACs reached the north end of the field, turned, and taxied to a stop. Hatches opened and unarmed Imperial Sailors and Marines dressed in the black and red of the Lusitanian Empire poured out. They immediately reminded Promise of Montanan fire ants. As they formed into ranks, Commodore Samuelson walked to the front of his lines. A Lusitanian Marine Corps lieutenant colonel shadowed Samuelson's port side at a respectable distance. Both men's chests glistened with fruit salad. The two men reached the head of their formation, and the colonel barked out, "Ten-*Hut!*" Hundreds of boot heels clicked together as a battalion of starched arms flew upward in a show of respect. Samuelson returned the millenniums-old gesture. Then he smartly turned on his heels to meet the Republican delegation.

Very nice, Commodore, Promise thought. *Go ahead and get your pomp and circumstance over with. I hope you like mine just as much.*

As Samuelson and the colonel approached their hosts, Planetary President Annie Buckmeister, Promise, and Gunnery Sergeant Tomas Ramuel stood their ground at the center of the field, waiting.

Commodore Samuelson pondered the large group of men assembled at the far side of the landing field, standing at attention. He guessed their ranks to be close to three hundred, a formidable unit for a neobarb world, and a much larger Marine garrison than he had planned for. He flexed the muscles in his right eye in a learned pattern, which made a hundred meters appear to be no more than ten. Upon closer inspection, he realized he wasn't looking at a modern formation of Marines at all. What he saw was an irregular assembly of men—*and women,* too. Most held antiquated weapons with rifle stocks made out of what appeared to be a facsimile of wood. *No, not all of them.* He spotted the frame of a modern energy rifle, and then another. Samuelson's eyes narrowed in concentration. He looked once more at the young Republican lieutenant that waited to receive him. *She's armed them.* The lieutenant met his gaze evenly, a fact that slightly unsettled him. He'd met other women in uniform from other star nations, but he'd never been received by one. The handgun on her hip looked irregular, too, and it struck him as a cheap shot from a little girl who was probably on the rag and one mood swing away from creating a conflagration.

As he approached his hosts, Samuelson made a point of noticing their sidearms while masking his displeasure. Wasn't this supposed to be a diplomatic function to discuss matters of state? As the guest nation, he and his men had come kitted out and unarmed, in a display of good faith. His weapons waited in the LACs behind him, which were at the moment a considerable distance away.

Now wait a minute. She's got one, too. A cursory inspection of the woman Samuelson recognized as Montana's president made him reconsider his assumptions. Perhaps weapons were customary on a backwater planet like the one he found himself on, and if that was indeed the case, his aide had missed a glaring fact in his brief on Montana social and political customs. *I'll have to have a chat with young Viany about this later.* Either way, it really didn't matter. What did matter was that they were armed. *And I'm not!*

Samuelson carefully schooled his face to radiate confidence and genuine interest. He turned to Lieutenant Colonel Saloman, who was faring worse, concern written all over his face.

The Republican lieutenant spoke first. Samuelson's eyes blinked twice, a tell he'd never quite mastered. He had expected the president to make the formal introductions. He covered his astonishment quickly as he was led to yet another conclusion. *If this is to be a military engagement, so be it.*

"Commodore Samuelson. I'm Lieutenant Promise Paen, commanding officer of Victor Company. Welcome to Montana." Promise extended her right hand, which Samuelson took and squeezed harder than protocol dictated.

"Thank you, Lieutenant. This is quite a welcoming party."

Promise smiled broadly. She'd seen his eyes briefly flicker to her side-arm and his mouth tense ever so slightly in response. "Indeed. Your visit was most *unexpected,* too." Promise thought she saw a trace of amuse-ment dancing in the commodore's eyes. Whether it was a small admis-sion of the truth or for some other reason, she couldn't tell.

She released Samuelson's hand and turned to the colonel. She snapped a parade-sharp salute to the decorated officer, one that he returned with equal amounts of panache and surprise. Promise was pretty sure she saw gratitude in his eyes, too. Then she turned to her right. "Allow me to in-troduce President Anne Buckmeister and my second in command, Gun-nery Sergeant Tomas Ramuel."

Commodore Samuelson nodded at the gunnery sergeant and quickly introduced Lieutenant Colonel Krystian Saloman. Then he took Annie's right hand in both of his.

"Madam President. It's a pleasure to meet you. Thank you for playing hostess. Considering the recent hostilities and the grievous losses my com-mand suffered, it is a relief and a great comfort to be upon solid ground again."

"Commodore Samuelson, I am truly sorry for your dead. As for the hostilities you mentioned, I feared your request to visit the surface may have been nothing more than a pretext for an invasion. Thank you for coming unarmed."

If Annie's bluntness surprised the commodore, he managed not to show it. "Why Madam President, I hope, if anything, this evening proves the purity of our intentions as official representatives of the Lusitanian Empire. As promised, my men left their weapons behind. I believe what happened between my vessels and the Republican cruiser was both re-grettable and something to be avoided in the future, at all costs."

Promise saw Annie open her mouth. She prepared herself to hear her president dress down the senior-most uniformed officer in the Lusitanian military present. She ended up surprised and all the more impressed when Annie edited her words, choosing a more congenial response instead.

"Commodore, I am relieved to hear you say that. I'm afraid that convincing me that you mean what you say may take some time. But perhaps tonight will help to redirect our relationship onto a more productive course."

The commodore gushed relief. "Madam President, I certainly hope so."

Annie slipped her arm into the commodore's and began to escort him to a small receiving area beneath an open-sided tent, where members of the Congress and senior officials from her administration waited. On her way, she turned toward Promise, looking rather pleased with herself.

Promise watched as Montana's head of state herded an aggressive foreign military officer like a head of cattle, talking niceties with him while simultaneously planning to ram a bolt through his skull if he stepped out of line. Promise wondered what nasty surprises Samuelson had in store for Annie and for her company of Marines, too.

Lieutenant Colonel Krystian Salōman dismissed his men, many of whom were already distracted by the horde of women disembarking from a wheeled transport at the far end of the landing strip. Then Saloman met Lieutenant Promise Paen's gaze, and he found a calm professional staring back at him. He'd been surprised at her military courtesy, and her salute had nearly made him piss his dress black and reds. And, if he was being completely honest with himself, he was grateful to the lieutenant for it. After all, he meant her no ill will. He and she just happened to be squared up on opposite sides of the line in this particular sandbox.

As if she sensed his appraisal, the lieutenant gave him a curt nod and then turned to watch his men, which gave him the opportunity to observe her directly.

"The man has wandering eyes," Sandra said.

Promise saw her mother out of the corner of her eye, standing next to the colonel. And she saw Saloman give her a once-over. Her jaw tensed.

This is exactly the sort of thing I expected from a male-chauvinist Lusie pig. I had hoped for—

"At least he's being discreet about it," Sandra added, though there wasn't much heart in her words. "That says something about the man."

Yes, it says he's a male. Chauvinist. Lusie. Pig!

"Maybe, dear. Do go easy on him. I suspect he hasn't been this close to a pretty woman in months. And he's not used to seeing curves in uniform either."

Point taken. But I'm not—

"I'm glad to see you acknowledge the obvious. He has a kind face, too. And your tailoring is spot-on. Modestly seductive, even. Makes it hard for a man not to rise to the occasion."

Great, I better do something about that. *I'm an officer, after all, and—*

"There's nothing wrong with making a statement, you know. You can lead and look good, too."

Stop interrupting my thoughts.

"I'm just saying. Please lighten up." Sandra cocked her head. "Hmmm—he's taken a keen interest in your GLOCK, too, or maybe it's your tail he's drooling over? I can't really tell from this angle." Sandra followed his line of sight to its target, and her lips turned upward. "Definitely your rear, dear."

The longer Saloman observed her, the farther south his eyes traveled. Lieutenant Paen had a small but interesting rack behind her mess dress short-waist jacket. Her trousers hugged a shapely rear, then flared at the knee and cinched above a pair of glossy boots. His eyes refocused on the curve of her derriere, and his mouth went dry. His uniform grew hot, and things started getting cramped down there.

Krys, you're a queen's officer and a Marine, not a frogging private who's looking to get his ashes hauled. There was also Maureen to think about. He hadn't seen her in more than six months. Thirteen faithful years. *I'm, sorry Mauri—you deserve better than this.* The holovids she'd made for him had helped a lot. He played them several times a week, in the privacy of his quarters. Version A, if he needed some TLC and QT from the Alpha unit, and version B for slam, bam, thank you, ma'am! *Hang on Krystie—here we go!*

Maybe I'll play B when I get back to my quarters, Saloman told himself.

That's right—let your Mauri feed you. Later. Right now, get your gear to-gether, Saloman. Time to lock it down. Saloman turned slightly and reposi-tioned himself. When he was righted and shipshape, he looked back at the lieutenant and tried to focus on three and only three matters: first, he was a *queen's* officer and a better Marine, and, woman or not, Lieutenant Paen wore the uniform of an officer from a belligerent star nation; second, her cold eyes said "trained killer," and he'd do best to remember that; third, she'd shown him respect, and he was, by stars, going to repay it in kind.

With his libido squared away, he started paying attention to the little details he should have noticed all along. Like the lieutenant's beret. Only LE special forces wore them. Regular Marines and Sailors wore the tradi-tional barracks cover with the quatrefoil embroidered on top. Berets flew in the face of hundreds of years of military tradition. Saloman thought berets were for the pricks in SPECOPS and lesser military traditions like the Fleet Forces of the RAW.

Just like the 'Publicans to toss tradition to the wind and go it alone.

Promise turned to face the colonel and caught him in the act.

"So, Colonel, a chit for your thoughts."

She followed his eyes to the GLOCK strapped on her thigh and de-cided to offer him an olive branch. "She's been in my family a long time. Nice piece, isn't she?"

It took Saloman a moment to catch on. But when he did, his shame got the better of him. "She's a beauty. I'm sorry—I couldn't help but notice. I've only read about them in the histories."

Promise thought she caught his double meaning, and this caused her to reevaluate her second impression of the man. *An apology—interesting.* She met Saloman's eyes directly and said, "I appreciate that. Thank you."

Saloman nodded uncomfortably and returned his attention to the parade field. It suddenly looked very different. He watched waves of estrogen rolling through his ranks as virgins in sheer sundresses passed out wel-coming baskets and batted their lashes. His hard-trained, hard-earned spit and polish was being pussy-whipped before his eyes. Saloman turned back to Promise and saw something else. *That's the look of satisfaction.* Lieutenant Paen was no longer just a woman or an enemy officer. She was the real deal, a citizen-warrior adept at battlefield tactics both on and off the field, and Saloman realized he respected her for it.

First round to you, Lieutenant. Well played, he thought.

Promise tapped the colonel on the shoulder and handed his basket to him personally. Saloman recognized the apology on her face. The basket included a note, which he read, read again, then a third time as he looked for what wasn't there. He glanced up at Promise and scanned the grounds for hidden dangers.

The card inside said:

**Welcome to Montana, members of the 57th Lusitanian
Imperial Marine Battalion
Please enjoy our planet and the following festivities:
Sauna and Shower
Nor' East Beer Garten
Dinner Featuring Local Montana Fare
Your Basket of Sundries and Parting Gifts**

"I like the bit about parting gifts," Sandra said. "Nice touch."

Promise rolled her eyes.

"Lieutenant Paen, your kind reception of my men is most appreciated and . . . unexpected. You have my sincere thanks," Saloman said.

Promise nodded smartly. "And you'll have mine, Colonel, providing your men behave themselves," Promise replied with a crooked grin.

"Well, Lieutenant, you have my word on that count. My shore patrol will ensure that any of my Marines that don't keep it zipped will lose a stripe and their liberty," he said with measured sarcasm.

"Hmmm, the signs are rather pointed, aren't they?"

"I'd say that's putting it mildly, ma'am," Saloman replied with a genuine grin himself. "The virgins in white were a nice touch, too."

Promise cocked her head and took a hard look at the colonel, one he returned matter-of-factly. He *was* trying to be professional. Ogling aside, there wasn't a hint of disrespect in his words or tone of voice. And "ma'am" was a term for a superior. *Why are you using it?* Was it out of deference to her rank as the senior Republican officer on the planet or out of some arcane code of chivalry? Or both? Saloman was proving to be not at all what she'd expected from a male-chauvinist Lusie Marine Corps officer.

Are you trying to tell me something? And if so, what is it? Perhaps I best find out.

"Colonel, I'd like this visit to be a positive one for both of our militaries. It's not everyday that Marines from our two corps meet each other on such pleasant terms, let alone get to socialize together."

"That's true, ma'am."

"Nor, if you don't mind me being so bold, did I expect you to pay deference to an officer of my status."

"Well, Lieutenant, we may not have many women in our Marine Corps, but you're the senior commander here, and I'm your guest. I believe common military courtesy should rule the day."

"If you say so, Colonel. You'll have to forgive me a second time if I find that a bit hard to believe." Promise decided to tip her hand a bit. "I'm afraid I know of no other way to say this without being undiplomatically blunt. What happened in the asteroid field wasn't at all courteous. It was a downright premeditated act of war, which resulted in a lot of unnecessary deaths, on both our sides. So, Colonel, why are you and Commodore Samuelson really here, and what are your intentions?"

Promise watched her words land hard in Saloman's gut. Anger flashed across his eyes, and what might have been a flicker of embarrassment. If it was, he quickly erased it from his face.

"Ma'am, I'm afraid I can't speak for the Commodore."

"I understand that. I'm coming to respect you as a reasonable and honorable man, Colonel, one that's willing to cut through the bull. So, let's do that."

"All right, just what did you have in mind?"

"Why don't we take a walk? I'd like to introduce you to some good people."

"Introductions?"

"Mmm, mostly ranchers and farmers, and members of the militia, too."

Militia? Her last word set off a screaming alarm inside Saloman's head.

Forty-three

Master Sergeant Kofi Achebe sat at a wood table nursing a local micro-brew, a head taller than his fellow ratings, all of them subordinates and most of them buddies from the HMS *Piedmont*. He hadn't been dirtside for months and hadn't seen a girl up close since reporting for this cruise nearly twenty-five weeks ago. He'd enjoyed ogling the little brunette who welcomed him with a flirtatious smile, one that promised more but he knew wouldn't deliver. As quickly as she'd said hello she'd disappeared, which hadn't surprised him either. *I wouldn't let my daughter, if I had one, near most of the enlisted sea donkeys I serve with either.*

Now, all Achebe saw were men, a lot of tall, beefy local men wearing leather boots and holstered weapons. And the more he looked, the more he found. They were everywhere, manning the food and beer stations, all the exits, and even the crapper. *Can't blame the locals, really.* Things hadn't gone well among the asteroids. He'd half-expected beams to fly when they landed. Not pretty women to stare at, fresh food to eat, and blessed ice-cold beer.

"So, Master Sergeant," Staff Sergeant Sam Johnson said from across the rough-hewn picnic table. The bald non-comm had stripped off his mess jacket and cuffed his shirtsleeves. Both forearms were muscled and brightly inked, right down to the wrists, and they made up part of a much larger "body suit" that was almost complete. He'd have tattooed his head and neck, too, if the Regs hadn't forbidden it. He had tattooed his tongue and was careful to keep it in his mouth. But his words had a way of getting away from him. "What do you think is really going to happen, even with the locals playing nice? Probably shaking in their backwater boots, if you ask me. I hear that 'Publican cruiser *Absalon* opened up on two of ours and destroyed both. She killed a lot of our Sailors in the process and didn't bother searching for our lifepods either."

"Staff Sergeant, do you believe everything you hear? Let me ask you something. How many ships did we arrive with? And how many did they have? You do the math, and it doesn't add up at all. The way I hear it, their ship was so badly crippled they barely rescued themselves."

"Well, I hear this Lieutenant Paen of theirs is a loose warhead. She's probably cycling and just a cramp away from pulling the trigger herself."

"Sam," Achebe said, since it was just beer and the guys and they were headed down that road, "just because their lieutenant has a vagina doesn't mean she doesn't have a pair. I've met your mother. The way I hear it, she pussy-whipped your daddy on the first date, and he never recovered." The table filled with laughter as Sam turned brick red and stood.

"Sit down, Sam." When he didn't, Achebe stood with his palms up. "All right, just cool it. I meant it as a joke, but probably went too far. I was an ass. Apologies?" he said, extending his hand in a truce.

"Yeah, all right," Sam replied. "You're my best friend, after all."

"I'm your only friend," Achebe pointed out. Sam's anger melted away as the master sergeant thought more carefully about his next words. "Don't underestimate their commander—this Lieutenant Paen—just because she's a woman. I've spoken with a few of the locals, who shared some interesting scuttlebutt about her. If even half of it's true, then Paen's a warrior, regardless of what's not flopping between her legs. She apparently hot-dropped into a swarm of very well-armed and well-financed pirates and took out over a dozen of them on her own, before she landed in the infirmary herself."

Staff Sergeant Johnson rolled his eyes. "Whatever."

"Pirates, Sam. A well-financed outfit on a neobarb planet like Montana, Sam. With modern weps. If she took out even half a dozen on her own, then she's no slouch."

Johnson grew quiet and crossed his arms. "Well, I don't buy it. She's a woman, and women have no business in uniform or in battle."

Achebe was about to respond when Lieutenant Colonel Saloman arrived, sending all the non-comms to their feet.

"As you were, men," Saloman said.

Achebe saw worry on Saloman's face, though no one else at the table seemed to notice. He'd seen that look in the colonel's eyes before, back in the Mudwater Campaigns on Helios 2. A small and well-armed paramilitary outfit had seized the planet's seat of government and captured the head of state. He'd been with Saloman when the man was just a captain, seen the same intel he had, and reached the wrong conclusions. They'd walked into a trap and barely crawled out with their lives. Now Saloman looked haunted, just as he had on Helios 2 after the dust settled and his men were done dying.

"Master Sergeant, would you accompany me for a moment?"

Achebe didn't ask why. He left his beer on the table and the bottom of his stomach with it.

Forty-four

APRIL 9TH, 91 A.E., STANDARD CALENDAR, 1140 HOURS,
LANDING COLLEGE SOUTH LAWN, PLANET MONTANA

Private First Class Vigor Rhia'an of Her Majesty's Imperial Marines knelt behind a thorny plant, examining the approach to the single-story building, 77.2 meters away. With the sky-blue eyes his mother gave him, he looked for sentries, while his suit sniffed for heat prints and electronic countermeasures. He turned to watch a midsize black vehicle disappear behind a hill.

The home was set in a wide clearing and was large enough for a family of four or perhaps six. A two-lane road ran the length of the property. *Quaint,* Rhia'an thought. But he knew better. The house was nothing but a shell, a humble ruse. Montana's backup satellite command center and an auxiliary node for Landing's power grid were inside, at the bottom of a deep shaft, accessible by lift with the correct codes and retinal scan. The locals called it the Ice Box. Rhia'an had them. According to his intel, the facility was manned by a skeleton crew of two. They'd just left for lunch only moments ago. But he wasn't sure about the grounds. Surely there were traps, perhaps low-tech, which posed a problem. *How am I supposed to find those?* Rhia'an's job was to infiltrate the facility without being detected and upload a self-replicating hunter-seeker program. The HuS would do the rest.

Three disks appeared on the HUD of his goggles and darted about his field of view like bats flushed from a cave, from the red doorway to the checkered panes and window-well coverings. A few moments later, a soft tone in his mastoid implant signaled the all clear.

He double-checked his readings. The HUD added technical data in the margins: Montana evergreen at three o'clock, thirteen meters, base to crown. A dozen small heat signatures in the highest branches. A local avian species called a russ. A blue-green shrub to the building's left glowed burnt orange—a minor threat because of its thorns, which would easily tear through the microfilaments of his suit. He heard a small animal rustling in the leaves nearby.

Rhia'an nodded to himself and checked again. *In, out, and no one will be the wiser,* he told himself. *I think I'll try the back door.*

Rhia'an duckwalked from bush to bush and winced as a twig snapped. The meshing of his SNEAK suit rippled as he moved, blending him imperfectly with his surroundings. When he stopped, the suit synced with the terrain, making him nearly invisible. Suddenly, he was dressed in thornwood, with it telltale greens and aqua-blues, down to the red spikes dotting his limbs. Unfortunately, the SNEAK suit did nothing to quiet his feet.

He slowly dropped onto his belly and pulled himself forward on his forearms, using his knees for leverage and thrust. A thorn caught the side of his calf, snagging a loop in his suit's meshing. Rhia'an felt the slightest bit of hesitation in his calf and shrugged it off. His suit changed colors again, from the blue-greens of grass and browns of bushes and twigs to the gray-on-gray of the road, right down to the dark fissures where underground stress had reached up and kissed the surface.

The patch of cold caught him by surprise. He'd missed the small bit of standing water at the road's edge. Different mediums radiated heat differently. And SNEAK suits could only do so much to mimic heat differentials, even small ones. Rhia'an swore under his breath as his suit's processor kicked into overdrive.

Unbeknownst to Rhia'an, an enemy whisker fluttered over the grounds, looking for stray Lusitanian Marines, courtesy of the RAW-MC. It happened to be circling directly above the house and PFC Rhia'an, moving in concentric circles. The whisker might have missed Rhia'an had his suit not had a small tear in the right calf the width of several millimeters. Might as well have been a kilometer-wide canyon, because it leaked a small but readably identifiable heat signature of 36.78 degrees Celsius.

The whisker altered course to investigate. Even then, it might have ignored him since the weather was about as warm, except for the water that found the tear in Rhia'an's suit and soaked through to his skin.

Gunnery Sergeant Tomas Ramuel reclined in the van's front passenger seat, nursing a cup of jet-black tea. His helmet was perched on the van's dashboard next to his gauntlets. His driver, a Montana Rotary member named Hale Christianson, sat in the driver's side, tapping the steering wheel while he whistled a tune unfamiliar to Ramuel.

"What's it called?" Ramuel asked.

"A local favorite named 'Steal Away.' Talks about going home and such."

"Humph. Home sounds nice."

"Sure does, no place like it. I don't suppose you get home much."

"Too little and never for long enough."

"You got kids?"

"A daughter," answered Ramuel. "A Marine, too. She's just out of infantry school and on her first deployment, planet Kafertine."

"Wife?"

Ramuel looked over at Christianson and frowned. Small chat was fine and good. The wife made it personal.

"Didn't mean to pry," Christianson said. "Me, I'm divorced. Couldn't stand the woman. Not even sure why I married her. Well, that ain't entirely true. If you saw her, you'd know why," he said. Christianson's eyes glazed over, and a dumbstruck look swallowed his face.

Ramuel chuckled freely. "Women have that way about them. My ex was all kinds of pretty. We just drifted apart. Too many long deployments can do that to a marriage."

Christianson nodded like he understood. He couldn't, not really. He wasn't a brother. Ramuel let it slide, then his HUD chirped. Ramuel bolted upright, nearly spilling his tea, and donned the helmet. A red icon was flashing angrily on his HUD, in a restricted area. *Looks like the Lusies decided not to listen.* His helmet pressurized as he commed the lieutenant. "We've got an unknown contact in quadrant sixty-three, which is near the node." Ramuel flexed his jaw to equalize the pressure in his ears.

"I know and I'm not surprised. Roger, that. Proceeding there now. Ramuel, out." He downloaded a set of coordinates from his HUD to the van's GPS and spun his hands fast, in a circular motion. "Let's roll." Then he pulled on his gauntlets and reached for his weapon.

"Okay, boss. I'm moving," Christianson replied.

The two drove another half klick before stopping by the side of the road. "Pull off here." Ramuel told Christianson to stay put and then he headed off toward the unidentified contact, disappearing into the trees. Private First Class Molly Starns exited the rear of the van where she'd been riding. Starns was a vivacious youngster who reminded Ramuel a great deal of his daughter, Agatha. Starns was also a fast learner and Ramuel was glad to have her with him.

The gunny had the itch. It'd been too long since his last target. He didn't particularly like killing people. But the deeper truth was that he didn't mind doing it either. Not one bit.

The crosshairs of his standard-issue pulse rifle traced the figure crawling across the open road several dozen meters away, stopped at the head, and settled back at the torso. Satisfied with the shot, the gunny fired. Instead of a deadly pulser fire, a broad beam of electromagnetic radiation bathed his target and the surrounding ground, burning through the nanocircuitry of the SNEAK suit. Ramuel smiled as the Lusie abruptly pushed back on his knees, tore his face mask off over his head, and vomited.

Ramuel walked up to the much younger man, who was, at the moment, still heaving up the contents of a late lunch. The gunnery sergeant gave him a moment. Finally, the spy wiped his mouth and looked up at his captor. Anger and a complete lack of fear registered on his face.

Ramuel shook his head disapprovingly. "Son, are you lost?"

"Looks like it to me," came from behind him in an unmistakable Montana drawl. "Maybe he's just stupid."

Ramuel turned slightly to greet a tall militiaman dressed in olive drab fatigues. He'd just stepped out from a cluster of trees and was crossing the road. His face was smeared green and black and his arms cradled an odd-looking shotgun.

"Hello, Jean-Wesley," Ramuel said. " Glad you could join the fun. It seems we have a party crasher here. What would you like to do with him?"

Jean-Wesley Partaine looked down at their captive with a wicked look in his eyes.

"I believe I know just what your lieutenant would do, Tomas."

"I believe I know, too, which worries me. The lieutenant isn't known for her diplomacy."

"No, she isn't, which is probably why I like her so much. That's her Montana roots showing their true colors."

Partaine reached into a pocket and came up with a zip cord. He bent down and scowled at the youngster. "Son, be a good Marine and get to your feet, slowly. Try anything cute, and I'll break that pretty jaw of yours."

"Commodore, it seems I need a word with you," Promise said.

Commodore Samuelson sat at a rough-hewn table with Lieutenant Colonel Saloman and an SNCO Promise didn't recognize. The three men were leaning forward, deep in conversation, when she threw a flashbang into their midst.

"Something wrong, *Lieutenant*?" Samuelson said as he pushed back from the table and stood to meet her.

"Why don't we take this someplace private?" Promise suggested. It was bait the commodore couldn't resist.

"Ah, I don't think that will be necessary. Whatever you believe is this important for me to hear may be said *here*, for all to hear."

"Fine. Here it is," Promise said. She noticed a bit of worry crease the commodore's brow.

"My men just apprehended one of your Marines in a SNEAK suit in one of our restricted areas. Would you help me understand what he was doing there?"

Lieutenant Colonel Saloman looked away. The SNCO gawked at Promise. And to her surprise, the commodore closed the distance with her, got nose-close.

"Anything else you'd like to say?"

Alarm bells went off in Promise's head. Though she hadn't really expected the commodore to back down if put on the spot, she hadn't expected this, either.

"As a matter of fact, there is. How many of your men do I have to apprehend or kill before you accept the fact that this planet isn't yours?"

As if on cue, Jean-Wesley Partaine stepped through the trees at the far side of the grounds, Gunnery Sergeant Ramuel at his side, wearing armor. An embarrassed-looking Lusitanian private first class was positioned in front of them with his hands tied behind his back. Partaine gave the kid a shove forward with his boot. The Lusitanian Marines nearby began to protest, some getting to their feet, a few reaching for weapons that weren't supposed to be there, when a full toon of Promise's Marines appeared, too, wearing mechsuits.

"Now look, fellas," Partaine said as he approached the outer ring of angry Lusies, "I'm not lookin' for a brawl. I just need to speak to your commodore and clear up this mess. Seems your friend here got a bit lost. I'm just taking him home."

"In cuffs?" said a Lusitanian non-comm. "And what are you doing with 'Publican Marines marching in tow, dressed in mechsuits? I'd say you're the one looking for a fight . . . Mister?"

"Senior Chief"—at least Partaine thought he was one, and he smiled as the petty officer's rank registered on his face, causing his temper to calm from a rolling boil to an irritated simmer—"take a good look at what your boy is wearing. Now you tell me what he was doing in a camo suit outside an access point to the city's communications grid?"

The senior chief hesitated and took another hard look at the armored Marines staring back at him through mirrored faceplates. Reluctantly, he stepped aside for Partaine and several tons of man and metal to walk through. Then the senior chief yelled out, "Make a hole so the old man can deal with them."

More Imperial spacers stood as the Republican prison detail marched by. But they kept their distance and held their tongues.

"Commodore, I believe this man is yours," Partaine said as he approached Promise's position. I could lock him up but thought it might be best if he went home with you, in the spirit of neighborliness and all."

The commodore took a deep breath and frowned down at Partaine's hand, which was greased with spittle. Reluctantly, he took it. "I don't believe I've had the pleasure."

"Jean-Wesley Partaine, friend of President Annie Buckmeister. Commander of the planetary militia."

"A militia? I must have overlooked the fact that you have one."

"You don't sound too surprised, Commodore. But you are overlooking several matters."

"And what matters might those be, Mr. Partaine?"

"Like the fact that Montana is under the protection of the Republic. And the fact the Rock is our only operational mining station. At least it was before your spacers shot it full of holes. And neighbors don't go ambushing each other in cold space either. And how about this one: you are guests here. We asked your men to stay on the grounds and not wander off. *Those* matters, Commodore."

"I am afraid that you are misinformed, Mr. Partaine. My ships were fired upon by—"

"Bullshit," Partaine said, which caused Samuelson to turn three shades of red. Partaine turned to his captive. "Hold still, son."

Partaine cut the zip cord with a folding blade, gave him a gentle shove forward. "Your liberty is revoked. I see you in my city again, or anywhere else on this planet, and you'll be seeing the inside of my jail cell. We clear, son?"

The Marine gave a quick nod before he retreated behind Lieutenant Colonel Saloman.

"Mr. Partaine . . . *Jean-Wesley*," Commodore Samuelson, said, "you will not treat me or my men in this manner."

"Sir, I'll do what's necessary to keep my city safe. You keep your boots in line, Commodore, or I'll toss you in a cell, too."

Partaine spun around before Samuelson could think of an appropriate response and stormed between a sea of parting Lusies.

Promise gave her Wolves several quick hand signals. They slowly faded into the background, and headed for their vans. Two followed behind Jean-Wesley.

Promise turned back to Samuelson and extended her hand.

"I believe we have an understanding, Commodore."

"Yes, Lieutenant Paen, we do indeed." Samuelson took her hand and leaned in to whisper into her ear. "You don't have the men or metal to handle what I can throw at you. Cross me and you'll lose." The commodore broke contact but held his ground.

"I just happen to know a thing or three about fighting outmanned and outgunned," Promise said while brushing a spot of dirt from the commodore's shoulder. Shock and indignation registered on Samuelson's face, and to Promise's satisfaction, he took a half step backward. Then she smiled sweetly and leaned in. "Commodore, go ahead and try. It will cost you more than you can bear."

Forty-five

APRIL 9TH, 91 A.E., STANDARD CALENDAR, 0130 HOURS,
CENTRAL LANDING CITY, PLANET MONTANA

"Subtle, Partaine, very subtle," Annie stared at the man until he blinked first. She rocked back and forth in her office chair, lips clamped shut to hold in the tongue lashing Partaine deserved, all 92 reckless kilos of him. "You just had to start a pissing match with their CO. To cap it off, you turned your tail, dropped your trousers, and wagged your comet and stars in his face. Then you scat on his boots. If all that ain't bad enough, you rubbed his sniffer in it . . . in front of his men. What the devil were you thinkin'? It's one thing to challenge a man in private, and God knows he deserved it after sending his man into a restricted area. But you—you kicked him in the privates while the whole 'verse watched you do it!" Annie nearly ran out of breath.

"I won't stand by while this Samuelson cowboy walks all over our planet, taking an almighty shit wherever he pleases."

"Neither will I," Annie said as calmly as she could. "But that doesn't mean you have to pick a fight we can't win."

Jean-Wesley seethed in his chair, without apology or concession. He raised a finger. "And another thing, I—"

"Shut it." Annie stabbed him with her finger. "I'll deal with you later. Promise, please tell me there's good news."

"Ma'am?"

Annie sighed and rubbed her temples. "That's what I thought. Well, did your men detect any more strays?"

"No, m . . . Annie." Promise was almost comfortable calling the president by her first name in private settings. "Samuelson seems to have taken every last one of his Marines and Sailors back up with him. But he's upped the stakes, too. Our satellite grid just went down. He took it out with kinetic strikes. And he released a number of whiskers around the grounds before launching. Our own whiskers tracked a lot of them, but we lost some and they could be anywhere. We've secured our most vulnerable spots. But there are a lot of holes in our defensive grid. Thankfully, Lusie flies are pretty unsophisticated. Tough to cram much capability into a platform the size of your thumbnail. They can't do much physical damage, but they can tap your communications. They can give the Lusies eyes and ears in a lot of inconvenient places."

"Then we're compromised," Annie said. She inhaled and looked around warily.

"Don't worry, ma'am. I posted enough whiskers around your offices, my barracks, the J-CIC, and a handful of other sensitive installations. You can speak freely here." *But not too freely. The hole in our net, which we intentionally left open, allowed one of Samuelson's whiskers in, and it's listening to us right now. Just stick to the script, like we rehearsed early this morning, and you'll be fine.*

"That's small comfort, though," the president said. She shook her trigger finger at Partaine, to remind him he wasn't off the hook for the mess they were in. Jean-Wesley shrugged his shoulders like he hadn't done a thing and stared back. When he blinked first, again, he kicked at an invisible table and swore under his breath.

"You never were any good at that." Annie smiled like a winner.

A muffled "humph" came out the corner of Partaine's mouth, which promptly shut like a barn door.

Then the president folded her arms and grew oddly quiet.

Promise saw a new look on Annie's face, one she hadn't seen before, and one they had definitely not rehearsed. *Not quite fear. Maybe indecision. She's going off-script—uh oh.*

"Ma'am, if I may make a few suggestions."

When the president didn't respond, Promise cleared her throat.

"Sorry. Um . . ." Annie shook her head and waved Promise on.

"Samuelson is gathering intel on us as we speak. He's deciding when and where to strike us." There it was again, Promise thought. *Us.*

"It will be Landing. I have no reason to think otherwise." Promise took a deep breath. "This is the planet's capital and the seat of your government, Annie. I think we need to get you and your administration to a secure location and put a curfew into effect for the local citizenry."

Annie gawked at Promise, clearly struggling to believe matters had come to this. She opened her mouth, but nothing came out. Her head twitched to the side, as if she hadn't heard Promise correctly.

Except you heard me on this exact matter only hours earlier. Your acting is exemplary, ma'am. At least I hope you're acting. Promise felt herself relax, and it occurred to her that perhaps the president had been acting all along and that she had been the one to panic. *Doesn't matter. Just get on with it, P.*

"Do you have a bunker, Madam President? Or a safe house? A fallback position for you and your administration?" Promise threw out the questions just as they'd rehearsed them, too.

"No, not exactly that. Ah—I have a second home up in the Fhordholm Mountains. It's covered in snow this time of year. It was my mother's, but I took control of her estate several years ago after her fall. She's still sharp as a bull's horn, though, and she'd be the first to tell you, too. Age has nothing on that woman."

Promise believed her. If Annie was any indication, age only made Buckmeister women more lethal, not less.

"Access points?"

"The only access road to the place is covered by more than two meters of snow at the moment. A hovercraft or tracked vehicle can make it in but not much else. The chalet is tucked up against two mountains that merge and form a V. The winds coming down and off them can be violent and unpredictable. Even one of your LACs with counter-grav assist might have a hard time of it."

"Hmmm . . . that has possibilities," Promise said. "How many know about it?"

"Few. That home isn't in the public records. It's very much off the grid."

"Annie, it's time you get yourself off the grid, too," Promise said. "With your permission, I'll detach two of my Marines to bolster your security team and give you a scatter comm capable of short-burst, encrypted transmissions. Since the commodore knocked out communications, we'll have to install a few ground-based towers to restore some semblance of a comm net. That shouldn't be a problem. We'll seed Landing and the surrounding areas with towers, too, to add confusion to the mix. We need the extra capabilities, and Samuelson will be hard-pressed to locate you. Our towers are shielded, too. He'll have to focus his sensors on your exact location to even pick up chatter, and the odds of that happening are about as likely as your local sun going nova."

"Don't talk odds with me, young lady. I'm not a gambling woman, but I do believe in Murphy, and he loves long odds. Unfortunately, I don't seem to have much choice. Let's just pray Samuelson doesn't get lucky and flush us out."

Annie pursed her lips and considered Jean-Wesley, who had been remarkably quiet for much of the conversation. "You," she said, "may help me with my luggage. I keep a bug-out bag at the capitol building, just in case. Saxena will show you where it is." Then she shooed him out the door. High above them, tucked into a corner of the room, a Lusie whisker recorded their every word.

Forty-six

The snow fell like a loosely woven blanket, covering the valley and the mechsuit of Gunnery Sergeant Tomas Ramuel with a fresh coating of powder. Ramuel's powered gloves rested against the base of a Montana evergreen, his rifle propped against the tree, locked and loaded. His hands wouldn't last long in the cold. But he didn't need much time, just a few uninterrupted moments to feel the earth between his fingers. Snow would suffice. He knelt down and plunged his hands into the snowpack and sensed the planet's life-force around him. He felt his spirit connect with it as he dipped his tongue into the loose powder.

The universe is God's, and everything in it belongs to Him.

He brushed the snow from his hands and crossed himself, repenting for the women and men he was about to end. To whom he prayed, he didn't really know. It really didn't matter. Tomas knew someone *great* watched out for him. There was no other explanation for the many times he'd gone into battle and come out unscathed. The work of an unseen hand had been present too many times for him to explain it away—far too many for him to count. That wrong turn on graduation night, which had saved his life. Missing his transport to boot camp, which had crashed shortly after launch. The frag grenade that didn't go off.

He raised his hand to his moustache, scraped off the excess snow that had frozen under his breath, and decided his hands had had enough.

With his gauntlets on, he could crush a man's skull between his thumb and forefinger. Without them, an innocent snowball could rob him of the touch necessary to fire his pulse rifle. He took another bite before grabbing his gauntlets and coupling them to his forearms. A soft click told him the seal was good. His suit's heaters began to warm his palms and fingers to a regulation 36.78 degrees Celsius.

"Don't eat the yellow stuff, Gunny."

Private First Class Nathaniel Van Peek lay prone next to Ramuel, his hands caressing the frame of an Assault-class Bi-Polar rifle coupled to a whirly mount. The pad of his gloved fingers nestled the trigger. The rail gun was a heavy weapon and typically part of the weapons mix of smaller stingships and troop transports or a three-man artillery crew. But Van Peek's mechsuit made the lifting easy. It took two unaugmented Marines just to carry one and a third to load and fire it. For Van Peek, it amounted to a small imposition that cut his speed by fifteen percent and required both of his hands to bring the weapon to bear.

"I'll take that under advisement," Ramuel said as he donned his helmet. "You ready?" His mastoid implant carried the question through a secure channel and into the younger Marine's ears.

Van Peek's visor dropped into place. *"Ooh-rah, Gunny. Just give the word."* His voice sounded distant and snowy, which reminded the gunny of just how far away from help they were.

Ramuel scowled at the young Marine from behind his helmet's faceplate. His demeanor softened almost immediately as he remembered his own youth and how young and stupid he'd been once, too. That had changed after his first kill. You never forgot the day you spilled blood, the day you became a Wolf. First blood always changed things. Van Peek wasn't blooded. *He still has a lot to learn. Today will be a good teacher.*

"The word is definitely not given, Private First Class. You know the op. We have the high ground and the element of surprise. Their Marines are expecting light resistance from the president's civilian armed detail and just a couple of our ilk. But we didn't come in light, did we?" Ramuel said. "We will give them the opportunity to surrender. But if they don't, you'll have all the targets your heart desires."

"Between you and me Gunny, I hope they don't."

"If they don't, we're gonna dye the ground red. Are you prepared for that?"

Van Peek didn't respond this time.

Good. He's thinking it through. Ramuel closed his eyes and remembered a particular day in the life of a much younger Marine. His toon had intercepted, lamed, and boarded the pirate vessel the *Majestic*. He still remembered the ship's scored paint and battered hull. The boarding was supposed to have been routine.

Ramuel had just made PFC—a very green boot at the time—and was the first to float through the air lock. The *Majestic* had started life respectably, but her crew had made a decisive career change after completing an unprofitable stint as a merchant vessel, transporting farm equipment to Rim-world colonies. *Majestic* terrorized several star systems for the better part of two months before the RNS *Bellerose* and Ramuel's platoon caught up with her. After heaving to for boarding, Ramuel took point and entered the *Majestic* just aft of engineering, near the ship's secondary collar. His platoon sergeant assigned him to cover the exit while the rest of his toon secured the engines and the bridge. An explosion instantly killed the sergeant and lance corporal. He'd watched his toonmates round the passageway as they ran for the air lock, only to be mowed down by enemy fire.

He'd killed that day to cover his own retreat, and he'd killed many times since in the service to his star nation. Most nights he slept fine. But on rare occasions, usually after drinking too much and wallowing in dark places, he saw the faces of the women and men who died on *Majestic*, haunting his dreams. Or faces of the young men and women he'd later commanded, most no older than his daughter was now, asking him if they could come home. In his dreams, they looked gaunt and lost. They'd followed his orders on subsequent missions and come home in caskets. They were his dead, and their faces never left him. They just faded like old stars. In the moments leading up to combat, he became acutely aware of their faint glow, and he always remembered.

Ramuel laid a hand on the PFC's broad, armored shoulder. "Just remember your training, don't get fancy, and stay on me."

The center of the gunny's HUD shifted as he focused on the valley's mouth below. It was clear of trees and covered in white. He looked upward and into the distance as two LACs appeared above the horizon. Enhanced the image until the designations on their hulls were visible; watched as they came in slow; and then descended vertically, touched down, and sunk into the snow. Lusitanian Marines in arctic gear poured out, their white suits nearly blending in with their surroundings.

He counted a full company of Lusie Marines. Eight toons of eight each, substantially more than the eight toons of five each the Republic used. And all he had was one reinforced toon at his disposal.

For this mission, Lieutenant Paen had assigned him a reinforced toon of six Marines, which he had divided into three squads of two each, one Marine with a heavy weapon, the others loaded with extra packs of Horde missiles. He checked his scanners and confirmed his troops' positioning. They were center, left, and right of the valley, covering all possible approaches to the chalet, except for an aerial drop. Only a crackpot or glory hound would attempt that idiotic move—dropping his men between two mountains in winds that were known to gust up to 225 KPH.

Ramuel smiled to himself and looked at where his arm was, where it should have been but wasn't. They wouldn't find him or his men. He and his troops were running cloaked, a recent upgrade to the mechsuit and still on the RAW-MC's official secrets list. The Bureau of Military Intelligence knew the Lusitanian Empire was working on a prototype, and BU-MIL figured the RAW had an eighteen-month head start, minimum. Ramuel's mechsuit was coated in billions of nanites that took readings measured in teraseconds—light, temperature, wind velocity, humidity, sound—then mimicked it in real time by projecting a holographic skin around his suit. Instead of blending his armor with his surroundings, like a SNEAK suit did, the Cloak imitated reality, and it eliminated his heat signature and any sound he made, too, by slightly phasing the space about him with a Null Field. Simply put, he both was and was not present.

Officially, he and his men were prohibited from cloaking unless they found themselves in dire circumstance. Even then—assuming he survived—he'd have to file an after-action report amended with a Justification for System Activation-15 form, all forty-five screens and fourteen thumbprints. In Ramuel's estimation, bureaucracy and an incompetent CO were the biggest obstacles to a Marine's getting the job done. The Bureau of Personnel could bust him down a stripe and put him on half pay for all he cared. The JSA-15 was worth it. This was one battle he intended to win, without losing a single Marine.

A Lusie with a heavy weapon caught his eye. The gunny shook his head, cleared the ghosts from his active memory, and focused on the enemy down-valley. The Imperial Marines wore arctic tactical gear, ablative vests, and light weapons. *No mechsuits, that's good. Probably worried about too much weight sinking in the snow.* And they were right to worry. If his men had to hump it out fast, there was a very real chance that they might not make it out at all. He envisioned his entire command buried in an icy tomb. Then he forced the thought aside. Sowing negative thoughts would only get him and his Marines killed. The Lusies outnumbered his men almost eleven to one; they had a full company of 64 Marines and all he had was a reinforced toon of six boots. But his toon's mechsuits and heavy weapons mix stacked the deck about even, and he was about to take them with their skivvies down.

He opened a link, and suddenly his voice echoed off the valley walls, which was the general idea. *Hello, Lusies, this is God.*

"Hello Lusitanian Marines. This is Gunnery Sergeant Tomas Ramuel of the Republican Marine Corps," he said instead. "Be advised. You are outgunned and you hold an inferior position. We can see *you.* Pull your cells, drop your magazines, and toss 'em. Lay facedown with your hands on your heads, legs spread-eagle. This is your one and only warning. You have thirty seconds to comply. After that, we will destroy your command. Ramuel out."

"Bet that got their attention," Private First Class Van Peek added.

Forty-seven

"*. . . one and only warning. You have thirty seconds to comply. After that, we will destroy your command. Ramuel out.*"

Master Sergeant Kofi Achebe of the Lusitanian's Imperial Marines nearly creamed his skivvies as he dove for cover without thinking, slammed his back into a large downed tree piled high with snow. Looked left and right to make sure his Marines had followed suit. Then cautiously turned to peer up-valley at the FUBAR he'd just dropped into.

"This is turning out to be a bad, bad day," he said under his breath, to no one in particular. He glassed the valley walls and the A-line roof of the chalet, which the casual observer might have overlooked as just another treetop. Absorbing Montana into the Empire was a matter he understood. He didn't like it, but he understood that his star nation needed buffer star systems between itself and the Republic, because tensions were mounting. No one disputed this, no one. It was just a matter of the right incident and the passage of enough time. For all he knew, he was about to fire the proverbial shot heard around the 'verse. But going after Montana's president like this was a fool's errand. He'd told the colonel in so many words before takeoff, and Saloman had nearly bit his head off. But Achebe didn't think hard of his superior. He knew the colonel better than that, and knew that this op wasn't sitting well with him either. But it didn't matter. He'd been suckered by the 'Publicans, the colonel had been steamrolled by the commodore, and the commodore was going to get them all killed.

Achebe knew better. A whole planet of rugged individualists wouldn't take kindly to their president's abduction. And if the 'Publican Marines holding the high ground came in force, with powered armor, too, a lot of his men were about to die.

Her Majesty's Marines—my Marines—don't need an insurgency piled on top of a planetary takeover.

Achebe ground his teeth in frustration. *This was supposed to be a simple operation, light resistance, in and out.* If Master Sergeant Achebe had learned anything as an Imperial Marine, it was that *simple* didn't exist.

"Give me a full-up scan of the valley. Find them," he said over his mastoid implant.

"Just like the readings we got coming in, Master Sergeant. Nothing," Private Kinsley Malarick reported. She sat at NAVCOM aboard LAC 2. Her hands danced over her holographic controls in a frantic search for the source of the transmission that had asked for their surrender.

Achebe grunted and turned to his second in command, Staff Sergeant Ryck Journere, a tall dark man with cobalt eyes and teeth as white as the snow about them. Journere was busy glassing up-valley, the business end of his sniper rifle looking for a reason to report, teeth bared in what Achebe could only conclude was a very pained expression.

"Staff Sergeant, what do you think?"

"Maybe they have us outmaneuvered, Master Sergeant. And maybe they are bluffing," Journere said.

"And maybe they aren't," Achebe responded. It was Journere's turn to grunt. "Where are they?"

They were too close not to get a read on the enemy: heat or a rad signature. Nothing in the valley walls was generating interference. Their orbital scans said as much, too. A remote broadcast perhaps. *A bluff, maybe. Or maybe not. Why can't we see them? See . . . see. Hmm . . .* The Ministry of Naval Intelligence didn't think the 'Publican's had it, let alone a field-ready infantry version. But they knew the Republic was working on it. Everyone was. The technology was mostly theoretical. But MONI had been wrong before.

Let's be honest, MONI is wrong a lot. It's unlikely, but unlikely is Murphy's specialty, isn't it? And we're talking about the 'Publicans, too. They don't always think conventionally.

Achebe didn't place much confidence in the spooks. He trusted what he could see with his eyes and feel with his gut, and both told him that the 'Publicans were out there. And if they were cloaked, Paen had just tipped her hand in a rather startling way. Revealing military secrets wasn't done lightly. If Paen felt her back was sufficiently up against it . . ."

The time ticked down toward zero. At T minus five seconds, Achebe made his decision. He wasn't wet behind the ears. Valleys like this one were perfect locations for an ambush. Though he thought an ambush highly unlikely, he'd come prepared for one. He never closed a door without leaving a window open . . . just in case.

"All units, execute plan Rebound."

Gunnery Sergeant Tomas Ramuel saw the launch plumes even as the explosions started around him. He turned in time to see the valley walls avalanching and his ride home, hidden under a camo net, crushed by a chunk of ice as large as a house.

"All points, down and out. Leave the heavies and kill every last bastard you . . ." A close call picked him up and tossed him backward through the trunk of a deciduous tree, snapping it in two and showering the snow with splinters. He shook off the blast, grateful that his suit had buffered his hearing and backside, and rolled to his feet. He stole a glance at his heads-up display and grunted in satisfaction; all five dots on his HUD moved in unison toward the mouth of the valley.

Private First Class Van Peek pumped his mechsuited legs in a dead sprint and ordered his AI to ping the rail gun he'd abandoned through a remote link with his suit. The AI brought up the weapon's targeting subroutines and ordered the gun to lay suppressive fire. Primary target, there. Secondary target, there. A split second later, a rain of depleted uranium slugs began pelting the Lusies downrange. Then two more rail guns joined the barrage.

The first slug hit the snow a meter shy of its intended target. Three more followed suit before the rail gun recalculated, fired another volley, and found its targets. Private Zara Dhodolar of the Lusitanian Imperial Marine Corps fell to her knees in penance. Her head exploded and bits of flesh showered the face and goggles of her nearby toonmate. The corporal felt something warm slap his cheek and enter his mouth. He doubled over and started retching as another round hit him squarely in the midriff, ripping through his torso. Two serrated legs stood at attention in a half meter of powder and blood until the avalanche swept over them.

The Republican Marines burst through a stand of trees to the sight of retreating Lusie boots climbing suspended ladders.

"All eyes on the nearest bird. Light her up!" Gunnery Sergeant Ramuel took a knee, dropped his targeting reticule on the vessel's forward intake, and fired everything.

Horde missiles, heavy penetrators, and energy beams knifed into the Lusitanian craft, penetrating armor and the ship's hull. Eight Lusies died in the forward crew compartment. In response, the pilot selected a surface-to-ground missile and fired on Gunnery Sergeant Ramuel's position. As the missile propelled clear of its hard point, a hyper-velocity penetrator hit the missile's nose, and the starboard side of the LAC and every remaining soul aboard perished in the explosion.

Ramuel watched as the retreating bird streaked out of range and dropped below a distant mountain peak. Adrenaline flowed through his blood and pounded in his ears. He forced himself to breathe deeply to help calm his nerves.

The SNCO took a quick visual roll call: *Lance Corporal Zahn Charn, Magellen*. Ramuel swore.

A quick scan located the missing two. Van Peek and Starns had gotten caught in the flow. Starns's icon glowed crimson red. Van Peek's was orange—critical—just less than dead.

"Van Peek . . . Private First Class Van Peek . . . Nathaniel!" Ramuel rushed toward the youngster's location, pushed his rifle to the side as he dropped to his knees, and started digging. *Have to reach him in time. Need to get through this ice, fast. I need . . .* Ramuel rocked backward and keyed his pulse rifle to wide-beam, minimum yield. Fired.

"Hold on, son. I'm almost there." He heard moaning over the comm.

The gunny tossed his rifle aside and smashed through the remaining snow with his powered gloves. He found one foot, then the other, and quickly scraped the last few centimeters of snow and rock off the young Marine. What he found nearly stopped his heart. One side of Van Peek's mechsuit was crushed. Blood oozed from the cracks in Van Peek's armor. His right arm was severed at the elbow collar, his faceplate split down the middle. Ramuel raised Van Peek's visor, and his heart sank. The young-ster's eyes were open and unfocused, and he was panting for air. A deep gash cut across his scalp, and his jaw hung awkwardly.

Dear God.

The gunny tried linking with Van Peek's suit and ran into an invisi-ble wall.

"Corpsman Zahn, I need you proto. His suit's offline. We need to jump it."

Lance Corporal Roxi Zahn came running, and dropped to the other side of Ramuel. Short threads of bleached hair were matted to her skull. Her hazel eyes were flushed with heat. She copied the gunny and withdrew a translucent cable from her wrist's collar, plugging it into the opposite port on Van Peek's armor. Juice started flowing, but nothing happened.

"No good, Gunny. His AI is slagged. We need to crack him."

Zahn reached into her thigh compartment and fished out a laser cutter. Slowly, the azure beam torched through armor until Zahn could wedge one hand and then both into the gap. She pried the chest cavity open the rest of the way. Reaching inside, she jacked into Van Peek's pharmacope. To her relief, the mechsuit's auxiliary MEDSYS spun up.

Van Peek's breathing slowed as the slight wind went still.

"Not much time. Routing his MEDSYS through my HUD, one mo-ment. Almost there . . . almost there . . . got it." A hologram of Van Peek's body materialized next to him, yellows and oranges and reds ranking in-juries by priority. Blue branches spread throughout his body, tracking blood flow. Zahn scanned the body, turned the image on its side, and then back. "His body's crushed. Pulse is erratic. The right lung's collapsed. In-ternal bleeding. Skull fracture. Hemorrhage at the L1 vertebrae. Gunny, I—I don't know where to start. He's—"

"Going to make it," Ramuel said. *"Understood?"*

"Gunny, he's too far—"

"No, he's not. You can do this, Marine. Deep breath. Take it one at a time. Get him stabilized."

Zahn nodded. "I'm going to need a stasis collar, fast."

"I'll comm Primara Hospital. You get him stable."

"All right. Yeah, Roxi, you can do this," she said unconvincingly. "You need to . . ."

An alarm shrieked, jerking Zahn from her indecision. She withdrew a mask and placed it over Van Peek's nose and mouth. Heard it seal and start rescue breathing.

A second alarm whaled.

"Shit. No . . . don't you dare crash on me . . ." And then Van Peek's heart flatlined. Zahn placed a thumper on his chest to start compressions, heard the *whomp, whomp, whomp* as pulsed gravity crashed into Van Peek's heart.

Epinephrine flooded Van Peek's system while energy stroked his heart. His body arched with each shock before dropping to the deck, totally still. The gunny grabbed a nearby stick and shoved it between the Marine's teeth. Zahn deployed nanites into Van Peek's body to seal the major arteries. Dialed the power up a setting and shocked him again.

"Nothing, Gunny." Zahn checked her HUD for life signs. Her voice inched upward. "His arteries aren't sealing fast enough. There's too many bleed-outs."

"*Hit him again.*" Ramuel looked skyward, spoke over the comm. "*I need that collar now. No, that won't work. I don't care what you have to do. He doesn't have time.*"

"C'mon, Nate, give me something to work with." Zahn bit her lip so hard it started bleeding. "God, please. It's not working."

Ramuel looked behind him. "*Just get it here.*" Then at Zahn. "*Lance Corporal, you will keep at it until he stabilizes.*"

Zahn's hands stared shaking. She hit Van Peek three more times. And then she did it again.

"Nothing. Gunny. I'm sorry. I'm so sorry." Zahn's vision was blurred by tears.

"*Do it again.*"

Zahn tried, but her hands were trembling so badly she couldn't key the right sequence.

Ramuel screamed at her. "*Then hit him again, dammit.*"

Van Peek didn't move. Zahn was on her knees, half-covered in snow and blood, hands shivering with cold, tears streaming down her face.

Ramuel took a deep breath and unclenched his fists. He reached over, put his hand on Zahn's, and spoke as calmly as he could. *"Lance Corporal, I'm sorry. One more time. Okay? One more. We owe Nate that much."*

Zahn nodded, took a deep breath. "Aye, aye Gunny. Step back. I'm dialing it to max and hitting him with another dose. Zahn counted down from three. The spike on her HUD startled her. "I've got a blip. And another one. And another. I've got rhythm, Gunny—it's extremely weak, though. What's my ETA on that collar?"

Van Peek's eyes rolled backward as he convulsed. Ramuel pushed him onto his good side as he coughed up blood and vomited. Then he began to groan.

"There, that should do it," Zahn said. A cocktail of painkillers and neuroinhibitors rushed into Van Peek's body and jerked his body calm.

"Hold on, son. I'm going to get you home."

"Ayeee, ayyyeee, Gunnyee," Nate drawled.

"Hush, son, help's on the way. Just lie still."

The gunny turned to Zahn. *"Medevac is en route. ETA: three mikes."* Just behind him lay a metallic object half-buried in the snow, roughly twenty meters away.

"Hold his hand until the medevac gets here."

Ramuel got up and walked toward it, heart in his throat.

He knelt down next to the battered body of Private First Class Molly Starns. A thick blanket of snow covered her up to her neckline, as if she'd treaded water. He reached down and brushed the snow from around her neck. He nearly fell backward when he saw her. He'd seen a lot of casualties, but Molly was different, and her death found a chink in his armor, struck deep. A splinter of stone sat wedged between her chin and collarbone. It had found the chink in her mechsuit's armor, where the helmet coupled to the breastplate, and pierced right through it, nearly severing her head from her body.

Ramuel's body swayed as he held Molly's half-buried gauntlet with both of his. He let go with one hand and pressed a small button just above her temple, retracting her visor. A shock of sweat-soaked, flame-red hair framed her face. He helped her close her eyes one last time.

At least she's not suffering, he thought, though it came as no consolation.

Water pooled in his eyes, and a single tear escaped and fell on the white snow, freezing almost instantly in the cold.

Gunnery Sergeant Tomas Ramuel quietly sobbed over the loss of Private First Class Molly Starns. He was the last to board the LAC with her torn body cradled in his arms.

Forty-eight

"I still can't believe the man came after me like that. What was he thinking?"

"To be fair, Annie, I don't think he planned things the way they went down—the way the gunny made them go down. He probably thought you'd surrender peacefully. I doubt he expected us to use you as bait to force a confrontation with him."

As Annie bared her teeth, Promise got a quick look at the predator beneath the presidential façade.

"At least Tomas made sure they paid for it," Annie said. "I don't think I'll ever forget the look on his face as he carried that young woman in his arms and . . . refused to put her down."

"I've never seen him like that myself," Promise said. "The gunny's a hard man. But he's got a soft side to him. He has a daughter Molly Starns's age. Looks a lot like her, too. I think Molly's death hit too close to home."

Both women sat staring at the other with moist eyes. They'd known each other for less than two months, and they'd buried far too many Marines and Montanans together. A bit of time and a lot of death had left indelible marks and aged them both immeasurably. As Annie put it, they'd been initiated into the club of crap.

"Still," Annie said, "I just don't understand Samuelson coming after me like *that*. He has to know that I'll talk and let everyone off planet know what really happened here."

"Not if you and your administration disappeared first."

Shock registered on Annie's face.

"Twice before, the Lusitanians seized Rim-world planets by manufacturing a domestic crisis. We can't prove it, but a hoard of circumstantial evidence and speculation leaves little doubt. In both cases, the governments met untimely deaths. A bioweapons accident on Herodotus took out the head of state and most of his administration before a crucial vote on RAW annexation in the Senate, and a shuttle crash on Coralin claimed the lives of virtually every member of the national assembly—a crash involving an unregistered civilian shuttle carrying an abnormally large quantity of fuel, which had the misfortune of plowing into the central government building during a presidential address to the planetary congress. In the aftermath, the Lusitanians moved in and declared both planets Imperial protectorates."

"Promise, we can't keep doing this forever." Annie tried to lighten the atmosphere. "And I don't know how much longer I can handle hiding on Jean-Wesley's ranch. Sending me here instead of to my mother's place didn't do me any favors. Believe me." Annie's voice dripped sarcasm. "The ranch dredges up memories of he and I doing things that I'd just as well forget. Well, there was that one time." Annie shook her head. "The man has a nice backside, but he can be a Montana jackass and a . . ."

Promise held up both hands, cutting her off. In point of fact, she was one of the few people close enough to Annie to get away with doing so.

"I don't want to know, ma'am. Some things are best kept private," Promise said with a lopsided grin.

"Fair enough. I have to give it to you, Promise. You read Samuelson just right."

"A bit of luck. A lot of it, really. Going after you was fairly obvious. Samuelson knew you weren't in his pocket. With you talking, he risks an interstellar incident. Either that or being court-martialed and shot by his government for going off the reservation."

"And what do you think the commodore is up to at this moment?" Annie asked.

"He's utilizing every asset at his disposal to track down your location,"

Promise said. "Without you, he's up to his neck in it and about to get a mouthful."

Annie smiled, a true genuine smile, which pleased Promise and brought a smile to her own face. Then, both women started chuckling, which turned into belly-busting laughter that blew the tension out of the room and capped off what had been a bloody and hellacious day.

Forty-nine

APRIL 10TH, 91 A.E., STANDARD CALENDAR, 2300 HOURS,
HMS *INTREPRID*, MONTANA ORBIT

Commodore Samuelson sat in his ready room, reading Lieutenant Colonel Saloman's after-action report. Saloman had mishandled the entire operation, badly. Getting half of his men killed merited a beam in the head, and Samuelson had half a mind to pull the trigger himself.

He rubbed his face, hard. How had things gone so off course? Clearly, the intel his whisker had gathered in the president's office had been planted. *Which led me to the wrong conclusion.* He didn't know where Annie Buckmeister or her staff was. It was possible she was buried underneath meters of ice, but he didn't think so. The 'Publicans had known he was coming, which meant President Buckmeister had known, too. She was hiding somewhere else, somewhere she thought was safe.

Which means she could be anywhere on the planet.

A soft chime sounded near the bulkhead door.

"Come."

Samuelson watched his Marine BAT-CO enter stiffly, stop in front of his desk, and salute.

"You requested to see me, sir!"

"Yes, I did. Thank you for coming so quickly. We have much to discuss."

Lieutenant Colonel Krystian Saloman prepared himself for the long fall from grace he was sure was coming, a fall he wouldn't recover from. A "light" colonel in Her Majesties Marines came fast when a commodore of the Imperial Navy and the task force commander told him to. The commodore hadn't offered him a seat or told him to "stand easy," which didn't bode well for where this conversation was likely to go.

After a few moments, and much to the Saloman's relief, the commodore pointed to one of the chairs opposite him. "Sit."

Saloman chose the center seat facing the commodore and squared up to meet his CO's wrath head-on. *The old man's going to rip me a new one, reach in and pull my insides out, and space what's left through a missile tube.*

"Colonel, your handling of this mission was, to say the least, disappointing." Samuelson shook his head slightly. "It leaves me with grave misgivings about the ground situation we currently face," Samuelson said, tossing his minicomp on the tabletop and folding his hands together.

Saloman had a few choice thoughts for the commodore's latest brainchild, too. He acknowledged his failure with a curt nod. "I understand, sir."

"Really?" The commodore leaned forward. "Then you'll understand why I'm sending you back down to the planet to reclaim the initiative and finish the job. But first, what I want you to tell me is if you believe you can do that. Can you, *Lieutenant* Colonel?"

The way the commodore used Saloman's full rank—emphasis on "Lieutenant"—made Saloman think that if things didn't turn out right, he'd never make "full bird."

Can I? I'd like to show you what I can do, sir, Saloman thought. But what he said came out a bit differently. "Yes, sir. I can, sir!"

Saloman blinked and waited for the bad news to drop-kick him into tomorrow.

"We need to secure the president and her staff. But she's in hiding. Find her. Mobilize your battalion and have them standing by, ready to launch on a moment's notice. I want options. Draw up battle plans for securing the city of Landing and get them to me by 0800 hours. I want the president's office and the congressional buildings locked down. I want their net disabled. I want the Republican Marines neutralized. We will deal with their militia if necessary—hopefully, we can convince them to lay down their arms and assist us in restoring peace to the planet. Once you've accomplished all of that, I want a curfew in effect for the city of Landing. But first, I need options to consider. Battle plans. By 0800 Understood?"

Saloman cleared his throat. "Sir, how will I explain our actions to the locals, without provoking them?"

"I've already released a statement and given Montana's president two days to respond. We picked up reliable intelligence indicating her life was in jeopardy. In response, we felt it was our duty to send a small contingent of Marines to ensure her well-being. We were met with augmented Republican Marines that butchered our men in response to our kindness. We cannot stand for this gross abuse of power, nor can we sit idly by in orbit while the Republic circumvents accepted interstellar laws and abuses its power and position on this planet! We have no choice but to declare martial law and restore order."

Saloman blinked.

"Your orders are to secure the government and neutralize all Republican military personnel and assets."

"I assume you intend to allow them to surrender, sir?" Saloman asked, to cover his own backside, in case he found himself court-martialed. *Which is exactly where I'm headed.*

"Of course, Colonel," Samuelson said, baring two perfect rows of white teeth. "But personally, I hope they don't get that chance."

Fifty

Promise set her empty mug down, already her second of the morning. It was still dark out. The pace of events and too little rack time was wearing her thin. Just like her command. Thin. *Like a piece of plexi. There are too many critical areas on this planet to defend and not enough Marines to cover them all.* Less than a week had passed since her altercation with Samuelson outside the beer garden. The botched presidential abduction had occurred merely two days ago. There was no doubt in her mind that Samuelson would return. The question was not if but when, where, and how. She leaned back in her chair, crossed her legs, and patted her GLOCK. With Samuelson up there, she knew her service pistol should have been in the holster. But she felt more at ease with her senior.

"It had the same affect on me, too."

Sandra sat on the opposite side of her desk, leaning forward and smiling warmly.

"When did Grans give it to you?"

"I was eighteen and packing for Landing to go to university. Grans said a young woman needed to pack heat. She told me in no uncertain terms that my six-shooter wasn't "adequate to the task." Then she handed me a duffle with it inside and four loaded magazines of hollow-points and told me her semi-auto—*my* semi-auto—would make any boy think twice."

"I wish I'd known her."

"Me too, munchkin. How's my girl holding up?"

"I'm trying, Mom, but I'm getting desperate." Promise looked up. "Sir, if you're there, I'm up against it."

"Desperate prayers are the best kind . . . because they're honest."

Promise nodded. *I'll give you that.*

"I'll give you something else. There's a time for everything—a time to live and a time to die." Sandra's expression grew serious. "But, dear, until you're dead, you're not. So stop acting like it."

The knock at the door was right on time. "Come on in." Her mother disappeared as Sergeant Sindri and Seaman Fingers walked in.

"Morning, Lieutenant," Maxi said.

"You both look like you're up to something." Promise noticed their disheveled appearances and a day's growth of facial hair. "Did either of you bag some sleep last night?"

"No, and for good reason. Jiggers and I stayed up playing with an idea, which is why I woke you so early this morning. I think you'll like it. Like it a lot, actually."

Promise crossed her arms and leaned back in her chair. "This sounds promising. Gentlemen, please take a seat. You have my attention."

"All right, Jiggers, why don't you share your idea with the Lieutenant?" Maxi said as he sat down. "It was yours, after all."

"Jiggers now, is it? Well, he got us out of a very tight spot once before. I've come to think quite a lot of his ideas," Promise said, speaking of the man as if he wasn't in the room. She turned her gaze to the ruddy young Sailor who hadn't said a word.

Seaman "Jiggers" and the newly promoted Sergeant Maxzash-Indar Sindri were a study in contrast. One man was the short, muscled Marine she trusted with her life. The other was a freckle-faced tomato on a stick who had, overnight, acquired a reputation as a tech whisperer. The description was accurate, too. After all, Jiggers had nursed a broken warship home and saved Promise's entire command while doing the seemingly impossible.

Promise smiled at the engineering apprentice. *'Jiggers'—nice work, Maxi. Always making new friends. God knows we need more of them, and I could certainly use more than one of you, too.*

"Well, ma'am," Jiggers began, "I asked the sergeant if I could play with the LACs on-board sensors. I wanted to try and tap into *Absalon*'s net and see what, if anything, was still operational."

"And how did you expect to accomplish that without *Absalon*'s command codes?" Promise asked. "*Absalon*'s captain and every officer aboard her died in our exchange with the Lusitanian warships. When command passed to me, so did the codes. No one else has them." The words came out sharply. She hadn't meant to dress the man down, but hacking a warship's net was a capital offense. *You better have a good explanation.*

Jigger's voice broke through in a rush of words that sounded more like a confession than a status report.

"Ma'am, I hacked into her net and overrode her security lockouts because . . . I had to try. We're up against it, ma'am, and I just had to see if I could help." With that off his chest, Jiggers sank back in his chair, exhausted though the day had only just begun.

"Jiggers, you are a man of many talents. I won't ask you to explain how you came by such skills. At least not now," Promise said. "But I assume whatever you found is the reason for this meeting. So please . . . enlighten me."

"Aye, aye, ma'am," Jiggers said. His voice cracked on the "ma" and scraped across the "am."

"You were saying . . . ," Promise said evenly.

"Uh, yes, ma'am. Right, ah, like you'd expect, most of *Absalon*'s systems are smashed. Hardware reduced to scrap. Code scrambled. Most of her net is down, too, and her auxiliary power is almost depleted. But a few of the weapons are still operable, and there's enough juice to fire them under local control."

"Which is a problem," Promise said, thinking out loud. "We have no one on that ship to fire her weapons manually. You already know I won't risk sending someone back up there. Which means you've figured out something else you shouldn't be able to do. Am I correct?"

"Yes, ma'am. I believe so, anyway."

"Why am I not surprised?" This time she couldn't help but smile.

Jiggers turned red in response.

"That was a compliment, Sailor."

"Well, uh, thank you, ma'am."

"Seaman Fingers, never hesitate to accept praise," Promise said. Then she opened her hands, palms up, for him to get on with it.

He cleared his throat. "Several weapons are still operable—three missile tubes, to be exact."

The revelation stirred something deep within Promise's core. She rocked forward in her chair and stole a glance at Maxi. He nodded back enthusiastically.

"And?"

"Well, ma'am, as you said, we don't have anyone aboard *Absalon* to fire her weapons manually. So anything we do must be done remotely. Which was a problem before—"

"You hacked the ship," Promise interjected, with a twinkle in her eye.

"Aye, ma'am. Before . . . before that. I began to think about that problem and how to solve it. After tinkering a bit, I wrote a simple program that I could upload from your LAC's computer to the *Absalon* using an encrypted microburst transmission. But a program without a data core to store it on and a computer to run it is pretty much useless. That's when Maxi here, uh—the sergeant, ma'am—suggested something really clever. What about using the launch tube as its own data core and processor? Which is ingenious, really. Tubes have built-in microprocessors that are normally slaved to the ship's net. They are hardwired into the net, but all launch tubes come with virtual backups. If the net goes down, the tubes can be accessed and operated manually, which frees up a lot of memory on the data core. This should theoretically free up enough space on the weapon's microprocessor for other purposes. Since we're not on the ship to input the commands directly, it's really a simple matter of writing a basic targeting program and a command sequence and uploading it directly to each tube. If we give the tubes a remedial education, they'll be smart enough to run the program. I can use the LAC's sensors for targeting."

Promise sat forward. "You know this will work?"

"No ma'am, but I *believe* it will work. I'd like to try. All the ship's weapons are hardwired to the net and are accessed the same way. But there is a virtual backup port, which can be accessed if you know the command codes . . . or, ah, how to hack a warship's net." Jiggers swallowed. "The worst that happens is we get a bad firing solution and miss or the weapon doesn't fire at all. We put *Absalon* in a geosynchronous orbit before we abandoned her. According to your LAC's sensors, the Lusie ships are about fifteen hundred kilometers off her starboard bow and holding station, which gives us two missile tubes with a direct line of sight and the third with a parabolic flight pattern."

"Jiggers, I'm distressed to know a capital ship can be hacked so easily."

Suddenly, Jiggers's nerves were back in full force.

Promise held up a reassuring hand. "That said, you've managed to start my day off with some very good news. And for that, you have my sincere thanks. Please, upload your program and keep me apprised of your progress."

"Aye, aye, ma'am!" Jiggers refolded his hands awkwardly and threw Maxi a hesitant look. The sergeant gave him a "might as well tell her everything now" response.

"Seaman Fingers," Promise said, "are you farther along with your scheme than you first led me to believe?"

Jiggers raised his shoulders and danced his eyes about before meeting her question head-on. He gave her a nervous nod up and down, then up and down two more times.

"Exactly how far along?"

"Ah, along about ready to fire." Jiggers dropped his eyes to the deck and then added, "ma'am."

Promise looked up. *Wow, sir, that was fast. Thank you.*

Promise heard her mother whisper into her ear. *Told you so.*

"See, I told you you'd like this . . . a lot," Maxi said.

"All right." Promise stood up and motioned to the door. "Why don't we head to the LAC and see what kind of targeting solution you've got for me."

Fifty-one

"**. . . which gives us three** full salvos and two partials."

Promise frowned at the sensor plot. She had a paltry number of birds to throw at Samuelson's ships, and nowhere near enough to take them all out.

"The forward tubes will fire simultaneously. Those birds will come in together for a coordinated strike. But the third tube is on a different plain. We'll be firing three birds simultaneously, but they'll be staggered in a two-one pattern. Wish I could synchronize them for you, but I'm afraid the code necessary to accomplish that is more than the launchers can handle."

A solitary green dot sat adjacent to three red icons, right where they were supposed to be in standard parking orbit about the planet, and just a hair over fifteen hundred kilometers from a very nasty surprise.

"At close to point-blank range on ships sitting with cold drives and unsuspecting point defenses, it may not matter."

"I believe you're right, ma'am."

Promise turned to the young rating. "Seaman Fingers, tell me this. Which ship is larger?"

"You mean which one is Samuelson on?" Jiggers said.

"Exactly."

"Can't be sure with this gear, ma'am."

Promise shrugged. "Then we'll just have to guess. Three staggered salvos and three ships. We don't have enough birds to take them all. I doubt we'll get off the third launch before they return fire and destroy what's left of *Absalon*."

Promise cycled through her options and settled on the ship closest to *Absalon*. She stabbed the screen. "Concentrate fire on this vessel. She's the right flank of their formation, the closest to us, and will benefit least from her sister ships' countermeasures. Throw everything at her."

"That will leave two very angry siblings, Lieutenant," Maxi interjected.

Promise nodded. "Can't be helped, but with a bit of providence, we'll have one less ship and at least one less company of armored boots to contend with. If we bleed them enough, perhaps they'll concede the day."

"Do you really think so, ma'am?" Jiggers asked.

"Nope." Promise slapped Jiggers on the back and interjected as much humor into her voice as she could muster. "But we are going to try and sway them."

Promise straightened up and headed for the LAC's hatchway. She stopped at the top of the gangplank and turned back to face her subordinates. Each man returned her gaze with equal measure. Suddenly, the moment felt sacred to them all. *Duty, Honor, Republic.* They all understood the call, what it asked of them each, and what it might ask of them still. They didn't say good-bye, for veterans never did.

"Stay here, close to your comms. Plug in your firing solutions and work to refine them as best you can. I need to make a few calls and confirm all of our assets are ready for a ground war."

Promise took a deep breath and bared her teeth. "All right, gentlemen—good hunting."

Fifty-two

The hour of reckoning followed a predawn thunderstorm, heavy rains, strong winds, and transient clouds stippled in shades of gray. By the time the sun crested the horizon, it had completely dissipated into an eerie calm. *Too calm.* Promise wondered if she was standing in the eye of the storm.

She surveyed the Mall, the seat of Montana's government, reviewing her preparations with her own eyes, knowing her planet would rise to this occasion as she did or else fall on the sword of her miscalculations. She wondered if, in the end, anything she did could defeat what was coming.

The fear of the unknown hit hardest. She spotted a small distant cloud near the horizon, lonely in a sky of blue. She looked up into the face of a great man. *Sir, we're not going to make it, are we?*

A tall statue of Montana's founder and first president, Matthew Hein, overshadowed her, reaching well beyond where she stood and crossing over a small pond. The arm extended west, reminding all Montana's citizens that hope was out there, just over the horizon. The sculptor had captured President Hein during his second term in office, when Hein's streaks of gray had overtaken a full head of otherwise jet-black hair. Shades of bronzes and browns colored the man's likeness from head to boots. Saddlebags hung over his shoulders, reminding all who saw the statue that Matthew Hein had been a working man first and foremost.

All about her, Landing's citizens casually sauntered by as if the day was, in every way, ordinary. But their faces and the guns they wore told an entirely different story. Sidearms were common enough in Landing. Shotguns and high-caliber rifles suggested all was not well.

She'd been furious to see them, not that she could really blame the people for staying. Most of Landing's population had opted to remain in the city and not evacuate it as she had ordered. Trying to round them up would have been futile. Only an act of Congress could technically force them to leave—Annie had made that point very clear—and Montana's Congress had rebuffed the suggestion. Virtually every elected official had also stayed to defend the capital.

Promise's eyes drifted from the likeness of Matthew Hein to the top of a nearby high-rise building, which sat adjacent to the Supreme Court. Three heavy Bi-Polar rifles and a small tracking array sat atop a modest high-rise's southern corner, each mounted to a whirly platform. They constituted all of her antiaircraft assets. Each gun was tied into her remaining LAC's command and control links. Jiggers sat at NAVCOM, several klicks away in the LAC, providing her with a thin screen and targeting solutions. Maxi manned the guns. Hopefully, they'd score on one or more of the LACs Samuelson was sure to send against them. If Maxi took even one in the air, it would go a long way toward evening the odds for her Marines and Partaine's Rotary on the ground.

Promise stood in the shadow of a great man and bowed her head. She prayed for her Montanans and for her Marines. She even prayed for the enemy and for a good death—theirs.

Seven minutes later . . .

"All systems nominal, ma'am."

"Good. Now do it again."

Her AI ran a full diagnostic on her suit for the second time that morning. It was a habit she'd acquired after her first tour in the Semus system. She'd been the fifth member of a toon running customs on the spaceport circling Bellanor, a Rim world with a severe axial tilt and violent weather. Pirates had struck there, too, ones less sophisticated than the Lusitanian-sponsored proxies she'd encountered on her birth world. She'd ordered her AI to run a complete diagnostic on that morning, too, but only one, and a glitch in a simple subroutine had looped where it should have returned. A second check might have flagged the anomaly and rerouted her sensors through her secondaries. Instead, she'd found herself in the blue flame of a firefight when her HUD died, leaving her without a targeting system or communications. She never wanted to be "gun blind" again.

Again, her mechsuit's systems blinked green. Nominal and ready for Promise to call upon them. Promise checked her scanners and saw the dots. Her AI handled a quick roll call, and all of her units acknowledged ready, including Maxi, who was manning the LAC with Jiggers. Her other LAC was down with an engine problem they didn't have the resources to fix. And *Absalon*'s spare was with the president and key members of Congress, on the opposite side of the planet, just in case. Her company was about as thin as it could get: one LAC, one stingship, and twenty-eight Marines, including her.

A blinking yellow starburst appeared on the upper right corner of Promise's HUD. The gunny. She turned to her right and looked down a gentle slope until she found him, about twenty meters in the distance.

Promise lased Ramuel's mechsuit, which established a direct, more secure channel with the much older SNCO. "Go ahead, Gunny."

"Lieutenant, with all due respect, I don't care for your AI. He's got a geobyte complex. Couldn't you give him a standard Republican accent? He sounds like a highborn Lusie prick."

"Gunny, he's not a Lusie. He's a Brit, from . . . oh, never mind." Promise sighed. "I like the voice, okay? It's calming. Just let it go." *She almost made it an order.*

"AI bonding. I've heard of that." Ramuel started laughing. *"Seriously, ma'am, if you don't mind me asking, what's the backstory? What's a Brit?"*

"Someone from Great Britain, of course—a nation from Holy Terra. Pre-Diaspora. Long gone, I'm afraid. I have a crush on Mr. Bond's handgun, by the way, not him. I've always wanted a Walther PPK. But I'll never be able to afford one, not on my salary, even if I could find one for sale. There aren't many floating around the 'verse."

"All seniors are alike—underpowered and outdated. I don't understand why you bother with them."

"Point taken, but you have to respect their simplicity and rugged power. Just you and the gun. No HUDs or data feeds. No molycircs. Just eyes-on-target and recoil."

"Right," Ramuel said sarcastically. *"What's so special about this Walther PP . . ."*

"PPK. It was a small police pistol dating back to the nineteen thirties. A twentieth-century literary character named James Bond made it extremely popular." *And here we go.*

"*I see. You can't have the gun, so you've settled for the next best thing: Mr. Bond.*"

Promise pitched her voice thoughtfully. "I've never thought of it that way. I like both, but for different reasons."

"*Uh-huh. Besides this Bond character, what makes the PPK so special?*"

"Well, Adolf Hitler shot and killed himself with one. The monster mostly got what he deserved, too."

"*Mostly?*"

"He cheated. He deserved a bullet in the head from a firing squad."

"*Sounds like a reason not to own one.*"

"Don't blame the gun. The PPK saved plenty of lives, too. Mr. Bond's Great Britain—like the PPK—is part of the histories for a reason, far more than just one. I try to be mindful of why."

"*Which is?*"

"If I have my time lines correct, Great Britain, which was part of a commonwealth called the United Kingdom, joined the European Union in the mid-twenty-first century."

"*So Bond's a highborn British prick.*"

"Think of the European Union as the precursor to the Terran Federation, back before Earth settled Mars, before the Terries invented the jump drive and planted the flag on Tau Ceti e, *long* before Hold was colonized or became a respectable single-system power. The EU's civil war followed a half century later, in 2092. Some historians think the day the United Kingdom joined the EU was the beginning of the end."

"*I'm sorry, ma'am. You've completely lost me.*"

"You are familiar with the Atomic Edicts, right?"

"*Of course, ma'am. All civilized star nations abide by it. That's why our Marines don't deploy in theater with tactical nuclear weps. Space navies were exempted. Life's not fair.*"

Promise smiled. "And the genesis of the edict?"

"*Things got messy on Holy Terra. A lot of people died. People said, never again.*"

"Essentially, yes. But it wasn't a lot of people. Over two hundred million died in what historians called the Great Terran War. Neither side used tactical nukes. Imagine dropping a *strategic* nuke on a major population center. And then on dozens more. Whole cities were wiped off the map. London, Kraków, Kiev, Tallinn . . . just gone. It's a miracle the EU recovered at all."

"Today, no star nation in its right mind will risk universal retribution by dropping a nuke on a civilian target. Not the Lusies, not the Terries, not even your run-of-the-'verse pirate."

"Okay, I think I've got the history."

"Mr. Bond's history—actually, what would have been his future—reminds me that no matter how bad it gets, it could always be worse. War is bad enough. The Lusies have us outnumbered. Commodore Samuelson controls the system, Montana's skies, and he has enough assets to swamp our forces. But he still has to bring the war to us the old-fashioned way, by putting boots on the ground."

"By bleeding for it, you mean."

"Exactly."

Ramuel grew quiet.

"It's time to bleed the enemy."

"Could have just said so, ma'am," the gunny said lightly.

"Could have. But history gives it context. That's why I read it."

Ramuel conceded. *"Time to bleed the enemy."*

"That it is, Gunny. That it is. You ready for this?"

"Ooh-rah."

Promise made two more calls. Because she didn't have LOS to Jean-Wesley, she slipped into proper voice procedures and call signs, in case the enemy had somehow cracked their net.

"Slipstitch to Hermes, over."

Jean-Wesley heard her voice come through the static of his handheld comm and frowned. She'd given him the call sign Hermes, which was growing on him like moss on a sun-kissed tree. Some kinda god from a place called Greece. Apparently, this Hermes character had played tricks on the other gods. Promise had mentioned his wit and cunning, too. He couldn't disagree there. But he thought the name sounded like something you caught at a brothel. He had scowled while Promise tried not to laugh.

He looked out across the Mall at the Supreme Court, the presidential offices, and the Congress. He'd wished Promise good luck from this very spot a less than a half hour ago and watched her lead her people off to the frontlines of a war he knew she might not come home from. *A home I might like to share with this native-born, off-world woman.* There was too much left unspoken between them, more he might have said had times been different. He saw it in her eyes then, but any trace of what might be happening between them was far removed. She had been all business, and the lack of emotion in her voice had caused him to hesitate. War had a way of distilling life's hopes and promises until nothing else mattered but survival. At the moment, his small part in defending his planet meant keeping the president alive if Samuelson's troops came searching for her.

Off to Jean-Wesley's right and a few steps above him stood an Annie Buckmeister look-alike, call sign Manticora. Fake Annie was at the moment holding a press conference on the steps of the capitol building. Janice Celleset possessed the same figure and flesh tones as Annie Buckmeister, a grade-A, 100 percent Montana woman. Makeup, Annie's own wardrobe, and a voice modulator completed the ruse. If Promise hadn't shown up a few months ago, he might have even gone for her.

"Hermes, do you read me?"

Partaine snapped the comm to his mouth. "Sorry, Slipstitch, go ahead."

"Hermes, give me a comm check, over."

"Slipstitch, I read you five-by-five. Had to round up a stray. I'm good to go."

"Roger that, Hermes. Is Manticora secure, over?"

"Secure and sassy, Slipstitch."

"Copy that, Hermes. Stand by."

Several klicks away, Promise smirked, wondering how Jean-Wesley had talked Annie out of the capital. She made a mental note to ask him later, after they had kicked the Lusitanians off their planet.

Lastly, she commed Jiggers and gave the word like a reborn Montanan.

"The steer is in the pen, Jiggers. Time to cut off his oysters."

Fifty-three

Captain Raikk Vasquez of the HMS *Python* sat in his command chair on the first watch of the day, which started at 0600 and ended promptly at 1430 hours. He'd arrived at 0545 hours, just like every morning before it, a tradition he'd started the very first day he heard a subordinate call him Skipper. His minicomp rested on his hip with a day's worth of reports waiting to be digested, annotated, and filed.

After finishing his first cup of the morning, the captain began scanning yesterday's download. The third memo was a bright spot in an otherwise starless list of files on routine sensor readings, engineering reports, and a foul debacle with the ship's sewage-treatment plant, which had backed up into the *Python*'s galley and ruined yesterday's breakfast. Twenty percent of his crew were walking improvised explosive devices, and laundry was struggling to keep up with bags of soiled uniforms. Vasquez shook his head as he skipped to the next file, which proved to be far more interesting. His XO has tagged the article from the nets and sent him a copy. Apparently, a team of Her Majesty's zenobiologists had found a primitive race of bipedal tool users on a recently charted G-type star. It was now a Lusitanian protectorate.

He suddenly found himself wishing he'd pursued a different career. Perhaps in survey or with the Ministry of Exploration. Commanding a starship had sounded so appealing at first. It had looked even better in the holovids. But in reality it amounted to a lot of busywork and boring patrols in backwater systems like the one he currently found himself deployed in. The only things he'd blown up in the last three years were targeting platforms and a couple of privateers. Hanging those bastards was always sublime. But in all of his years in space, he hadn't discovered a single thing of interest.

HMS *Python*'s Electronics Warfare Officer, Second Lieutenant Mia Pham, had run every targeting solution on the derelict *Absalon* that she could think of. She was, to put it mildly, bored.

Pham was in many ways the most striking member of HMS *Python*'s crew. She had a shock of snow-white hair she'd inherited from her mother, set against the dark olive skin of her father. Her hair had turned prematurely white by nineteen standard years of age. The second lieutenant owned a cool, level temperament and rarely raised her voice more than a few notes, and never a full octave. In the black of space, she was white contrast. An even keel and preternatural façade had earned her the nickname Ice.

Pham decided to assuage her boredom by navigating her holopanels blindly with eyes closed to inject an element of uncertainty into the mix. Slowly, her hands began inputting commands, but her mind wandered off.

A soft tone sounded in her ear as her console flagged a discrepancy. Eyes opened as a window materialized, directing Pham's attention to a Priority-3 alert. She focused on the puzzling activity that appeared to be emanating from RNS *Absalon*. Confirmed it with furrowed brows. For all intents and purposes, the Republican vessel had been dead for a number of days. The fact that it was now showing signs of life was at the very least alarming.

"Sir, I'm picking up an energy signature from *Absalon*."

Captain Vasquez brought up the anomalous data on his chair's screen and punched in several queries.

"What do you make of it, Lieutenant?"

"Skipper, if I had to guess, I'd say we're picking up a small power bleed from a capacitor, maybe in one of the forward missile tubes. There's still some juice bleeding out. It could be nothing."

"Keep monitoring it. Let me know if something changes."

Pham's spine went rigid. "Sir, something just changed. I'm now picking up multiple power fluctuations. Cross-referencing their positions with what we know of *Absalon*'s schematic . . . One moment, sir." Pham spun around in her seat. "All three match the locations of known launch tubes."

"Bring up our point defenses."

"Aye, aye, Captain." Pham spun back around and began inputting commands furiously.

"Tandra, get me Commodore Samuelson's ship on the horn. I'd feel a whole lot better if that ship wasn't sitting over there, derelict or not. If the commodore doesn't object, I want to send her to the breakers."

"Junior Lieutenant Tandra Sanders, communications officer, a wiry young woman with black hair and a streak of irregular blue running through it (but not strictly nonregulation blue) raised a hand to cover her earpiece and began subvocalizing with her counterpart on Samuelson's ship, which was sitting in parking orbit nearby.

"*Python* to *Intrepid,* I have a Priority-One, over. Repeat, I have a Priority-One, over."

Pham's defensive grid came up as her scanners recorded three incoming warheads from a vessel that had, moments before, been nothing but a derelict. She heard the skipper yell out, "Action stations" and "Helm—Evasive Maneuver Echo-4" as she initiated defensive fire Delta-2, without orders. Her initiative swatted two of the three missiles from space and saved the lives of several hundred members of the crew. The third bird bore down upon the *Python* and struck the ship's forward hammerhead, to the starboard side of the command deck.

None of *Python*'s crew members were wearing vacsuits as *Absalon*'s missile blew through armor and opened up her bridge to space. Captain Raikk Vasquez, Second Lieutenant Mia Pham, Junior Lieutenant Tandra Sanders, and the rest of the watch died in the blast, and the *Python* fell out of Samuelson's command net.

Fifty-four

Promise heard Sergeant Maxzash-Indar Sindri in her mastoid implant. *"Shamrock to Slipstitch, over."*

"This is Slipstitch. Go ahead, Shamrock, over."

"Slipstitch, be advised: we have in-bound," Sergeant Sindri said flatly. *"Six Assault-class LACs just hit atmo. ETA eleven mikes. Their trajectory has them on a zero-intercept with the spaceport. By the book, just like you called it."*

"Copy that, Shamrock. Stand by." Promise spoke over the battlenet. "Drain it, dump it, wolf it down, and pack it up. We go in five mikes."

A toon's worth of males formed a staggered line and pretended to hold their members as they drained their mechsuits. Five streams of yellow arched out and watered the ground. Promise heard *"I pee straight"* and *"Wow, Sergeant, that thing is huuge!"* and *"What you been drinking, Corporal—piss like mustard ain't healthy."* When they'd "drained it," Lance Corporal Talon Covington drew their attention, raised a pointer, and held it out for the first taker. Newly promoted Corporal Vil Fitzholm, a stocky man with a dry wit and well-groomed eyebrows, did the taking for him. Tal's trapdoor opened and out dropped a pellet, prewrapped in sani. *"Like I said, boys, MREs can build 'em."*

Promise shook her head. *Men.* She tried to keep the mirth out of her voice and failed. "All right boys, enough chatter. Put your guns away and grab your rifles." More laughter shot across V Company's battlenet.

As the chatter calmed to a prefire hum, Promise forced herself to refocus, south. She'd planned for two possible scenarios: Samuelson would either go directly for the Mall, the president, and Congress, or he'd land at the partially repaired spaceport and secure it first, then take the more cautious approach, working his way into the city on foot. It was a fifty-fifty proposition, so she'd split the difference and positioned her troops as near the middle as the local terrain allowed for, on the highest piece of ground she could find. The spot was called Laci's Main. It was a meager piece of rock famous for its panoramic views and for a young woman named Laci Stryke. On a blue-sky morning almost five years ago to the day, Laci had hooked four weather balloons to her ATV and launched herself heavenward, without counter-grav. Laci rose to four thousand meters before her balloons started failing. But since she was a resourceful gal, she'd packed silk and a tank of O_2 and floated back to Montana clay no worse for wear. A local contest grew up around her maiden voyage, and each year since, Landing's best (and dumbest—depending on whom you asked) took part in a contest to see who could go the highest, fall the quickest, and land the softest. So far, Laci held the record—five consecutive years running. Scores of smashed ATVs littered the ground. Promise wondered which ones were Laci's.

As Promise looked about, she saw Marines kneeling down to triple-check their gear. Others reclined on a rock or boulder to record a final thought to a loved one. One more vid, just in case.

"Is there a certain someone you'll be makin' a vid for?" Sandra Paen appeared on Promise's HUD, a head without its body, and kissably close.

"Mother, I don't have time for this."

"This being Mr. Partaine?"

"This being a man, any man. *This* is not the time for a mother-daughter talk on the opposite sex."

"That so?" Sandra's eyebrows rose in unison. "My little love martyr. Well, if it were me, I'd comm him. Now."

"If I do, will you get out?"

"Yes."

"Done."

Sandra said, "Good girl," before she disappeared.

PFC Kathy Prichart stood off to Promise's right with her helmet racked on her hip, a spork in one hand, and a half-eaten pouch in the other.

Promise popped her visor. "Ick, of all the food options, you chose that?" Promise shook her head at her guardian in disgust.

Prichart made a face as she shoveled another mouthful and tried to talk at the same time. "Calories, Lieutenant. We're gonna need them." Kathy offered her some. Priority one, ma'am—fuel."

"Keep it. I'll refuel later," Promise said.

"*Actually, Private First Class, the first priority of a planetary assault is to secure the air, then the ground.*" Her AI quoted from the Republican Marine Corps *Small Wars Manual*, in academy-clipped fashion, over Promise's externals. "*Your pharmacope is more than capable of maintaining your body's caloric needs in an extended campaign, enabling you to focus your attention solely on the battlefield and not on eating.*"

"Why, I ought to—"

Promise raised a hand, made another mental note to give her suit's AI that frontal lobotomy she'd been promising.

"Technically, he's right. But wars are fought with stomachs, and some of us prefer them full."

"*Touché, ma'am,*" said Promise's AI.

"I didn't realize we were fencing."

"Neither did I," said Kathy.

"Shut up, Mr. Bond."

"*Shutting up, ma'am.*"

Promise recalled a lecture from boot camp. One of her classroom instructors, Gunnery Sergeant Cable Thornbottom, had been a legend in the Marine Corps for his volcanic temper and a mess of glittery earned the hard way. His essay "Battlefield Initiative" was required reading for every Marine, from the lowly private to the mythic four-star. As she recalled, Gunny Cable had quoted himself, daily and often:

> She who fires first has the luxury of thinking ahead; she gets to plan her attack, execute it, and set the tone of the engagement. But if she

takes too much time to plan, her enemy will act and take the initiative from her. He who fires last yields the initiative and must react without the benefit of careful planning. And once you start reacting, it's nearly impossible to stop.

The section of the essay that Promise remembered verbatim was the same one every Republican Marine committed to memory from day 1, lest she risk the displeasure of the gunny and earn a five-klick run for it:

Taking the initiative is easy, but it requires a disciplined mind and a steady hand. Taking it back from your enemy is much harder. Your job as a Marine is rather simple and straightforward. Shoot your enemy first. Don't let him shoot you.

She'd chosen the former—fired first. Barely five minutes ago, Seaman Fingers had "knocked" on Samuelson's command. She checked her chrono again. The commodore and Lieutenant Colonel Saloman ran a very tight outfit. Almost time to go.

A soft chime caught her attention, and she dropped her visor for privacy.

The rugged face on her HUD caused the bottom of her stomach to fall away.

"Hello, Promise."

"Hi." Her smile was automatic.

"We're supposed to be following proper voice procedures, in case the Lusies crack our comm net. Visuals tend to make call signs irrelevant, don't you think?"

Promise's mother cut in. "Looks like he beat you to it."

Get out.

"Getting out dear. Bye."

Jean-Wesley continued. *"I wanted to see you again . . . before the fit hits the shan."*

"Well, it's nice to be seen." *It's nice to be seen?*

Partaine's cheeks warmed as he looked skyward on his side of the feed. *"Didn't take them long, did it?"*

"We've got their attention all right. Is the Rotary ready?"

"*Sure as shi . . . tah, yes, ma'am,*" Jean-Wesley said.

"You know, you don't have to change your language for me."

"*I would change a whole lot of things for—*"

"Jean-Wesley, tell me about that later, when you have all of my attention."

Partaine looked encouraged. "*I'll do that, ma'am.*"

She heard an impatient chime in her mastoid, sighed. "Hermes, stand by." She made it a three-way comm.

"*Shamrock is standing by, over.*"

"Very good. Shamrock, you are to hold position until you hear otherwise from me."

"*Roger that, ma'am.*" Sergeant Sindri replied.

"And tell Jiggers to keep me posted if their ETA or trajectory changes."

"*Aye, aye, ma'am.*" Maxi disappeared from her HUD.

"Mister Partaine, good hunting."

"*Thank you ma'am.*" Jean-Wesley hesitated. "*Anyone ever tell you how your eyes sparkle?*"

Promise didn't know what to say.

"*Didn't think so. Well, they do. You take care. Bye.*"

Promise took a deep breath and shook her head to focus her thoughts. She activated the company-wide channel. "Slipstitch to all points. Danger close. We have in-bound in . . ."—she paused to check her suit's chronometer, which was already ticking down in the upper right quadrant of her HUD—"eight mikes. That gives us light-years of time. It's five mikes to the spaceport. Remember: act fast; look slow."

Promise thought of her mom and dad together and happy. She skimmed over her recently formed memories of her birth world. A shared chocolate bar and little Emily's smile. The Rotary and the young man she owed a shooting lesson; she couldn't for the life of her recall his name. *All good reasons.* Her mom's advice about desperate prayers rang particularly true. *Sir, all hell's about to fall upon us. Would you help me hold up my hands and bear it?*

Her HUD chimed. *Time to move.* This fight was going to be up close and personal. She figured the COMSEC should be, too. "All points. Call signs from here on out. Activate your Witches. Sync your chronos for countdown. We go in sixty. On my mark."

All twenty-six mechanized Marines gathered by toon, pounded each other on the back for good measure, waiting for her to give the word. One by one, they phased, then disappeared.

Promise watched the ticker drop. She had the sudden sensation that she was lifting off and her stomach was staying behind.

"All points, on my mark."

Promise double-checked her readouts. All greens, just like she liked it. And then she heard the voice again, the one from the shuttle she'd nearly died in, which sounded a lot like her mother's. *MOVE!*

Aye, aye, Mama.

That's my girl.

Promise glanced at her chrono and counted. "On five, four, three, two, one, mark!"

Her small, determined army surged in unison toward the partially reconstructed spaceport. Then Ramuel's toon broke left and pulled away from the rest of V Company.

"ALCON, maintain radio silence. Slipstitch out."

Promise followed the five silhouettes of Third Platoon for a brief moment as it ran away from the bulk of her command. Even though they were phased she could still see them on her HUD thanks to her onboard Phased Tracking Array, the PTA. *Good hunting, Gunny,* she thought. *Godspeed. Hell's teeth.*

Her suit's leg actuators groaned as she pushed them into a full military sprint, settled her breathing, and rehashed her strategy in her head.

Once the LACs finish taxiing (breath), we'll have five seconds at most before their troops start deploying (breath)—and that's when we hit them hardest.

The most pessimistic force estimate puts them at 256 in mechsuits (breath) and another possible 700 Navies—if Samuelson brings them all—in unpowered armor with light to medium weapons, APCs, and artillery.

Promise broke through a stand of trees.

Priority 1 is to cover the gunny's toon (breath) as they pull back and to neutralize the enemy boots in mechsuits. (Breath.) The Witchfield will mask your thermal footprint but not your weapon's signature once you fire. (Breath.) Remember: Run; Gun; Evade; Survive. Once the gunny's unit is clear (breath), fall back and scatter to the rendezvous point.

With eighty-nine seconds left, Promise was redlining her suit, breathing quickly and evenly like a long-distance runner midkick with the finish line in sight. The landing strip came into view as she crested a grassy hill. Her suit's internal sensors tracked her company as they formed up on her; they looked like green dots roughly in the shape of a tree. Then the tree became a column as she slowed, and then the column became a tight cluster as the chrono ticked down to zero. Her command came to rest 257 meters from the edge of the strip, twice again that distance from the gunny's toon, with time to spare. Their elevation gave them a sniper's view.

As they fanned out and took up their positions, a small bit of worry lodged in the back of her mind. It was the worry she always felt before combat, the worry that told her she'd missed something or misread something else. Only this time she had far more to worry about than herself.

Fifty-five

APRIL 13TH, 91 A.E., STANDARD CALENDAR, 0756 HOURS,
WAKE CANYONS, LANDING CITY OUTSKIRTS, PLANET MONTANA

Over thirty klicks away, hiding in a narrow ravine just wide enough to touch down in, Sergeant Maxzash-Indar Sindri sat strapped into the bowels of a Republican light attack craft. He wore gunner's glasses that condensed his weaponry's point of view. Time-to-target counted down on the left. A target lock danced about his right eye, waiting compliantly for the approaching vessels to enter his engagement envelope. The trio of makeshift antiaircraft guns anchored to the roof of a ten-story commercial building in the heart of Landing waited for his commands, twitching slightly left, then slightly right as they kept eyes on target.

As the enemies closed within seven klicks, Sindri activated his AA assets, and three rail guns opened fire on the nearest Lusitanian LAC. Parallel magnetic fields accelerated ordnance to many times the speed of sound. The guns had a slow rate of fire, and the ordnance, once in flight, was committed to a single straight-line trajectory—what the Marine Corps called dumb ammo. But it was all Sergeant Sindri had, and he wasn't complaining. What he had was adequate to the task at hand. *And adequate gets the job done,* he reminded himself.

Given the LACs' closing velocity, he figured he had enough time for three shots before the LACs dropped bellow his arc of fire.

Sindri's computer designated the first LAC Zulu 1. His first three shots closed on the vessel at supersonic speeds. Two rounds scored direct hits on the ship's midsection and engines and opened her up to the elements.

The vessel careened out of formation and corkscrewed before crashing into a rolling hill.

Definitely not complaining now. He smiled. Maxi took a play out of his lieutenant's battle book. *I believe that's "one."*

The sergeant's guns fired again, grazing Zulu 3. A stream of gas and debris blew out from multiple wounds in the vessel, but she managed to remain flight-worthy and continued her approach. Her crew was no worse for wear either. Modern space navies prepped for such things, which is why her entire complement sat in armor or suits as the outside winds howled about them.

Once the barrage started, Zulu 2 opened her reach hatch and disgorged two stingships, which fell toward the ground and circled back toward the launchers. Both spat missiles at the base of the low-rise building as Maxi got off a final salvo. Then all ten stories, and Maxi's guns, fell straight to the ground.

"That was a good bit of overkill," Promise said. She heard Prichart's laugh from several meters above her. Both women had popped their visors, preferring fresh air to canned in their last moments before combat.

"Men always try to compensate for their inadequacies," Prichart replied. "Hold this a sec?"

Promise looked up into a tall leafy tree in time to catch Kathy's tri-barrel pulse rifle as her guardian jumped down from her perch. The rifle fell into phase, visible just long enough for Promise to catch it. Then Kathy thumped down beside her. The ground beneath her caved, leaving two boot prints in the grass and mud.

Promise heard smacking and smiled, felt something slop across her right boot.

"Nut butter and honey—want some? Oops, sorry 'bout that."

"I don't believe I have a choice."

The whine of shuttle engines caught their attention. There, from the east, moving supersonic. And one was dropping fast. Too fast.

Kathy and Promise both looked grim.

Lieutenant Brenda Whispers of the Lusitanian Imperial Marine Corps swore as her LAC took enemy fire and became heavy, then dropped like an arrow toward the deck.

She barked into her mike. "Counter-grav's down. All hands prepare for crash landing." Whispers gripped her controls and pulled back, hard. Watched the altimeter drop below 500 meters, 300 meters, 100 meters. Then, "Brace yourselves!"

She'd come in hot, like a conventional aircraft instead of a VTOL, which meant she needed time and strip to bleed speed. Her craft's front skid snapped upon impact and brought the nose down with a sickening crunch, which prematurely slowed the craft, nearly flipping it end over end. Whispers bit through her lip and tasted copper. But the craft was pointed in the right direction, and she breathed a sigh of relief.

Unfortunately for her, the other ships in her formation were close behind her, and the LAC next in queue was moving too fast to change course. The pilot, Warrant Officer Melissa Preen, had only just earned her wings. Her inexperience caused her to panic. Her miscalculation dropped her rear skids into her sister LAC's cockpit and killed Brenda Whispers instantly.

As two of the Lusitanian shuttles collided on the ground, Victor Company opened fire. Promise's Marines armed with heavy weapons targeted LAC engines with ruthless efficiency. Her Marines carrying sniper and assault rifles killed individual Marines as they poured from their carry-alls. Frag grenades lobbed overhead, split open, and filled the air with magnetic rain. Thousands of small circular disks pelted the Lusitanians below and stuck to their battle armor. Moments later, more than a dozen Imperial grunts exploded. One unfortunate Lusie raised his arms in horror a second before he blew apart.

In the midst of the confusion, Third Platoon, led by Gunnery Sergeant Tomas Ramuel, rushed out of its fighting hole and frog-jumped toward the nearest LAC. Each member of his toon, including himself, had swapped out nonessential gear for extra Horde missiles, which they unloaded mercilessly on the Lusitanian vessel. The ship's portside disintegrated.

The gunny's toon fired again, this time thermal rounds, which ignited upon impact. As the LAC sped across the tarmac, it lit the ground behind it on fire, burned everything and everyone inside. Ramuel's toon continued to jump and fire until it cleared the other side of the landing strip.

Behind them, mines cooked off like bullets in a frying pan, clouding the entire field in debris and fire.

With their initial objective met, the gunny and Third Platoon fell back to the nearby forest, through a shroud of haze, thick with energy fire. LAC-mounted autocannon turrets turned on them and fired thousands of penetrators into their backs. Ramuel's fourth point, Corporal Val Na'go, ran through a solid wall of enemy fire that dropped her to her knees. As she hit the deck, she rolled sideways and sprang forward. She came down on her right foot as energy fire hit her in the small of the back and tore through what little armor remained there. The beam severed her spine, and her icon turned crimson.

Enemy mortars started thumping, everywhere. Promise's HUD tracked a flight of ten, heard the telltale whine and thud of incoming and impact. Then several casings about the size of an adult hand sprouted legs, popped up, and sprinted toward her Marines.

"Walkie-talkies!"

"*Hit the deck!*"

Promise swung her rifle around when a blur knocked her over and into a slight depression. The explosion sent up a small cloud of debris and killed one of her Marines.

"Slipstitch to all points, fall back!" Promise barked across the company channel as she clawed her way to her feet. She took a knee, dropped her reticule on a platoon of nearby Lusitanian raiders, and fired. As her people fell back, she continued to pepper the enemy. She took one down—a center-mass shot. Took another—this time a head shot, beam clear through and into the Marine behind. Kathy fell in beside her with her tri-barrel, finished off the remaining three, and rapped her on the shoulder.

"It's go-time, Lieutenant."

Untamed land flickered by as Promise ran and quickly reorganized her command. Victor Company was down to half of its original strength. Numbers scrolled across her mind as she reorganized five partial toons into four full-strength units, two reinforced with a sixth. She remembered Corporal Na'go's harsh laugh, and thought it ironic that her customs inspector had survived the destruction of the Lady only to fall in the first military engagement on Montana's soil. Lance Corporal Talon Covington's loss weighed the heaviest. The lance corporal had died at Promise's side, firing his BP rifle to the very last. He'd pushed her aside and thrown himself on top of the spider-like grenade. Now, her toon needed a new heavy-weapons handler.

Private First Class Kathy Prichart bound in front of her, sweeping for hostiles. Armor marred by blood splatter and dirt, rifle arching from nine to three, waiting for the next kill.

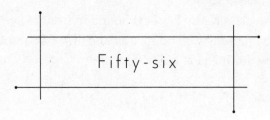

Fifty-six

Jean-Wesley Partaine glassed the streets below his location. What he saw filled him with pride. Block upon block of Montana's manufacturing sector sprawled toward the horizon. Buildings, most low-rise, sat full of products that were made on Montana by Montanans: farming and agricultural equipment, workbots, textiles, and guns. A small bioresearch firm was churning out hybrid seed, and a modest hovercar plant was bringing down the cost of modern transportation to within the reach of the middle class. It all amounted to tens of billions of chits of infrastructure and over a dozen years of favorable tax policies and corporate investment incentives. With the unwavering encouragement of its president, Montana had thrown everything it had at the 'verse, hoping to draw frontier venture-capital firms planet-side, and with them the means to claw Montana's citizenry out of the cesspool of Rim economics. It was working, too. Montana now enjoyed an average planetary standard of living that was forty percent of the Republic's core worlds. Still a third-rate world by most standards. But how many verge planets could boast as much as Montana could? And Mr. Jean-Wesley Partaine worried that all of it was about to go up in flames.

Partaine dialed up the magnification and looked across the city's sprawl to the fires and explosions in the distance. The Lusies were getting closer to the predetermined choke point, where Montana's forces would make their last stand. Several nearby subdivisions were already under siege. Promise had commed him a few minutes ago and told him, only after he'd pressed the point, that she was down to seventeen Marines—she'd lost a full toon just moments ago and was low on cells and ammunition. Once they ran out of grenades and missiles, Promise would have to take more risks to engage the enemy, and that meant that her troops would die faster. Matters would soon grow desperate. Jean-Wesley knew Promise had given far better than she'd gotten. Three shuttles completely destroyed, the others grounded—probably permanently, seeing how Montana didn't have a repair facility up to the task.

I've stayed off the dance floor long enough, he decided.

He grabbed his Marine-issue pulse rifle, dialed it to the highest setting, and double-checked his backup cell. He picked up a belt of antique-looking shotgun shells that belonged to his semi-automatic hog and wrapped it around his chest. He slung the weapon over his shoulder and pulled his head through the strap. The shotgun was one of his designs, a spread weapon with a mull kick. Each shell carried an anterior charge that blew upon impact or at preset distances, with a hollow inside full of dozens of explosive pellets. It would take a few to penetrate battle armor. He didn't plan on getting that close to one of the Lusies.

Partaine pressed his chin to his right shoulder and hit the TRANSMIT button. "Hermes to all units: stay out of sight. Hold your fire until I give the signal."

At Partaine's command, three hundred armed Rotarians double-checked their weapons, waiting for the battle to come to them.

Lusie artillery fire was killing them at an unsustainable rate.

Promise paused in a makeshift fighting hole near the center of a small lot overgrown with weeds and shrubs. Her guardian, Kathy, as well as newcomers Lance Corporal Roxi Zahn, Corporal Richard Morris, and Corporal Fitzholm, fanned out around her. They were the orphans of First, Fifth, and Eighth Platoons. Sergeant Richelle Felix's loss weighed freshly on her mind.

"I'm done, Lieutenant," Sergeant Felix had said. *"Le-eave me. I'll s-slow 'em down."*

Promise's platoon sergeant sat propped up against a pile of rubble, convulsing in pain. Blood trickled from her side. Her breastplate was split, and the armor over her right thigh was completely gone, the skin underneath blistered and oozing. Richelle looked down and typed a series of commands into a small display on her wrist, which started blinking red, slowly at first, then with increasing haste.

"Not this way, Sergeant. We'll hump you out."

Felix had slapped Promise's hand away. Her words suddenly turned wet and mushy. Her visor popped up as she spewed blood. Richelle wiped her mouth. "Na wi-ou loosin mo Maeens."

Promise knelt by her fallen toonmate, intent on getting her to her feet, but Richelle punched her in the breastplate.

"No, dammi." Punched again. "Ge ou o here. I'm al-edy dea."

Felix winced as another round of painkillers dripped into her veins, and then she noticeably relaxed. An unnatural smile spread across her face. She shook her head and almost sounded like herself. "Go, Lieutenant. Just go."

Promise raised her visor. A tear slipped down her cheek as she reached out and grasped the older woman's forearm.

"In the next life, I'll look for you."

Felix tried to respond.

"Don't speak. Here—take these." Promise handed Felix her last frag grenade and two magazines for her Heavy Pistols. "Make the bastards pay."

Semper paratus. Always ready. *Semper fidelis.* Always faithful.

I'm so sorry, Promise thought. As she ran, she felt every bit the betrayer. The Corps never left a boot behind. She felt the explosion shake the ground. Her scanners told her three of the enemy had perished with Richelle Felix's final deed.

The words of Dimitri Tsveokiev, once *Absalon's* CO, spoke for the dead, for Richelle. *Make sure this story gets told.*

Promise pushed the pain aside, rounded a blackened street corner, and took up a position against a meter-high retaining wall. A terraced garden spread out behind her. A pond of dead fish and water plants was all that was left.

She heard scramjets above and a telling rumble coming from a block away. Her HUD showed over thirty enemy pinpoints closing on her position. "All right, people, we take them one at a time. For Sergeant Felix."

A rushing sound followed a skirted APC that floated into the intersection and slid sideways, at a diagonal. It had an ungainly, patchwork look. The single-barreled turret at its top started rotating toward Promise's locus. When it more or less pointed at her, the turret stopped and remained silent. Instead of weapons fire, a voice rang out from the vehicle, a voice that spoke with the ease of command and the benefit of eyes in the sky.

"We don't have to keep doing this, Lieutenant."

Promise didn't hesitate as she flipped on her externals. "Then call a cease fire and pull your men back, Commodore."

"I'm afraid I can't do that. You do understand."

Promise didn't answer. There was nothing left to say.

"So it is to be like this. Your people dead . . . or dying. Your planet's capital in ruins. I can be a reasonable man, Promise. You don't mind me calling you Promise, do you? Perhaps it is time for you to accept the inevitable. You can't win."

She was losing. The mounting dead were chipping away at the granite walls of duty to her country and service to her star nation. Admitting defeat was a means to an end, a choice that would save lives and spare the living unnecessary suffering. Promise had wondered if she would face such a time during her career. What choice would she make? Would she hold the thin red line? Promise closed her eyes and saw her unit and the ghosts of those who had passed on. The few living would continue to fight and die. *Can I ask more of them?* She thought of her father, hands raised in surrender. She heard her mother's voice say, *I'm proud of you, not because of what you do but because of who you are.* And then she remembered little Emily, the bar of chocolate they'd shared, and what she had said about Promise. *When I grow up, I want to be just like her.* In that moment, Promise knew she would never be worthy of those words if she surrendered to the commodore.

Her voice echoed over her externals, with a deadly purpose that screamed more loudly than any shout could have. "You haven't won yet, Commodore. What are you waiting for?" She never heard Commodore Samuelson's response. Instead, she saw flames leap from the APC and engulf her position. The Lusies had learned quickly—they'd started using fire to nullify the Witchfield's advantage. She'd lost three Marines from such hunter-killer tactics.

Promise screamed and charged the APC before Kathy could stop her.

Ran right into the flame and through it. Her suit's internal heat spiked into dangerous levels as she let loose her last salvo of Hordes. The diminutive missiles blew a small hole in the side of the troop transport. She rolled under the return fire, came up, and unloaded several bursts of energy fire into the wounded craft. One moment the vehicle was there and the next it erupted into a cloud of debris. Two battered Marines stumbled from the rear of the vehicle. Kathy's tri-barrel blazed from behind Promise and put a quick end to them. The lead Marine got lucky. He only lost a leg from the knee down before blacking out. The other was reduced to a mound of metal and flesh.

Promise looked skyward as a high-pitched whine approached. Promise and Kathy dove for the ground. Even in mechsuits, their hands went for their ears and their mouths fell open, both out of habit. Several loud thuds kissed the ground all around them. Kathy flew backward into a pile of rubble that had once been a small private bank.

Promise shook it off, rolled to her feet, checked her guardian, checked her damage readouts. Her AI beat her to the punch. *"Your portside armor is down to thirty-two percent. The feed to your pulse rifle is damaged."* Promise grunted in acknowledgement. With the feed, her mechsuit's fusion plant kept her cells continually charged and negated the need to reload. *Without* it, she was down to the cells she had on her. When she bled them dry, she'd be out of ammo.

Promise filed away the information and gave her guardian a quick fist pump, and the two fell back into the building behind them, where the rest of Victor Company had already assembled. Morris and Fitzholm took up positions next to open wounds in the structure, where a door or window had once been. Kathy and Zahn secured the second level and the high ground. They all released their remaining whiskers to secure the perimeter while Promise got on the comm with Maxi.

She looked up to see fast-moving contrails heading east.

"Slipstitch to Shamrock, over."

"This is Shamrock, Slipstitch. Go ahead, over."

"Shamrock, be advised, they're using stingships as spotters, coordinating their ground efforts with artillery. I need eyes in the sky and those ships neutralized. You are to go for Soaring Gale, over."

"Wilco, Slipstitch, go for Soaring Gale, stand by."

Promise had held her two remaining aircraft in reserve, waiting to learn if the commodore was keeping a reserve of his own to surprise her with. But a couple hours of intense fighting and her own mounting losses had finally forced her hand. She didn't think Commodore Samuelson had an air wing on standby. But even if he did, she could no longer afford the luxury of holding back her own birds.

During a long and unforgiving minute, her motley crew hunkered down in a shelled-out department store. They checked and rechecked their gear, and those that had extra ammo to spare shared out of their need. They exchanged raucous humor, and they all rode the thunder. The building shook from blow upon blow, and the ground threatened to crumble beneath them. And then twin plumes of jet wash passed overhead and a small, fledgling hope rose in their spirits as Promise's air support made its battlefield debut. Corporal Porter sat at the helm of the stingship, and Maxi piloted the LAC. Both vessels formed into a two-point formation and streaked toward Samuelson's stingships. The two enemy star powers met in the air over Central Landing, above the power plant and primary communications node.

Maxi's targeting reticule dropped over the lead stingship and turned solid green. His forward-mounted pulse cannons opened up and tore the ship's left wing from its fuselage. The smaller Lusitanian ship dove in an uncontrollable spin and struck the belly of the Landmark Building, which housed Montana's stock exchange and a substantial portion of the planet's banking industry. The second stingship broke for higher elevation, and outclimbed the larger and less maneuverable LAC, which left Corporal Porter in an even fight.

"Shamrock to Big A, she's all yours."

"Roger that," Corporal Porter said. *"Watch and learn, Shamrock. Big A, out."*

Maxi smiled as his wingman outclimbed his position and disappeared into the stratosphere.

The two combatants climbed higher and higher, through Montana's thinning air and out into space, twisting in and out of target lock. They danced at the edge of gravity, hunter chasing hunter, until Porter's targeting computer chimed in her ear. She let loose a flight of missiles and one struck behind her enemy's cockpit, severing it from the rest of the craft. The pilot sat encased and unable to punch out as gravity pulled him and the remains of his craft toward Montana.

Corporal Sammi Porter let out a whoop and pushed her flight stick downward, back toward the planet's surface, when an energy mount from the HMS *Petrograd* acquired lock and fired.

Fifty-seven

The shelling stopped abruptly and an eerie calm settled across the city of Landing. Promise looked up and heard Maxi's voice echo over the battlenet.

"*Those guns still giving you a problem, Slipstitch?*"

"Strange you should ask, Shamrock. Things just got real quiet, over."

"*Roger that, Slipstitch. Might be because I dropped a few cluster bombs in response, nice and neighborly like, over.*"

"Bravo Zulu, Shamrock. Stay high and out of SAM range. I don't want to write a letter to your mother, not now. Not *ever*."

"*Wilco, Slipstitch. I do try to please, especially my momma.*" Maxi sounded pleased with himself. "*Climbing. Deploying atmospheric whiskers for additional coverage—should improve communications dirtside, over.*"

"Much obliged, Shamrock. Slave a few to my mechsuit, too. I'm out, and I need to see what Samuelson's men are up to. Stay high. I plan on seeing you shortly, over."

"*Roger that, Slipstitch. You can count on it. Shamrock, out.*"

The remnant of Victor Company converged on the east side of Landing's warehouse district, at the heart of the Rotary's forward operating base— X-ray FOB. Jean-Wesley and a light company of Rotary members greeted Promise's Marines with MREs, MRSs, and charged energy cells. Both uniformed and irregular soldiers ate quickly, one eye on the meal and the other on the horizon.

"SITREP?" Promise asked Jean-Wesley as she squeezed out a mouthful of blue potatoes and cheese."

"I'd sure love to sit a spell, ma'am," he replied.

Ramuel scowled at him from a distance, but kept his peace.

Promise set her food down and picked up a clean cloth to towel off her sweat-soaked hair. After that, she grabbed her pulse rifle and checked the settings, popped the cell, and loaded a fully charged one. When she looked up at Partaine, she was all business.

"Sorry, ma'am, that was this civilian's lame attempt at humor."

Promise's lip curled upward and she risked a glance at Partaine. The sun accented the flecks in Jean-Wesley's eyes, reminding Promise of fall. She stared a bit too long for common propriety, finally breaking away when Jean-Wesley smiled at her, when she heard the gunny clear his throat several meters away.

Ramuel shook his head and looked upward.

Partaine sat across from Promise with a minicomp in his hands. He placed it at the center of the makeshift table between them and fingered a 2D map, which instantly grew into a hologrid. "If it's a SITREP you want," he said, looking from Promise to the gunny and back, "then I have three hundred men in position in an L formation at this intersection, from here to there." Partaine drew a line across the map with his finger as the gunny drew up close. "Samuelson is taking the bait—you," Partaine said as he circled a second location. "We've drawn the bulk of his troops to this position, about three klicks from us."

"He won't say there for long," Promise added.

"Agreed," said the gunny.

"According to our intel," Partaine went on, "their boots are rearming before they come at us again. When they do that, they won't like what they find. With your Marines out of the way, he can hunt for Annie and anything else his heart desires. But that isn't going to happen. I figure to use you as bait one more time, for a grand last stand, like that Custard fellow from Earth's history."

"I don't like the sound of that, Jean-Wesley. It's actually General Custer, and he died," Promise said dryly.

"Didn't say I was playing for the losing team, Promise. Let's trap these bastards and send a few live ones home with their tails between their legs."

Promise shook her head. "You . . . we may not have enough to hold him. If he breaks through our lines . . ."

Jean-Wesley leaned into the table and stared intently at her. "Ma'am, I believe I owe you another dance. I left you abruptly on the floor last time. I don't intend to do that again."

Her insides began to tingle. She grabbed a cup of cold water and downed it.

"Right." Then louder, for her Marines to hear. "Mount up."

Promise tapped into Maxi's sensors and brought up an aerial view of the Imperial Marines' current position. She slaved Partaine's minicomp to her mechsuit as they talked. Then she reached into the holomap and enlarged a section due south of their location. "Looks like the bulk of Samuelson's men are here. I'll take my Marines to this intersection, here, to draw in their right flank." Promise waved the gunny over. "Gunnery Sergeant Ramuel will take his command to this field, here, and pull in the left. Together, we will lead them back to you and funnel them through this alleyway, just outside of the warehouse district."

"Don't worry, Promise," Jean-Wesley added. "Those Lusies will pay dearly for setting foot on our planet."

Fifty-eight

APRIL 13TH, 91 A.E., STANDARD CALENDAR, 1202 HOURS,
CENTRAL LANDING CITY, PLANET MONTANA

"Danger close . . . Two toons bearing down on my six . . . Falling back to your position . . . Request covering fire once I crest the hill, over."

Private First Class Kathy Prichart had scouted ahead, roughly three hundred meters from her platoon's position. She was on the other side of an elevation, between two ranch-style homes, when several enemy mech-suits spotted her. She'd been cloaked, near a large shrub, when a mutt decided to defend his territory. It didn't take long for the Lusies to realize the dog wasn't barking at thin air, and the dog's peeing on her mechsuit hadn't helped. She ran right through the nearest door and dove through a back window. Moments later, the home's windows blew out and the roof caved in.

"*Wilco, Carbs. Make haste, over.*"

"Roger that, Slipstitch. It's getting hot out here and—"

"*Carbs, do you read me . . . I repeat, Carbs, do yo—*"

"I read you, Slipstitch. The edge of a scatter field knocked me out of the net for a cycle. Ninety-five meters out. Approaching the crest, over."

Kathy jumped over a rover and ducked. Rounds whizzed overhead and into the vehicle behind her. Several fast-moving pinpricks appeared in her compressed full-wrap field of view, to the extreme right and left of her HUD. *Mortar fire.*

Kathy swore. Seconds later, she heard the high-pitched whine before the thud.

Promise crouched behind an overturned shuttle bus riddled by weapons fire and scanned twelve o'clock. The sun was setting low and directly into her face, making her eyes all but useless.

"Bond, switch to infrared and shop the sun." Her vision abruptly changed to a primary color palette dominated by greens, with oranges and yellows. A splotch of red roughly shaped like a human popped up into view and started down the rolling hill toward her position. Prichart had crossed a quarter of the distance when the first Lusies appeared. They came in ones and twos, too spread out to concentrate their fire or to form up into a proper wall of battle.

Big mistake. Advantage mine. Promise zoomed on the right hip on her guardian's suit and snarled. The blue streaks bleeding through the red indicated a coolant leak and extensive internal damage. She switched to a modified thermal scan. Her HUD turned black, except for the humanoid blotches of red and orange bouncing behind Kathy. She counted eight signatures, then ten. Thankfully, what she was looking for wasn't there.

"They left the heavies behind them," Promised relayed to her platoon. "Hold positions and remain cloaked. When they pass within fifty meters, neutralize them." PFC Prichart had ditched her heavy gear, including her tri-barrel. Promise brought the sights of the tri-barrel up and waited for her first target.

When the distance to the lead Imperial Marine hit five-zero meters, Lance Corporal Zahn stroked the trigger of her mini Bi-Polar rifle. The shot punched cleanly through her target's faceplate and out the back of his skull. Gray matter and bits of flesh sprayed the Marine behind the target, who tried to avoid his toonmate, and went down himself. Promise locked up the downed trooper with Kathy's tri-barrel. That Marine never got back up either.

The third Lusie to cross the line fared slightly better. Promise fired. Her target lost an arm and his right shoulder joint before he bled out.

Twenty-two. Or was that twenty-three. Promise had lost count over a double-kill involving Zahn and herself.

"Mine or yours, Lance Corporal?"

"How 'bout we share, ma'am," Zahn said.

"Fine by me."

Promise fired again, added one to her number.

Enemy artillery fire tore up the ground all around PFC Prichart and lifted her body into the air.

Prichart's arms cartwheeled as she rotated through a cloud of rock and sand and over onto her back. Her ears started buzzing and her vision blurred. Kathy slowly rolled onto her side, raised her right arm, and fired her Heavy Pistol—set to full-auto—at the blur of metal running toward her. She emptied the magazine before a blast of energy took the pistol in her hand and the armor on her forearm. She raised her arm instinctively above her head and felt rounds ricochet off her suit.

"*Hold on, Kathy.*" The lieutenant's voice sounded hollow and distant.

Promise dropped her targeting reticule on Kathy's attacker, pulled the trigger, and held it back. Her tri-barrel fired a sustained beam that tore through her target's right leg, up through the torso, and out the left forearm. Her thermal vision blurred momentarily to all red before fading back to its normal color palette. Switching back to normal vision as the sun dipped below the hill in front of her, she let the drained cell drop free as she loaded her last charged one, acquired a new target, and tapped the trigger. This target let loose a flight of Horde missiles, which spent themselves on the shuttle bus's undercarriage. Two low-yield energy blasts followed them and made short work of the mover's rear axel before punching through, vaporizing precious armor on Promise's mechsuit.

"*Right leg at seventeen percent, breach on the lower chin,*" her AI said.

"Seal it," Promise said as she returned fire and scored a belly shot. She watched a pair of legs run a few more meters before they fell over. The rest of the Marine sat in the dirt some distance back, barely half of a self.

"Twenty-four."

Her AI summarized her predicament. "*Smartmetal has closed the gash, which will help keep the muscle lubricated so it won't seize on you. But you'll lose the leg if you take another hit there.*"

"Acknowledged."

Private First Class Kathy Prichart came barreling through a patch of shrubs. She took several shortened paces before leaping over a brick-and-mortar mailbox. While she was in the air, a burst of autocannon fire slammed into her left heel, causing her to overrotate and land harder than she'd anticipated. She rolled out of the fall, broke right, and catapulted up and over the shuttle bus, coming down on one knee and almost adjacent to Promise. A quick scan of her lieutenant told her everything. Kathy grabbed the tri-barrel from her commander and commed the gunny.

"Carbs to Rabbi, over."

"This is Rabbi. I'm occupied—make it fast, over."

"Slipstitch's taken critical damage, and we're tied down. Her energy feed is off-line and her cells are dry. Can you get her out of here?" Kathy shoved Promise down, popped up, and fired her tri-Barrel in harmony with Zahn's MBP rifle. Together, they ripped loose several bars of music and scored two key changes.

"Negative, Carbs, over," the PFC heard back, intermixed with the sounds of distorted explosions booming over the link. *"Two toons . . . battle armor ambushed our scout . . . hacked our net and traced our locus before we could . . . ,"* the gunny said between a string of expletives punctuated by small-arms fire. But Kathy read his meaning. They'd almost been compromised. *"Falling back to the rally point. Up to you . . . get Slipstitch . . ."* Ramuel's end went dead. Static and silence answered back.

"Rabbi, do you read me . . . *Rabbi!* Prichart yelled over the comm. Silence and static followed.

Shots rang out from the top west-facing window of a three-story palisade home, consuming their attention and threatening their location.

Promise scanned their exit roughly forty meters away. The path to it was largely exposed, which fed into the alleyway that narrowed at the end and funneled back to Jean-Wesley's position. She did some quick calculations and realized her math was worse than rusty.

Promise motioned inside the bus. "Kathy, in, fire out—suppress them." Kathy crawled through a gap in the floorboard into the shuttle bus's cabin and found a reasonable amount of cover and an opening in the roof to fire through. Promise racked her weapon and grabbed the frame of the vehicle. "This piece of junk is our ticket out of here. On three. One, two, pull!"

Their first tug was awkward and ill-timed. It earned them mere centimeters of ground.

Kathy swore as she lost her balance, which sent her beams wide of their intended target.

Zahn told her she could do better.

Corporal Fitzholm reached up and in to get a better grip.

Promise screamed at all of them. "Come on!"

Kathy fired.

Promise counted down from three and yelled so loud her ears rang in her helmet "Come on!"

On their second tug, the remnant of V Company fared better, Kathy found joy, and Zahn grunted in satisfaction as another enemy soldier fell down dead.

Their third try moved the wrecked people mover almost a half meter. And then a meter, and then a bit more than a meter. "Pull!" *Tug, tug, fire.* "Pull!" *Tug, tug, fire.* "Pull!" Mechsuit actuators and artificial muscles strained as the bus's weight exceeded their mechsuits' design tolerances. On the twelfth tug, Zahn's right arm gave way and fell limp at her side, exposing the suit's internal muscle and a mass of molycircs. Promise pushed the young woman toward the alley's mouth, just over ten meters away now. As she fell back, a burst of rounds penetrated the joint and took Zahn's arm just below the shoulder, and her to her knees.

The remnant of V Company abandoned the people mover and closed around their fallen toonmate, weapons up and tracking. Kathy grabbed Zahn's severed arm as she ran past, and secured it to her suit. She took up a covering position with the tri-barrel along with Corporal Fitzholm, who wielded the toon's only grenade launcher. Promise and Corporal Morris grabbed the handholds on each side of Zahn's suit and humped her out of harm's way. A split second later, a mortar landed on their last position.

Prichart and Fitzholm spit the alley, fired, and fell back, returned fire and retreated, again and again, skirting the walls from door to door while their toonmates ran behind them. Once they cleared the alleyway, Prichart waved the corporal back out of the killing field and used her much larger weapon to hold the line. As she fell back, a beam of pulser fire struck her injured heel and sheered the foot off at the ankle. Inhibitors and grit kept her moving.

Fifty-nine

"Here they come, people," Jean-Wesley Partaine said into his handheld comm. "You are to hold fire and stay hidden until the Lusies cross into the open." Partaine watched anxiously as Promise and her Marines traversed the last few hundred meters of exposed parkway. Once Samuelson's people were out in the open, it was his job to spring the trap.

Partaine thought he knew what his people were thinking. "It doesn't sit well with me either. But this is what they signed up for. They're the decoys. Let's make sure we are worthy of their sacrifice," he said slowly to bring the point home. "When they hit the line, give our Marines cover and give the Lusies a one-way ticket to hell."

Promise and Corporal Morris broke through first with PFC Zahn lumbering between them. On the opposite end of the park, the remains of Gunnery Sergeant Tomas Ramuel's toon burst into view. Three metal suits, charred and blackened, ran for their lives. The gunny brought up the rear, not a single weapon on his mechsuit operable.

The gunny closed the distance with Corporal Wintry Charng and Lance Corporal Zozo Magellen. With safety in sight, Corporal Charng glanced over at the gunny and flashed his ivories through his cracked visor. The smile froze on his face as he toppled forward. A split second later, Lance Corporal Magellen ran into a "walkie-talkie," caught air, and flipped end to end before crashing through a park bench. The gunny gritted his teeth, grabbed his last grenade, spun, gunned and spun again, and kept running. Then heard the boom.

Corporal Fitzholm came next. He ran a quarter of the distance to safety before he slid to his knees, completed a one-eighty, and raised his grenade launcher, all in one fluid motion. His last two frag grenades arched over Kathy's head as she exited the alley and detonated. Hundreds of small magnetic charges packed with micronite fell to meet their targets. The first three Lusies through the alley's neck took the full brunt of the fusillade and were still running when their organs exploded.

Corporal Fitzholm tossed the launcher as he dove for cover behind a ferocrete sculpture of a draft horse. More than a toon of enemy suits opened fire on his position. Adrenaline and poor firing solutions drove most of their shots far short of the retreating Republican Marines and into the equine or the landscaping. Then several more toons broke in the clearing, and the park became a shooting gallery. The horse lost its hindquarters and toppled over. Fitzholm found himself pinned and looking backward. He saw the lieutenant and Corporal Morris running hard, Zahn between them, injured, and knew they were going to make it. Then his heart felt like it burst as Zahn slumped over, a hole the size of a fist burned through her back. Fitzholm screamed and muscled the horse off his body and got to his feet.

Corporal Fitzholm palmed both of his Heavy Pistols and charged the Lusitanian Marines. He swept his arms through two diverging arcs, raking Lusitanian troops with deadly precision.

"Lieutenant, make sure my vid gets home," the corporal panted over the battlenet.

"Corporal Fitzholm—Fitz! You tell her yourself. Get your tail back here!" Promise barked.

"Not gonna happen, ma'am," he said as a Lusie took the full brunt of both pistols and dropped. "Too many of them. Not enough of us." He grunted as pulser fire ripped through the armor on his thigh and caused him to stumble. Fitzholm's knee joint froze as he bored into an Imperial boot, crushing the enemy's shoulder.

Promise turned to aid her Marine when Kathy, wounded and limping, rushed up to her and grappled her to the ground. Kathy almost lost her grip on her lieutenant before she overrode Promise's AI and took control of her mechsuit.

"No! Kathy, let me go. Let. Me. Go!"

Kathy pressed her helmet against Promise's, visor to visor, so Promise could see her talk.

"No, Lieutenant, you have to let him go so you can live. Bond, get her out of here!"

Promise screamed as her mechsuit ran against her will. Behind her, Corporal Fitzholm smashed through flesh and metal for the Marine Corps, for the Republic. For her.

Fitzholm fired at point-blank range until his guns ran dry. He let the clips drop free, hammered the guns into his thigh mags to quick-load them, and ran his guns dry a second time. Out of ammo, he dropped one gun and used the other as a hammer, cracked a faceplate and the face behind it. Tossed it, then engaged in hand-to-hand combat. As he ran past one Imperial Marine, he thrust his gauntlet into the crack in his opponent's helmet, yanked, and snapped her neck. Let go and spun around. His reverse knife-hand crushed a Lusitanian sergeant's collar. He rotated the opposite direction and caught another Imperial Marine in the helmet with his forearm, momentarily stunning the man and knocking him over. Then he executed a spinning roundhouse and caved in the chest plate of yet another enemy soldier.

Exhausted, Corporal Fitzholm fell to the ground, his arms at his sides, his leg angled badly. Time stilled as he looked up at the mêlée around him. Knew this was it. No less than five enemy Marines were training their weapons on him. He saw the other side of death as he unsheathed his force blade. Made his peace and knew all would be well. The force blade was millimeters thin and nearly invisible, which he brought up and around as he leapt to his feet. His muscled right arm swung with the full and practiced extension of a trained swordsman, taking an enemy boot square in the torso and coming out surgically clean on the other side. The corporal brought his arms together and swung the blade downward into the shoulder and out the right hip of a young Lusitanian woman. Her two halves fell apart like a piece of trimmed meat. Fitzholm nearly broke through the Lusitanians' ranks, his blade held high in preparation for yet another

thrust. The blast from a tri-barrel hit him in the chest and stopped his ber-
serker charge. The corporal looked down at his chest, muttered something,
and fell asleep. Moments later, his suit exploded, taking five nearby Lusitanians with him.

"Open fire!" Three hundred Rotary members unleashed enough firepower
to raze a city block. The park rippled with kinetic energy and burned with
blue flame. Playground equipment splintered into armored Marines,
knocking some off their feet, impaling others. Over twenty pulse weapons scored a single target, leaving nothing but smoke and ash where flesh
and metal had stood a split second before. Frag grenades exploded from
above and rained death. Fifty-nine Rotary members and virtually all Victor Company lost their lives, in exchange for almost every single Marine
Commodore Samuelson had thrown at them during the entire day of
battle.

After a long minute, Partaine barked over the comm. "Cease fire! Cease
fire!" But staccato burps continued for several seconds more.

Promise overrode the comm. "All units, cease fire now, or I will cease
fire for you!"

Overwhelming silence followed. A noxious stench rolled across the
grounds, causing militiamen to wretch. Smoke hung in the air, masking
the full extent of the carnage from the eyes of those who had caused it.

Promise sagged against the doorway of a bakery, surrounded by the
remains of her company. She looked over at Prichart, Morris, and the gunny.
So few left. Maxi was in the sky, safe for the moment. The sign above her
head swung gently in the breeze. FRANZ'S BAKERY.

Promise reached for her clamps. The helmet came off with a slight pop
and fell to the ground. She stepped into the open, flexed her jaw to equalize the pressure, and drew the only weapon on her that still had ammo.
But Kathy got in her way first.

"Get out of my way, Private First Class."

"No, ma'am. Let me secure the perimeter first." Kathy met her CO's
gaze and blinked, looked down at Promise's 'senior,' which was pointed at
her chest. She took a step sideways and lowered her weapon.

"No, Kathy." Promise pulled back the slide of her handgun. "Please,
don't make me do something I'll regret."

"Lieutenant." The gunny spoke evenly. "You did it, ma'am. We stopped the Lusies. Stopped them cold. Now, lower your weapon."

"I need to make sure."

"Roger that, we'll take you out," Kathy said. I'll take point. Corporal Morris, would you take the right flank? Gunny, the left?"

Kathy took a deep breath. "All right, then stay on me. If it makes a move, kill it." Kathy skirted around Promise and swept her field of view for threats. Her left hand rose and motioned forward. "Watch your six."

Promise walked through dozens of bodies, some injured beyond recognition. Acrid smoke and the smell of burning blood nearly made her vomit. Severed hands clung to weapons, refusing to let go. Midway in, Promise found a Lusitanian mechsuit slumped on its side, against a stone park bench. The Lusie's chest was mangled, and the Marine had lost most of a right arm and a leg. A thin strip of metal connected the other leg to the torso. Promise heard the death rattle before she rolled the body. The Lusitanian's visor was up, revealing an anguished face. Promise cupped the woman's head and pressed a hypo to her tongue.

"This will hurt. But it will kill your pain."

The woman started screaming and arched her back, then grew oddly calm. "Thank you." The words were garbled and barely audible. Promise simply nodded.

She's no older than I was when I enlisted. The name on her armor said M. V. Jakartash. "Corporal, I'm sorry."

Jakartash's eyes were glazed over, clearly unfocused. "Did we get them, ma'am? Did we . . ." Jakartash's eyes fluttered and then fixed on something in the distance.

Promise closed Jakartash's eyes and pulled her close. She removed the helmet, tossed it aside. The woman's hair was matted and wet with blood.

"Yes, Corporal, you did your duty. Go with God. Go in peace."

Promise lay the girl down. Her face was so young it was hard to call her a woman. More a kid, really. Rage boiled up inside her. Promise retrieved Jakartash's helmet and turned it round.

"Samuelson!" Promise pulled the helmet closer to her mouth. "Commodore Samuelson, do you hear me? Your Marines are dead. They're. All. Dead. And their blood is on your hands. This didn't have to happen. How many more, Commodore? How many more have to die?"

The commodore stood on his flag deck, listening to the impossibility of it all. *This woman, this* Lieutenant *Paen, has obliterated my command. And now she dares to mock me?* Anger and fear crept up his back and circled around to his top lip, which began to twitch involuntarily.

Lieutenant Colonel Saloman heard his commanding officer in his mastoid implant. *"Colonel, what do you have in reserve?"*

The message reached Saloman instantly. He spent a small eternity wondering where he had gone wrong in his career before he answered. "Not enough, sir. Our birds are grounded, our supply lines are stretched thin, and almost all of my mechanized armor is either heavily damaged or destroyed."

Saloman thought very carefully about his next words. He realized there was no way to salvage his career. So he chose the one course of action he could faithfully commit to with a clear conscience.

"Sir, I have wounded, critically wounded, men down here. You have two shuttles in reserve, sir. I need an immediate evac and all available medical personnel on standby to receive our wounded. And, sir, I suggest we broker a truce—and soon—so our medics can deploy and retrieve those that can still be saved, while they still have a fighting chance."

Commodore Samuelson cursed providence. He'd had every advantage, more warships, more Marines, more intelligence, and decades more experience than Lieutenant Promise Paen. But events had still turned against him.

"Very well, Colonel. Call a truce and see to our injured."

Samuelson walked back to his command chair and sat down, slowly. His ship's arsenal began to scroll across his holoscreen until he reached the missile manifests, various nukes and ship-killers of specific yields, and a substantial list of bunker busters. His eyes found the GEHAKs—Gravitic-Enhanced High-Altitude Bunker-Killers. The GEHAK missile was the heaviest nonnuclear ordnance at his disposal.

"Colonel, notify me when you've evacuated our wounded and are three minutes out."

He muttered to himself. "We aren't finished yet."

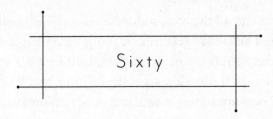

Sixty

Promise sat across from Annie in the president's office, nursing a cup of oily caf. She watched the president drop a third sugar in before changing her mind. The brew was from an old pot and had grown stale. Promise added more sugar to hers, stirred, took a sip, and gave up on it. Annie looked at Promise questioningly as her finger joined the rhythm of the ticking wall clock.

"No good, ma'am. You give yourself up, and we lose Montana," Promise spoke quietly, though she might as well have yelled her thoughts at Annie. The president winced at her tone.

"If I don't give myself up, Samuelson will start bombarding my planet. He will destroy everything we've worked so hard for, and kill God knows how many people doing it."

Promise opened her mouth, saw the president cross her arms in challenge, and closed it. This was one of those times when it was best to be seen and not heard.

"What I don't understand," Annie went on, "is what Samuelson hopes to gain at this point. Much of Landing is in shambles, thanks to him, and news of this will spread fast. He can't possibly win over the public, not after all that's happened."

"No, but does he really have to? He wants your planet and the system, even if he can't have your allegiance. Either way, he won't settle until you surrender." Promise wanted to say the man was bluffing. She wanted to and she couldn't.

"For the present, all the commodore needs to do is silent the planet's government and keep the press from leaking what's happened here into the nets. He can spin his own web of lies until he casts enough doubt around that some of the locals start believing him, too. You've reminded me, on several occasions I might add, that most of Montana doesn't think too highly of *my* Republic. And my Marines, the few of us left, may not fare well in the court of public opinion." Promise's eyes hardened. "But consider this, Madam President: When Samuelson finished off *Absalon*, he also destroyed every satellite in orbit, and your communications grid on the ground went with it. Your planetary net is down. As far as the neighboring systems are concerned, let alone many of the ranches and homesteads across Montana, none of this has happened. We're cut off. Samuelson plans to keep it that way until it no longer matters. But, I'm still praying for a miracle. Chief Swanson and the Maven are still out there. Even now, he could be en route with help. We just need to hold on a bit longer."

"But we can't bank on that. I guess I know what I have to do."

"Ma'am—I didn't mean to say—"

Annie held up a hand, cutting her off.

"Annie? Please. Not like this. Chief Swanson's out there. He's coming ma'am. We just need to give him time."

"We're out of time, Promise. This ends. Now. Understood?"

"Yes, ma'am."

Promise looked away. The ticking of the clock grew louder. Annie's pictures and placards and presidential mementos were hung with care, covered in flat glass that told you nothing of the world staring back at them. Everything appeared righted, as it should be. Ordinary and orderly and fine-tuned. *And the rest of Landing is a wreck. Dear God, what have I done?*

Promise heard the president continue speaking without really listening to her. "I know you don't agree, Promise, but I don't see how I have much choice. Please don't take offense at this—it isn't directed at you—but your superiors and mighty Fleet Forces put the Rim worlds low on their list of priorities decades ago. And I have little hope that our situation will change anytime soon. Either I throw my planet at the mercy of the Lusitanians and hope for better days under Her Majesty's watch, or I watch Samuelson destroy our industrial base and roll back decades of progress. What would you have me do?"

"You can only work with what you've got, ma'am." *And trust the Maker with the rest. At least my dad always thought so.*

Both women fell silent. Promise found herself staring at the president's bookshelf. It was lined with volumes of various heights and thicknesses. *War and Freedom*, by Mallory Brick, stood next to Thomas Heinrick's *The Lost Colony*, which was inspired by the mysterious disappearance of a twenty-fifth-century colonizer en route to Kathmandu. Lost in jump. Several titles appeared to be bound in leather, including a copy of *Love Him, Hate Him, Marry Him* and *Shoveling Sh*t: Lessons I Learned at the Business End of Life*, by the famous Montana poet Elton Blaze. She'd never seen so much printed text in a single room. Her eyes drifted over the shelves and back to Annie's desk, and to the book that lay there alone. A name was embossed in the lower corner. Promise reached for it before she realized what she was doing.

"Go ahead," Annie said. "I read it most every day."

The worn binding reminded her of her father's copy. The fire had claimed it along with her childhood mementos, and she hadn't thought of it since. Thumbing through the familiar onionskin pages almost fooled her into thinking Annie's book and her father's were one in the same. She fanned to the passage with a reverence she thought she had abandoned many years before. Palms facedown on the page, eyes closed, she mouthed the words.

> *There is a time for everything,*
> *A season for every activity under heaven.*
> *A time to be born and a time to die.*
> *A time to plant and a time to harvest.*
> *A time to kill and a time to heal.*

With each word, her voice grew stronger, and somehow surer of itself. Promise wondered if the men and women she'd lost in combat were speaking to her now, perhaps even through her, lending her their strength from beyond the grave. Tears tried to come but wouldn't. Now wasn't the time to mourn but a time to see to the living. She kept going.

A time to tear and a time to mend.
A time to be quiet and a time to speak up.
A time to love and a time to hate.
A time for war and a time for peace.

"It's true, you know." When Promise opened her eyes, Sandra was sitting next to her. Promise thought her mother looked uncharacteristically staid and distant, as if lost in another time. "I've read that passage more times than I can count, and drawn strength from it twice over. You don't know how many arguments your father and I had over you. Me longing to teach you to stand up to evil. Him telling you to turn the other cheek. Turns out, we were both right." Sandra shook her head and looked at her daughter. "Just remember, sometimes you have to help peace along before it has a chance to take root."

Promise smiled and did a double take. *They are so very similar.* Both women affected the people around them in eerily similar ways. They could ionize the room. And here they were, sitting across from each other, mere meters apart, with Promise in the middle, swinging like a pendulum between life and death. That neither woman could see or speak to the other made the moment more real, and a bit tragic, too.

"Ma'am, do you remember what I said in the hospital room, back when I was injured?"

Annie looked puzzled and slowly shook her head. *No.*

"I said you reminded me of someone." Promise paused. "I sure wish you could have met my mother. I think the two of you would've been good friends."

Sandra nodded her head. "Promise, I believe you're right. Maybe even kindred spirits. Your president's a good woman. Keep her close, you hear?"

Promise shook her head. "Yes, ma'am. Good friends."

"That's about the nicest thing anyone has every said to me, Promise. Your mother must have been a fine woman."

"That she was, ma'am. And she taught me there was a time for everything. We've had our day of war, just like the good book says. Now it's time to sue for peace."

"Sue for peace? With what? We have nothing left to bargain with," Annie said in bewilderment. "*That* book has given me a lot of hope and direction over the years, but as I see it, the only hope left is to surrender and *pray* for peace."

"Or bluff our way to it," Promise suggested. "The mechsuit's cloaking ability is still on the Navy's official secrets list. You know about it because our defense of Montana relied upon out ability to hide in plain sight. By now, Samuelson's men have seen more than enough to figure out what we're using and how we're doing it."

"Okay, meaning . . ."

"Meaning, we tell Samuelson the same cloaking technology was scaled and installed on a small jump-cable ship, which just departed from Montana's system. The ship witnessed what happened here and is at this very moment en route to Nouveau Paris, where BATRONs 15 and 22 are berthed. We're not even stretching the truth, at least not by much. I did dispatch the chief and the *Maven* and I still believe they're out there. Suppose we tell Samuelson his war crimes are about to be broadcast across the 'verse, and let him do the math."

"That's a tall bluff, Promise. Can you sell it? Do you think Samuelson will buy?"

"His Marines saw enough against my Marines to put two and two together. He knows the Witchfield exists. Hiding an entire ship in one is entirely another matter. It's theoretically possible, even if we haven't yet figured out how to do it. Miniaturization is in some respects always harder, though the principle tends to work in reverse where the Witchfield is concerned. But Commodore Samuelson doesn't need to know that. The *Maven* might arrive today, she might arrive tomorrow, or she might never reappear. But if there's even the slightest chance the chief was successful, we owe it to him to give him time. Time, Annie. We just need to stall for time. That's all I'm asking for."

Annie pursed her lips.

"Madam President, if nothing else, I can appeal to Samuelson's sense of self-preservation and remind him that human beings fight wars."

"Remind him of his own mortality, you mean."

"Yes. If the tide turns against him, his government might turn on him, too, which leaves him few options: carry out his plan, bombard the capital, and murder countless innocents, which probably will get him court-martialed; or return home and possibly face a court-martial anyway; or disappear into the 'verse."

"And if he doesn't go?" Annie asked.

"If he doesn't leave, we're back where we started from. We can say, with a clear conscience, we tried everything before we surrendered."

Annie nodded. "All right, Lieutenant, I'm not sure it will work, but if anyone can pull this off, you can. We'll give him our answer in the morning."

"And in the end, you will have done all you could do," Sandra added.

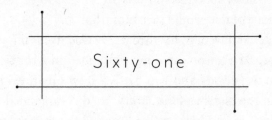

Sixty-one

APRIL 14TH, 91 A.E., STANDARD CALENDAR, 0713 HOURS,
HMS *INTREPID,* GEOSTATIONARY ORBIT, PLANET MONTANA

Commodore Samuelson listened to the message in his quarters. His hands massaged a weary brow and tried to ease the steady migraine building behind it. His mind tried to wrap around all the possibilities, but there were too many shifting variables and unknowns at play. A sleepless night had robbed him of clarity. And then there was Lieutenant Paen's blind luck.

She can't keep winning, not forever. Yet her luck seemed to have no end.

What if there was a ship, one with enough sensor data to repudiate his actions? If a distorted version of what happened on Montana spread through the nets, he'd lose everything and rot somewhere in a Lusitanian penal colony or worse—hang as a rogue officer who went off mission and tried to scalp a bunch of backwater neobarbs.

Samuelson cursed, slamming his desk with both fists again and again until they throbbed, the pain a kind of narcotic. He forced himself to breathe slowly. Each breath brought a measure of clarity until Samuelson saw the truth. He even surprised himself by how quickly he accepted it. Word was going to get out about what had happened on Montana. He'd destroyed a defenseless mining installation, invaded the planet, tried to abduct the president, and threatened to shell the city and butcher civilians to sate some twisted need for power. That's how it would go—the hatchet job would ruin him. They'd lie about his motivations, malign his character, and twist the truth. In the end, it wouldn't matter what he said in his own defense. It would all be meaningless in the end. Why he'd done it—to preserve Her Majesty's interests in this sector and to secure his empire's borders. No, none of that would save him from . . .

Samuelson's hand went to his throat. *My God, what if I went too far?*

Commodore Samuelson sat alone, entombed in a starship built from the keel out to wage wars and win battles. It was manned by one of the finest navies in the history of humanity. He'd commanded thousands of Sailors and Marines and his word had carried the weight of law. A life in the service to Her Majesty's Navy had brought him here, to power and to the breaking point . . . And all of it was meaningless.

Samuelson stood and walked over to the side of his bed. He placed his palm against a small black cabinet and leaned into the retinal scan. Inside were four handheld pulsers, each with a fully charged cell, in case of emergency—not that there'd been a mutiny on an Imperial vessel, ever.

He selected the third pulser from the left and walked back to his desk. He dialed the energy setting to a low-yield burst and placed the weapon in front of him with the business end pointed toward the opposite bulkhead.

A soft chime interrupted him.

"What?"

"Sir," said Commander Mouser, and then he hesitated. *"We just detected a large jump print, at least a dozen contacts. CIC makes it a heavy BATRON and expects to find screen elements, too. Sir, they aren't ours."*

"ETA?"

"Eight hours."

"Thank you, Niall. That will be all."

The silence was palpable. *"Sir, your orders?"*

Samuelson killed the link, closed his eyes, and looked inside. No family or friends. No one to record a message to. He regretted doing this to Niall, but at least his XO's career would survive. He looked at the weapon on the desk in front of him and reached out for it with two steady hands. A smile crossed his face as he met his death without hesitation.

Sir Geoffrey Theodore Samuelson fed the weapon into his mouth and aimed high, just to be sure.

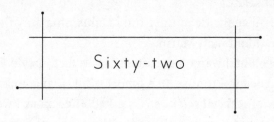

Sixty-two

The sun burned unrepentantly in Montana's eastern sky, having long since warmed the steps of the capitol building and the grounds of the Mall. President Matthew Hein's statue stood nearby, several families encamped in his shadow, their blankets staking claim to the Montanan's legacy. Landing Monument wasn't far away, cradled in an embankment one had to walk up and then down to appreciate. The original module sat open to the public, a ringed interior with twelve webbed cushions that had cradled the survey team during first fall nearly three centuries ago. High overhead, the rippling silhouette of Montana's planetary flag fluttered across the manicured lawn. The Republic's own standard and the RAW-MC's colors stood to the right and left, all three noticeably lowered to half-mast. Below, forty chairs sat in rows of five each, with one welcome addition, all abutting the capitol's steps. A transparent podium stood empty to the side, squared in red material that pooled generously on the hallowed ground.

In the distance, the slow cadence of a drumbeat could be heart.

Two rows of armed Rotary took to the field—"Left, left, left-right-left"—halting just short of the stage. They wore Rotary jackets, holstered sidearms, and proud, somber expressions forged by combat none of them ever imagined. Jean-Wesley Partaine's amplified voice rang out from the side of the formation. "Militia, officer on deck!" They came to attention—"Left-face"—and turned inward. At "Present-arms," they held their imperfect salutes.

Citizens of all ages rose to their full heights, shielding their eyes for a glimpse of the "Montanan Marines."

None of them had wanted the attention. In fact, they'd flatly refused, at first, and turned to Promise for support. And what about the survivors from the crew of RNS *Absalon*? she'd asked after an awkward moment. Surely they deserved just as much credit. Why single us out? she'd pressed, when so many militia had fallen, too. Annie had nodded and reminded Promise that the folks who'd bled and died with them only wanted to say thank you. How do you say no to that? Besides, the soon-to-be-renamed planetary spaceport and multisensory memorial would guarantee that *Absalon* and her crew lived in perpetuity. *Absalon*'s crew and the militia would have their days, soon. And with the BATRON burning in system, things were going to change in a hurry.

"As long as Montana remains free." So President Annie Buckmeister had promised them.

Duly prodded and chastised, the Montana Marines walked through the ranks of Rotary militia in solemn time, in the white and gold mess dress of the RAW-MC, wearing full glittery. Engineering Apprentice Fingers followed close behind, eyes scanning the assembled crowd wildly, arms mostly keeping time in Navy black and gold. Promise had insisted he be honored, too, only to discover the president was three steps ahead of her on the matter. The reached the stage and found their seats but remained standing, at attention.

Sailors and Marines all wore the standard Fleet Forces' white beret, with the Seraph, Globe, and Anchor affixed to the crown, canted just so.

The twin doors behind them at the top of the capitol's steps opened, and Montana's president, alone, walked out, down with measured step, and up the short flight to the stage. She carried a small black folder, which she placed on the dais, and scanned the documents before looking out at the masses. Her face flooded with emotion, making it nearly impossible for her to speak. She had to clear her throat, twice, before a glass of water appeared.

"Nearly three centuries ago, our founders came to Montana seeking to build a new world upon old, time-tested principles. These simple ideas beat in our hearts today as they did in the hearts of our brave ancestors. Our first president, Matthew Hein, spoke of the Montanan dream in his inaugural address. In it, President Hein talked about the riches of Montana, which in his estimation weren't found in currency or land but in the inalienable freedom of the human heart. He said that freedom 'enriches our soil and binds us together as neighbors and as friends. We are all born free. We can, through hard work and the Maker's blessings, secure our freedom. And governments should get the hell out of our way as we do it.'

"Notice that he did not say government, but *governments*." Annie paused. "His words are oddly prescient and as appropriate today as they were then."

Applause raced across the crowd like a wind wrinkling the sea. Children waved Montanan and RAW-MC flags with vigor. Many wore RAW-MC shirts picturing the Corps's universal slogan and Aunt Janie's pointed finger, encouraging the young and adventurous and brave to begin the journey of a thousand light-years. In the days following the Second Battle of Landing, enlistments had risen tenfold.

Annie paused and swept her eyes over the audience. She turned her head upward to the flags. To one flag.

"Today is a day of remembrance, a day we celebrate a hard-won peace in the defense of our homeland and in defense of our first principles. The Lusitanian Empire tried to rob us of our freedom and failed, largely because of these brave women and men of the Republican Fleet Forces, who stand before you."

Annie opened her hand to the Sailor and Marines on the platform. Their stand-up collars and turned-down berets. The crowd cheered, and more applause swept over the audience, this time with an intensity that seemed to shake the ground about them.

"My fellow Montanans, look closely. They are among the finest souls I've had the honor of meeting. They wear Republican uniforms and have sworn to protect the Republic's member planets and plebecites from enemies both foreign and domestic. Not that long ago I wondered if the Republic really cared about our *uncivilized* world. But today I am proud to be a Montana citizen and a citizen of the Republic of Aligned Worlds."

"I am—" Annie stopped as raw emotion swelled up from the crowd, almost dragging her down into it. The crowd melded together until their voices became an unpredictable wave, which rose and crested without warning, nearly drowning even the rushing of the wind. As the volume refused to die down, the president added her voice to the chorus of praise. Live feeds carried her words to every school and park and central meeting area across Montana's Federated States.

"Seaman Fingers, Marines of Victor Company, Charlie Battalion, Fifth Brigade, Twelfth Regiment—look closely. All of Montana is with you. We see you and we honor your sacrifice. Today, you are one of us, too."

For a brief time, intermittent gunshots and uncultivated applause filled every continent, in every city and rural area, across the blue globe.

President Annie Buckmeister stepped back from the lectern and walked over to the remnant of Victor Company and the sole representative of the crew of RNS *Absalon*. A small camera hovered overhead, recording each moment, relaying it to the screens placed throughout the crowd.

"This is the Protector's Medal." Annie's assistant, Saxena, walked up the stairs with a stack of small rectangular boxes in her hands. Saxena opened the one on top, and Annie removed the commendation tied to a purple sash, turning to face the young Sailor. "And I believe the name speaks for itself. It's a small token of this planet's affection for each of you, for your truly exceptional service and sacrifice to Montana and her people."

The crowd grew still as the camera focused on the medal and then on the face of the man who would wear it.

"Engineering Apprentice Jerry I. Fingers, with the gratitude of my homeworld, and that of her people."

Fingers swallowed hard. "Th-thank you, ma'am. I don't know what to say."

Saxena handed Annie another medal, this one for the SNCO of V Company.

"Gunny?" Sandra held up her hands and cocked an eyebrow at him.

The gunny bowed sheepishly, low enough for Annie to place the ribbon around his substantial neck. When he came back up, his face was noticeably flushed.

"Gunnery Sergeant Tomas Ramuel, you have my gratitude and that of the Montana people."

"Thank you, Madam President. I am truly honored."

Annie withdrew another medal and moved to face the next Marine in line.

"Sergeant Maxzash-Indar Sindri, for your selflessness and service to this planet, you have my sincere thanks and the gratitude of my people."

Maxi smiled up at the president as she placed the ribbon over his head. "The honor is mine, Madam President."

And so it continued.

"Corporal Richard Morris, with the thanks of a grateful planet."

"Thank you, Madam President."

"Private First Class Kathy Prichart, for your extraordinary service, you have my thanks and Montana's." The private balanced between her crutches with the right ankle of her uniform pinned back.

"It's an honor, Madam President."

The president remained in front of Prichart and held out two more medals. "Private First Class Nathaniel Van Peek and Captain Ffyn Spears can't be with us today because of their injuries. I'm told, with time, both are expected to make a full recovery."

The president's words came out like a question, and Kathy Prichart nodded in the affirmative.

"Well, then, Private First Class, please make sure they get them."

And then the president stood in front of her. Promise couldn't meet her eyes, not at first. But she willed herself to and found that hers were just as inconsolable as Annie's. In that moment, both women realized something. Though they weren't flesh and blood, they were cut from the same fabric. They understood each other. Believed in doing hard things and learned that it was better to do them together than alone.

"Lieutenant, this is becoming a habit." Their laughter was a great relief. Both women dabbed their eyes and smiled. The camera zoomed in, and the audience grew solemn, still. As the president spoke, her words thickened with emotion. "Lieutenant Promise T. Paen, for your heroism in the face of truly . . . overwhelming odds, for leading Victor Company and my people by example from the frontlines, for your service to your homeworld, you have the gratitude of all Montana. And you have the love and admiration of all of *your* Montanans."

Annie stepped to the side and began clapping. And it seemed only fitting for Promise to join her, then her Marines and Seaman Fingers were clapping as enthusiastically as Annie was for all Montana, and for the Rotary, and for the mothers and fathers and husbands and wives who had walked their sons and daughters and partners into eternity. The ovation grew to deafening proportions and went on for over a minute. When the moment finally retreated, Annie spoke again.

"My fellow citizens, this stage in noticeably empty. Over 80 percent of Victor Company—in total, thirty-three valiant Marines—lost their lives so that you and I might stand here today. Nearly all of them sustained wounds, some grievous. To them we owe a debt of gratitude we can never repay. Please offer them your silence in return."

Gunnery Sergeant Tomas Ramuel broke rank, pivoted smartly on his heels, and took to the podium. Tradition held that the unit's longest serving member—regardless of rank—gave the final roll call. Tomas Ramuel removed his beret with practiced care, blinked several times. His hands felt heavy on the podium as he mustered his breath. He pictured each Marine in turn, their faces indelibly burned upon his memory.

As he called the names of the fallen, one by one, a surviving member of Victor Company answered final roll call.

"Lance Corporal Talon Covington."

"Present, Gunnery Sergeant," Promise said. She'd barely uttered the word before a fresh layer of mist clouded her vision.

"Staff Sergeant Moya Hhatan."

"Present, Gunnery Sergeant," replied Sergeant Maxzash-Indar Sindri in a firm yet strained voice.

"Corporal Vilhelm C. Fitzholm."

"Present, Gunnery Ser-geant!" barked PFC Kathy Prichart. The young Marine refused to dry her cheek, for the fallen Marine, and for her friend.

The gunny's voice grew strained. "Private First Class Malory 'Molly' Starns."

"Present, Gunnery Sergeant," said Corporal Richard Morris.

Gunnery Sergeant Tomas Ramuel called, "Captain Paul Remus."

Promise tried to speak, but no words came. The skipper's loss pressed down upon her, as if he were reaching up from the grave and dragging her down with him. Captain Dimitri Tsveokiev's last words filled her mind, words said in the midst of certain death. Words spoken by a warship captain who was out of options. Words that unraveled whatever re-solve Promise had carefully stowed away.

She felt a hand against her back. Heard Corporal Morris say, "Go ahead, Lieutenant, the skipper passed command to you, ma'am. He would have wanted you to do it."

Make sure their story gets told. The orders of a dying warship's captain, spoken to her because there was no one else to speak them to. Then other words, more intimate and familial. *You did your best, munchkin. All you could do.* The words changed, no longer *their* story but *my* story, *our* story, yours to sell. Tell them, Lieutenant. And so she did.

"Present, Gunnery Sergeant."

After all the living and dead had been honored, they stood together one last time, resolute, as the faithful and the fallen of Victor Company, Charlie Battalion, Fifth Brigade, Twelfth Regiment.

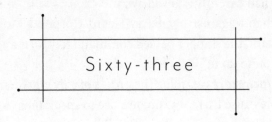

Sixty-three

Jean-Wesley guided Promise across the dance floor to a local favorite, "I'll Make You Smile." An ensemble of helix guitars, strings of various size, and percussion played in six-eight time.

"Whatever that is, I like it," Promise said.

"Just aftershave, ma'am."

"I was talking about the music. But your aftershave is nice, too."

"Then it's working."

"Maybe . . . just a little"

Jean-Wesley chuckled.

"I wouldn't get your hopes up. I'm an old-fashioned girl, Mr. Partaine."

"Jean-Wesley."

Promise swallowed hard.

"Wouldn't dream of it, ma'am. Besides, I like to move at my own pace, steady and real slow." His hand moved down the small of her back, just a smidge.

Promise's insides turned to goo. "That sounds perfect." Jean-Wesley had no idea how perfect it, he, everything felt.

The rest of the evening unfolded like a perfect fairy-tale, too. The two Montanans danced through the last number of the evening, a ballad about two lovers who reunite in midlife. "Wiser and in Love." When the music faded to silence, Jean-Wesley leaned in.

Everyone whooped. Her Marines—Maxi, Tomas, Richard, and Kathy—Annie Buckmeister, Jerry Fingers and even crusty old Kauffee. Promise's mother, Sandra, stood off to the side and toasted her with a glass of red.

Promise punched Jean-Wesley in the chest, but there was no heart in it. Then she kissed him back. That brought the house down.

Promise excused herself and headed off to the ladies' room to fix her lips. The face in the mirror looked oddly relaxed. She thought over all they'd experienced together. The joys, the losses, those she'd buried and the few who remained. Command had come to her the hard way, unexpectedly, and she'd done all she could to bear up underneath it, for her Marines and for the Republic. Even for herself. A part of her wondered if she'd done enough.

Promise shook off the doubt and turned her thoughts to the dark skies above her and the blackness of space beyond. It was all punctuated by stars, without the white hulls of Lusitanian warships parked in near orbit.

They'd left quickly. BATRON-15 had made sure of it, thanks to Chief Mark Swanson, the *Maven*, and the miners from the Rock. The heavy task force of battlecruisers with screening elements had jumped in system and made a bold statement. But Promise suspected something else had happened to expedite the Lusitanians' departure. An unfamiliar captain had commed her to say he was breaking orbit. Their conversation was terse and brief. No Commodore Samuelson.

After the battle of Landing, Lieutenant Colonel Saloman, with the Rotary's help, had evacuated his wounded and left the planet in a hurry. The help had shamed him, and he had stumbled through one of the most awkward thank-yous Promise had ever heard. She suspected a decent man lived somewhere inside of Saloman. Part of her wanted to tell him not to blame himself. But doing so would have shamed him further. And the other part of her enjoyed watching him squirm anyway.

When Promise returned from the washroom, Jean-Wesley was waiting for her with a fresh cup of hot caf.

"Anything in that?"

"Just sugar and cream." Jean-Wesley's arm went around her possessively. She looked up into his eyes and saw the wanting, and knew it couldn't be.

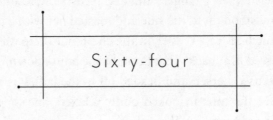

Sixty-four

APRIL 15TH, 91 A.E., STANDARD CALENDAR, 0830 HOURS,
RNS *SYKES VAN SHIPLEY,* MONTANA ORBIT

She was leaving and she couldn't bring herself to open his letter.

Promise hit TRANSMIT, killed the screen, and pushed back from the desk in her officer's cabin. She looked across her quarters to the mirror on the bulkhead and saw an incongruous mess of fruit salad. Commendations from two different traditions fought for attention over her heart. The regimented life of the RAW-MC sparkled next to the asymmetrical, almost garish medals of her birth planet. She'd sworn allegiance to the Republic and simultaneously sworn off her homeworld, but the latter had wormed its way back into her heart, had slowly won her over, had shown her that she could still love.

She thought of Jean-Wesley, again. She'd just been with him the evening before—a few good drinks, a few more dances, and a sweet kiss. Well, several kisses, but who was counting? But it felt like an eternity ago, and she was glad it did. She needed to put it behind her and move on. BATRON-15 had swept in with six Mandrake-class battlecruisers, plus another half-dozen heavy and light CZs, and a protective screen of destroyers, and established a battalion-level garrison force with a lieutenant colonel commanding dirtside. The new CO, a plain-looking woman named Krenshaw, had commed her at 0430 hours, apologized for the ungodly hour, and told her directly that she and rest of Victory Company were being recalled, immediately. To the *Sykes Van Shipley,* which was headed back to Nouveau Paris. There, she'd be debriefed. Departure at 1430 hours.

A quick comm to Jean-Wesley and a fierce embrace with Annie at the spaceport was all she was given time for. He'd offered to come. She'd brushed him off. *Easier that way.* She packed her seabag first before waking her people. Annie had shown up in jeans, just before dust-off, with her hair pulled back and her face washed of color. The ride up in the LAC had been too quick and she'd stepped off the gangway disoriented. The gravity felt wrong. The artificial light hurt her eyes. But then the bosun's pipe had sounded three times, two shorts and one long. The call reserved for flag officers and important guests. Her eyes went wide as she spotted the receiving detail in mess dress waiting below.

Every hand on deck rocked upward to salute her.

Promise paused and cleared her throat. Finding the captain of the vessel, she said, "Lieutenant Promise Paen requesting permission to come aboard, sir!"

"Permission granted."

And like that she was home.

Jean-Wesley's letter came up just before they broke orbit, written with care, in neat and precise script, on real paper. She should have said more to his face, and, to her shame, her fear had bested her. "Duty calls. I wish we had more time together" and "I'm sorry" seemed pretty insensitive now. Jean-Wesley had just nodded from his side of the screen. He hadn't even asked her when she might return. Watching the fight go out of him had nearly done her in. She'd almost hitched a ride to the surface. And then it had hit her—he hadn't tried to stop her from going. The lack of surprise on his face told her why. She was military, and he understood enough to know what that meant.

Relationships weren't like command decisions. They were messy two-way exchanges, and she'd had no practical training in them. She recorded several vids before selecting one that she hoped struck the right balance. She confessed the truth to him, about her feelings, what she wanted, and what she knew she couldn't have. Her life was elsewhere. The Corps was her family. She'd be sure to write. Most of it was true.

Promise pressed her thumb against a small pad on the center desk drawer, which obediently slid outward. She removed the handgun and crossed her cabin to her rack. Sat down and cradled the weapon to her breast and said a final good-bye to a tall drink of water that would have given her acres of room and a heart of gold. *God, I don't want to let him go.* But she was Corps, through and through, and it was time to get on with it.

"Mom, I just need to know that you're here, okay?"

The air around her warmed—her mother's smell—and a soft voice began to sing a lullaby she hadn't heard in twenty years.

*I'll hold you
Now and forever
I'll hold you
Closely and tight
I'll hold you
Now and forever
I'll hold you dear
T'will be all right*

Promise turned over and cried into her pillow until she fell asleep.

Epilogue

The RAW-MC is many things. It isn't a whole lot more. Love, fatigue, war, and grief. Pick any three, as long as it isn't the first one.

Her debrief on Nouveau Paris turned into a month of mandated therapy with a psychobabbler, hours of staring at white walls, three bland meals a day, and meeting after meeting with the spooks at MARINT. NAVINT, too, because the Sailors didn't quite trust the Marines to get their facts straight. Doctor Corilla Yathil, a dark-haired woman of Indian descent, poked and prodded her until she was satisfied that Promise had a lid on her demons. Even so, the nightmares continued for months. Filled with the same faces of those she'd ordered to die. Sedatives helped her sleep the nights away. Exercise, grit-on discipline, needles and yarn, and stimm-tabs pushed her through the days.

Promise had once read that the living gave themselves medals to help them stomach burying their dead, and, in the end, they never did feel any better about it. Her battles on Montana taught her this was absolutely true. The RAW-MC awarded her the Silver Star for her leadership, resolve, and heroism in the face of overwhelming odds. The Navy awarded her the Nebula Cluster for distinguishing herself in ship-to-ship action against a superior enemy and with outstanding heroism. She also received three Skull and Crossbones for confirmed kills of enemy officers and the Purple Heart for being wounded in action. The medals did nothing to slake her pain.

The Republic of Aligned Worlds, at the specific direction of President Jack Carroll's office, filed an official complaint against the Lusitanian Empire for its blatant acts of aggression in the Montana system. The RAW stopped short of calling what happened an "Act of War." Ambassador Kenneth O'Leary delivered the communiqué, in person, to Queen Aurilyn the II of the Lusitanian Empire. It was carefully worded and specifically directed at one of the queen's officers, who happened to be deceased. Promise wasn't surprised when the Lusies took the bait and repudiated Commodore Samuelson's actions. *The man was probably better off dead,* she thought. She didn't buy the story of his aneurysm either. The Lusitanian Empire refused to make reparations, citing its enormous losses in both manpower and hulls.

After she was cleared by BUMED, she was ordered to the capital planet of Hold, where the official inquiry began. She testified before the Senate Intelligence Committee, the Senate Frontier Defense Committee, the Office of Frontier Security, and then before the Marine Board of Inquiry. Her answers were brief and matter-of-fact.

"Why did you exceed your command authority as a Republican officer by mobilizing a planetary militia? Why did you accept combat bonuses for yourself and your company, bonuses paid outside of authorized channels? Why did you fire preemptively on a Lusitanian warship? Do you understand the legal headaches you've created for the attorney general's office?"

She'd listened patiently and answered each question in turn.

Eventually, her field decisions were examined from every angle and exonerated post facto. Her tactics and deployments scrutinized and dissected and later written up for future forms of Marines to study and learn from. Her person and performance held up as that of a model Marine, in every way. Then it was three weeks' mandatory leave before Officers Training School at Camp Watain, to make her field-promotion permanent.

The rest of her "Montana Marines" spread out across the 'verse for much-earned leave, followed by their own schools and training. The gunny filled a last-minute vacancy at the RAW-MC's School of Infantry. And Kathy added a third stripe to her belt at the Corps' Mixed-Martial Arts Academy, third in class, earning her junior instructor patch, too. Maxi blew his pay on bad bets and other crap he didn't need. Van Peek convalesced, received a new arm, and retrained his brain to use it. Morris took a short leave of absence to care for a failing parent. Promise knew she'd see them all soon enough.

She'd see her old company lieutenant soon enough, too, now Captain Spears. He'd been reassigned to his own company in Charlie Battalion. And because he could regen, his new hand and leg were doing nicely.

In the 287-year history of the RAW-MC, no single company of Marines had faced a battalion of enemy troops, with support elements, and won. She had. No field-promoted lieutenant had ever bested a ring of well-financed pirates and subverted a planetary takeover by a hostile star nation. She had. No mere "boot" with zero training in starship command had patched up a warship with a broken keel, assumed command of her crew when every officer aboard had been killed in combat, managed to restore power to her critical systems, and jumped her back into harm's way. She had. And no Republican Marine of any rank had ever stared down a Lusitanian Navy commodore and called his bluff. She had done all of these things.

First Lieutenant Promise T. Paen took one last look in the mirror. She tugged on her short-waist jacket, adjusted the single gold first lieutenant's bar to her collar points, and canted her white beret just so. The Seraph, Globe, and Anchor sat on the crown of her head, front and center, the emblem of nearly three hundred years of fleet pride. The unit patch on her left shoulder was new—a green and gold snake wrapped around the keel of an enemy battlecruiser, crushing it to death. Promise locked eyes with the woman in the mirror. There were more lines now, particularly around her eyes, and telltale shrapnel scars. She could have erased them, but that wasn't her style. Wasn't the way a proper RAW-MC officer did things. *You look fair, Lieutenant. Pretty good. But not great. Humph—it will do.* Her reflection nodded back sharply. She exited her officer's cabin, did a hard to port, and advanced down the ship's corridor. Gunnery Sergeant Tomas Ramuel, Sergeant Maxzash Indar-Sindri, recently promoted Sergeant Richard Morris, and newly promoted Lance Corporal Kathy Prichart all waited for her at the end of the passageway.

Prichart stepped to the front and led the rest of the way.

Promise looked over at her guardian and raised an eyebrow in question. "Now is not the time for a snack."

"What?" Prichart asked and looked at the energy bar in her hand before taking another bite. "I'm hungry."

Promise shook her head. "Just finish that before we reach the bulkhead door."

They stopped outside of KS-17, which split apart, allowing them to enter. Inside was the barracks of the newly reconstituted Victor Company. Every Marine present jumped to attention as Prichart announced, "Lieutenant on deck!"

"Stand at ease," Promise said calmly as she came to a hard stop. Her Marines rocked their hands back to a parade rest, backs stiff and chests flared, eyes straight ahead.

"I'm Lieutenant Paen. Welcome to Victor Company, Charlie Battalion, Fifth Brigade, Twelfth Regiment—the Pythons."

"*Paen's* Py-*thons!*" the gunny barked. Promise's eyes went wide, head snapped around to face her second in command. The gunny simply nodded and patted the new unit patch on his left shoulder, then returned his attention to the assembled Marines of V Company, the newly christened Pythons. Someone at Battalion HQ had started calling V Company that after Montana, and the name had held fast despite Promise's objections. "Too bad, Lieutenant," she'd been told. "Winning battles comes with consequences."

Promise cleared her throat. "Please, lend me your eyes."

As she examined her command, she recalled the day she'd met her first company CO. She'd been just as young and as sure of herself as the boots before her were now.

"Ours is a proud company." Promise paused. "We are one of the best." She paused. "We never stop. We never quit. We can go where others can't. Each of you will add to that tradition. I know you'll rise to the occasion and make us all proud."

Promise motioned to the gunny. "Gunnery Sergeant Tomas Ramuel is my second in command. He will personally command Second Platoon, too. Normally, my number two would be a second lieutenant. As you know, the Corps is strapped for bodies and actively enlisting every poor jane and jack it can lay hands on." Some of her Marines—most privates and PFCs—didn't how to take that, but several of the veterans smiled and tipped off the rest. "Given that, I asked to keep the gunny because he is the best at what he does. And the Corps, being the accommodating mother hen that it is, obliged me."

A few of her veterans cracked smiles, but most stood up straighter as if their collective reputations had just grown by several centimeters. If anything, the Corps didn't mother anybody. If you cried to momma, the RAW-MC told you to square up and stop pissing in your boots, which meant the gunny was better than Promise said he was. And because Promise was only a first lieutenant, not a captain like most company COs, she was better still.

She'd debated whether to bring her "Montanan Marines" with her, rather than simply greeting them with the rest of her new command. In the end, it had seemed the right thing to do. She was trying to build something special, and the "old guard" would be at the core of it.

"To his right is Sergeant Richard Morris. Sergeant Morris will command Third Platoon. I'm still getting to know the sergeant. And though our time together has been short, our battles have been hard-won and fierce. I trust him implicitly. You will come to as well.

"To my left is Sergeant Maxzash-Indar Sindri. He will command Fifth Platoon. For those of you that gamble, watch out! And watch your chits even closer."

A couple privates did a quick double take and promptly gave themselves away.

"And to his left is Lance Corporal Kathy Prichart, my guardian." Promise looked at her young warden with true devotion. "Some of you outrank her. Lance Corporal Prichart is a good subordinate. She knows how to follow orders and she *will* follow yours. But make no mistake about it—she's pulled me out of fires more than once, and she is the only Marine in this outfit that has the right and the God-ordained authority to tell me what to do. Give her a wide berth and you'll be just fine."

Promise stepped into the aisle and began walking through her people. Aboard ship, Marines slept like Navies, in racks two-high, instead of clusters. To Promise, the compartment felt cramped, and she found herself longing for terra firma and a proper Marine cluster.

As she appraised her command, she made contact with each Marine, matching the name to the face in each Marine's jacket.

Private Sig Patoursburg . . .

Private First Class Ronald W. Vaden . . .

Lance Corporal Matthue Childs . . .

She stopped in front of newly promoted Corporal Nathaniel Van Peek. "You're looking good, Nate." Promise held out her arm. The folds of her eyes tightened slightly. "I didn't expect you until tomorrow. How's your grip?"

"I've been tossing fruit, ma'am. I only crush one out of three." Van Peek grabbed her hand with his synthlimb and pumped it vigorously. "See? The neuros say my brain is shipshape even though my body rejected the regen therapies. And I dropped a lot of mass. But I'm working on getting it back."

Promise retrieved her hand and flexed it protectively. "Keep practicing," she said dryly. "Third Toon needs a level head and a heavy-weapons expert. Can do, Corporal?"

"Can do, ma'am."

Promise slapped Van Peek's shoulder and moved down the line.

Sergeant Portia M'Dvokorsky . . .

Private Race Atumbi . . .

Private C. J. X. Bohmbair . . . "Charlie, correct?" she said. The private beamed, clearly pleased that the lieutenant already knew his first name.

"Yes, ma'am!" he replied, perhaps a bit too eagerly.

"I believe we have something in common, Private."

"Montana, ma'am." He answered without hesitation. Bohmbair stood a bit taller and gazed at the bulkhead behind his lieutenant. He risked a quick look at his CO and saw her face soften for a moment.

"They're a tough lot, Montanans. I know—I've fought alongside some of the best of them."

It took her several minutes, but she finally reached the end of the line and turned to face her command, her Marines, her company. Most of the women and men before her looked too young to serve, perhaps as young as she had to her CO just after she'd joined Victory Company as an unblooded cub. Now, it was her job to worry about the new recruits and her own cubs, worry about blooding them into mature Republican Wolves. Promise drank them in, the next generation of Victor Company, their discipline and crisp uniforms, their zeal and strength. Potential, every one. Victor Company would soon be deployed, with her in command.

Together, they'd face unknown adversities, and she would face hard decisions. Her orders could leave some of them wounded, perhaps even critically. She'd give orders that others might not survive. Her thoughts sobered her and made her grateful for the present, for the combined strength of her Marines, here and now.

As Lieutenant Promise Paen inspected her command, she saw her commission for what it truly was—a single link in an unbroken chain spanning generations of Marine Corps officers, bound together by honor. It was both an opportunity to lead and a great burden to shoulder. The choices she made to get to this day had great costs, and she realized if she had to do it over, she'd willingly pay them again. To live a life worthy of a Republican Marine, and to do her share of the task, no matter the cost.

GLOSSARY
(not at all exhaustive)

A.E. after Earth

AI artificial intelligence

ALCON all considered

ANDES Android Enemy Soldier, but commonly used to refer to android sentinels, friendly or foe

APER armor-piercing explosive round

Armorplaste a clear, high-strength, military-grade polycarbonate material (pronounced armorplasty); sometimes shortened to "plaste"

Aye yes

Aye, aye "I understand and will comply"

Bag-drag to be transferred, or to ship out

BAT-CO battalion commander

BATRON battlecruiser squadron

Beegees the underarmor worn by mechsuit drivers, which prevents chafing while "suited" and affords the wearer some protection against small-arms and energy fire; beegees are acceptable attire in place of utilities while aboard ship and sometimes referred to as a "body glove"

BMR Battlefield Mapping Reticule (projects a compressed three-dimensional display of energy signatures into the wearer's field of view)

Bravo Zulu well done

BUMED Bureau of Medicine, or Bureau of Medicine and Surgery

BUMIL Bureau of Military Intelligence. BUMIL is the shortened form of BUMILINT (BU-MIL-INT), with "intelligence" omitted and understood, and is the source of many jokes in several military traditions. In the Republic of Aligned Worlds, for instance, BUMIL also refers to the

collective intelligence communities of the entire military, including
NAVINT (Naval Intelligence) and MARINT (Marine Intelligence).
One may insult the military's intelligence—BUMIL—without specifi-
cally disparaging a particular branch of service.

BUPERS Bureau of Personnel

BUWEPS Bureau of Weapons Development

CAR short for "carbine," a long arm with a shorter barrel than a rifle

CIC Combat Information Center, or Combat Intelligence Center

Civvie a civilian

Civvies civilian clothes

Comm communications device (adjective, verb, or noun)

COMSEC communications security

Copy as in, "copy that"—or, "I heard what you just said"

Crossed Anchors and Charger the official emblem and insignia of the
Lusitanian Imperial Navy

CRURON cruiser squadron

CZ cruiser

Deck the floor or surface of the earth

Delta sierra DS, or "dumb shit"

Eve or Echo-Victor-One, a code name for a female prisoner

EWO Electronics Warfare Officer

Fruit Salad also called glittery; medals and service ribbons worn by uniformed military

Ferocrete a military-grade material that is poured to make roads and
landing pads for light attack craft and shuttles

FGL Flexible Grenade Launcher, capable of firing an assortment of explosive ordinance

Fighting hole a defensive position dug into the ground

FOB forward operating base

FTL faster than light

GEHAK Gravitic-Enhanced High-Altitude Bunker-Killer

GLOCK a popular twentieth-century semi-automatic firearm created by
Gaston Glock that revolutionized the small-arms industry with its
polymer frame; became known as the "plastic gun"

Gunny nickname for a gunnery sergeant (but not for a master gunnery
sergeant)

HALO High-Altitude, Low-Opening (e.g., "HALO drop"; "HALO jump")

HAWC Health and Wellness Center

HG heavy gravity (e.g., "HG world")

HMS His/Her Majesty's Ship, used before the name of space-faring warships

Horde missiles small antipersonnel/antiarmor missiles launched in packets, or "hordes," that are designed to swamp an enemy's defenses

HUD heads-up display

HV hypervelocity (e.g., "HV round")

HVT high-value target

ILW Independent League of Worlds, a now-defunct coalition of non-aligned planets in the Rim, or verge. The planet Montana initially led the league before joining the Republic of Aligned Worlds. After Montana's departure, the ILW fell apart.

J-CIC Joint Combat Intelligence Command

JSA Justification for System Activation (which is a PITA to fill out)

Klick kilometer

KZ kill zone

LAC light attack craft, the workhouse of most space Marine Corps. A LAC is typically a system-bound (i.e., non-jump-capable) craft capable of interplanetary and atmospheric flight. There are several classes of LAC, which range widely in size. Most warships carry a small complement of LACs to support their Marine detachments.

LE Lusitanian Empire, a constitutional monarchy with a hereditary king or queen as the head of state, a lower House of Commons composed of elected officials, and an upper House of Lords

Liberty authorized free time ashore or off station that is not counted as leave

LIDAR or LiDAR, a remote sensing technology from the twentieth century that measures distance by illuminating a target with a laser and analyzing the reflected light; the terms originated as a combination of "light" and "radar"

LOS line of sight

Lusie a derogatory term used by Republicans and citizens of other star nations when referring to the Lusitanians (from the LE)

LZ landing zone

MARINT Marine Intelligence

MBP mini Bi-Polar rifle, an electromagnetic projectile launcher (an electromagnetic rail gun)

Mechsuit mechanized suit of battle armor. Before the advent of powered armor, the word "mechanized" referred to soldiers equipped with armored vehicles. Mechsuits are roughly humanoid with interlocking plates of armor that protect the driver. Modern militaries prefer a plug-and-play platform and semiautonomous AI assists.

MEDSYS medical emergency triage system

Mess dress uniform worn at formal occasions and roughly equivalent to civilian black-tie

Mike minute

Mike-mike millimeter

MOLLE Modular Lightweight Load-Carrying Equipment (pronounced "molly")

MONI Ministry of Naval Intelligence (pronounced "money"); this division of the Lusitanian Empire is roughly comparable to NAVINT (Naval Intelligence) in the Republic of Aligned Worlds

MOS Military Occupational Specialty

MRS Mobile Recharging Station (for handheld energy weapons); also Misses

NAVCOM Navigation and Communications

NAVINT Naval Intelligence

NCO noncommissioned officer

Non-com noncommissioned officer

Ninety-day wonder an officer commissioned in a military branch after an unusually short training period

OCS Officer's Candidate School

Overhead ceiling of a building or ship

Peristeel an alloy used to make mechsuits, small land and aerial craft, and warship armor

Pharmacope a Marine's personal bank of drugs, typically implanted in the thigh; a mechsuit's MEDSYS contains a backup

PF platform or space station, often but not always a military installation

PFC private first class

'Publican a derogatory term used by Lusitanians when referring to Republicans (from the RAW)

Rack a bed

RAW Republic of Aligned Worlds, a democratic republic of worlds that won its independence from the Terran Federation in 2481 C.E.

RAW-MC Republic of Aligned Worlds Marine Corps

RAW-FF Republic of Aligned Worlds Fleet Forces, an umbrella term referring to the collective military branches of the Republic: Marine Corps, Navy, and Sector Guard

Regular dress roughly equivalent in form and function to a civilian business suit

Rim the outskirts of human civilization—a Rim planet or Rim world is typically poor and nonaligned, often plagued by rampant poverty and lawlessness; the term is often used interchangeably with "verge," although it is considered a derogatory term by Rimworlders

RNS Republican Naval Ship (or, Republican Naval Warship—with "war" being understood), used before the name of Republican space-faring warships

Roger as in, "Roger that"—or, "I understand what you just said"

SAC Standard Atmospheric Conditions

SAM a surface-to-air or ground-to-air missile

SAR search and rescue; also, "sounds about wrong"

SARG Semi-Autonomous Reasoning Grunt, a mechsuit driver's AI assist

Scuttlebutt gossip or a rumor

Seabag a duffle bag

SECCOM Sector Command

Semper Fidelis "Always Faithful" or "Always Loyal"

Semper Paratus "Always Ready," the official slogan of the RAW-MC

Seraph, Globe, and Anchor the official emblem and insignia of the RAW-FF

SERE Survival, Evasion, Resistance, and Escape school

SITREP "situation report"

Skipper nickname for the captain of a warship or the captain of a company of Marines

Skivvies undergarments, including skivvy shirts and skivvy drawers

SNCO staff noncommissioned officer

Snotty cruise an ensign's first mission after successfully completing her or his officer's training, often at a service academy

SNEAK Stealth-Navigation-Evasion-Adaptation-Kill suit

SOP standard operating procedure

SPECOPS Special Operations Forces, or Special Operators, or Special Forces

Striker sniper

Tango Down target eliminated or neutralized

TF task force; also, Terran Federation, the first and largest star nation in the 'verse (Terrans consider the abbreviation a veiled insult)

UAV unmanned aerial vehicle; broadly used to mean a drone that can operate in atmospheric conditions as well as in vacuum

Utilities designed for wear in the field, the standard working uniform for deployed and most garrison Marines and Sailors

Vacsuit garment capable of withstanding harsh environments, vacuum, and the extreme cold of space; often worn inside warships and small craft during combat as a precaution in case of loss of atmospheric containment and necessary for extravehicular activities

Verge derogatory term for the outskirts of human civilization—a "verge" planet is typically poor and nonaligned, often plagued by rampant poverty and lawlessness; the term is often used interchangeably with "Rim"

VTOL Vertical Takeoff and Landing vehicle

Webs short for "webshorts" and "webvests," loose-fitting clothing with MOLLE gear woven into the fabric

Whisker a small drone used for reconnaissance by many militaries and clandestine services across the 'verse

WILCO I have received your last message, understand it, and "will comply"

Wolf a "blooded" Marine (i.e., a Marine who has killed in combat)

XO executive officer, the second in command of a military unit

Turn the page for a sneak peek at
the next book in the Chronicles of Promise Paen

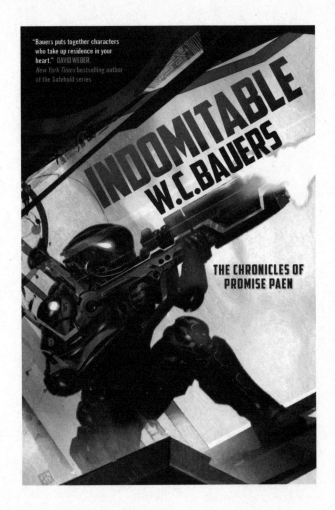

Available July 2016

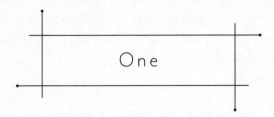

One

A round the size of Promise's trigger finger hit her like a maglev. It tore through her mechsuit and mushroomed in her chest, just above her heart. Miraculously, it didn't go off. Promise stumbled backward and off the cliff's face, into a thousand meters of darkness. Neuroinhibitors flooded her system almost as fast as the pain. *This is it* flashed across her mind as her body flatlined. *Tomorrow I'm hero-dead.*

Her vision grayed out and she lost all feeling in her hands and feet.

Promise rag-dolled in her mechsuit . . . fell and fell and fell, perilously close to the cliff's face. Her heel caught an outcropping several hundred meters below. Her AI, Mr. Bond, sealed the hole in her chest, and patched and packed it with cauterizing goo. Then Bond isolated the round kissing her heart in a null field, in case it decided to go off on its own timetable. Removing it was out of the question, and beyond the mechsuit's capabilities. A Marine Corps cutter would have to brave that. And there were more pressing matters to attend to. Her heart had stopped beating.

The mechsuit intubated her and zapped her pumper. One, two, three . . . six times before her heart's arteries and connective tissues remembered how to work in concert. A single stroke came followed by another, and then a stable *thrum thrum thrum*. Promise gasped, and came to. Her heads-up display blared with error messages she couldn't process. Her ears weren't discriminating sounds. Her body felt disemboweled, as if someone had ripped her soul clean out and now someone else was trying to stuff it back in but the fit was wrong. Insert leg there. No, not there, *there*. The tube down her throat was the worst violation. Mercifully, Bond pulled it out.

"SITREP," Promise said, the words a faint, hoarse whisper.

"You're in an uncontrolled descent. There's an armor-piercing explosive round in your chest."

"Is the APER hot?"

"Negative."

Thank the Maker for that. Promise blinked hard but still couldn't make sense of her HUD.

"Today is a bad day to die." Her voice was stronger now, the sky a starless void. "Why aren't my lamps on?"

"Stand by," said Bond at the same time that her proximity alarm howled.

Promise's forward lamps lit several milliseconds later. She gasped, and threw her hands out in front of her, which sent her tumbling backward end over end. Meters away, the rock face somersaulted in and out of view.

"Could . . . have . . . warned . . . me," she said through clenched teeth. Down became up became down until she couldn't tell the difference between them anymore.

"I tried, Lieutenant." Bond sounded mildly put out. "Tuck your arms to your sides. I'll right you."

Her mechsuit's ailerons bit into the wind, stopped the tumble, and reoriented her: head down, feet up, knifing toward the watery deck. The distance opened between her and the wind-carved face at her six o'clock.

"Altitude?"

"Twenty-five hundred meters."

"LZs?"

"There's an island up ahead, ten degrees to starboard, three klicks out. Because of the headwind, you'll cover one-point-three klicks before splashing down."

That means a long swim . . . if I survive impact. "Comm the gunny."

"Your comm is out. The APER pulsed when it hit you, and the pulse knocked out most of your systems, including your heart. *My* secondary shielding held. *You've* lost weapons, scanners, countermeasures, braking thrusters, and the gravchute. You're going to hit hard."

"Suggestions?"

"Bail out."

". . . Of my armor? You've got to be kidding."

"You tweaked my personality chip to make that impossible, ma'am." Bond sounded a bit too sure of itself for Promise to be sure her tweaking had fully taken hold.

"Mr. Bond, I don't believe *my* tweaking worked."

Her AI made a *tsk*ing sound, three times. "Let's debate that later, ma'am, during my next inspection. Your beegees were recently upgraded. Use your microgravchute embedded in the fabric between your shoulder blades." Her beegees, or standard-issue mechsuit underarmor, were good for a lot of things. Prevented chafing. Absorbed energy fire. Made using the head while suited tolerable. Barely. The microgravchute was going to come in handy. But first she had to bail . . . out of her armor . . . which was the only thing keeping her alive at the moment.

"It's double-shielded and should still work. Theoretically. I lost my link to it so I can't tell if it's operational. You'll have to manually activate it."

"And if it doesn't work?"

Not one *tsk* now. "Passing one thousand meters."

This is going to be fun. "Did I see lights overhead while we were flipping?"

"Someone went over the cliff's face with us," Bond said. "But I can't tell friendly from foe, not without my scanners."

"It won't matter if we botch the landing," Promise said. She stretched her limbs to slow her fall, and then made a slight correction with one hand, and rotated onto her back. "Open up on three and stay level. I'll rise. You fall away."

"Roger that," Bond said. "Good luck, ma'am."

"On my mark." She counted down from three. "Mark!"

Her mechsuit's chest, arms, and shanks unsealed. The air chilled her to the marrow. She felt the slightest movement upward before the suction ripped her out of her suit and into the open sky. For a moment she felt like a leaf blown about the air by an unrelenting gale. She wrestled the wind for control for a solid half mike. Far below her the lamps on her mechsuit grew dim.

Promise spread-eagled to kill as much speed as possible. She pressed her right thumb against her pinkie for a two-count. Her mechsuit's lamps vanished. *Bond just splashed down.* She flexed the thumb again. Prayed the drive-by-wire backup transmitted the impulse from her thumb to her mini-gravchute. She was nearly panic-stricken when the chute deployed a second later and dislocated her left shoulder.

Her descent slowed to a survivable fall before reaching an all-stop. Her night vision intensified until the darkness around her lifted. The sun crested the horizon. Howling winds fell silent. Promise looked down, looked between her mechboots, looked at the endless indigo ocean for as far as the eye could see. Her arms flailed widely for something to grab hold of as the fear of falling warred with her other senses; contrary to the laws of physics, she was standing on air. No, she was floating. Flying, maybe? Somehow she was hundreds of meters above the watery deck but holding station. After a few moments of abject terror she willed herself to calm down.

I'm not falling. I'm safe. Relax, P, you can figure this out.

A far-off object entered her field of view. A door perhaps, maybe a person. It was moving toward her. The door became a human silhouette and then a heavily damaged mechsuit: armor crushed; helmet lost somewhere in the clouds. The driver's eyes were open, lifeless. Now she could see the rank on the driver's armor and her bloodshot eyes. Then another mechsuit floated into view. Promise turned her head and saw not one but three lifeless bodies, all suited, all closing in. None wore helmets. Their faces were cadaver blue. Their hair waved gently in the air though no breeze stirred it. With nothing to grab ahold of or push off from, somehow Promise was able to rotate in the air and look behind her. The sky was raining dead Marines. Above her. Below her. The nearest boot opened his mouth to speak.

"Lance Corporal Tal Covington, present." The voice howled like a wind-shot cavern. Covington's eyes rolled up into his head and began to bleed. Then his body blew apart.

Promise threw her hands up without thinking, slammed her eyes shut to blunt the bright flash of light that followed. A moment later it dawned upon her that she was still alive, not blown to quarks. When she dared to look, Covington was still floating in the sky, two meters away, but his body was rent asunder. The explosion had frozen in process milliseconds after happening. Covington's armor was cracked a thousand ways, his organs and bones stitched together with little else but air.

To her right, Promise heard labored breathing, followed by an anguished cry that punched her squarely in the gut. A blast of heat swept over her, blistering the side of her face, her lips, and the inside of her mouth; the taste of death was on her tongue. Turning, she saw a mechsuit engulfed in fire. The wearer was desperately trying to put the flames out with what was left of his gauntlets. She couldn't look away from the hands. Metal and flesh clung stubbornly to skeletal hands. Then, as unexpectedly as the blaze had appeared, it simply went out. The smoking remains of a scorched mechanized Marine came to attention, and a blackened skull opened its mouth. Bits of charred flesh dangled from its upper lip. "Corporal Vil Fitzholm, present."

"Private First Class Molly Starns, present," came from Promise's opposite side. Starns started convulsing. She ripped her tongue from her throat and threw it at Promise. Starns's head rolled to the side and off of her shoulders. Bits of connective tissue refused to let go.

"Staff Sergeant Moya Hhatan, present." Hhatan was floating dead ahead of Promise. "All boots present and damned for eternity." Hhatan's lips curled upward, exposing shaved canines stained with blood.

No, this isn't possible, Promise thought. Hhatan was trying to swim through the air toward her. *I watched you die. I tried to save you but your wounds . . . and the enemy was so close. You sacrificed yourself for me. Told me to go and then . . . I ran away.*

"I'm so sorry, Staff Sergeant," Promise said. Hhatan was nearly on her. "I tried, really. I did my best but I couldn't stop them all." Promise raised her hands palms-up in front of her and kicked her legs to try and get away. "Please. *Please* . . . you have to believe me."

Staff Sergeant Hhatan drew a Heavy Pistol from her holster and took aim. "You don't deserve to live, Lieutenant." Then something peculiar happened. The staff sergeant's face grew young. Years of experience melted away, the eyes changed from blue to green. "You left me on Montana." The voice morphed so quickly that Promise barely registered the change. Now complete, Hhatan's appearance was for Promise a looking-glass mirror. "Your time is up. Good-bye, Lieutenant."

Promise heard her own voice say, "I'll see you in perdition."

Hhatan's gloved finger tensed around the trigger of the Heavy Pistol, took up the slack. The air cracked in two. Muzzle fire blossomed. When Promise opened her eyes the bullet had traveled half the distance from Hhatan to her. A second later it was a meter away, and then half a meter off. Promise screamed as the bullet pierced her temple, drilled through the crown of her skull, and tore her mind apart.

APRIL 14TH, 92 A.E., STANDARD CALENDAR, 0549 HOURS
REPUBLIC OF ALIGNED WORLDS PLANETARY CAPITAL—HOLD
MARINE CORPS CENTRAL MOBILIZATION COMMAND

The screams told her to wake up.

First Lieutenant Promise Tabitha Paen bolted upright, fully alert, First Wave blaring in her mastoid implant. The band was surfing high across the nets with "Alternate You," a throwback of classic metal and new-groove rage, set against a track of cosmic background noises. Week-one sales had topped all previous records. Promise dropped her feet over the side of her rack and hit the cold polished deck of her government-assigned quarters. Back straight, shoulders squared, and eyes focused dead ahead. She started counting "One, two, three . . ." as First Wave's lead singer screamed in perfect pitch. "There's another you who's stalking true, better run the 'verse, better strike-back-first!" At forty-nine, Promise fell over, laced her hands behind her head, and stopped when her abs gassed out and her "alternate you" found her "jumping dreams" while her "real self screams."

"Enough." Promise shook her head to clear out the dissonance and pursed her lips. "Um . . . play Chiam's Sonata in G Minor." Melody flooded her ears as her pulse settled down to normal.

The nightmares are getting worse, she thought as she rolled again onto her arms, pushed up, and started counting down from fifty. *Forty-nine, forty-eight, forty-seven . . .* To this point, the nightmares had been a rehash of her battles on Montana. She'd watched her Marines die again and again and again, each death more gruesome than the last. *Forty-three, forty-two, forty-one . . .* Perhaps it was her penance for failing them, for leaving so many dead on her birth world, or so she thought. *What doesn't kill you makes you stronger, right?* But that was a hollowed-out truth. What failed to kill you still exacted its own pound of flesh, and not even sleep offered an escape. The nightmares were definitely getting worse.

A jolt of pain caused Promise to cry out at *twenty-nine*. She collapsed onto her side, clutching her hands over her pounding chest. Surely there was a gaping hole in her heart that must have turned black by now. Perhaps all that remained of it was a deathly hollow, carved out by the worst kind of flesh eater. Survivor's guilt.

I know because most of my first command is dead, she thought.

Her dead wouldn't stop coming to her mind. *The Skipper is dead, Lance Corporal Tal Covington shielded me from that blast and got hero-dead, Staff Sergeant Hhatan is dead because I left her behind, my mother—dead, father—dead, all turned to dust except for me.*

Tears pooled in her eyes. "Sir, if you're so good, how could you have let this happen?"

Promise willed herself up off the floor and on with her morning. She had a busy day ahead of her. The gunny was expecting her in less than an hour. She didn't bother drying her eyes as she force-marched herself to the head, shedding clothes as she went. "On." A bad memory flashed across her mind. Promise drowned it out by turning on the water as hot as she could stand it. A quick dunk under the faucet rinsed most of the night terrors away. She blindly felt for her towel on the wall. Dried. Stood up straight and punched her reflection in the face. Crack. The woman in the mirror was familiar except for the glass fractures—same eyes colored like sparkling ocean, same pale skin—but where Promise's hair was short, the reflection's was long. Where Promise was angles the woman in the mirror had curves. She was old enough to be Promise's mother.

"Warn me next time." Promise forced herself to breathe.

"Sorry, munchkin. I came as fast as I could." Sandra Paen was dressed in a silk robe with a low neckline. An ornate tail curled over her shoulders, and coiled around her heart. Promise drew a circle around her breast, mimicking the coil of the dragon's tail in the mirror.

"You remember." Sandra's hand was over her heart.

"How could I forget?" Of course Promise remembered the robe. It was the same one her mother had worn shortly before her death.

The gold band on Sandra's hand caught the overhead light. The band symbolized a bond that was supposedly unbreakable. Life had proven otherwise.

"Look, Mom. Now is not the time. My unit has morning PT. I'm needed out there. I have to go."

"The gunny can handle it." Sandra dared Promise to deny it. Sandra reached out of view and came up with a towel. "You need to talk about the dreams," she said as she dried her hair.

I already have. BUMED cleared me for duty, Promise thought. She didn't feel like discussing this particular matter. Besides, her mother was adept at reading minds. Well, hers anyway.

"That's not what I meant and you know it. You told the psychobabbler what he wanted to hear, not what's really going on inside of you." Sandra hung her towel on her side of the mirror and folded her arms.

Promise glanced at the empty hook on the wall and knew she was going mad.

Sandra cleared her throat. "Correct me if I'm wrong."

I told them enough . . . and I didn't lie. A Marine never lies, but that doesn't mean I have to tell the whole truth either. I've got this.

"For how long?" Sandra asked. "We both know you're running on damaged cells. What happens when they fail?"

I'll survive. But Promise knew it was a lie. She was as close to lying as she had ever been comfortable with. But, it was just a thought. *I'm not responsible for every thought that crosses my mind.*

How long could she hold it together? The question was unanswerable. Promise had started seeing visions of her deceased mother shortly after her father's murder, just before she'd enlisted in the Republic of Aligned Worlds Marine Corps. Raiders had hit her birth world, Montana. Her father's pacifism had gotten him killed. She'd been too young, too inexperienced, too far away, and too frightened to help him. She'd tried to outrun the pain ever since. *How's that working out for you, P?* She never knew when her dearly departed mother would appear and read her like a well-worn book, but it was always at the most inconvenient of times.

Look, I need to get in my morning run. If I swear I'll talk with someone will you let it go?

"Yes."

Good. Talk later.

Promise turned away from the mirror and opened a drawer on the opposite wall. She selected a fresh pair of skivvies, and her PT uniform. After dressing, she removed the two polished onyx bars of a first lieutenant from the small box in the corner of the drawer, and pinned one to each side of her collar. When she turned back around she nearly jumped out of her skin.

"I love you, munchkin, you know that, right?"

"Yeah, I know," Promise said aloud. *And you know I hate being called that. But I'm tired of telling you because it never makes any difference.* She heard her mother's laughter echoing in her mind, and then Sandra was gone. Promise couldn't help smiling, and she shook her head. "Don't stop laughing" was one of her mother's mantras.

Promise took a deep breath and told herself that the morning could only get better. *I'm sure some of my Marines talk to their ancestors too. I know some of my boots pray to them. This isn't as weird as it seems. I'm doing fine. Right.* Promise raked her short-cropped hair. A swipe of gloss completed the battlefield makeover. She grabbed a pair of socks and her boots and headed for the door.

Hold's rising sun peeked over the horizon as she stepped outside, inhaled the cool morning air kissed with a hint of rain. She reached over and activated her minicomp, which was strapped to her arm above the biceps, flicked to the next screen, and selected a preprogrammed sequence called "Dawn Up":

One—molded soles for running uneven terrain.
Two—activate Stevie.
Three—send Stevie for the usual: extra-hot caf with cream and sugar,
and egg and chorizo roll.

"And turn the music off. I want to hear what I'm running through."

The soles of her boots morphed for light trail running, the sides with extra support for her ankles. Promise set off at a modest pace and looked left, nodding over her shoulder. "Right on time, Stevie. Stay on me." Stevie's humanoid metal carcass dropped back on her six, and settled into a slow hover on a plane of countergrav. It cradled a thermos of extra-hot caf in one hand and a breakfast roll in the other, fresh from the chow hall. Promise's pulse rifle was slung over its back, the muzzle pointed skyward.

In the next seven and a half minutes, Promise covered two klicks to the Saint Sykes training field, over hills, through a light patch of woods, and past Great-Grans's house. The RAW-MC's old lady was actually Lieutenant General Felicia Granby and her house was the RAW's Central Mobilization Command. CENT-MOBCOM wasn't much of a house either, just an unpretentious four-story seated on a foundation of one hundred underground levels. Grans was something of a legend in the Corps. She was pushing eighty and hadn't deployed in over a decade but still rated expert with heavy weps, and she held the record for most orbital insertions by a RAW-MC officer. Two hundred sixty-eight . . . and counting. Grans was lethal in a mechsuit. Out of mech she owned a near-vertical side kick and twelve grandchildren who didn't mess around. Eleven were Fleet Forces: eight Marines and three Sailors. The twelfth was the black sheep in the family. Johnny. He'd become a man of the cloth and was now a bishop in the Episcopal Church. The general's scarred hands had molded the RAW-MC over the last two decades, and more than one boot had assumed the position and taken a wallop in the ass from Lieutenant General Felicia Granby.

Promise sighted the open window in the upper story's northwest corner—Great-Grans's office—and Grans's personal ANDES standing watch below it. Only the truly brave approached the stoic sentinel and made a bet with Great-Grans. Promise slowed to a jog and fast-walked to the ANDES. She raised her sunglasses so the mech could scan her eyes. "Morning, Lieutenant Paen," said the ANDES in a perfect imitation of Great-Grans, grizzled voice and all. "Want to play Great-Grans says?"

"I'm game," replied Promise. Grans liked challenges and she liked to hand them out too. If you volunteered to play, Grans came to you on her terms, and it might be tomorrow and it might be a month from now. The record was five years.

"Grans will comm you at her convenience," the ANDES said.

Right. "Thank you, ma'am," Promise said, and pulled down her shades. "I'm off to the range."

As Promise took off, a gravelly voice boomed from the heavens. "Oohrah girly—send one downrange for me." Promise almost ran off the path and into a patch of basil thornwood. Grans herself had been listening.

Promise arrived at the earthen track feeling at ease, limber, ready to face her Marines. The hulking girth of Gunnery Sergeant Tomas Ramuel crested the hill a moment later. Victor Company was struggling to keep up with the veteran senior noncommissioned officer. And, Promise noticed at once, the gunny looked pissed. *Uh-oh.*

Ramuel and Victor Company jogged past Promise and circled the field. Her Marines were dressed in PT uniforms with pulse rifles cradled in their arms. All accept one. Private Atumbi had forgotten his, again.

Promise's eyes narrowed and zoomed on the Marine's face. "Figures." *Why can't he remember his wep?*

As Victor Company circled back to Promise's position, the gunny called out his first preparatory command. "Company, double time, march!" The company dropped out of a steady run and into step with the gunny, at a slight jog. A squat Marine fell out of formation and promptly threw up.

Private Race Atumbi was admiring Private First Class Jupiter Cervantes's backside when the gunny's order came, and his reaction time was far too slow to avoid a collision with her. When the company slowed, Atumbi plowed through Cervantes and burst through a platoon of Marines, sending every one of them to the deck.

Cervantes ended up on top of Atumbi. "Don't get any ideas," she said as she backhanded him across the mouth.

"Hey, *chica!* What was that for?"

"For your wandering *ojos*. Keep your eyes on target and off of me."

Cervantes stood first, and then offered a grudging hand to Atumbi. Her grip was like a vise, and she kept squeezing until he cried out. "What was *that* for?" he said, rubbing his hand, which now hurt worse than his throbbing jawline.

"So you don't forget." Cervantes looked pleased with herself as she shoved Atumbi forward. He fell in beside the Marines he'd just knocked down, and Cervantes joined him on his right.

"Where did you get a grip like that?" Atumbi asked as they jogged.

"Bion-*ics*," she said, and held up her right hand. "I don't regen. I lost the original in a training *accidente*."

Atumbi took a closer look at the skin's color. It was slightly off but pretty good for synthetics.

Colorful metaphors and insults erupted all around Atumbi as he found his place in formation.

"You fool. The gunny's gonna make us frog-jump around the field."

"Hey, Atumbi, you make me believe in reincarnation. No one gets so stupid in one lifetime."

His one-word nickname earned in boot camp—a solitary, cold dismissal—rolled off the lips of the woman who'd caught his eye. "Trip."

He brushed each aside with the dirt on his PT uniform. Jupiter's next words knifed the deepest. Cervantes eviscerated his manhood, shot through two magazines without so much as reloading. *"Tirar de su cabeza fuera de su asteroide."* His Spanish was north of rusty, but he caught the gist. Because they'd come from her they cut him to the core.

Atumbi's stomach sank when he realized the gunny had turned around and was marching backward with his eyes on him. They weren't quite smoldering. Then Ramuel did an about-face and started singing "The Old Lady."

Here we go again, Atumbi thought.

ABOUT THE AUTHOR

W. C. BAUERS's interests include Taekwondo, reading and writing military science fiction, toting gear for his Alpha Unit, and French Press brewing. He lives in the Rocky Mountains with his wife and three boys. *Unbreakable* is his first novel.